MARK'S WAY

by

Thomas Willis

TIFTON PRESS 2023

For permission requests contact the Tifton Press: tiftonpress@gmail.com

Book Cover by Stewart Williams

Logo design by by Bill Baffa

First Edition: Published 2021

Second Edition: Published 2023 by Tifton Press

10 9 8 7 6 5 4 3 2

ISBN: 979-8-9893052-0-9

Printed in the United States of America

Contents

PART ONE

If there were no tribulation, there would be no rest;
if there were no winter, there would be no summer.
St. John Chrysostom, Homilies

Big Bend Wildlife Management Area

West Coast of Florida-1988

Well after midnight, a full moon lit up the coastal marshes with a light almost as bright as daytime. The shoreline and forest emitted a cacophony of sounds that were almost orchestral, as the frogs and insects competed to be the loudest. The small finger of land that reached out of the dense pine forest and into the marshes of the Gulf of Mexico seemed to be far removed from civilization, desolate except for a few cabbage palms and patches of palmettos.

The peaceful scene was disturbed by the faint sound of an approaching motor. As the sound grew louder, a faint light could be seen emerging out of the dark forest and onto the finger of land. A pickup truck, jacked up high on huge wide tires with its dim running lights giving the driver enough light to navigate the narrow trail leading out of the dense pines, slowly emerged onto the open land. The driver turned the truck around and left it facing the way it had come before two men and a woman climbed down out of the truck. The woman reached back into the truck's cabin, pulled out two large suitcases and walked toward the water's edge carrying one in each hand. The two men walked behind her, each carrying assault rifles with long curved magazines protruding ominously from each rifle.

One of the men handed the woman a large lantern-type flashlight that she pointed out toward the open gulf and flashed several times. Her signal was quickly answered by a faint light blinking from the outer marshes and was soon followed by the sound of an outboard engine. Within a few minutes a small flat-bottomed boat approached the shoreline. One of the three occupants jumped out and pulled the boat partially up onto dry land. The man steering the boat remained in his seat holding a small automatic weapon leveled toward the shore. Reaching back into the boat, the other men brought out two military type duffle bags and carried them over to where the occupants of the truck were waiting. The woman pushed the suitcases toward the two men from the boat before she knelt down and began to examine the contents of the duffle bags. So far, not a single word had been spoken by any of the people. It was a well-rehearsed and orchestrated event that had obviously occurred many times before and everyone knew their part.

Each of the participants were so focused on the ongoing trans-action, no one in the group was aware of the ghostly figure, only a few feet away, that rose up from a clump of dead palm trees. The automatic weapon cradled in his arms erupted in a blazing inferno of smoke and noise, creating a virtual hail- storm of lead that continued steadily for several seconds. When it stopped, there was a pause before two more shots, different from the first, erupted in large explosive blasts. For several minutes the silence was palpable. A gentle gulf breeze had dissolved the pungent smell of gunpowder and it seemed that the tranquil scene had been restored. That illu-sion of peace was lost once more when a plaintive, almost animal like wail of pain, fright, and utter desperation, rose up into the sky before being overridden by the sound of the revving truck engine. Both sounds were soon swallowed up by the dark forest while an indifferent and smiling man in the moon continued to watch from above.

CHAPTER 1

Death Row- Raiford Prison

1998

The execution was on schedule. There was no last-minute reprieve coming for the man sitting in a death watch cell, who was scheduled to die for a brutal crime he'd committed and continued to brag about. Leroy Augustus Jones, covered with swastikas, death head and snake tattoo's, suddenly lost all his bravado and imploded like a dirtdobber's nest falling on concrete when he realized that his last-minute appeal had not been granted as they always had been in the past. The mood across all of Death Row, always gloomy in the best of times, hit an even lower point.

In another wing of Death Row, lying curled up in a fetal position on a hard mattress, his back pressed tightly against a cold cinderblock wall, fighting to keep back the bitter bile rising up, Jim Herbert knew first-hand what the condemned man must be feeling. Only a few weeks earlier, he'd been sitting in a death watch cell himself, watching the seconds he had left to live, one by one tick down toward zero. He'd given up any hope by the time his appeal was granted. He was only given a temporary reprieve while his attorney continued to look for some way to block the next death warrant which he knew would be coming.

The man scheduled to die today was guilty as sin according to creditable eyewitness and forensics. The murder he'd committed was cruel. There was no sympathy for him, and Jim realized the similarity between himself and Jones. The evidence against Jim was overwhelming as well. The murder was also brutal, and Jim was considered to be as guilty as Jones. The public held no sympathy for him as well. But there was one major difference between himself, and the man currently scheduled to die. Unfortunately, as only Jim himself knew, he was innocent of the crime he was waiting to die for. Jim fought against the urge to relive the past but as he'd done a thousand times before, he went back in time and tried to understand why.

Chapter 2

Jim Herbert-Orlando,Florida

1995

Like the little bug that went kerchoo, the most insignificant choices sometimes lead to significant consequences. How many times had he tried to go back and change his decision to stay instead of leaving?

Three years earlier Jim had been working for a large engineering firm finalizing construction plans for a new expressway in Orlando. He was staying at a large downtown hotel that was convenient to the office his firm was working out of. He'd worked late on a Friday afternoon before going back to his hotel room. He remembers debating whether to pack his things and drive back home to Boca Raton that night or to wait and drive down the following morning. He chose to stay and no matter how hard he tried to turn back the clock, the decision had been made. It was both cold and wet outside and he was tired from a long grueling week of work. He decided to treat himself to a good meal, a good night's sleep, and drive home the next morning.

After a hot shower, he put on a pair of jeans, a clean white dress shirt and a light jacket. Glancing at himself as he walked out of his room, he couldn't help but notice that his full head of hair was beginning to show traces of grey around the edges. At least, so far, he'd managed to avoid any sign of a potbelly, but he was afraid it was coming.

When he reached the lobby, he walked over to the front entrance and looked outside. It was raining even harder and when someone opened the front revolving door, he could feel a cold blast of air. Orlando only gets cold a few times a year and this was one of those few times. Orlando's definition of cold is anything below sixty degrees and when it's combined with rain and wind, an Orlando native thinks a new ice age has arrived. He'd intended to drive to Charlie's and get a steak, but he changed his mind. Again, another small choice he'd made. The hotel he was staying in actually had a decent restaurant, so he decided to have a drink at the bar and eat in the hotel.

The bar was large, and it was packed. Apparently, he was not the only one choosing to stay inside. It was also happy hour, and the bar was a popular after work gathering spot for local professionals. He'd almost circled the bar before he found an open seat that was surrounded by people wearing pinstriped suits and wingtip shoes.

The group closest to his seat was clearly comprised of attorneys. One young woman was verbally castrating a judge, a known misogynist, for mistaking her for a court reporter. She obviously didn't see any humor in it because she'd proven herself to be the best attorney in the courtroom. She'd been better prepared than the opposing attorney and her arguments based on previous rulings had persuaded the judge to rule in favor of her client. A couple of the pompous men in the group still seemed to have a hard time accepting that she'd made such a brilliant courtroom presentation. When she asked one of the men in a loud voice to tell her what case he'd won today, Jim almost choked on his drink.

Starting on his second drink, he became aware of the woman around the curve of the bar to his right. He hadn't noticed her because she was sitting in the middle of another group of suits, but after watching her it was obvious she wasn't a part of the group. She was not wearing a suit like most of the women, but was dressed in a casual blouse, sweater, and skirt. Jim guessed that she was thirty to thirty-five years old. She was not movie star beautiful but there was something about her that attracted Jim. She had short cut bleached blond hair and an angular face with a Romanesque nose. When he caught himself staring at her, she smiled at him and gave a slight nod of her head as if they were co-conspirators sharing a secret. He was not egotistical enough to consider himself a lady's man, but it did feel good to have a woman smile at him. Immediately after his divorce he'd chased everything in sight that wore a skirt. He was successful in his field, decent looking enough so he had no problem in relating to women, but he'd soon realized that there was a hollow satisfaction in the bar life. He loved women but had absolutely no desire for a relationship with anyone at this point in his life. As the group between himself and the girl around the bar began to break up, the lady lawyer looked at her watch, made a comment about time to go back to work and left along with several others. The girl continued to stare at him and finally got up and walked around the bar to where Jim sat. She could not have been over a hundred ten pounds, and she moved with an easy unaffected grace.

"I hope you don't mind," she said. "I'm Tanya," and she held out her hand. "Somehow I was left out of that conversation."

"You mean you're not a lawyer?"

"Not quite."

"What do you do?"

"I work in a doctor's office filing insurance claims."

"That sounds like fun."

"Are you kidding me? I used to think the doctors were the parasites feeding on the patients. Now, I'm not sure whether I dislike the tort lawyers or the insurance companies the most. Then you throw in the drug companies and you've got the perfect clusterfuck."

Jim couldn't help but laugh.

"Sounds like you've got it all figured out."

"No, I really don't have it figured out but someone sure as hell needs to."

He bought her a drink and ordered himself another one. Already, a little voice inside told him, "You're being stupid. Say goodnight, go to your room and go to bed," but he felt himself being drawn to her as the alcohol began to have an effect. It wasn't long before Jim had any doubt about where the evening was going, and he wasn't going to fight it. From that point on the conversation turned into one sexual innuendo after another and at some point, Jim realized that she had her hand on his thigh and was slowly moving higher. Jim remembered glancing around to see if anyone was watching them.

Finally, Jim said, "Let's go up to my room. I'll show you my tie collection," and immediately felt like a complete fool for making such a stupid statement.

She laughed. "No, let's go to my place. It's not far. Hotel rooms seem cheap."

"It's cheap no matter where we go," Jim thought.

He signed for the bar bill, and they walked out to the parking lot. He followed her to her car, a small older model import of some kind. She unlocked the door, opened it, and turned around to face him. When he pulled her close, her hands were trying to open his zipper and his hands were all over her chest. He put his hands behind her, pulled up her skirt, and cupped both cheeks in his hands. Neither one of them noticed the cold or the slow drizzling rain. Only when a car started to turn in to park close by, did they separate.

She said, "I'll wait by the front entrance. Follow me."

Panting like a dog in heat, Jim ran to his car and pealed out of his parking space. She was waiting at the entrance and took off with Jim close behind. She drove like a maniac and Jim had to really work to stay close, all the time hoping they didn't pass a cop. He knew he was being stupid but, in his alcohol induced state, there was no turning back.

Chapter 3

No Turning Back-Orlando

1995

Jim followed her out West Colonial just past the fairgrounds before turning off onto a side street, made a couple more turns and finally drove into a large apartment complex. It was one of those places that was not yet seedy but was turning the corner in that direction. The cars were mostly older with a few outright rust buckets. Many cars were backed into their parking spaces possibly indicating the prospect of having to make an unexpectedly fast exit. There was a lot of dead shrubbery that needed to be replaced and a few broken riding toys laying on the sparse grass. They wound around several buildings before she pulled into a parking space. Jim had to stop and back up a few places to find another open spot. He followed her into a hallway with an apartment on both sides and a set of stairs leading to the second floor. There was a heavy smell of fried food in the hallway, and he could hear sounds of a loud television playing. Her door was on the left at the top of the stairs. She fumbled for her key and dropped her key ring. Jim bent down and picked it up for her. She picked out a key and unlocked the deadbolt lock, then tried the bottom passage lock.

"God dammit, this is always hard to open."

"Here, let me try it." He took the key and after a little jiggling the passage lock opened. When they went inside Jim was surprised because the interior was decorated simply but with surprisingly good taste. The inside of the apartment was a contrast to the exterior of the complex. Everything was neat and orderly. He immediately noticed a couple of children's toys on a bookcase shelf.

She saw him looking and said, "My son is five. He's staying at my mother's house tonight."

She took Jim's hand and led him down a short hallway and into a bedroom. The room was filled with a king size bed that left almost no room to walk around. The headboard was all glass, and a huge mirror was built into the ceiling. He remembered thinking that someone had spent a lot of money decorating this room. He didn't have a long time to look because she was pulling on his belt, and he started pulling her sweater over her head and then fumbling with the buttons on her blouse. He remembered buttons popping off and when he got to the catch on her brassiere, he just jerked on it. Her breasts spilled out and he immediately had his mouth on her nipples. She dropped to the floor and pulled his pants down with her. She started up his thigh with her tongue and he lost his balance with his pants around his feet, and he fell across the bed. She followed him without losing her place. Everything after was a blur of tongues and lips and soft places. It had been a long time since he had made love with such total abandon, and he just let himself go. At some point, he was totally spent as he passed out in a fuzzy alcoholic haze.

He woke up lying cold and naked with a pounding headache. Somehow, he still had his watch on, and he forced himself to focus on the time. It was 1:15 a.m. He turned to look at her and she was lying on her back with her legs still spread as if she hadn't moved from their final position. Her mouth was open, and she was snoring loudly. He forgot his headache as he was suddenly overwhelmed by a wave of nausea. He quickly forced himself up and on very unsteady feet went into the open door across from the foot of the bed hoping it would be the bathroom. He couldn't find the light switch and his stomach was about to unload. Thankfully he could see the outline of the toilet. He got his head over it just in time before his stomach exploded. He didn't remember how long he remained on his knees with his head hanging over the bowl violently retching. When the convulsions finally eased, he was so weak he remained on his knees gripping the toilet for several minutes and cursing himself for drinking so much alcohol.

When he got back up on his feet, he reached for the faucet handle on the sink. As he did, his hand hit a glass sitting on the sink and knocked it off. It hit the tile floor and glass exploded everywhere. He could see light reflecting off a large piece of glass and without really thinking he reached down to pick it up. He knew it was a deep cut as he jerked his hand back up. He could already feel blood running across his hand and down his arm. He knew he had to find the light switch before he dared to take a step with all the glass on the floor. He leaned over and felt along the wall until he finally found the switch. The fan came on and the sudden noise made him jump. His foot jerked as a shard of glass punctured his heel. He managed to turn off the fan switch and turn on the light switch. It was a god-awful mess. He was bleeding all over the floor. There were pieces of glass everywhere. He took a towel and began to clean up the mess. He had to wrap his hand with a small hand towel and keep it pulled tight to slow the bleeding. He put the glass in a small trash can being very careful with the large piece that had cut his hand.

By the time he'd finished cleaning up as well as possible, his nausea had eased but his head was still pounding like a base drum. He went back into the bedroom and got dressed. Blood had already soaked through the towel, and he was getting it on his clothes but there was nothing he could do about it. The girl had still not moved one inch and her snoring had not let up. The last thing Jim did before he left the room was to pull up a sheet and blanket to cover her. She snored on, oblivious to the movement. He realized that he didn't even remember her name, but he knew he wouldn't see her again anyway. When he went out the front door, he made sure the passage lock was engaged before he closed the door, but he obviously couldn't lock the deadbolt.

When he started down the stairs, he suddenly realized that he'd left his belt on the floor by the bed. Color it gone he thought.

It was a good one and the buckle had his initials engraved on it, but it wasn't worth the trouble to try to go back and get it. When he walked out of the building, it was still drizzling rain and the cold damp wind cut into him. There was nothing moving in the parking lot, but he had a strange feeling that someone was watching him. The hairs on his arms stood up and he had the urge to run to his car. Once he was in his car and moving out of the complex, his heater was beginning to push out warm air, and he felt a little better.

Colonial Drive was almost totally deserted as he drove very carefully back to his hotel. He parked in an outside parking lot and went in through the front entrance still holding the towel wrapped around his hand. At least the bleeding seemed to have stopped.

When he walked through the lobby, a front desk clerk and a doorman who was standing by the desk, both stared at him. That's when he realized how bad he must have looked. His eyes were bloodshot, his hair stuck out in all directions, and his shirt was stained with blood. He gave them a stupid smile.

"If you think I look bad, you should see the other guy."

He walked on to the bank of elevators where a door was open and waiting and went up to his floor. He went into his bathroom, took a heavy dose of Tylenol, washing it down with a glass of Alka Seltzer, took off his clothes and got into a hot shower, still protecting his hand with the towel. Before he got out of the shower, he carefully unwrapped his hand and rinsed the blood off. It wasn't as bad as he had thought but it probably needed a few stitches. He decided that if he kept if wrapped tight it should be ok. He carefully rewrapped it with a hotel towel, turned off the lights and literally crawled into bed without trying to set his travel alarm or asking for a wakeup call. He passed out for the second time of the evening.

When he woke up, bright light was pouring through the open curtains. He was dying of thirst, and he couldn't tell whether his head or his hand hurt the most. He tried to remember the night before and it seemed like one of those dreams you have that are so real that you have to focus hard to separate it from reality. In any case it was a night he wanted to forget, so he pushed it aside and started getting ready to go home. After another hot shower, an order of Eggs Benedict with a pot of hot coffee, he was beginning to feel a lot better. By 11a.m. he was headed for the Florida Turnpike and south to Boca Raton. As he got closer to Boca and home, the events of the previous evening began to fade from his memory. It was probably good that he could forget the past night. If he only knew the consequences the night would bring, all of his hair would be turning grey.

CHAPTER 4

The Morning After

1995

Jim lived in a townhouse condo just off Glades Road. His patio overlooked a lagoon that created a relaxed, restful setting. He spent Saturday evening cooking a steak and watching a basketball game on television. The next day, Sunday, was Jim's favorite day of the week because he always spent it with Libby. Libby had been born prematurely and she had suffered both mental and physical development challenges. But she was making great progress, and everyone was optimistic about her future. It was the initial pressure of caring for her that was largely responsible for Jim and Julie's divorce. They were both strongly career oriented, and their jobs and schedules caused conflicts they simply couldn't handle at the time. Fortunately, both Julie and Jim were mature enough so that eventually they let their love for Libby transcend the acrimony of the divorce.

At ten a.m. the next morning Jim arrived at Julie's home. Libby and her mom, lived in one of the newly developed areas in Plantation where Julie worked as a drug rep for one of the large pharmaceutical companies. She had climbed the company ladder and was in charge of the southeast region of Florida. She'd chosen Plantation as a place to live both because her parents lived there and because her work involved a lot of travel. Her parents were a tremendous help with Libby. She knew that Jim would always help but his job took him away even more than hers. She, like Jim had never remarried. She had dated a couple of men seriously but eventually she always felt a lack of their acceptance of Libby, and Libby was the most important thing in her life. When Jim walked up to Julie's front door, Libby had been watching for him from the window and before he could ring the doorbell, Libby threw open the door and leaped into his arms. Julie walked up behind Libby.

"Somehow, I get the idea she's glad to see you. And it's only been a week. I don't think she could stand to go any longer without you."

"I couldn't go any longer either," Jim said.

"I think she's catching a cold. You'd better take this box of tissue and these cough drops just in case."

"What happened to your hand?" Julie asked as Jim reached for the box of tissues.

Jim shrugged nonchalantly replying, "I broke a glass and cut myself trying to clean it up."

Immediately changing the subject, he said, "We'll try to stay inside today."

Jim took the tissues and cough drops in one hand, Libby's hand in his other, and walked to his car. Libby was ten now and any of the problems she'd had up to now were difficult to detect. It was apparent to any observer that she was a happy and loved child. Jim took her to her favorite restaurant overlooking the Intracoastal Waterway and let her pig out on fried shrimp, french fries, and lemonade. Libby loved to watch the boats and Jim planned to one day buy a boat that he could take her out on. Afterward, they went to a new Disney movie and then for ice cream. She went to sleep on the way back to her mom's house and Jim had to carry her inside and lay her in her bed. He gave her a kiss on the cheek and wiped a sweaty strand of hair out of her eyes. She had a big smile on her face that melted Jim's heart as he reluctantly stood up to leave. Julie was standing in the door, and he didn't see her turn her head and wipe the tear from her eye. Jim went out to his car and brought back the tissues and cough drops.

"It was only a four-tissue day," he said. "Maybe she'll be ok."

"Let's hope so. I'll let you know how she does."

"I'll plan on picking her up Wednesday afternoon unless I hear different from you," Jim said as he left. He returned to his condo feeling good, the memory of the past Friday night replaced by the warm memory of his daughter hiding the nightmare that was coming.

CHAPTER 5

Jim's World Collapses

1995

The following week was a good week for Jim. He spent the week working in the company's home office in Boca and was able to spend time with Libby on Wednesday as planned.

The next morning Jim had showered, dressed, eaten breakfast, and was getting his briefcase ready to go when the doorbell rang. He didn't have many visitors at eight a.m., so he was curious when he opened the door. Standing there were two men in dark suits and two sheriff's deputies standing behind them. One of the suits was a heavyset man with a ruddy complexion. His nose was large, bulbous, and redder than the rest of his face. He looked to be in his mid-fifties, and he had a disheveled appearance looking as if he had slept in his suit. The second man was younger and dapper in his appearance. He was wearing a light-colored linen suit with a paisley tie that matched his blond hair which was parted down the middle. The older one spoke first.

"Are you Jim Herbert?"

Jim, standing in the open door replied, "Yes. Can I help you?"

"Would you step outside please?" the heavyset man said.

Jim realized that even though the man had said please, it was not a request, but an order. Puzzled and alarmed, Jim stepped outside. The older man held out a badge for Jim to see.

"I'm detective Martin Schloss from the Palm Beach County Sheriff's office. We have a warrant for your arrest."

As he started to ask what was going on, the two deputies had quickly stepped behind him, one on each side, grabbing both his arms, pulling them behind his back and snapping on handcuffs.

The florid man said, "Jim Herbert, you are under arrest on suspicion of murder. Anything you say can be held against you."

Jim couldn't hear the rest of his rights being read because his head was pounding from the sudden rise of his blood pressure. He almost passed out as they led him toward one of three Sheriff's vehicles, an unmarked car, and a patrol car. A small van with Palm Beach County Crime Scene written on it, sat in the street as well. His mind was frantically trying to figure out what was happening. This had to be some terrible mistake. He even wondered for a moment if this was one of those money raising events where you were arrested, and someone had to contribute money to a charity to bail you out. But after he was seated in the back seat of the patrol car and the door slammed shut, it became too real to be any kind of ruse. He felt like a caged animal as he sat helpless in the patrol car.

He watched the van doors open and two men dressed in jump suits get out, one of them putting on rubber gloves and the other carrying a camera as they entered his condo. By now there were neighbors coming outside to see what was going on. This was the most excitement on their street since Ruth Rosenbaum came home from grocery shopping at Publix and drove her new Lexus into the lagoon. They pulled her car out of the four feet of water with Ruth still sitting in the driver's seat holding a loaf of bread over her head to keep it dry. Meanwhile at Jim's front door, the two detectives were pulling on rubber gloves and following the technicians in coveralls into his apartment. Within a few minutes two deputies came back out, got into the car and without speaking, drove away with Jim sitting in the back seat in complete shock and disbelief.

CHAPTER 6

A Surprise Visitor-Raiford Prison

1998

Jim was startled back to the present by a voice outside his cell. Clarence Jenkins was a death row guard who although had a very stern appearance, was a kind man who treated the inmates probably better than they deserved.

"Jim, you have a visitor that's not recorded on your visitor list."

"What newspaper wants to write their version of my life this time?"

"This time it's not a reporter. Do you know a Mark Price?"

Jim immediately sat up.

"Yes, I do. I'll see him."

Jim had met Mark Price before his divorce. He and Julie were living in Boynton Beach and Jim happened to meet Mark at a sporting goods store where they were both looking at tennis racquets. It turned out that they both played at the same USTA level, and they began to play whenever Mark was staying at his oceanfront condominium in Boynton Beach. They enjoyed each other's company and since they were so close in ability, they always had a competitive match. Mark told Jim that he owned a condominium in South Florida only for the fishing. He kept an offshore fishing boat near the Boynton Beach Inlet, and he took Jim out on several occasions. His "boat" was a thirty-eight-foot Bertram that was equipped for big game fishing in the gulf stream which was just offshore. Jim knew that the upkeep of the Bertram alone must require substantial wealth. After the disruption caused by his divorce, Jim had moved to Boca and had unfortunately lost contact with Mark but still missed his company. Mark had always been reluctant to talk about his past and the only thing Jim ever learned was that Mark had been a college history professor who had suffered some sort of personal loss in the past. He never offered any details and Jim in turn, never pushed Mark for details.

Jim was led to a room with a small desk and a section of glass separating it from another small room. At a first glance, the man standing on the other side of the glass was well tanned and he was big. Not big as in fat, just big. He could have been a poster boy for a tight end on a professional football team. He had broad shoulders and looked as if he didn't have an ounce of fat on his body. He was casually dressed in khaki trousers, a blue button-down dress shirt and brown loafers. His full head of hair was a light brown that fell just over the tops of his ears and looked as if it was a few weeks past needing to be cut. His blue grey eyes seemed to focus like lasers, and it was hard not to notice that his nose was slightly off center as if it had been broken but never set back straight. A long scar ran from his forehead downward past his ear. He had a relaxed demeanor and as he looked at Jim through the glass, he smiled warmly. A guard stood a few feet away carefully monitoring every minute of the visit. Communication was through a type of speaker built into the bottom of the window so that nothing could possibly be passed from visitor to inmate.

Mark spoke first.

"I guess you're not interested in playing tennis today?"

Jim forced himself to smile back.

"Not unless you can make like Houdini and get me out of here."

"I've been out of the country most of the time for the last three years and I never heard anything about what happened. I just went to a boat show in Ft. Lauderdale, and I ran into Julie in a restaurant later. She was meeting with some drug company reps and when I asked about you, she turned white. I thought she was going to faint. She agreed to meet me later that day and told me the story. She was adamant about your innocence."

"Mark, I am innocent. When I left that girl, she was snoring loud enough to wake her neighbors. I also know I left the door locked when I left. I was hung over, but I knew what I was doing. When I cut myself on the glass in her bathroom, I sobered up fast. The police said the deadbolt on the back door was locked but the front door was unlocked. Somebody else had to have left the front door unlocked. Traces of her blood were on the front door handle. When I left the only blood in that apartment was mine."

"From what I hear, you have a good attorney representing you."

"I don't fault Karin Stills for anything. If I could start over, I'd still use her. It was like we were caught in a tsunami. Everything seemed to be stacked against us."

"Would you mind if I talked to Stills about your case?"

"Mark, you've got my permission to talk to anyone. I'll make sure Stills has my permission to talk to you. I'll admit that I'm running out of hope. I don't think there's much you can do for me at this point."

"Who knows, Jim? I'd like to try anyway. I have the time and maybe a new set of eyes can find something that's been overlooked."

Although Jim didn't really believe that Mark could do anything to help him, he did feel a certain degree of strength and confidence coming from Mark that he hadn't felt from anyone else for a long while. After Mark left and he was back alone in his cell, he realized that he was only grasping at straws at this point, and he sank back into a deep and dark depression.

CHAPTER 7

Mark Price

While Jim Herbert was sitting on death row for a crime he was innocent of, Mark Price was a free man, even though he was guilty of multiple murders that were cruel, heinous, savagely brutal, premeditated, and totally devoid of any remorse on his part.

Eight years before he first met Jim, Mark had been a history professor at a state university located in Jacksonville, Florida. He had grown up in a small town in the northwest Florida panhandle where his dad had owned the local hardware store that also served as the sporting goods store for the area. Growing up, hunting and football appeared to be the two most important things in Mark's life. Although by all outward appearances he was a classic Florida redneck, both his parents and his teachers knew better. At an early age Mark developed a love of books. He would read anything he could get his hands on, and it was reflected in his ease of learning in school. Because he was blessed with a photographic memory, everything he read, he remembered. But he could also apply what he learned. As an only child, his parents doted on him, and he should have become a spoiled brat. Fortunately, his parents made sure he never took himself too seriously and kept him well grounded in reality.

Mark's love for hunting led him to spend a lot of time in the North Florida pine forest and swamps. He killed his first deer at seven years of age and over time he lost count of the number of deer he'd killed. The family freezer was always well stocked with venison and was a staple part of his family's diet.

Deer hunting in the rural south is an integral part of life for many people. Different methods of hunting vary from group to group and region to region. Some areas favor hunting with dogs. The dogs are released in an area where deer are commonly found. After picking up a scent, the dogs will chase the deer until they cross the path of a waiting hunter. It's usually a good old boy social event where the hunters stand around drinking coffee or hot chocolate, often laced with something stronger, and try to keep warm while bragging about the last deer they'd killed. When they hear the baying dogs getting close, they check their rifles or shotguns to be sure a round is chambered and ready to fire. Then they spread out to cover the possible paths of the approaching deer. This form of hunting is not really about killing deer. It's actually all about the dogs. The dogs are never expected to catch the deer who can move through the woods much faster than any hunting dog. Instead, it's whose dogs can distinguish bucks from does and whose dogs will be closest behind the running deer. Whose dogs will obediently come back to its owner after the chase? Many men have been accused, sometimes rightly so, of loving their hunting dogs more than their wives.

By far though, the most common method of deer hunting and what Mark grew up with was "still" hunting from a stand. A deer stand could be anything from a fancy house on stilts with a heater and comfortable easy chair, to a board nailed to a fork in a big live oak tree. At an early age Mark developed a reputation of being a lucky hunter. Everyone said that whichever stand Mark would be sitting in would be the one where the deer would appear. It really wasn't luck at all. Mark would get bored very quickly and though it was frowned on, he would leave his stand and go to the deer rather than wait for the deer to come to him.

Because of his dad's store, he had his choice of just about any type of hunting rifle he wanted. But the rifle he'd used to kill his first deer remained his favorite rifle. It was a Savage model 99 lever action in 300 Savage Caliber with a 4x Redfield scope. It was a classic and no other deer rifle ever felt as comfortable in his hands.

Leaving his stand required him to be careful and know exactly where the other hunters were located in order to avoid becoming a target himself. But Mark knew the woods and he knew the habits of the deer, which gave him an uncanny ability to know where they would most likely bed down during the day. His hunting buddies wondered why his deer always ran so far from his stand before they fell. They thought Mark probably couldn't shoot straight and the wounded deer had run some distance from his stand before falling. Somehow it never dawned on them that there was always only one bullet wound in the deer he killed, and it was always placed perfectly in a vital spot.

By the time Mark was sixteen, he was bored with hunting deer. It was too easy. He sometimes thought that if deer were dangerous animals like Bengal Tigers or Cape Buffalo, then it would be a real sport. If the animals could pose a real threat to the hunter, then it might be fun. He started taking a book with him but he had to hide it under his coat so his high school friends wouldn't see it. Trying to explain to Leroy Seldon and Horace Monk why he was reading The Mayor of Casterbridge or Thucydides and The Peloponnesian War just wasn't worth the trouble.

Mark's other passion was football. By the time he was a senior in high school, Mark was six feet two inches tall and weighed close to two hundred pounds. He was fast, tough, and he had good hands. He played quarterback on offense and linebacker on defense, but he was overshadowed by Lorenzo Brown who was an unstoppable running back. Even though their team was terrible, Lorenzo was being recruited by several major colleges including The University of Florida where he would eventually become a Heisman contender. Mark really wanted to go to Florida, but they didn't need another quarterback and even if they had needed one, every recruiter who came to see his team play was only there to watch Lorenzo. Mark really didn't begrudge Lorenzo his success. Lorenzo was really talented. He was a good guy, and he was a good friend. Besides, football might be Lorenzo's only way out of their small town.

Mark ended up with a football scholarship to a small college in Mississippi where he did get to play all four years. Because of his grades and especially his SAT scores, he could have gone to a lot of places on an academic scholarship, but he wanted to play football just because he liked it so much. He majored in History with a minor in Spanish, and still managed to graduate Magna Cum Laude while playing football.

During Mark's last year in college, his dad died suddenly from a heart attack. Mark knew his mom would need all the financial resources his dad had left her, and he did not want her to spend money she might need, on himself. He had no desire to borrow money for grad school and end up in debt so soon after graduation, so Mark enrolled in the Army. The military had always appealed to Mark, and it was an easy decision for him to make.

If Mark had been looking for action, 1964 was the time to enlist. In Vietnam, the stage was being set for the years of conflict that followed. By 1962 the United States was steadily increasing its aid to South Vietnam and by the end of the year, there were up to 12,000 military "advisers" in South Vietnam. In 1963 the President of South Vietnam was overthrown and the Viet Cong from the north were close to overrunning the South. This fact combined with the Gulf of Tonkin incident where North Vietnamese patrol boats fired on US Navy vessels, led the US Congress to give approval for military action in the region. By 1965, there were 200,000 US combat troops serving in Vietnam.

As soon as he enrolled, Mark qualified for the Special Forces. He was made for it. He loved everything from the physical challenges to the firearms training. His natural skills as a soldier were obvious to his superiors and rather than send him off as a grunt solder with the rest of his contemporaries, he was held back and assigned as an instructor for new troops in the US. Outwardly, Mark was a quiet, polite, and easygoing person. However, when placed under stressful situations, he always seemed to instinctively make the best choices. Whether it was skill with firearms, hand to hand combat or tracking and ambushing in the woods, Mark excelled. He always quickly gained the trust and respect of the men around him. One incident that became a legend at the base made him a hero to the men around him.

During Mark's time as an instructor in the Special Forces, a new man who once fought professionally in the heavyweight boxing division, joined the company and immediately became the company bully. His sheer size intimidated most of the men. He began to extort things such as watches and cameras from some of those who were terrified of him. He sent a couple of men to the infirmary for trying to stand up to him. Complaints made to the company commander were ignored, the prevailing opinion being that these men were the toughest of the toughest and they should work out their differences themselves. The new man's name was Sylvester Dorch. He was six feet four inches tall and weighed close to three hundred pounds. His neck was as thick as his shaved head.

When Sylvester was twelve years old, he would steal money from his passed-out, dead drunk, alcoholic father. His favorite trick was to take a handful of coins to school and get a group of younger kids to gather around him looking at the coins. He would then throw the whole handful into the street and laugh like crazy when the kids dashed out into traffic picking up the coins. It was a miracle that a kid was never hurt. His reputation spread around the school and the teachers watched him around the clock. After once masturbating in study hall and later attempting to set the principal's car on fire, Sylvester dropped out of sight. The next time anyone heard from him, he was boxing professionally. He was mean and he was a good boxer, but he never made it to the top. After being twice charged with felonious assault and somehow getting off, he joined the army hoping to distance himself from his shady reputation.

When he walked past Marks bunk, he stopped at the one next to Mark and said to the guy lying there, "I think that's my lighter."

Joe, a new guy, said, "No, I bought it before I got here."

Sylvester walked over to him, grabbed his shirt and said, "You calling me a liar, asshole?"

A quiet voice behind Sylvester said, "Leave him alone. I'll vouch for him. It is his lighter."

Everyone in the barrack had been watching Sylvester from the moment he had come in, but you could feel the tension intensify the moment Mark spoke.

Sylvester whirled around at Mark's words. His eyes narrowed as he stared down at Mark.

"I'm not talking to you, ass wipe."

Mark, who had been propped up in the bottom bunk reading, very slowly sat up on the side of his bed and just as slowly stood up, his face only inches from Sylvester. He looked into Sylvester's eyes and again said loud enough to be clearly heard through the entire room, "I think you're the liar and the asshole."

By now everyone in the barrack was watching, aware that something was about to happen.

Sylvester led with his right hand. It was as if a huge piston was directed toward Mark's face. Later those that had a direct view, swore that Mark didn't move at all. Actually, the only thing that moved was his head and even then, it moved ever so slightly. When Mark rolled his head to the right the split second before Sylvester's fist would have crushed it, the fist grazed Marks cheek and continued straight on and into the metal railing supporting the upper bunk. The force of the blow bent the rail inward, but it also crushed Sylvester's knuckles and shattered his wrist. The intense pain that shot up Sylvester's arm suddenly became secondary to the pain Sylvester felt when Mark's knee exploded into his groin. Holding his hand, Sylvester doubled over just as Mark slammed both of his ears simultaneously with cupped hands rupturing both of Sylvester's eardrums. Mark then half led, half dragged, Sylvester to the barracks door and pushed him out. There were several wooden steps and as Sylvester rolled down them, you could clearly hear his head hit every step. When he reached the ground, he lay still, curled up in a fetal position, moaning pitifully. Later, all the witnesses would testify that Sylvester had tripped and fallen down the steps.

Three weeks later Sylvester limped back into the barrack. His hand was in a cast that reached to his elbow and his head was still wrapped with gauze. He headed directly for Mark. Everyone was holding their breath and expecting the worst as Sylvester approached Mark. But something remarkable had happened to Sylvester. Mark stood up to meet him and Sylvester put out his left hand since his right hand and forearm were useless.

"Thank you." Sylvester said. "I was a total jerk. I deserved everything you did to me. This is something I'm not used to doing, but I want to apologize."

A sigh of relief was felt throughout the room. Sylvester sat down on the bunk next to Mark to tell him that the first few days, all he could think about was how he would kill Mark as soon as he got out of the hospital. That was before he started talking to a sergeant in the bed next to him. The sergeant had broken his leg during a training exercise. It had been a compound fracture that was severe enough for the sergeant to be hospitalized for several days. His wife and five-year-old son came in to visit him every day. The five-year-old was under treatment for an aggressive type of leukemia. He was bald and wore a protective mask but otherwise seemed to be a happy child. The boy's father confided to Sylvester that the doctors gave him a guarded prognosis.

"There was something about the boy and his parents that got to me. I didn't know I had a heart but somehow, I felt a pain I'd never felt before. I was fighting the world for my own selfish reasons and here was a child and both his parents fighting a battle a lot bigger than any problem I'd ever had. Something in me just broke. I left that hospital bed determined to change something in my life."

Before Mark left active duty, Sylvester had actually become a friend and sometimes followed Mark around like a puppy dog. Sylvester's transformation led to his becoming a friend and protector to the men around him and he later left the army with a clean record and an honorable discharge. He continued to communicate with the sick child and his parents and years later was said to have broken down and cried when he watched the boy graduate from high school. Mark was pleasantly surprised at the changes in Sylvester, and he took no credit for it although everyone who knew the story, credited Mark with the change. After they left service, they stayed in touch and in time Sylvester ended up being elected sheriff in a Florida panhandle county near Mark's hometown. One day in the future their paths would cross again.

One day while serving as an instructor during his first two years of service, Mark was abruptly summoned to his base commander's office. However, the base commander wasn't present at the meeting. One of the office orderlies later said that he watched a Two Star General accompanied by two men wearing dark suits and dark sunglasses, enter the office ahead of Mark. After being in the office for about thirty minutes, Mark came out of the room and without saying another word to anyone, went straight to his barrack. He came out in a couple of minutes carrying his duffle bag still dressed in his fatigues, climbed into a waiting jeep, and was driven away without uttering a single word to anyone.

Mark essentially disappeared for the next eighteen months. He reappeared seemingly out of nowhere with severe injuries as a patient in the military hospital in Fort Sam Houston. Although he received an honorable discharge after recovering from his injuries, he refused to talk to anyone about where he'd been or what he'd done. His army records only contained a brief statement indicating special assignment stating, "Records retained by the pentagon, Special Operations Branch. All access denied."

Chapter 8

The Professor

When Mark reappeared at the end of his fourth year of duty, he was quietly discharged with honor. Since he had no intention of making a career of the army, he applied for a graduate program at the University of Florida. Because his college grades and his GRE scores were so high, he was accepted into the program. Within five years he'd earned a master's and PhD in history specializing in South American studies. Money he'd saved from active duty and some unusual education perks from the army, enabled him to finish debt free. During those five years he met and married his wife, Marge. By the time he received his degree, he and Marge were the proud parents of a beautiful daughter. He accepted a position teaching at a state university in Jacksonville, Florida. Marge was from Jacksonville and she wanted to be near her parents who both had serious health problems. Mark also had no desire to go back to the panhandle to live.

He and Marge wanted to have more children, but it didn't happen. They both spoiled their daughter Kim by giving her everything she wanted. According to all the accumulated wisdom of child rearing, Kim should have been a real brat the same way Mark, as an only child, should have been. She was not. She was a beautiful child in every way. It was probably a good thing she was an only child. Another one would never have measured up to Kim. As it so often happens, if the first child is so perfect, it leads parents to think they have the secrets of raising children. The second child usually soon dispels that notion. The teenage years were a challenge for Marge and Mark, but they survived. Mark learned the meaning of a bumper sticker he once saw that read, "Ask a teenager while they still know everything."

CHAPTER 9

Kim Price-Orlando

1988

Kim's high school grades and entrance exam scores afforded her many options of schools to attend. She especially liked the University of Richmond as well as Vanderbilt. She also was attracted toward the emerging University of Central Florida because of its proximity to Disney and its developing communication programs. Because she qualified for state scholarships, it would almost be a free education if she attended a Florida school. A little parental bribery with the offer of a new car if she attended UCF, plus two of her best friends going there as well, tipped the scales in favor of UCF.

Even though Orlando was two hours away from Jacksonville, Kim seemed to draw even closer to her parents while she was away. As expected, Kim had done well in school and even though she was in her junior year, Marge and Kim talked almost daily by phone. They talked for a long time on a Thursday night and Kim was excited about a date she had planned with a star athlete on Saturday. Marge knew Kim had a busy weekend planned so she didn't really expect to talk to Kim again until Sunday night. Around eight p.m. on Sunday evening Marge answered the phone expecting it to be Kim, but it was Kim's roommate Ann instead.

"Mrs. Price, did Kim come home this weekend?"

"No, Ann. I thought she had a busy weekend planned there."

"Well, she left Friday and she hasn't been back since. I went to the beach early Saturday, and I just got back. No one here has seen her all weekend."

Marge didn't know whether to be angry or scared.

"Will you put a big note on her bed telling her to call home no matter how late she gets in?" Marge asked.

After hanging up the phone Marge told Mark what Ann had said. They both began to think of possible explanations, none of which were good. Neither of them were able to sleep Sunday night.

Monday morning after calling the sorority house and learning that Kim was still unaccounted for, they packed a few things and headed for Orlando. They went straight to Kim's sorority house. Mrs. Zimmer, the house mother, met them with a distressed look on her face as they came in and took them straight to Kim's room. The room looked as if she might have just walked down the hall to talk to someone and would walk back in the door any moment. Ann told them that she and Kim were both working on papers so they could have the rest of the weekend free. Ann said that around ten thirty Kim had gotten a phone call. Ann overheard Kim say, "Don't worry. I'll be there in a few minutes."

Kim had picked up her car keys and wallet before telling Ann, "I'll be back in a little bit. If I don't see you, have a good time at the beach," and had left in a hurry.

Mark asked, "You don't have any idea who called her?"

"No," Ann said. "I left soon after Kim did. I spent the night at an apartment with a couple girls and we left early on Saturday to go to Daytona Beach."

Mark asked Ann if she knew the boy that Kim was planning to see on Saturday.

"She was supposed to be going to a fraternity party with Don Rich. Let me see if anyone knows when he picked her up."

A girl was coming up the stairs and Ann asked her if she knew when Don picked Kim up. The girl had a surprised look on her face.

"I thought everyone knew that Kim stood Don up Saturday night. It was apparently the first time he'd ever been stood up and he didn't take it too well."

By now Mark and Marge were really becoming frantic. Mark called the campus police from Mrs. Zimmer's office and was told to come to the station and file a report.

At the campus police office, they again went through their concerns with the officer. They filled out some forms and answered more questions. The police were polite but there seemed to be no sense of urgency. They said they would follow up on her scheduled date first. They probably thought Kim was nursing a hangover in someone's off-campus apartment. They asked how they could get in touch with Mark. He said he and Marge would be checking into a hotel nearby and he would call the office back and give them the number where they could be reached.

He and Marge got a room at a motel near campus and when Mark called them back with the hotel number the officer told him about the call Kim had gotten on Friday night. It came in on a sorority phone line and had been made from a payphone outside a convenience store on 17/92 in South Orlando. Otherwise, they didn't know anything else at the moment.

Mark couldn't sit still and do nothing so even though it was almost dark, he left Marge at the hotel and drove to the area of the convenience store. He took the cross-town expressway from UCF and got off on 17/92 South, also known as South Orange Blossom Trail, or as locals call it, "The Trail."

When he took the exit, and merged onto The Trail, it was like he had descended into a war zone. What had once been a major north-south route for happy tourists was now an embarrassment to the city of Orlando. Before the Florida Turnpike had been built, the Orange Blossom Trail had once been lined with prospering motels and restaurants filled with excited families headed south to sun and fun. By the middle seventies, a large part of the Trail had disintegrated. It was reduced to a series of adult motels with rentals by the hour. There were hubcap stores, used tire stores, junk cars sitting on dirt streets leading into areas that looked like forbidden zones in an armageddon movie. There were nude dancing places, gentlemen's clubs, and adult bookstores. Young male drug dealers stood on street corners, their hands stuck deep in pockets of baggy pants that hung to their knees, waiting to make eye contact with the driver of a passing car. Prostitutes maintained a presence both day and night, sometimes alone and sometimes in pairs. Some were young and pretty, taking their first steps into their own personal hell. Some were thin and frail, their bodies already destroyed by drugs and disease. Mark shuddered to think that Kim may have driven down this street alone and at night.

He found the convenience store and the phone booths where the call to Kim had come from. He parked and went over to the phones. The phone books had been ripped out of their binders. One of the phones was broken and the phone dangled by its cord. The other phone was so filthy Mark wondered how desperate someone would have to be to put their mouth and ear anywhere near it. Several young males with pants hanging almost to their knees were leaning on an old car in front of the store watching him closely.

Frustrated and with an increasing sense of dread, Mark returned to the hotel. Marge had fallen into a fitful sleep out of sheer exhaustion and Mark tried not to wake her up as he came into the room. Almost immediately the ringing phone did wake her as Mark answered it quickly.

"Sorry to wake you Mr. Price. This is Bob Johnson from campus police. I wanted you to know that Kim's car was found in the parking lot of a fast-food restaurant on the South Trail. It was only a few blocks from the pay phone the call had come from. I was told there were no signs of violence but from this point forward, the Orlando Sheriff's department is assuming authority. It's now out of the campus police jurisdiction and it's now officially a missing person case."

Mark tried to ask more questions but Johnson either didn't know anymore, or he just wouldn't tell more.

The night was the longest night of his life. Mark tried to watch television, but it was impossible. Marge was becoming a basket case and Mark was trying to keep his composure for her sake. However, he was dying inside. They both stayed awake most of the night. In the early morning hours Marge fell asleep again, but Mark was still wide awake. As the morning light began to chase away the darkness, Mark began the darkest day of his life. For Marge, it was the beginning of the end of her life.

At around six-forty a.m. the hotel phone rang, and Mark literally dove across the bed to pick it up.

"Mr. Price, this is Bob Johnson again. Someone from the sheriff's office just called. They'd like you to come in as soon as possible. I wanted to give you the directions and the person you need to ask for when you get there."

"Bob, did they tell you anything else?"

"I really can't tell you anymore Mr. Price. Let me give you a name and directions."

Marge was awake and was looking expectantly at Mark as he tried to keep her from seeing his shaking hand as he wrote the directions down. With a foreboding sense of dread, Mark set the phone back into its cradle.

CHAPTER 10

Shock and Disbelief-Boca Raton

1995

Jim sat in the back seat of the sheriff's cruiser in a complete daze. He felt like he was sitting in a cage like an animal in a zoo, which he now was. The two uniformed deputies didn't speak as they followed Glades Road to I-95 and headed north. Within thirty minutes they exited I-95 onto Southern and then to Gun Club Road. The Palm Beach County Jail could be seen well before they reached it. The jail was a massive concrete structure that rose into the sky like some monolithic Egyptian structure standing alone in the desert. They turned off Gun Club into the Palm Beach County government complex and entered the jail detention area toward the rear of the building.

With a deputy on either side, he was escorted through a large booking area, down a hallway and into a small room with a single table and three wooden chairs. No one was rough or rude, but he clearly sensed that he was not among friends.

"Can I use a restroom? I really need to pee."

The two deputies looked at each other and shrugged.

"Come with us," the taller one said after removing Jim's handcuffs. They escorted him a short distance down the same hall and entered a restroom with a couple of urinals. They both stood inside the door and watched him as he used one. When he was finished, they took him back to the same room. He was told to sit, and the deputies left him alone in the room. Jim had seen enough crime movies to know he was sitting in an interrogation room.

There was the usual large glass mirror, and he had no doubt that someone was watching from the other side.

Jim sat for what seemed to be hours but was probably only a few minutes before the door opened and the two detectives, Schloss and the dandy one entered the room. They sat down on the other side of the small table and this time it was the young one who spoke first.

"Jim, I'm detective Jason Armstrong from the Orange County Sheriff's office. I'd like to make this as quick and easy as possible. I'm sure you agree. I imagine this has been weighing heavy on your mind. Do you need anything to drink before we get started?"

He spoke with a soft easy voice accompanied by a relaxing smile.

Jim, who was still in a partial daze, said, "Make what quick and easy? I still have no idea why I'm here."

Schloss leaned forward with his arms on the table, his narrow eyes only inches from Jim's.

"You know damn well why we're here. You can't run away from it and you sure as hell can't talk your way out of it."

Jim wanted to shout but he tried to control his voice.

"Out of what?"

In a calm soothing voice Armstrong said, "Jim, we know everything that happened. If you can help us, you'll be helping yourself. Maybe there were things that would give some perspective on what you did. Was it alcohol, drugs, maybe self-defense? Was there anything that would explain why you killed the girl in a different light?"

Jim's head felt like it was about to explode.

"Kill? I never killed anyone! Ever!"

Schloss leaned forward and pointed his finger at Jim and said, "You met Tanya Griffin at the bar in your hotel last Friday night, got her drunk, took her home, raped her, beat her, strangled her with your belt, cut her throat and other parts of her body and left her bleeding out on her bed. We have your blood, your belt, your semen, your fingerprints all over the crime scene including the glass you cut her up with. We don't have a DNA result yet, but I'm sure it will be a match. Plus, we have witnesses of you leaving the bar with her and entering your hotel later wearing bloody clothes. And you're telling us you didn't do it. Sorry, my friend. The longer you deny this, the worst it's going to be."

Armstrong reached over and pulled Schloss back into his chair. Again, he looked at Jim with pleading eyes.

"Jim, I'm the lead investigator in this case and I might be able to help you but not unless you talk to me."

"Talk to you? Yes. I'll talk to you and I'm only going to tell you once. When I left the apartment, she was sleeping on the bed, and she was snoring like a freight train. I knocked a glass off the bathroom sink, and I cut myself trying to clean it up. I locked the front door passage lock when I left. That's all I can tell you, period. I want to see a lawyer now!"

Armstrong looked like he'd been slapped in the face and Schloss was looking apoplectic, his face turning beet red.

"Jim, that's too bad. I had hoped you'd be a little more reasonable. You can get your lawyer and meantime you'll be booked and charged with first degree murder."

He and Schloss both stood up as Armstrong spoke.

"We're done here. I'll see you in Orlando."

They both walked out leaving Jim stunned and overcome with fear and dread.

CHAPTER 11

A Nightmare

1988

After Mark hung up, he explained to Marge what Officer Johnson had told him. They wasted no time dressing and heading downtown. The directions Mark had been given were easy to follow. They got on the crosstown expressway, went west to John Young Parkway, and followed it north for a few blocks to the sheriff's main office complex. They had to circle the building once before finding the right entrance.

After finding a space to park, they entered a reception area and went to the designated visitor area. They identified themselves to a pleasant lady in a deputy's uniform and were told to please have a seat and someone would be with them soon. As they sat down in the waiting area, Mark watched as the deputy picked up a phone and spoke while looking in their direction. It was no more than three minutes before an adjoining door opened and an older deputy approached them.

"Mr. and Mrs. Price? I'm Sergeant Kelly."

Marge and Mark practically jumped up at once, "Yes!" they replied in unison."

"Would you come with me please?"

They went back through the same door and down a hallway to a set of elevators. The door opened immediately, and they went up to the second floor. The deputy was silent, and Mark was afraid to ask any questions. After going down another hallway lined with busy offices they were ushered into a large room. On one side of the office was a large desk and the other, a small sitting area with a sofa and two chairs. The officer behind the desk rose as they entered the room. His uniform was impeccable, and Mark recognized the Major's pin he was wearing. He came around the desk and introduced himself as Major Gene Rankin. He indicated for them to sit on the sofa. Sergeant Kelly walked over and closed the door to the office before sitting down next to the Major who was already seated. As he sat waiting for one of them to speak, he had a flashback to his time in the army as he looked at their spit shined shoes, perfectly creased uniforms, and neat, close-cropped haircuts. Major Rankin had the appearance of a very confident, take-charge person but he was visibly uncomfortable as he started to speak. There was no small talk. The major knew there was no way he could make this easy.

"Mr. and Mrs. Price, I'm afraid I have to tell you what no parent should ever have to hear. Your daughter's body was found early this morning."

Marge leaned forward and let out a wail of anguish. Mark's premonition had partially prepared him for bad news, but the scene felt surreal, and he felt as if he were outside his body looking down. His eyes were focused on the many photographs on the walls of the room, and he was having a difficult time hearing the major's words. He heard certain words, "homicide," "foul play," and "further investigation." He had his arm around Marge and tried to comfort her but was having little success as she continued to sob and rock back and forth. He finally managed to refocus on what the major was saying.

"And we need you to make a formal identification of her body before were start the autopsy."

Barely able to form the words, Mark asked "Can you tell us what happened? How did it happen?"

"Mr. Price, our investigation is just starting. I'm sorry that I don't have anything to tell you this minute. I can assure you that we'll let you know when we know. Her body has been removed from where it was found and has been taken to the coroner's office.

If you don't feel like you're able to identify her right now, is there anyone else that might do it?"

Mark took a deep breath, "No. I'll do it myself."

"We'll drive you to the coroner's office and we'll bring you back here to your car. It might be easier for you," Sergeant Kelly offered.

"I can't leave my wife here by herself."

"That's okay. She can ride with us. She won't need to see anything she doesn't want to see."

Marge had calmed down from her hysterical state to an almost zombie like one and she let Mark support her as they followed Sergeant Kelly and Major Rankin down to an enclosed parking area. The sheriff's office had obviously repeated this scenario before as a small van was already waiting near the entrance. Sergeant Kelly got into the driver's seat while Major Rankin helped Jim and Marge into the second-row seat, and he sat in the front passenger seat.

They had to cross downtown Orlando to get to East Michigan Street where the county coroner's office was located and the traffic as usual was heavy. During the ride Marge remained in her silent stupor while Mark struggled to gain some semblance of control over his thoughts. There had never been a time in his life that he felt as helpless as he did now.

They eventually arrived at a one story, nondescript building in a neighborhood that was mixed residential and commercial. They entered into a rather small waiting room furnished with heavy duty commercial furniture.

"Mr. Price if you'll come with me, we'll let Mrs. Price wait here. Sergeant Kelly will get her something to drink and wait with her."

For the first time Marge spoke. "I want to see her."

Major Rankin looked directly at Mark and said, "Trust me. Now would not be a good time Mrs. Price. You'll see her but not today."

Mark led Marge to a chair and helped her sit.

"I'll be right back Marge. Wait here."

Marge seemed to slip back into her comatose state and remained sitting.

As Mark followed Rankin down a series of hallways Rankin finally stopped before a double set of metal doors.

"Mr. Price, I made a judgment call back there that I hope is the right one. I don't think your wife can handle this. Sometimes it's the woman with the strength to make an identification but this time I'm judging you're the right one. Your wife is understandably in a state of shock and seeing your daughter right now won't help. I will tell you now before you see her, her body was just brought in. She's not a pretty sight. I want to give you one last chance to change your mind before we go in."

Mark took a deep breath before speaking, "I'll do it."

Mark followed Rankin through the double doors and into a large room that seemed to be all stainless steel with white cinderblock walls. The floor was concrete with multiple drains. The smell of strong commercial disinfectant was almost overwhelming. They were met by a lady in her mid-forties and an older black man. Both were wearing scrubs with plastic booties and the woman had a plastic cover that looked like a shower cap over her hair.

"Mr. Price this is Dr. Lucus. She is one of our medical examiners here and this gentleman with her is Mr. Ben Moore. He's one of our longtime assistants."

Major Rankin gave a nod to Moore who walked over to another wide metal door and pulled it open. Mark could feel the rush of frigid air even though he was standing at least several feet away. The assistant disappeared into the open door and immediately emerged pushing a gurney with some sort of fabric covering the object lying on it. Mark felt as if he was suffocating as he stepped up to the gurney and watched Dr. Lucus pull the cover back. Mark was not prepared for what he saw. It was Kim. But it was not his beautiful smiling daughter that he saw. Her entire face was cut and bruised. One of her eyes was open and staring vacantly into space. The other eye was closed, swollen and almost black. Her hair was tangled and matted. A dark blue line circled her neck. The vision of Kim's face was burned into Mark's brain, and he knew it would be there as long as he lived. He groaned and clutched the gurney for support. Rankin reached out to give him support but Mark straightened up and waved him off.

"This is my daughter Kim. I don't need to see any more."

When Mark went back out to the waiting room where Marge was sitting, she looked up at him with a pleading expression that screamed, "Tell me it's not her."

Mark could only reach out his arms to her and hold her tight as she stood up and started sobbing again as her worst fear was confirmed.

The deputies drove them in silence, back across town to the sheriff's office. Major Rankin asked Mark if he needed help to get back to their hotel.

"No. I'll be okay. Can you tell me anything else about what happened?"

"Right now, I can only tell you that Kim's body was found next to a Chinese restaurant early this morning by one of its employees. The restaurant is in a strip mall on South Orange Blossom Trail. Mr. Price, I can assure you that we're focusing every available resource on this but we're just now getting started. The autopsy should tell us more about the time and cause of death. I really wish I could tell you more but at this moment I don't have anything else I can tell you. Believe me. We want whoever is responsible and we plan to find them. Are you sure you don't need help getting back to your hotel?"

The Major's words offered no consolation to Marge and Mark. Like two zombies, they found their way back to their car in the parking lot and headed back to the hotel. Marge had retreated back into her fugue. Mark drove and wondered how his mind and body could continue to function on such a mundane activity as driving and his feeling of total helplessness continued to grow.

CHAPTER 12
West Palm Beach County Jail

1995

After his humiliating booking, Jim was again escorted to a small room and seated at a table. He was now dressed in a bright jail jumpsuit that smelled like the janitor's closet in grade school. One of the guards brought a phone and connected the line to an outlet, handed Jim a phone book, and told him to make his call. He left the room and waited outside the door which had a window. One of the deputies watched though the window while Jim tried to use the phone.

Jim's hands were shaking when he opened the phone book to the attorney section. The only person he could think of was Kevin Knight, the lawyer who had handled his divorce. When he and Julie were separated and eventually divorced, it had been an amicable one largely due to Libby. It was not a very profitable divorce for either of their attorneys and he didn't have to spend much time with his attorney. Consequently, Mark really never knew him very well. But right now, Kevin Knight was the only name he knew. That's when Jim realized that the phone book was for The North Palm Beaches and didn't include Boca Raton numbers.

His frustration finally boiling over, he threw the phone book at the door causing the deputy waiting outside to jump. When the deputy opened the door, Jim asked for a phone book for South Palm Beach County.

"Buddy, if you can't find a lawyer in that phone book, you must not need one very bad. If you really want to make a phone call, do it quick. You don't have all day."

The only thing Jim could think of now was his office in Boca. He called the main number, and the phone was answered by the receptionist.

Trying to keep his voice as calm and normal as possible, Jim said, "Morning Kelly. Will you do me a big favor and look up a phone number for me? My attorney left a message for me to call but I lost the number."

"Sure Mr. Herbert. What's the name?" She looked it up and gave it to Jim.

"Thanks Kelly. By the way, I've had a little emergency come up and I won't be in today. I'll call back later."

He had no idea how much later it was going to be.

He immediately dialed Knight's office. The phone was answered by the same secretary Mark remembered from past calls. After he identified himself, he was put on hold until he heard Knight's voice.

Kevin Knight specialized in two things, family law and golf. He was good at both. He was an excellent attorney, and he was very personable. This enabled him to deal with almost everyone. His relatability and his honesty helped him to excel in family law. He was also a scratch golfer. He'd played on his college team and his love of the game had continued.

"Mark, how are you? What can I do for you?"

Mark didn't know where to begin, and his first few words must have been incoherent.

"Mark. Hold on a minute. Are you telling me you're in jail right now?"

"Yes! They're accusing me of killing someone. They plan to take me to Orlando and charge me with murder."

"Let me make sure I understand. You're in the Palm Beach County jail right now?"

"Yes."

"Has anyone talked to you?"

"Yes."

"Have you confessed to anything or signed anything?"

"No. They wanted me to cooperate by explaining why I did it. I told them I didn't do any of the things they were saying I'd done."

"Good! Now Mark, listen very carefully to what I'm telling you. Do not, I repeat, do not talk to anyone until I can get there. You're probably going to need a criminal defense attorney, but I need to know more before I can help you. I'm going to get in my car as soon we hang up. It's going to take me thirty to forty-five minutes to get there from Boca. That's assuming I-95 isn't at a standstill anywhere. Try to hang on. Okay?"

"Thank you, Kevin. You don't know how grateful I am."

When Kevin hung up the phone he called out to his secretary, "Gail, will you call Doc and tell him I can't make our tee time this afternoon? Tell him this time I'm the one with an emergency patient."

Chapter 13

A Cold Case

1988

When Marge and Mark finally turned onto Alafaya Trail near the UCF campus and parked at their motel, they were met by a crowd of crying red eyed students. The detectives had wasted no time in starting to interview Kim's friends and the word of Kim's death had spread quickly. They wanted to offer help but really weren't sure how. They did help with Marge and that took some pressure off Mark. The next few days were a blur. Mark had Marge seen by a local psychiatrist who put her on a strong medication, and she remained in a zombie like state.

It was over a week before Kim's body was released for them to take her back to Jacksonville for burial. They had a grave side service with a closed casket, but Marge and Mark were able see Kim one last time before her body was taken to the cemetery for the service. Mark was very apprehensive about how Marge would react. A mortician had done an excellent job of preparing her face, but Mark could only see her face as he remembered it in the coroner's office. Marge, no doubt due to the medication, held up better than he expected. She stood and stared and reached out once to touch Kim's hand. It was only when the casket was closed that Marge, without saying a word, simply collapsed. The graveside service turned out to be an unexpectedly large event with many students from UCF and a large number of Kim's high school friends attending. It was a testament to how many people had been touched by Kim during her short life.

Mark took emergency family leave from the university and tried to help Marge for the first few weeks. He tried to get information on the investigation from the Orange County Sheriff's office but was told little. When Mark called Major Rankin after the funeral, he was very sympathetic.

"Mr. Price I can't imagine how frustrated you must be. I'm going to introduce you to Detective Garcia. He's the lead investigator on the case. He actually will know things before I do, and he can keep you updated better than I can. Please don't think I'm trying to put you off. You can still call me anytime you want. Stay on the line. I'm going to get him on the phone and introduce you so he'll know who he's talking to."

"Alright, I'll hold."

Mark was put on hold but within a minute Rankin was back on the line.

"Mr. Price, I have Detective Thomas Garcia on the line with us. Thomas, this is Mr. Price. He wants to be kept updated on every step of the investigation. I explained to him that you could keep him better informed than I could. I'm going to hang up and let you talk to him."

There was a click as Rankin's line closed.

"Mr. Price, first I want to offer my most sincere condolences. I have two children and even though I have to deal with violence every day, I can't begin to comprehend what you and your wife are going through. Understand that we are going to find the animals who killed your daughter."

"You said animals. You suspect more than one person?"

"Yes. For starters, Kim's body appeared to have been almost thrown into the back of a dumpster. It would have been difficult for one person to have done it."

There was a long pause before Garcia continued, "There are other things that point to more than one person."

Mark hesitantly asked, "Like what other things?"

"Mr. Price I'm hesitant to give you details over the phone. There are things that may be difficult for you to hear."

Mark was gripping the phone so tightly his hands were turning white.

"I had to identify her body. I need to know everything that happened."

"Mr. Price, Kim was sexually assaulted by more than one person."

Mark was gripping the phone so tightly his hands were turning white.

"What was the cause of death?"

"Even though she'd been severely beaten and strangled, the actual cause of death was an overdose of heroin."

Mark was stunned and emphatically blurted out, "Kim didn't use heroin or any other drug."

"We don't believe it was used voluntarily. There was no sign of any previous drug use, and the coroner believes the heroin injection that actually killed her was not consensual."

"Do you have any suspects?"

"At the moment, no. We weren't able to lift any definitive fingerprints from the scene including her car. We're still processing all the garbage that was in the dumpster. We're looking at anyone in the area with a history of related offenses or any predilection toward violence. I'm still hoping we'll find someone who may have seen or heard something. We're looking at any possible connection to anyone from UCF as well."

"What about the phone call she received?"

"That phone call is critical. It's also why we still think someone is out there who saw something that night. There is always a lot of foot traffic around that store at night. We're putting pressure on our contacts to come up with something. We just haven't found anything yet. Let me give you my phone number. The best time to reach me is between seven and nine a.m. I'm usually in the office then. I promise to let you know when we have something more."

Mark was too stunned with what he'd been told to ask any other questions.

"You have my number. Please call me as soon as you know anything."

Three weeks after the funeral, Mark realized there was nothing he could do to help Marge by staying at home. She was now under the regular care of a psychiatrist in downtown Jacksonville who indicated to Mark that it might take months for her to recover from the mental trauma. Mark resumed his teaching at the university, knowing that if he continued to sit around the house, he'd be needing psychiatric care himself. He immersed himself in his work at the university and tried to remain patient with the progress of the investigation. He wasn't able to get any more information from the sheriff's office. The problem was that there was almost no progress on the case, and it was fast becoming a "Cold" case.

At home, Marge, after some initial improvement, was slowly regressing again. He spent every moment he didn't have to be at the university with her. A couple of faculty wives who had been close friends tried to reach out to her, but she didn't respond at all. She only wanted to be alone and even Mark was having a difficult time communicating with her.

One subject that had been a taboo topic was Kim's upstairs bedroom. Since the weekend that Kim disappeared, the only person who had entered her room had been a detective from Orlando who had examined her room accompanied by a detective from Duval County.

As they left, the Duval County Detective told Mark, "We left everything just as it was. We took some pictures, but we didn't find anything helpful. I'm sorry we had to come in at all, but we don't want to take a chance on missing anything that might help."

"I understand. Thank you for trying."

When the detectives left, they closed the door to her room, and it hadn't been opened since. Mark knew that at some point they would have to go through Kim's room. Marge insisted that it be left alone, and Mark realized that now was not the time to push the issue. Later Mark would realize what a mistake he made by not recognizing the full extent of Marge's grief.

CHAPTER 14

Lawyers

1995

I-95 was running smoothly for a change and Kevin turned off onto Gun Club Road in record time. He was familiar with the main jail and the visitor area. The week before, one of his clients had been arrested for forgetting he had a handgun in his briefcase as he went through airport security. He was rewarded with a night in the West Palm Beach County jail before Kevin was able to bail him out. Since he was familiar with the jail, it only took him a few minutes to get through the check points and into the area set up for meetings with inmates.

Jim looked like a real basket case when Kevin walked into the small room where Jim was seated.

"Kevin, I can never thank you enough!"

"Mark, my job is helping people. I hope I can help you. Let's start at the beginning. Remember, what you tell me is privileged attorney-client information. This can't be recorded in any way."

"Kevin, I really don't care if it is recorded. It's the truth. I've done nothing wrong."

Jim started at the beginning where he met the victim in the bar and ended with the interrogation by the two detectives.

"Mark, everything you've told me is all circumstantial evidence, but I've got to tell you it is serious. It's not a question of whether or not I believe you. My advice is twofold. First, as I told you earlier, say nothing else except what you're told to say by your council. Secondly, you are going to need a criminal defense attorney. I don't mean one just out of law school or someone who defends DUIs for a living. I'll help you find someone who's qualified to help you. I would recommend someone from the Orlando area who'll be familiar with the people from the prosecutor's office as well as the judges there. I'm certain they'll move you up to Orlando as soon as possible, probably tomorrow. Even if they move you to Orlando tonight, don't worry. Either I, or someone I recommend, will be seeing you. Just continue to refuse to talk to anyone without your lawyer by your side."

"Kevin, will you do one more thing for me and call Julie? Let her know what's happening and tell her I'm being charged for something I didn't do."

"Of course, Jim. Try to keep calm and remember that innocent people are very rarely convicted for something they didn't do."

Kevin's statement was partially correct. Jim was held overnight and early the next morning, he was handcuffed, placed in the back of a van with no windows and driven north to the main Orange County jail in Orlando. He was told that his first appearance was scheduled for the next day. When he asked to call his attorney, he was allowed to make the call.

"Jim, I've talked to several other attorneys that I trust, and they all have pointed me to the same person. I've been told that one of the best criminal defense attorneys in the state is in Orlando. Her name is Karin Stills. She was a marine before she went to law school. She's defended some high-profile cases and has an excellent track record of success. Everyone says not to let her appearance affect your opinion. Apparently, she's a tiny lady but she's a pit bull in disguise."

"Kevin, I don't care if it's Smoky Bear, as long as they can help me. They've told me that my first appearance is scheduled for tomorrow morning."

"Karin will be seeing you this afternoon. And, by the way, I've talked to Julie. She'll be seeing you soon as well."

"Thank you, Kevin. I can't tell you how much I appreciate your help."

"Let's get you through this, my friend. Then you can thank me."

Later in the afternoon he was taken into a small conference room. He'd only been in the room for a couple of minutes before Detective Armstrong entered the room. He was accompanied by another detective who reminded him of the TV figure Columbo. Armstrong introduced him as Detective Johnson. Armstrong spoke first in a friendly way as if he and Jim had been best friends for life.

"Jim you've had some time to think about all this. Is there anything you want to get off your chest? I know this is difficult and we'd like to help make the process easier for you."

"Tell me how you want to help me?"

"If you could just give us some reason why this happened. Understanding why, would be a big help to us all. Was it self-defense or were you provoked in some unusual way? Just give us a reason."

Without warning, the door to the room flew open and a small figure carrying a black briefcase entered the room. She could not have been more than five feet two inches tall and maybe weighed one hundred pounds wet. She wore a severe black suit with a white blouse buttoned at the neck. Her hair was pulled up into a tight bun and she wore no jewelry at all. Her presence immediately dominated the room. She only glanced at the two detectives once before saying, "Get the fuck out!"

It was not a request. The two detectives shook their heads and left the room without saying a word, looking like kids caught with their hands in the cookie jar.

Mark's immediate impression was one of a sense of relief. It was immediately obvious that her size had no bearing on her strength, and she wasted no time with small talk.

She held out her hand and said, "I'm Karin Stills. What did you tell them?"

"Nothing."

"Good. Never talk to them unless I'm in the room with you. And by never, I mean never."

She sat down and took a notebook and pen out of her briefcase before she spoke again.

"Now, start from the beginning and tell me what happened."

Mark told her everything from beginning to end. When he was finished, Stills took a deep breath before she spoke again.

"Mr. Herbert, I can't stress enough how important it is that you disclose every single fact to me now. Even if it's uncomfortable, or you feel it's irrelevant or mundane, if you want me to give you the best representation, I've got know everything. If the prosecution knows something I don't know and I'm taken by surprise, then we're screwed."

"I've told you everything. Yes. I was there but she was alive and well when I left her apartment. I did not kill that woman! I'll gladly take a lie detector test. I'll do anything to prove I didn't it."

"Okay. Here's how it's going to work. Your first hearing with the judge will be tomorrow morning. Your bail will be discussed and I'm sure the state will want you held without bond. Do you have any history of criminal offenses?"

"No. I've never even gotten a traffic ticket."

"You are employed?"

"Yes. At least until yesterday."

"Do you own your own home?"

"A condo. Or I should say I almost own it."

"Do you own any firearms?"

"None."

"Do you have a passport?"

"Yes."

"You will need to let me have it."

"Tell me about your family."

Jim proceeded to give her a brief summary of his divorce and current relationship with his wife and daughter.

"I'm going to try to get you released on bail. I'm sure the prosecution is going to fight it, but I think we can show that you're not a flight risk. I should be able to get something reasonable set. Stills had been taking notes during the conversation.

"Can you think of anything else you want to tell me?"

"I want to move as fast as possible to get this whole thing over with."

"Okay. You will have the right to request a speedy trial. We'll discuss the best strategy in that regard as soon as the bail is set. I'll see you tomorrow morning. Follow my lead and let me do all the talking. If asked, the only words you will say are "Not guilty." I'll try to have you out of here as soon as possible. In the meantime, remember what I said. Don't talk to anyone."

CHAPTER 15

Moshe Gersten

1988

Mark and Marge's home was a two-story house sitting on the bank of the St. Johns River. The house was of solid masonry and stone construction built to withstand Florida's hurricanes. There was a three-car garage with a separate shop and laundry room at one end that was connected to the house by a covered walkway. A second floor over the garage contained a one-bedroom apartment. The main house was two-story as well with a large eat in kitchen, dining room, great room, and master suite with a small study, on the first floor. Four bedrooms and two bathrooms were on the second floor. Kim, being an only child had commandeered two of the upstairs bedrooms. One was her bedroom and the other was her playroom/study. On the riverside of the house, a wide stone patio extended out toward the St. Johns River. With the lot sloping sharply downward toward the river, the patio seemed to be suspended in the trees looking down. The view from all rooms facing the river and from the patio was breathtaking. A stone walkway led from the patio down to the river and to a dock. The dock led out into the river to a small boathouse with a screened sitting area.

As it runs through Jacksonville, much of the St Johns River is lined with commercial property that ranges from shipyards, condominiums, shopping, and entertainment areas. The areas of private homes have slowly eroded away due to simple economics. Even though condominiums and apartments are moving in like an unwelcome rash, there are still a few beautiful neighborhoods remaining. These are, as would be expected, very expensive and desirable areas. Normally, as a college professor, Marge and Mark could have never afforded a home in one of these neighborhoods, especially one directly on the river.

Mark's mother had passed away soon after he'd received his PhD and began teaching in Jacksonville. Being an only child, Mark inherited his mother's house and the twenty acres it sat on just outside the small panhandle town he'd grown up in. Having no intention of ever going back there to live, he planned to sell the home and twenty acres for whatever the appraised value might be. He contacted a realtor in the area whose name he remembered and discussed listing the property. He was surprised at how easy it was going to be. The realtor told him that it might just be Mark's lucky day because he just happened to have a client who was interested in purchasing the property. He told Mark that he would send him a realtor's contract today by overnight mail. If Mark would sign, notarize it, and send it back, he reassured Mark that it would be sold in record time. Mark did receive a large package the next day. He assumed it was standard language and he was almost ready to sign it and send it back, but a small voice in the back of his head told him that this was too easy. He wisely decided to have a lawyer look at it before he signed it.

Mark remembered that a professor from another department who Mark liked and trusted, had mentioned that his brother had taken and passed the Florida Bar and was moving from New Jersey to Jacksonville. The friend, Larry Gersten, had told Mark that his brother Moshe, was the smart one in his family and was leaving a large law firm in New York where he had already been made a partner. Mark called his friend Larry, who was pleased that Mark was asking about his brother and gave Mark his brother's office number. Mark called the number he had been given and a lady answered on the first ring. Mark identified himself and explained what he needed. He also mentioned his friend Larry. The lady's accent was a strong "somewhere from the northeast" accent. She was pleasant and asked Mark when he would be available. When

Mark said "As soon as possible," she asked him if he could come now.

Mark gladly replied, "Yes. That would be great. Just give me directions."

The Office was located on University Boulevard, just off the Arlington expressway. It was easily accessible from his office at the university, and he was in Gersten's building's parking lot within thirty minutes. The building was a three-story office building that appeared to be a form of office condominiums. A directory on the first floor indicated MDs, DDS, insurance agents and multiple attorney's offices in the building. Gersten's office was near the elevator on the second floor. He entered a tiny waiting room that contained two chairs and a reception desk. The lady sitting at the reception desk smiled as Mark walked in.

"You must be Professor Price?"

"Please call me Jim. I've got a way to go before I'm a full professor."

As he spoke, a tall slender man with a full head of prematurely graying hair came out of one of the two doors leading off the reception area. His facial features were striking. He had a prominent hooked nose that gave him a decidedly hawkish appearance. For a minute, Mark thought he was looking at Abraham Lincoln. Mark's surprise was obvious, and he hoped it didn't show. Moshe's brother Larry was short and stocky with a receding hairline. As Mark returned his handshake, he said, "I was expecting a clone of your brother."

Moshe gave a good-natured laugh.

"No. We don't look very much alike. My dad used to mention it to my mother a lot. By the way, this is my wife, Carol. She was a paralegal in another life. She's starting all over again."

Carol smiled, "I've got a demanding boss but I'm trying hard."

"Come on into my office and tell me how I can help you," Moshe said as he pointed Mark in the direction of his office.

Mark had been a little apprehensive about trusting someone he knew so little about, but after listening to Moshe explain why he left a large law firm in New York to start out on his own, any reservations he may have had soon disappeared. Moshe explained that he had picked Jacksonville because he and his brother's families were very close, and they'd spent their summers at Ponte Vedra Beach during their early years. They had always liked the area. Moshe had also developed a valuable working relationship with several prominent people in Florida and they'd encouraged him to move south.

"Besides, I could never get my nose warm during the winter," he said as he laughed at himself.

Mark eventually explained his concern and questions about the property left in his mother's estate. Moshe took the contract from Mark and quickly glanced through the pages.

"Mark, will you give me until either late this afternoon or tomorrow morning and let me read this. I've got some real concerns already, but I want to read it all before I say anything. If they're so hot to buy the property, a day or two won't stop the sale."

"That's fine with me."

Mark thanked Moshe and Carol as he left their office and drove back to his own office, feeling good about his meeting with Gersten.

Mark was grading test papers well after five o'clock when his office phone rang.

"Mark, this is Moshe Gersten. You were smart to be suspicious about this deal. First of all, it's not just a realtor's contract. When you dig through all the fine print, and there is a lot of it, it ends up being a binding contract agreeing to all of the buyers terms the minute you sign it. What they've done is not illegal, but to say it's deceptive is being far too kind. I've put some inquiries out to friends in Tallahassee who have a lot of connections and I'd like to get more information especially related to the proposed buyers. I've got a feeling that there's a lot we don't know."

"Thanks. I feel more comfortable already. Let me know what you find."

The following day after finishing a class, there was a message light on his phone. The message was from Gersten who asked Mark to call him back ASAP. Moshe himself answered Mark's call.

"Mark, are you sitting down? I have some very interesting things to tell you. Have you followed the news about the proposed interstate highway from Jacksonville west through the panhandle of Florida? It's been on the table for some time but nothing concrete and especially no specifics on the exact route. What do you think your property might be worth if the interstate were to split your twenty acres in half and your property fronts on a state highway where there will be an interchange as well? It may be the only interchange within forty miles east and twenty miles west."

"How did you find this out?"

"Let's just say I have some friends in the right places in Tallahassee. The group that wants to buy your property is tying up land from Jacksonville to Pensacola. You have a very valuable piece of property that you were about to sell for a fraction of its real value."

"What would you recommend that I do next?"

"I'll be glad to sit down with you and look at your options. One of your biggest concerns is going to be the tax implication. If this road goes through as planned, it could involve a substantial amount of money."

"Okay Moshe. It is a good thing I'm sitting down. This is unexpected. I'll get all the information related to my mother's estate and the trusts. Before Mom died, I'd made sure all the inheritance issues were addressed. All that effort should help, especially now."

And so, it did. Within the following year and a half, the proposed turnpike became a reality, and it did in fact split Mark's property in half. Mark's property became even more valuable since one of the other two corners of the interchange was covered by a lake and an old country church surrounded by a cemetery filled the other corner. Only Mark's two corners would be available for any commercial development. With Moshe's help and guidance Mark was able to use one corner for a long-term lease with a major oil company. It ended up including a truck stop, motel, and two fast food chains. A portion of the other corner was utilized in a property swap for the dream home Marge and Mark would never have thought possible. Several acres were held in reserve for future development.

Early in Mark's teaching career and while Kim was a baby, they would drive through neighborhoods and look at their dream homes. Their favorites were homes on the river. When the property negotiations began, their property search became a reality and ultimately through Moshe's continued help, they were able to secure the river front home. The income stream from the property leases alone easily covered insurance, taxes, and related expenses and what was left over was still more than his teaching salary.

But even though he and Marge had been able to live very comfortably for many years, their affluence provided little consolation to the stark reality of their current grief.

Eventually, Marge began to show gradual signs of improvement. Mark continued teaching but his heart wasn't in it. He had worked hard during his first few years of teaching. He had recognized the paper chase game early on along with the politics of academia. By now he had achieved both Full Professor and tenure. But for the first time in his teaching career, he was only going through the motions.

"It's a good thing I'm tenured. Otherwise, I'd have been fired by now," he thought to himself.

Weeks had passed since Kim's murder and there was still no evidence of progress on the case. Mark was growing more and more impatient.

One morning before Mark left for work, he and Marge were sitting on the patio drinking coffee and watching the sun come up over the river. Out of the blue Marge said, "I'm going to start cleaning Kim's room this morning."

Mark was elated at her statement.

"If you'll wait until I get home, I'll help."

"I'm Okay. Go on to work. You can help when you get home."

Mark went on to work both encouraged and a little bit scared at Marge's state of mind. He called her after lunch to see how she was doing but got no answer. He was concerned but she often didn't hear the phone every time he called. He called again sometime after two pm and still no answer. Now he was concerned. He cancelled his last class and headed home. There was an ominous silence as he entered the house.

"Marge!" No answer.

He ran up the stairs two at a time. What he found when he reached the second floor, rocked his world again.

CHAPTER 16

Formal Charges

1995

Jim's first appearance before the judge went as Stills had predicted. The state was charging Jim with murder in the first degree and was insisting that he be held without bail. Even so, Stills seemed to have total control of the situation. She immediately argued that with no previous criminal record, a stable job, a homeowner, and most importantly a close relationship with his special needs daughter coupled with his intention to ask for a speedy trial, he was not a flight risk. The Judge agreed with strict conditions. She imposed a two hundred and fifty-thousand-dollar bond along with house arrest. He would have to wear an ankle bracelet and stay in his home in Boca. He would also have to surrender his passport. Neither the state nor his attorney was happy with the judge's decision, but at least Jim would get out of jail for the time being.

Apparently, the murder was making front page news on a daily basis. Popular public opinion was screaming for Jim to be used as an example for equal application of justice. As more and more details of the brutality of the murder became known, it only grew worse. The evening news repeated the mantra of inequality. It was time for white privileged males to suffer the same fate as poor minorities did. Although the judge followed all the prescribed guidelines concerning flight risk, she was under a lot of pressure to keep Jim in closer confinement.

The date for Jim's first hearing was set for two weeks. The judge did give Jim the right to drive back and forth from Boca to Orlando as necessary for court appearances leading up to his trial.

Fortunately, Jim had enough equity in his condo to enable him to satisfy the bail requirement and by late afternoon he was being driven back to his home in Boca.

As soon as he was home, he called Julie. She answered on the first ring.

"Where are you?"

"I'm home, finally."

"Libby is staying with my mom. I'm coming up right now. I want to know what's happening to you."

"Okay. I need someone to talk to. This has been a bad dream. I keep expecting to wake up from a nightmare."

"I'll be there in about an hour."

Julie made it to Jim's condo in under an hour. There were several reporters outside Jim's condo when Julie arrived. The reporters tried to stop her and get her to make some sort of statement. She did make some comments that would have made a sailor blush as she pushed them aside.

When Jim opened the door, Julie was shocked by Jim's appearance. He looked almost shrunken, like someone who had slept in their clothes after a night of binge drinking.

As always, Julie was brutally honest.

"Jim, you look like shit."

"Right now, I feel worse than I look."

"Tell me what happened."

Jim started at the beginning. There was no shame in his description of his encounter with the girl he met in the bar. Since their divorce, they both had had relationships with other people, and they were long past any feelings of jealousy or judgment of the other. Julie listened to Jim's recounting of the encounter with an unemotional attitude and made no judgments.

"Why are they blaming you for her murder?"

"Because I was there. She was killed sometime after I left. They think it's a slam dunk case. They have evidence against me and no evidence against anyone else."

"How do you feel about the lawyer?"

"I like her. I think she's a good choice."

"What's next?"

"I'll have another hearing in two weeks. Naturally I'll plead not guilty and I'm not sure how fast it goes after that."

"So, for the moment, there's nothing you can do. I think you need a shower and clean clothes. Go clean up and I'll find something in your kitchen for you to eat."

Julie found some frozen things in Jim's freezer which she nuked and then she opened a bottle of wine. After Jim finished the food and wine, Julie left and promised to bring Libby back next time. Before she left, she gave Jim a hug and a kiss on the cheek.

"Jim, I believe you. I know you can be an asshole sometimes but you're not a killer. Try to stay strong."

She left him standing in his doorway watching her drive away.

CHAPTER 17

Mark's World Is Rocked Again

1988

When Mark reached the second floor, the doors to both of Kim's rooms were open wide. He found Marge slumped on an ottoman in Kim's study. The first thing he saw was an open bourbon bottle on the floor next to her. The bottle was laying on its side and some of the liquid had spilled out on the floor. The smell of alcohol was strong, but even more concerning was the empty pill bottle laying on the floor next to the bottle. Marge's lap was covered with pictures of Kim. She was unresponsive and her breathing was shallow, but he could feel a faint pulse. Mark immediately called 911 for help, and then continued to try to wake her.

The emergency response was quick, and he met them at the door and led them up to Kim's room. Mark rode with the paramedics who were hovered over Marge all the way to the emergency room. Mark waited in the waiting room for what seemed to be an eternity before a nurse came for him and took him back to a small room where a young physician in scrubs was waiting.

"I'm sorry Mr. Price. We've done everything possible to save her, but all of her systems just shut down.

"Can I see her?"

"Yes. Come with me."

Mark followed him a short distance into a room filled with beeping, blinking and humming devices. There were wires and tubes everywhere. Marge was lying on what looked to be an operating table. All the tubes and wires had already been removed from her body and she appeared to be sleeping. Mark thought she looked more at peace than anytime since Kim's death. Mark stood next to her body as a wave of loneliness like he had never felt before enveloped his entire being.

Marge was buried next to Kim on a wet and windy Thursday afternoon. This time the service was small with only a few of Mark's and Marge's friends in attendance. There were a few people from his department at the university as well as his friend Larry Gersten along with Carol and Moshe. Mark was able to convince them all that he was fine, and he sat in his car at the cemetery until everyone had left. He waited until the workers had finished with their work at the gravesite before he walked back to the deserted gravesite. As he stood where his wife and daughter lay, his grief was slowly replaced with a burning rage. He knelt down and placed a hand on each grave as he said out loud, "I swear to you both, I won't be back until everyone responsible for this is rotting in hell."

CHAPTER 18

The Noose Is Tightened

1995

A week before his scheduled arraignment, Jim was told by Karin Stills that he would not need to be present for it. She was only going to make the declaration of not guilty and set a date for discovery. Because Jim was house bound, he was spending a lot of time watching television. He was dismayed to see that his case had become a major news item with his name being prominently mentioned. The media was emphasizing the brutality of the murder as well as dwelling on the young son left without his mother.

On the day of the arraignment, the courthouse in Orlando was besieged by a mob chanting "Justice for Tanya." The demonstrations were further fueled by a recent trial where a local wealthy businessman had been acquitted of a hit and run which had left a young child dead. Again, the press pushed the narrative that this was a chance to do the right thing and balance the scales of justice. Jim realized that his presence would have further fueled the fires of retribution and he was thankful he didn't have to be present.

Shortly after the arraignment Jim received a call from Stills.

"Jim, I'm glad we didn't have you come up today. It was a circus. Now, because of all the negative publicity, you're going to have to be extra careful. Don't talk to anyone on the phone unless it's family or myself. Don't answer your door unless you know who it is."

"Karin, it looks like I've already been convicted."

"Try not to worry Jim. All this publicity could work to our advantage. I'm going to keep things moving as fast as I can. We've set a date for discovery a month from now which is unusually fast. We need to see just what evidence the state has so I'll know what we're facing."

"How about the simple fact that I didn't do it?"

"I wish it were that simple. Let's wait and see."

On the date of discovery, Jim drove up to Orlando and went with Karin Stills to the courthouse for the discovery hearing. Fortunately, the discovery hearing hadn't attracted the amount of attention that the arraignment had, and the onlookers were mainly members of the press. According to Stills, the judge who had been assigned to oversee the trial, was an even-handed lady who was respected by most of the attorneys who had been in her courtroom.

The proceeding turned out to be a one-sided affair with the prosecutor, Leonard Knotts, putting on a show almost like a carnival barker. He brought up one damning piece of evidence after another. The list included Jim's blood, semen, fingerprints on the glass used to cut the victim, Jim's own belt, an anonymous phone call and witnesses from the hotel bar and later from the front desk people. Jim felt overwhelmed by the sea of evidence from the state while his defense seemed to consist of only "I didn't do it." Also, for the first time Jim saw the pictures of the crime scene. He watched wide eyed as he saw pictures of the apartment which had been torn apart like someone was searching for something. He almost gagged at the images of the dead girl and had to turn his eyes away while shaking his head. Knotts watched Jim through the entire proceeding like a predator waiting to pounce on his prey.

After all present had agreed on a trial date, Jim went back to Still's office.

"Jim, we have a lot of work to do. One of the first things I'm going to do is to use a private investigator to look closely at the victim. There was a reason she was killed. I don't for one minute believe that it was a random act of violence. The state could care less because they are so sure of your guilt, they're under no pressure to look anywhere else. There are also some questions related to the evidence they submitted. During the upcoming depositions, you'll just continue with what you've told me. Just relate what you know to be true. I think now you realize that your innocence is not enough. The state isn't worried about proving you guilty. We're going to have to prove your innocence."

The next three months were a lifetime for Jim. He left his condo only for his depositions which left him feeling humiliated after each one. It seemed that every question was a curve ball designed to get him to contradict himself or to openly admit guilt for the murder. Karin continued to tell him that he was doing well by staying true to his version and continuing to express total innocence. Jim didn't feel that convinced and sank deeper and deeper into an overwhelming sense of helplessness. There were moments when he seriously thought about running away. He could go to Mexico, get a job on a cargo ship and disappear. The only thing that prevented him from running was his daughter Libby. He knew he was innocent, and he didn't want to leave any doubt in his daughter's mind, no matter how limited it might be, that he was guilty of murder. He was grateful to Julie who continued to be convinced of his innocence. She brought Libby up weekly and even let Libby to stay overnight with him on several occasions. He was anxious for his trial to begin, still believing there was no way he could be found guilty of something he was innocent of. Had he known what was coming, he would have headed to Mexico.

CHAPTER 19
Painful Details

1988

On the day after Marge was buried, Mark got up early and drove the two and a half-hour route down I-95 and west on I-4 to the sheriff's office in Orlando. He went straight to the reception area and asked the deputy if he could speak to Detective Garcia.

"Sir, if you don't have an appointment, he might not be able to see you. I don't even know if he's in the building. I'll try his office and see."

"Please try. He knows who I am."

"If you'll have a seat, I'll try to reach him."

After several minutes, a huge man came out of a hallway into the reception area and the receptionist pointed toward Mark. Detective Garcia's voice on the phone had sounded very southern. When he walked over to Mark and introduced himself, his appearance didn't match his voice. He was tall, with very broad shoulders, dark bronze skin and jet-black hair parted down the middle of his head. Mark had the thought that if there were such a thing as an Aztec king, Detective Garcia would be one. He didn't wear a uniform but was dressed in a dark blue blazer, khaki slacks, and a light blue dress shirt and tie.

He greeted Mark warmly.

"Mr. Price, you've caught me by surprise. I didn't realize you were coming in today. You're lucky to have caught me in the office this late in the morning. Usually, I'm out on the road by now. Let's go back to my office so we can have some privacy."

After Garcia sat in his desk chair and Mark sat down opposite him, Mark quickly told him about his wife's death coupled with his frustration and anger.

"At least the act of driving my car down here is better that sitting at home." Garcia was quiet when Mark talked about his wife's death. He seemed to understand the grief and frustration Mark felt.

"It's still seems like a bad dream and I sometimes think I'll wake up from it."

Garcia noticed Mark staring at several framed football photographs on the wall.

"I was lucky enough to get a football scholarship to the University of Miami and I was even luckier to have survived all four years with all my body parts still intact."

"If you got a scholarship to Miami, it wasn't luck. You must have been good."

"Good enough for college, but not the pros. Mark, I'm embarrassed to have so little to tell you. I would have bet the farm that we would have more information by now."

"I had hoped so too. What I would like to know now are some details. I really didn't feel like I could handle learning what happened until now."

"Are you sure?" Garcia replied.

"Yes."

Garcia leaned back in his chair and took a deep breath before he started.

"As you know, Kim's car was found first. It was locked and there was nothing to indicate any type of foul play. We've interviewed everyone we can find who could have been at or near where her car was found. Employees, delivery people and some customers have been questioned. Nada. Kim's body was found in the dumpster behind the Chinese restaurant. The restaurant was closed Sunday but was open for dinner on Monday. Her body was found by an employee of the restaurant early Tuesday morning. An employee had gone out to throw a box of trash in the dumpster and he had a set of keys in his hand that accidentally went into the dumpster with the trash. He had to climb over the side to look for the keys. The dumpster was about two thirds full, and he was digging in the back for the keys when he saw Kim's hand. He scrambled out, ran inside and called the police. They did a good job of isolating the scene and the forensics people went through every piece of trash with a fine-tooth comb. Because of the way the trash was stacked in the dumpster, we think her body was placed there late Sunday or early Monday. The restaurant put most of its trash out around midnight on Monday and there was some trash on top that was placed there on Monday by the store next door. The approximate time of death was sometime late Sunday. If the employee hadn't lost his keys in the dumpster, there's no telling how long it would have been before she was found, if ever. Again, we have interviewed anyone who might have seen something. So far, nothing. Mark, are you sure you want me to keep going? If I continue to talk, you won't like what you're going to hear."

"I've got to know the truth and I'm the one who'll have to deal with it."

"Okay, Kim was nude. She had been beaten and raped. She obviously put up a fight. There was skin and traces of blood under her fingernails. Her death was due to an overdose of heroin. It was high quality and very concentrated. We don't believe that it was self-administered because it was in her left arm and as you know, Kim was left-handed. Also, the angle of the needle insertion would indicate that another person had injected it. We think the key lies with the phone call she got on Friday night but all we have is a pay phone with no leads. We've talked to every informant we have in the area plus anyone on the street we can put pressure on. Either no one knows anything, or everyone is running so scared of something or someone they just won't talk. Mark, we've spent hours talking to Kim's friends and classmates. Can you think of anything or anyone we may have missed, even if it's a long shot?"

Mark had been gripping his chair while listening to Garcia speak as his brain tried to cope with the horror of Kim's death.

Garcia continued, "Mark, I will tell you straight. We've cut no slack on Kim's case. We do this for a living. We have to develop a tough skin to keep our own sanity, but Kim's murder has gotten to us all. We won't let this one go until it's solved. Trust me on that."

"I really appreciate your saying that. If you'll keep me informed on the status of things, I'd really appreciate it. I'll let you know if I think of anything that might help."

He stood up, shook Garcia's hand, and left the office.

Garcia had said something that Mark couldn't quite put his finger on. He was troubled on the drive back to Jacksonville, thinking there was something he should remember but couldn't.

By late afternoon, he was pulling into his garage. As he went through his kitchen, he took a Red Stripe out of the refrigerator and sat out on his patio and stared at the river deep in thought. Mark had started smoking along with Marge when they were married but both had quit after Kim was born. Marge had started smoking again after Kim's death and now Mark was overcome by a need for a cigarette. He went back into the house, found a pack of Marge's cigarettes, went back out on the patio and lit it. As he stared out across the river, he let his mind float. He was halfway through his beer when he suddenly sat up as if an alarm had gone off.

"Roe!" he muttered to himself as he ran up the stairs to Kim's room. The room was in the same state of disarray as it had been when he found Marge unconscious on the ottoman. He quickly picked up all the photographs, put them in a pile, and started looking through them. He lay them aside and took a large photo album off a bookshelf. He found the time period covering Kim's freshman year at UCF. When he found the photograph he was looking for, he realized what had been nagging him on the drive back from Orlando. He was looking at a smiling Kim and her one-time best friend, Roe Estes. They were standing in front of the sorority house with arms linked and both were wearing big smiles. The date indicated that the picture was taken at the beginning of

Kim's first semester at UCF. Mark looked at his watch. It was just past seven when he called Kim's roommate Ann.

Ann was in her room getting dressed to go out for the evening when Mark called.

"Mr. Price, I heard about Kim's mother. I am so sorry."

"Thanks Ann. I hope she's with Kim now. I'm sorry to bother you but do you remember Roe Estes?"

"I remember the name, but I was a year behind Kim and Roe was gone when I joined the sorority. There were a lot of rumors about why she left, but Kim would always change the subject when her name came up. Mrs. Zimmer could probably tell you a lot more than I can."

"Thanks Ann. I appreciate your help."

Mark knew the main number for the sorority house was also Mrs. Zimmer's number and his luck continued when she answered. She had also heard about Marge's death.

"Mark, I wish there were something I could do for you. No one should have to go through what you have."

"I'm doing okay. You might help me with one thing."

"Of course."

"Do you remember a girl named Roe Estes?"

"Of course, I do. She's a tough one to forget."

Mark knew that Mrs. Zimmer would likely be questioned again by the investigators, and he didn't want to raise any red flags, so he said, "I've found some pictures that Kim had taken in their freshman year that I'd like to send her. Do you still have a phone number or home address for Roe?"

"Can you hold for a minute Mark? Let me look." She was gone for a couple of minutes before she returned.

"You know she was from Gainesville. She was a brilliant girl. I remember that I would get Roe and Kim confused at first because they looked like twins. She and Kim were very close right up until Roe left. I can remember when Roe's personality began to change, and she became very unpopular with the other girls. Kim still stood up for her."

"What happened to her?" Mark asked.

"We think she was using some type of drug. She changed so fast, and she dropped out of school before the end of the first semester. Oh, here's her Gainesville address and her parents phone number. It's been over three years, so I don't know if it's still good."

Mark wrote down the information and asked one last question, "Did Roe have any contact with anyone else in the sorority house after she left?"

"None that I'm aware of."

Mark thanked her and hung up. He looked at his watch. It was too late to consider going to Gainesville tonight, but he did call the number for Roe's home and got an answering machine with a female voice identifying the Este's residence. He didn't leave a message but was encouraged that he had found Roe's family.

CHAPTER 20

Sid Estes

1988

Mark spent a sleepless night tossing and turning. He got up by six a.m. and by seven he was on I-10 heading west. He picked up 301 at Baldwin and turned south. Stopping at a Huddle House in Stark, he ordered scrambled eggs, cheese grits, sausage, raisin toast and lots of black coffee.

The road from Stark to Gainesville was like going back in time. Driving south on highway 301 was almost like driving through a museum. It had once been one of the main north-south routes into Florida but now it was lined with aging motels, some still being used to house migrant farm workers from Mexico and Central America. Some remaining structures were literally caving in with trees pushing up through rotted roofs. There were a few faded leaning signs that advertised, SEE LIVE FLORIDA PANTHER or 12 FOOT GATOR still standing in front of dilapidated curio shops. One shop was still open for business with a huge Confederate flag in the front and a sign that advertised Florida orange juice and "real" Indian moccasins. Mark was lost in his thoughts and oblivious to the scenery, either old or new.

During the drive to Gainesville, Mark tried to remember everything he could about Roe Estes. Kim had met Roe at orientation during their freshman year. They were very similar in size and appearance. From a distance, they were difficult to tell apart. They had become friends immediately and had gone through sorority rush together. Roe went out to eat with Kim, Mark, and Marge on several occasions. Mark remembered how excited Roe and Kim had been.They were practically inseparable. They decided to join the same sorority and had plans to room together as soon as they were able to live in the sorority house. During their first semester Kim had gone home with Roe for at least one weekend and Roe had come to Jacksonville twice. Roe had seemed to be very mature for her age and seemed to be very poised and confident. She was friendly and easy to talk to. Once when Roe was visiting, they were all sitting on the patio after dinner and Roe and Kim were talking about some of their classes being difficult. Kim had jokingly said, "Well if I flunk out, I can always be a dancer like Roe."

Mark remembers how Roe had blushed and Kim had quickly changed the subject. Mark had not thought about that comment since that night and even now he didn't know why it had surfaced in his mind. Sometime during her second semester Mark and Marge realized that Kim had not mentioned Roe for a while. When Marge questioned Kim about Roe, she had been evasive and only said that Roe had some personal problems and had to work them out. Marge, although curious, didn't push the issue and Kim said nothing else about her. For Mark and Marge, memory of Roe faded away.

Mark was so preoccupied that he almost forgot to slow down as he approached the small town of Waldo. Waldo had been blacklisted as a speed trap. Maybe in the distant past the rumors may have been true but today Waldo was only a small town that enforced the speed limits which were clearly marked. Mark always wondered why Waldo was criticized for expecting people to obey the law. Probably because the speed limits were so rarely enforced elsewhere. People were somehow offended that Waldo had the audacity to enforce their law and so the town's reputation lived on.

When Mark reached Gainesville, he stopped at a hotel on Thirteenth Street overlooking a lake and used a pay phone in the main lobby. Mark took a deep breath, crossed his fingers, and dialed the Este's home number. A woman with a deep but very pleasant voice that brought up images of Roe, answered the phone and Mark introduced himself. It was Roe's mom and she remembered Mark immediately. When Mark asked if he could talk to her, she insisted that Mark come to her house. She gave Mark directions which he wrote down. Fortunately, Mark was familiar with Gainesville having spent time there as a graduate student. He also lectured at the university on a regular basis, and he even attended many of the football and basketball games. He sometimes joked that the biggest vice in his life was in becoming a Florida Gator sports fan.

The Estes home was in an older but obviously well-maintained neighborhood near the university campus. The entire neighborhood seemed to be covered by a canopy of huge live oaks, aged pines, and tall sweet gum trees. Because of the numerous creeks that flowed through the area, the terrain was uncharacteristically hilly. The house was set back from the street and blended in with the trees. The landscaping was all natural using mostly native growth. A walkway of slate steppingstones led from the gravel drive up to the front door. The doorbell was answered by a very attractive woman who had to be Roe's mom. She wore jeans and a baggy purple sweatshirt with the letters GHS across the front. She appeared to be in her middle to late forties and her tanned face suggested time spent in the sun. She had a pleasant smile and she held out her hand to Mark.

"Mark, it's so good to meet you. I'm Sid. We are so sorry about Kim. She was a real friend to Roe, and we appreciate that. Come on in."

Mark followed her through a large great room with a high vaulted ceiling and out onto a large patio. The patio had the same fieldstone on the floor that the front walk was made of. It was bordered by a stone and wrought iron railing. The view looked down on a creek flowing through a deep ravine. The canopy of trees kept most of the sunlight from reaching the creek.

"What could I get for you? I have sodas, iced tea or a beer if you like."

"Iced tea would be great."

Sid disappeared into the house through another door and left Mark sitting and looking out at the scenic view. Sid returned quickly with a pitcher of dark tea, two glasses filled with ice and a small bowl of sugar. Mark was still standing at the edge of the patio and turned when Sid walked back out onto the patio.

"It is a relaxing view."

Sid frowned before she spoke.

"But it won't be for much longer. Our city fathers who know what's best for everyone else, plan to build a jogging /nature path through this ravine. Anyone, anytime of the day or night, will be able to meander through what is basically our back yard. Of course, it won't affect any of the people who planned it."

She poured Mark and herself a glass of tea and sat down on the other side of the patio table.

"Roe told us so many nice things about your family. I'm sorry we didn't get to meet you and your wife. Her name is Marge, isn't it?"

"Was. She died this past Monday."

A look of shock passed over Sid's face.

"Oh Mark, I'm so sorry. What happened?"

"I think Marge started dying at the time Kim died. It took a while for her body to catch up with her mind."

There was sincerity in Sid's voice when she said, "Roe will be crushed to hear about your wife. She really liked her."

"The feeling was mutual. We really liked Roe and we never understood why she seemed to vanish. Kim wouldn't talk about her at all. What happened? She seemed to have it all together and then she disappeared."

Sid took a deep breath and paused before speaking.

"Mark, Roe was a wonderful child. John and I thought that if raising children was as easy as raising Roe, we'd have a dozen. Something happened during her first semester, and she changed. Drugs are a terrible thing. We know firsthand the pain they can cause. We don't know how she started and maybe its best we don't know. Her dad would be in jail for murder if he knew who was responsible. He wouldn't hesitate to kill anyone who might have been involved in her addiction. Roe dropped out of school and refused to come home. She told us she was working as a waitress but would never give us an address or phone number. She came home for Christmas, and she looked terrible. She'd lost weight and seemed irritable with everyone including her younger brother.

"We finally had to give her an ultimatum to shape up or ship out. We watched her pack a bag and walk out the door and down the street. It was the lowest point in our life, and we kept trying to second guess what we'd done. But it was done, and we couldn't go back. Her brother Rick tracked her down later from a phone number she'd called from. It had been made from a topless bar and she was working there. Rick didn't even try to talk to her. He drove straight back to Gainesville crying all the way. John wanted to go to Orlando and bring her back, but I was able to stop him. It would never have worked and when John calmed down, he agreed that it wouldn't. Coming home would have to be her decision and not ours. We could only hope and pray and be here if she ever needed us. During the last few months, she has called us. She told Rick that she had saved up a lot of money and she wanted to go back to school again. That was a few weeks before she called us about Kim."

"When did she call about Kim?" Mark asked.

"I can look at a calendar and tell you. It was on a Sunday night, or I should say on a Monday morning about three AM. You know how scary it is when the phone rings after midnight. Roe was hysterical. All she could say was 'She's dead.' When she calmed down, she said she had just found out that Kim was dead. We asked her how she knew, and she said a friend had heard and remembered that Roe had been a friend. There was a small note on her death in the state section of the local paper a few days later."

Mark's head was spinning, and he was almost hyperventilating.

"Can you check on the date?" Mark asked.

"Just a minute," Sid said as she quickly got up and went inside.

She was only gone a couple of minutes and returned with a small planner.

"It was the last weekend in April. Rick played a spring football game with his high school on Friday and was invited to watch the Florida spring game on Saturday. He stands a good chance of getting a scholarship offer."

Mark was desperately trying not to show the emotions he was feeling. Roe had known Kim was dead more than twenty-four hours before her body had been found.

"Do you know where Roe was calling from when she called you about Kim?"

"No. We could hear music in the background, but Roe didn't say where she was. We had assumed she was still in Orlando but she said she was in Tampa and would call and give us a number there. She called a few days later and talked to her brother and told him that she was dancing at a large club in Tampa. She sounded okay. She still didn't have a telephone number."

"Did she give him the name of the club she was working at?"

"No. I'm sure because John and I both grilled him pretty good. That was one of our main questions. She did say that she was rooming with two other girls who worked with her but again, no address or phone number."

It was clear to Mark that Sid was suffering in her own way over her daughter, and he didn't want to push her farther. Mark talked with Sid a few more minutes and she invited Mark to stay for lunch and meet her husband, but Mark politely refused and rose to leave.

"I really would like to talk to Roe. If you find out how I could reach her, would you please let me know? I'll leave my phone number."

"Of course."

She reached out and gave Mark a hug as he stood up.

"It looks like we both have our heartaches to bear."

Mark thanked Sid again as he left.

Mark headed back toward Jacksonville almost overwhelmed with what he'd just learned. He knew he was at a crossroad. Intellectually, he knew he should have already called Detective Garcia and told him what he had learned. Emotionally, he knew he would not. Between Gainesville and his home in Jacksonville, Mark crossed another threshold in his mind. Until now he had tried to let the system do its job. No longer. He was no longer going to remain passive. It was time to become the predator. He knew there would be no turning back but after making his decision he began to feel a certain sense of purpose that he hadn't felt since Kim's death.

CHAPTER 21

Guilty and Condemned

1995

Jim Herbert's trial was a nightmare for him. He watched help-lessly as the evidence against him piled up piece by piece. It was overwhelming. And when the jurors were shown the murder scene pictures, Jim realized that he had no chance. From that moment forward, Jim didn't dare to look toward the jury box. The juror's eyes said it all. Karin Stills did everything she could possibly do with what she had to work with, but the circumstantial evidence was overwhelming.

After closing arguments were completed, the jury was recessed but was back within an hour with a verdict of guilty of murder in the first degree. Sentencing was scheduled for the following week. This time Jim did not go home as he was placed in handcuffs and led away.

The sentencing was only a formality. Although Karin Stills spoke eloquently and argued that the conviction was based totally on circumstantial evidence alone and the death penalty should not be considered, there was never any doubt about the outcome. The crowd outside the courthouse cheered when the death sentence was announced, and Jim Herbert's fate was sealed.

CHAPTER 22

Burning Bridges

1988

When Mark was within a few blocks of his house, he stopped at a large grocery store, went in, and bought a large thick T-bone steak, tomato, frozen baked potatoes, a key lime pie and a bottle of Pinot Noir. After reaching his house and placing the wine in the refrigerator to cool he lit the grill on the patio. He took a hot steaming shower, put on an old pair of jeans and a faded sweatshirt. The coals were perfect when he dropped the steak on the grill and by the time it was well seared on both sides, he had a tomato cut up and the potato was ready. He opened the chilled wine, sat on the patio and enjoyed the rare red meat. When he finished eating, he took a notebook and pen and started making notes as dusk settled over the river and the entire bottle of wine slowly disappeared. Mark didn't even bother to go to bed. He crashed on his favorite sofa with a view of the river and slept better than he had for a long time.

Mark woke up early Sunday as the early light began to push the fog off the river. He put on a pair of shorts and running shoes leaving on his sweatshirt and started slowly jogging north on Riverfront Drive. Mark had stayed in good shape before Kim's death but since then his physical activity had been limited. After the first block, Mark knew he had a lot of catching up to do. He went all the way to the first bridge crossing the river and after catching his breath, turned and headed back. He couldn't do the distance without stopping and walking to catch his breath several times and it was only five miles total distance. He put on a pot of strong coffee, sat on the patio and cooled down.

After showering and dressing in old casual clothes, Mark walked out to his garage through the open breezeway. The garage was large with room for three cars, a shop on one end, and a laundry room next to it. Just before entering the garage from the breezeway, a stairway went up to the second floor. It was originally built as a maid's residence, but he and Marge had planned for it to become an in-law suite. Since it was never needed for a parent, they had used it mostly for storage.

Mark went into the garage and stood looking at the two cars inside. His car was an older model Ford Explorer, but he had maintained it well even though it was past a hundred thousand miles. The other car had been Marge's. It was a bright red BMW roadster convertible. Kim's car had been sold immediately after her death. Mark went over to the roadster, opened the door, and began to clean out the glove box and console. When he opened the trunk to clean it, he found a bag from a large department store. Inside was a sweater in Kim's size that was the same color as UCF's colors. The ticket was in the bag with the sweater and the purchase date was after Kim's death. A surge of remorse rolled over Mark as he realized how complete Marge's denial had been. He should have done more to help her than he had. He almost lost his composure as he lay the sweater aside.

Going back into the house he found the title and keys for the BMW. He placed both in the center console of the Explorer next to a Smith and Wesson Model 39 pistol. He spent the rest of the day going through Kim's room hoping to find something that might lead him to Roe. But other than a couple more photographs that included Roe in the picture, he found nothing useful.

Monday morning, he got up early and jogged again. After showering and eating he dressed and headed out in the Explorer. Crossing the river, he turned onto one of the main roads heading toward the beach area. For a couple of miles there were scores of auto dealers. Almost every make of car could be found in the area.

Sandwiched between two large new car dealerships was a small used car lot. It had no more than a dozen new model high-end cars visible. There was a small, new building with a showroom only large enough for two cars. One of the two cars was a red Bentley convertible. The other was silver Aston Martin. The small sign in front read Honest Abe's Auto. It was an "in your face" kind of name. But the truth of the matter was that Abe Levin was one of the most honest and honorable men that Mark knew. He'd developed a reputation of serving his customers well and after buying a car from Abe, few people ever went anywhere else. His loyal customers ranged from college students buying their first car, to corporate executive types who would be looking at the two luxury cars that were sitting in the small show room.

Mark had originally met Abe when he had taken one of Mark's history courses. Abe was in his fifties, well over six feet tall, three hundred pounds and his hair was snow white. Sitting in Marks class among young college students, Abe stood out like a purple polar bear. But as Mark soon discovered, Abe had been a history buff most of his life. He probably knew more about the American Revolution than everyone in the entire history department combined. Mark asked Abe once why he hadn't become a teacher at some level and Mark had to laugh when Abe said, "I wanted to make enough money to be able to eat and have a roof over my head."

Mark parked directly in front of the showroom window and had hardly gotten out of his car before Abe came outside to meet him. Abe reached out, took Mark by the shoulders, and gave him a bear hug.

"Mark I'm so sorry," he said. It was not pity but genuine concern.

"Thanks. It's not been a good year. I do appreciate your selling Kim's car for us."

"Mark, you know I'd do anything to help."

"I do have a couple things you can help me with. I'd like for you to sell Marge's car for me. It's not something I plan to drive anytime soon."

"It seems like only yesterday that you bought it. How much do you want to get out of it?"

"Just sell it Abe. You know what its worth. I'd also like to get a newer model SUV with four-wheel drive like this old one."

"How soon will you need it?"

"I'd like to get something within the next day or two if possible."

"What are you looking for?"

"Another Explorer would be okay."

"Mark, the auction isn't until Thursday so I'd need to find something a dealer would have on hand. If you have any free time today you could look for something along this strip and if you found something you liked, I could get it for less than you could and with a lot less hassle."

"That's a good idea. That would eliminate any guesswork on your part. Let me see what I can find, and I'll let you know as soon as I've found something."

"I'll be here until six at least or you could leave me a message if it's after six."

He got back into the Explorer and drove a couple blocks to a Ford dealer. By some miracle he parked in the front of the dealership and walked unnoticed by any salespeople into the used car section. He saw a grey explorer with a for sale sign on the window and he walked over for a closer look. It was only one-year old, and it looked brand new. The sticker on the window indicated just over eight thousand miles and it was four-wheel drive. He went back to Abe's place and told him what he'd found.

"Abe, if you'll make sure it hasn't been wreaked or dunked in water and drives okay, it's good."

"Mark, I'll take care of it. Unless I find a problem, I'll have it ready by tomorrow afternoon."

After thanking Abe, Mark drove to the Landing, an area of shops and restaurants directly on the river. He parked and walked to a favorite restaurant where he found a table outside on a deck overlooking the river. It was still early, and he sat almost alone on the deck. After a Tanqueray martini he realized how hungry he was. He ordered a seafood casserole and hot sourdough bread, washing it down with a glass of cold house chardonnay. As he sat and looked out at the river, Mark was confident that what he was planning to do was the right thing. He watched a young couple with a small child walking along the railing next to the river and was able to watch them without feeling totally lost. His new focus had brought a sense of peace and he was able to go forward without the burden of his grief controlling his every thought.

When he returned home, he spent more time with a notebook and pen making sure he wouldn't forget anything. He sat at his desk in his study and organized the documents he'd taken out of his safe earlier. He set his alarm to wake him early Tuesday morning so he could run again. By eight thirty Tuesday after a long run, he was dressed and ready to go.

After first calling Moshe Gersten's office and making an appointment for later in the afternoon, he used the roadster to drive to the university's main administration building, going directly to the president's office. Mark had been considered to be a rising star on the faculty and he'd always had an open door to the president's office. He was well aware that he was violating protocol by going over the head of his department chairman but at this time he really didn't give a rat's ass whose feathers he ruffled. He didn't have to wait before he was warmly greeted by the president. The president was fully aware of the double tragedy that Mark had suffered. After thanking him for his concern, Mark explained his intentions.

"Mark, if I thought I had any chance of changing your mind, I'd try. I know you well enough to know I can't. You'll always have a position on my faculty anytime you want it."

"I'm grateful to you for everything you've done for me. I never expected to be doing this."

"In this life, shit happens."

The comment took Mark by surprise coming from the President, but it did sum things up pretty well.

"I wish you the best Mark," the president said as Mark left his office.

Mark went over to the HR office in the same building and went through the necessary routine of paperwork associated with taking an extended leave. From there he went to his department and talked to the department secretary, making some suggestions on how to cover his scheduled classes. He went into his office and picked up a few personal things and left. Fortunately, other members of the department were either in class or their doors were closed. He really didn't feel like talking to anyone and the bottom line was that most of the other people in the department would be glad to see him go. It was not personal. It just meant one less academic adversary to compete with. He knew how some faculty would be pissed because they'd have to cover an extra class and not be able to slip out early on a given day, but Mark's conscious was clear. Over the years he'd paid his dues many times over by covering for other faculty. Besides, the generous leave policies of the state university system helped compensate for the teacher's low salaries.

Mark left the campus, drove downtown, and parked in a lot next to a tall office building near the river. He took the elevator to the tenth floor. The lobby he stepped into as he left the elevator had a small plaque on the wall that identified the office as Gersten and Gersten.

Moshe Gersten had been more than successful since he opened his practice in the small three-room office on University Ave. His oldest son had also joined his practice immediately after graduating from law school. Moshe's office now occupied the entire riverside of the tenth floor.

A receptionist sitting at a desk recognized Mark and smiled.

"I'll let Mr. Gersten know you're here."

"Thanks," Mark said as he sat down next to a coffee table covered with expensive magazines. He picked up a copy of Architectural Digest but before he could even open it, Moshe walked out to meet him. Moshe appeared not to have aged a day since he first began helping Mark with his mother's trust years ago. If anything, he looked even more like a hawk ready to drop on its prey. His legal adversaries learned the hard way that his appearance was well deserved, and he had earned great respect from the legal community in the area. Mark had continued to trust Moshe over the years for his legal and financial advice. Moshe and his wife had been at Mark's side at both Kim's and Marge's funerals and Moshe knew better than most what Mark had been through.

"Come on back," he said as he shook Marks hand. "I know you'll drink a cup of coffee."

On cue the receptionist got up and went out another door. Mark followed Moshe down a hallway and into his office. If Mark had not been in Moshe's office so many times before, it would have taken his breath away. It was a corner room with fourteen-foot walls of glass. The view out across the curving St. Johns River was breathtaking. There was the usual large impressive mahogany desk, but Mark followed Moshe to an alcove on one end of the room. The space was designed as a small sitting area with a comfortable sofa, chairs and a coffee table that could serve as a writing table. They sat down and Moshe asked Mark if he was doing okay.

"Moshe, I'm fine. But I need to get away for a while without any distractions. Trying to continue to go through the motions of teaching wouldn't be fair to the university and especially not for the students. I'm also frustrated with the lack of progress in Kim's case."

Mark didn't want to go into all that he had learned on his own. Even as good a friend as Moshe was, he didn't want to involve him in any way. Of all people, Moshe understood. As close friends, Moshe and Carol had truly grieved with Mark, and each would have done anything they could to help him.

The receptionist came in with two mugs of strong, black Columbian coffee. Moshe, like Mark was a coffee addict. He searched for the perfect coffee like some people search for the perfect wine. His favorite though was a Columbian coffee that was sold in bulk in grocery stores in Columbia. He had found a Latino market in Orange Park that could get it and the owners keep it in stock for him. They both drank it the only way a coffee aficionado would, black. Mark began to explain to Moshe what he wanted him to do. He and Marge had set up a trust for Kim, which was probably larger than necessary, but Kim was an only child and they felt more was better. With Marge's and Kim's deaths, the trust reverted back to Mark and added to his already considerable wealth.

"Moshe, I'd like for you to invest most of the money in whatever you're putting your money in. But, put two hundred thousand in my checking account so I can access it from money machines anytime I need it. I want you to continue to manage all the lease property income. Keep doing what you think best. I don't want to have to think about money right now. Also update my will to reflect what's happened to Kim and Marge. If anything should happen to me, Pet Rescue, St. Jude's, and the other charities get everything. We've talked about it enough, so you know what I mean.

What Mark was referring to was his passion for helping children and animals. They were the defenseless ones. Animals included anything from cats, dogs, ferrets, or elephants. Mark still had no problem with some types of hunting of animals whose numbers needed to be controlled. The white-tailed deer population had to be controlled. Otherwise, overpopulation would be followed by disease and starvation. Although statistics indicated that the black bear population needed to be controlled by limited hunting, Mark was never comfortable with legalizing bear hunting. The Florida bear, along with Florida's panther population suffered enough losses from roadkill. Because of increasing population and loss of habitat, the black bear was doomed and before long would become as rare as the Florida panther. In any case Moshe knew how he felt and would honor his request if the need arose.

"It'll take a couple of days to get this done. I'll call when everything is ready. We'd love to have you over for dinner one night."

"Moshe, I appreciate it but let me get a few things settled first and I'll be much better company."

"You know you're welcome anytime, Mark."

"I know that, Moshe. I consider myself lucky to have you and Carol for friends. I'll see you again later this week."

Mark left Moshe's office knowing that Moshe would take care of everything. He drove to Abe's car dealership where the Explorer sat in front of the showroom. It took less than thirty minutes to complete the paperwork for the Explorer and BMW.

"Mark, the Explorer is pristine. I think it was only driven be a gentle, white-haired grandmother," smiling as he said it.

"Thanks Abe. I wouldn't have expected anything else," Mark replied, laughing at Abe's humor.

"Actually, it was driven by the dealer's wife. It's got the big engine and all the bells and whistles." As he drove the newer Explorer home, Mark was pleasantly surprised at how well the new car drove. He should have bought it sooner.

When he entered his house the land line phone was ringing. He managed to pick it up just before the answering machine kicked in. The voice on the phone was speaking in a whisper and Mark had to hold the phone tight against his ear to understand what the caller was saying.

"Mr. Price, this is Roe Estes. My mom told me you were asking about me."

"Yes, Roe. Where are you calling from?"

"I'm calling from a phone in a drug store, and I only have enough change for one minute."

"Give me the number of the phone and I'll call you back."

"No! I can't be seen talking to anyone right now. I really do need to talk to you Mr. Price but I've got to be careful."

"Where do you work?"

"I'm working at a place in Tampa on Dale Mabry called Bottoms Up. I'm living in a house off Nebraska. The address is," Roe was saying as the line went dead.

Mark got a beer out of the refrigerator and went out onto his patio. He sat in deep thought for a long time and slowly sipped his beer. When he stood up, he moved quickly. He went out to the garage and into the shop room. One wall backed up to the laundry room. It appeared to be made of heavy plywood and it had brackets for hanging different tools. When Mark pulled down on one of the hanging brackets, the wall loosened and swung outward revealing a huge walk in safe hidden between the walls of the laundry room and shop.

Years earlier when Mark's dad died, Mark had come home from college and stayed for enough time to help his mother close out his father's hardware and gun store. Somewhere in the past his dad had acquired the safe from an old bank building which was being remodeled. It was literally a walk-in vault, and his dad used it to store his most valuable items. With the help of some of his old high school teammates adding the muscle, Mark managed to move the safe from the store and into his mom's garage. Years later after the real estate deal was closed, he was able to find a moving company able to move it across the state and into his garage. Mark himself built the wall to close it off so that it would be hidden from view.

Years earlier, when his dad's store was closed down, Mark had inventoried the firearms and picked out the ones he wanted to keep as well as several coin collections stored in the safe. He could have opened a gun store himself between the ones he had kept and the ones he had added to his collection over the years. Of course, he had kept his Savage Ninety-Nine as well as his Browning Belgium A5 twelve-gauge shotgun. Probably his most valuable firearm was a Thompson sub machine gun with a classic round drum magazine. It was in new condition and was still wrapped in its original oil paper. Many years ago, a customer had traded it with his dad for a new lawnmower. His dad had greased it up, rewrapped it the oil paper, put in the safe and forgotten about it.

Mark reached up on a shelf where boxes of ammunition were stacked and took down a box of nine mm hollow point ammunition. He debated a minute and considered taking a Colt forty-five Commander but decided to stay with his Model Thirty-Nine. The colt may have more stopping power on paper but the Thirty-Nine had such great balance and it fit his hand perfectly. Mark always thought that placement of a bullet was the most crucial factor in the stopping power of a handgun and the Model Thirty-Nine was well known for its inherent accuracy. He also took out a hunting knife in a nylon scabbard along with a pair of compact Nikon binoculars along with the ammunition.

Although Mark owned more firearms than he really needed, he didn't consider himself to be a "Gun Nut." His value system strongly supported the right of self-protection. If the day ever came when no one had to fear a home invasion, a carjacking, a strong-arm robbery, or a rape attempt, then maybe there might be a valid argument against the need to carry a gun. He just happened to have grown up in a society where gun ownership was the norm, and the right of self defense was a basic god given right. He actually hadn't even considered a concealed carry permit until Kim was in middle school. Mark had taken Kim and two of her friends downtown to their ballet rehearsal. He parked in a dimly lit parking lot and walked them toward the auditorium. Before they exited the lot, three young gang bangers all wearing dark hoodies and baggy pants that were worn so low they looked like they were about to sit down on a toilet, appeared out of the dark. One of them demanded loudly, "Gimme me your wallet."

Mark stood between the three young bandits and the girls and asked, "So, what happens if I don't give you my wallet?"

The shortest one pointed a small silver revolver at Mark and said in a high-pitched voice, "I'll put a cap in yo ass, motherfucker."

At the same moment, a large group of people walked into the parking lot prompting the would-be thieves to change their plans and run away empty handed. The next day, Mark had started the application process for a Florida concealed weapon permit.

After closing up the safe, he went back into his bedroom, took a small sports bag out of his closet, and put a in few overnight items along with what he'd taken from the safe. After making sure everything was locked up, he backed out of his garage and headed toward Tampa.

CHAPTER 23

The Bottoms Up

1988

Mark retraced his route from the past Saturday and took 301 south past Gainesville and onto I-75 at Ocala. It was past six p.m. when he finally left Jacksonville and he knew it would take over four hours to reach Tampa. Although it would be late when he got to Tampa, for what he had in mind, later would probably be better.

Mark stopped in Wildwood at the West side Waffle House to eat and fill up on hot black coffee. The place was crowded but he found an open seat at the counter. During his meal, he was entertained by the men sitting on either side of him. They carried on their conversation over and around Mark as if he didn't exist. It seemed that they had something in common. Somehow, they discovered that they'd each shared the same psychiatrist while they were doing hard time in Raiford Prison. The one sitting on Mark's right wore a wife beater undershirt and his arms were covered with tattoos running up his neck. The one on his left wore a grubby baseball cap turned backwards and was in need of a shower and shave.

"He told me I had an anger management problem," the man on Mark's right said.

"God Damn. He told me the same fucking thing," the one on the left replied.

Mark was glad to finish his meal and leave without having to join that conversation.

Because the restaurant's parking lot had been so crowded, Mark had parked at the rear of the building. It backed up to an auto repair business and just across the curb from where he'd parked were several cars in various states of damage. A couple of them were covered in dust with weeds growing up through the bumpers. They had obviously been sitting there for a long time. On an impulse, Mark reached into his car and took a heavy multifunction knife out of the driver's side door pocket. He looked around to be sure no one was near and stepped over the curb and into the adjacent lot. Unnoticed by anyone, he quickly removed the current license plate from a badly damaged Chevrolet sedan. He dropped the stolen plate on the passenger side floor and drove back onto the interstate toward Tampa.

It was eleven p.m. when Mark reached Tampa and turned onto Del Mabry Avenue. He stopped at a convenience store with a phone booth and parked in a dark spot on one side of the store. He looked up the address of the Bottoms Up club and found that it was only a few blocks away on the same street. Before he drove out of the parking lot, he removed the license plate from his car and replaced it with the stolen one.

As he approached the bar, he felt as if he were entering a carnival. There were enough neon signs advertising nude dancing and "Gentlemen's Clubs" to light up the night. The Bottoms Up club was easy to spot. It was one of the larger bars and had a large flashing neon sign with the outline of a martini glass. Even on a Tuesday night, business was obviously booming and finding a parking spot was difficult. Mark finally managed to find a spot on a side street that ran alongside the bar. He walked up the street and around to the front of the bar and into the festive air around the entrance. Taxis were lined up, and people were coming and going. There were a couple of girls wearing short tight skirts and see-through blouses lounging on the fringes of the parking lot. They smiled at him and one of them motioned for him to come over. Mark ignored her and continued up to the entrance. Two huge bouncers stood guard at the door, and both looked as if they could play defensive tackle on any NFL team. Just inside the entrance was an alcove where a girl sat behind a small counter. When Mark looked at her, she simply said, "Ten dollars."

Mark gave her a ten-dollar bill and she stamped the back of his hand with a rubber stamp.

Mark had been in topless bars during his military days, but he was taken back by the Bottoms Up. The music was deafening, cigarette smoke hung thick in the air, and he found himself surrounded by drop dead beautiful girls. Many of them were totally nude and the ones that were "dressed" were only covered by a black or red diaphanous see-through negligee that left nothing to the imagination. They were walking around talking to the patrons as if they were at a chamber of commerce mixer. It was crowded with as many girls as there were guys. Mark shouldered his way in and could see a large circular stage with seating around the entire periphery of the stage. There were three brass poles extending from the floor of the stage to the ceiling and three naked girls were clinging to the well-polished brass in varying positions of gyrating, blatantly sexual poses. Occasionally one of them would leave the pole to approach the side of the stage, drawn by someone holding up a one or five-dollar bill, which they would let the patron place under the only item of clothing they wore, a single garter belt positioned high up on their thighs.

A young dark-skinned girl came up to Mark, took him by the arm and pulled him toward a dark area along a side wall lined with vinyl covered seats.

"You look lost," she said with a big smile. "Let me help you."

Mark let himself be led to a vacant seat in the darker area and sat down. The girl sat down next to him and casually put her hand on his thigh.

"My name is Melody. What's yours?"

Mark hesitated for a split second before he answered, "Joe."

"Nice to meet you, Joe. Have you been here before?"

"No." Mark replied.

"You must be from out of town then. Everyone who lives in Tampa has been here sometime or other."

"I can see why it would attract a lot of people. Actually, I'm from Atlanta and a friend who comes to Tampa a lot told me about this place. He was here last week, and he was really impressed with one particular girl."

"Why don't you let me dance for you and you won't want anyone else. I'll give you a twenty-dollar lap dance for half price."

Before Mark could reply, she had straddled herself on his lap facing him and pushed hard up against his groin.

"I won't dance until the next song starts," she said. "Did your friend tell you her name?"

"No. Only that she was a tall, almost skinny, blond and that she apparently was fairly new here."

Mark didn't want to use Roe's real name and he assumed that she danced under an alias anyway.

"I bet you're talking about Starr," Melody said as she began to move with the music. During the entire time Mark's eyes had been searching the bar hoping to see Roe. As Melody began to move faster with music, she pressed her pubis harder and harder into Mark's lap and he found himself becoming aroused even though sex was the last thing on his mind.

Melody whispered into Mark's ear, "You don't need that skinny white girl. She's too stuck up and she don't go out on dates like I do."

"Dates?" said Mark.

"You know, to your hotel room," she replied. "I'll make you forget her."

"I'm flattered by your offer," Mark said, "But no thanks."

The song ended and Melody stood up.

"Thanks for the dance. It was worth more than ten dollars," Mark said as he handed her a twenty-dollar bill.

"You're nicer than most people who come in here. I'll look around for Starr and send her over."

"Thanks."

As she walked away, he realized he couldn't help but stare at her perfectly shaped derriere. He lit a cigarette and continued to scan the bar. Several girls approached wanting to dance for him, but he only smiled and said, "Maybe later."

Mark saw her long before she saw him. Across the crowded bar on the far side of the stage, Mark recognized Roe as she emerged from a door that led to a private area. She was as beautiful as he had remembered her and the sight of her brought back images of happier times and with them a sense of sadness. She was thinner than he remembered her. She was wearing a black transparent cover that hung partially open. Mark watched as she worked her way through the crowd. As she approached his section, she began to look around. Because it was so dark where he was sitting, she was no more than ten feet from Mark when she recognized him. Her eyes opened wide in surprise, and she turned around in embarrassment with her back to him. She tried to pull her scant cover tight around herself while crossing her arms over her breast. After Mark finally convinced her to sit down, her head was turned away as if she were afraid to look at him. Mark instinctively put his arm around her and when she turned her face toward him, tears were streaming down her cheeks.

"It's alright, Roe. I'm not here to judge you."

"I didn't really think you would come here. You have no idea how dangerous it is for you to be here. If they have any idea who you are, we'll both be dead."

"Who is they?"

"We can't talk here, and I don't want anyone here to think I know you. We've got to get out of here. Where are you parked?"

"On the side street."

"Good. Go to your car and drive about a mile north on Dale Mabry. There's a Burger King on the right side of the street. I'll come in a taxi so watch for me. They expect me to leave in a taxi. I'm going to get sick and need to leave early. Meet me there."

Roe stood up and started working her way through the crowd toward the private door she'd come from.

As Mark sat and watched her go, he should have been looking toward the main entrance as Melody approached a woman who was standing next to the ticket counter. The woman was probably in her thirties. Her hair was bleached and almost white. She was slim and would have been attractive except for the excessive makeup and her hardened features, which made her look older. The other employees, both dancers and bouncers seemed to defer to her. It was obvious that some of the girls were actually afraid of her and tried hard to avoid being anywhere near her. She was well dressed in an expensive designer pants suit with matching shoes that some exotic reptile gave its life for. Melody was talking in her ear with cupped hands in order to overcome the loud music. A couple of times she looked toward the area where Mark was sitting. Mark casually stood up and walked toward the front entrance.

As he passed the ticket counter, Melody came up to him and put her arm around Mark's waist.

"Why are you leaving so soon? Wasn't that the girl you were looking for? She didn't dance for you at all."

"That was her. She said she was sick and was about to throw up. I'm going back to my hotel and get a good night's sleep."

The woman in the pants suit was listening to Mark and Melody's conversation while staring intently at Mark before she spoke.

"Come visit us again, Joe."

Mark realized as he walked out of the bar that Melody must have told the woman his name was Joe. He thought about it briefly and let the thought pass. As he passed the throng of people and taxies and walked toward the side street where he was parked, he could have sworn that a short stout man with shiny, jet-black hair, was following him. Mark stopped walking and lit a cigarette as the man walked on past him without even a glance in his direction. Mark walked on to his car, got in, and used the first driveway to turn around in before heading back toward the main street.

CHAPTER 24

First Blood

1988

If Mark had looked in his rearview mirror, he might have seen the short man step out from behind a parked car and read Mark's license plate not realizing Mark had switched plates. Without his knowing it, Mark's paranoia was paying off. He drove north on Dale Mabry as Roe had instructed until he reached the Burger King. He parked toward the rear so that he had a view of the entrance and waited for Roe.

While he was waiting Mark reached into his duffle bag and took out his pistol, confirmed that there was a shell in the chamber, clicked the safety on, put it back into its holster and tucked it securely inside his waistband. Twenty minutes had passed and still no sign of her. After thirty minutes Mark was about to start his car and head back to the bar when a yellow taxi pulled into the Burger King parking lot. Mark watched as Roe got out of the cab and appeared to be arguing with the driver. She threw what appeared to be money in the driver's window and the taxi left. Mark got out of his car and waved to Roe to get her attention. She hurried over to where he was standing. She was dressed in jeans and sweater and her hair was pulled back in a ponytail. The lighting wasn't good, but Mark could easily see the swollen eye and a small trickle of blood coming down her forehead.

"Let's get out of here. I'm in deep shit now," Roe said as she headed for the passenger side of Mark's explorer.

"Go right," she said and Mark turned north on Dale Mabry.

"Are you okay?" Mark asked and Roe turned her head away.

"They gave me a hard time about leaving early. Mr. Price you need to drop me off at my place and get out of Tampa. These people will hurt you really bad if they find you with me."

"Roe, answer one question for me. Did any of the people you're afraid of have anything to do with Kim's death?"

Roe leaned forward in the seat and covered her face with her hands and began to sob uncontrollably for several moments.

When she spoke, it was almost a whisper, barely audible, "Yes. And if I hadn't called her, she wouldn't be dead."

Her words cut through Mark, and he was overwhelmed with an avalanche of emotion. He almost ran off the road before gripping the steering wheel tightly. It took him a couple of minutes before he found the words to reply.

"Roe, I know you wouldn't have hurt Kim intentionally. If I can help you, will you let me?"

Roe lifted her head and spoke so softly Mark had to strain to hear.

"I'd do anything to hurt them but I'm too scared to cross them."

"Roe, if you'll trust me, I can and will help you. I'm going to go after everyone responsible for Kim's death, with you or without you."

Roe was silent for several minutes and seemed to be deep in thought before she took a deep breath.

"Let's go by my house and get a couple of things I need. Then we can find a safe place to talk. I'll tell you everything I know."

Roe indicated that they should go east on Busch Blvd and soon pointed to a side street. Mark turned into the street, which led into a dark seedy, rundown area with many trees and only an occasional working streetlight. The houses were small and most needed of a lot of repair and maintenance. There were cars with open hoods sitting on concrete blocks. Screen doors hung loose on hinges and many carports looked like junk bins. Roe pointed to a grey house with an out of place picket fence. There was a dim porch light on and faint light showing through window shades.

"I'm sharing this house with two other girls. They're both still working at the bar."

Mark intentionally turned the car around and parked it a couple of houses away from Roe's house so that it was facing toward the way back out of the neighborhood. The street was dark where he parked.

Roe turned to Mark before they got out of the car.

"Wait here, Mr. Price. It'll only take me a minute to get what I need."

"No, Roe. I'm coming with you."

"Then let's go fast. I wouldn't be surprised if they sent someone to check on me. They didn't buy my sick story. I wouldn't even have come back here at all except for a couple of things I need to get. When you see what I'm talking about, you'll agree," Roe said as she climbed out of the Explorer.

Mark followed Roe up the small sidewalk to the front door. Roe unlocked the door, and they went into a small living room which was surprisingly clean and neat. There was a door into a kitchen straight ahead and a door leading into a bedroom area on the right.

"I'm going to get a few things together. Can you make us some coffee? We'll take it with us. Everything you need should be in sight."

Mark opened the door into the small kitchen and went in. There was one window over the sink and there was a menorah sitting in the windowsill. The stove was an old gas stove that would easily qualify as an antique. Mark found the coffee maker and coffee and by the time it was brewing, Roe had come back into the living room carrying a small duffel.

"Who does the menorah belong to?"

"It's mine. I know. Don't say it. I'm not a very good example of my faith. Sometimes though, it's the only thing that keeps me sane."

Walking into the kitchen, Roe reached up on a shelf for a screwdriver before opening the refrigerator. She used the screwdriver to separate the plastic lining on the inside of the door, reached into the insulation and pulled out a huge roll of cash and a small black notebook.

"Emergency money," she said as she went back into the living room and stuffed the money and notebook into the duffel. She looked out the front window and jumped up.

"Oh hell. I was right. That asshole taxi driver must have gone back and told Charity that I didn't go straight home."

Roe had turned off the living room light and was looking out a corner of the window blind toward the street. Mark came up and looked. Parked directly in front of the house was a large black Lincoln Town Car.

As Mark watched, the driver and the front passenger got out of the car.

"That short one is Fernando. He's really bad news."

Mark recognized him as the man he thought was following him earlier. The car's windows were tinted enough so that anyone sitting in the rear seat couldn't be recognized. There was definitely someone in the rear seat because both men were leaning back in and talking to someone in the back seat after they got out of the car. Mark quickly made sure the front door was unlocked and then pulled Roe into the kitchen. He took the menorah off the window frame and taking a lighter from his pocket, lit all the candles and set the burning menorah just inside the living room on the floor next to the door. He then quickly opened the oven door on the stove and turned on the gas to the oven as well as all the stovetop burners. It was such an antique that it didn't have any of the safety cutoff features all newer ones have to have. There were no working pilot lights so the hissing gas immediately began to fill the room.

"Outside fast," he said as he tried to open the back door. The door wouldn't budge.

"We had it nailed shut because we were robbed twice through this door."

The gas was rapidly replacing the oxygen in the room as Mark desperately pushed on the window over the sink.

"Let's hope you didn't nail the window shut."

At first it looked like it wouldn't budge but it moved an inch or two and suddenly slammed upward. There was no screen and Mark threw Roe's duffel out the window and literally shoved her out headfirst. By now, Mark was getting dizzy from the gas, so he dove out headfirst as well. Fortunately, there was nothing but dirt under the window and he came up gasping for air. As soon as he could stand, he reached up and pulled the window shut. Roe was still sitting down but she was okay as Mark helped her to her feet. He handed her the duffel, took his gun out of its holster, and clicked the safety off.

Taking Roe by the arm, he pulled her across the dark yard and into the neighboring yard. He hoped he was going in the direction of his car since the combination of the gas and the headfirst exit had left him slightly disoriented. The first fence was only three feet high and easy to cross but the next yard, although it was lit with a flood light had a higher wood fence. From the corner of his eye, he saw a movement coming from the back part of the yard. He pointed his gun at a huge dog lunging toward them. Just before he fired, the dog was suddenly stopped in its' tracks by a heavy chain which limited its range. Hoping the chain was a good one, he lifted Roe up and over the fence, threw the duffel across, and climbed over himself. As he rolled over the top of the fence, the night erupted with a deafening whoosh and a blinding fireball. Without the wood fence shielding them, they would have both been singed by the blast. They crossed to the other side of the yard and Mark followed Roe over the fence again.

The street was visible from this point and as they came out from behind the house, there were lights coming on and sleepy faces coming out to see what was happening. By now, Roe's house was engulfed in flames and the Lincoln was gone as well. Fortunately, Mark had chosen the right direction. There were no more dogs, and the Explorer was right in front of them when they come back out onto the street.

They jumped in the car and quickly drove out of the neighborhood and back onto Busch Blvd. As Mark turned onto the main street, both were watching the approaching fire trucks and failed to see the black Lincoln parked next to a closed gas station.

When the house had exploded, it was obvious that the two men who had gone into the house would not be coming out. The woman who was sitting in the back seat had quickly jumped over the seat and into the driver's seat leaving her henchmen to their fate. Once safely out on the main street she parked in a deserted station so she would have a view of cars leaving the same side street. She watched the Explorer turn onto Busch Blvd., and she recognized it from Manual's description of the vehicle that Mark was driving when he left the club earlier. As it turned the corner, she could see enough of the license plate to be sure it was the same vehicle. She would have followed them, but at two a.m. it would have been obvious. Anyway, she had the license number and she mistakenly assumed she could have it traced and find out who this guy was.

Mark's mind was on overload with questions, but he was careful with his driving and continued on toward the interstate passing several police cars with flashing lights and screaming sirens, all headed in the opposite direction.

Before he turned onto 275 North, he pulled into a deserted parking lot and quickly replaced his own license plate back on his car. As he headed north on the interstate, he turned to Roe to ask a question and realized she had shut down from sheer exhaustion. Her head was leaning against the window. She was sound asleep.

Mark drove straight through to Jacksonville, only stopping once for gas. Roe didn't wake up even after he had safely parked in his garage and closed the door. He half led, half carried Roe and her duffel inside and not wanting to carry her up the stairs, put her on a sofa in the study, leaving her covered with a blanket. By the time he'd turned off the lights and closed the door, she was sound asleep again. Mark was exhausted by now but still not ready to sleep. He went to his wet bar, filled a glass with ice, covered the ice with Tanqueray gin and squeezed a little lime juice on top. He put on a warm coat, took his drink and a pack of cigarettes out onto his patio. He replayed the events of the night over in his mind realizing that he needed Roe's help even more. After two cigarettes and the glass of gin, he went inside and crashed on the sofa in his family room.

The sun had risen over the St. Johns River and was flooding Mark's family room with bright light when he woke up with a pounding headache. He forced himself to get up and put on a pot of coffee. There was not yet any sign of Roe. He took a quick shower and when he walked back into the kitchen, Roe was looking in cabinets for a coffee cup.

"I've never smelled anything better than that coffee." Her eye was still slightly swollen. She still looked tired as if she hadn't had enough sleep.

"I guess I wasn't very good company last night."

"You looked like you needed the rest. I was too tired myself to get you up to a bedroom, so I dumped you on the sofa. Get yourself a big cup of coffee and let me show you a room where you can shower and put your stuff."

Mark filled a large coffee cup and handed it to Roe.

"Get your bag and follow me."

After Roe got her meager bag of belongings, she followed Mark up the stairs and into the guest bedroom.

"The connecting bath should have soap and towels. I'll be getting something for us to eat. Take your time."

Mark went back downstairs and loaded two trays with some orange juice, sweet rolls, and cheese along with a cut-up apple.

A few minutes later when Roe came back downstairs, she looked like a different person. It was as if the slime of the Bottoms Up Club had washed away and she looked fresh and revived. Mark could see signs of the Roe he remembered. They each took a tray with fresh coffee out onto the patio, which was warming up with the rising sun. They ate in silence while watching the traffic on the river. Mark could tell that Roe wanted to talk but he let her take her time.

"I don't know how to start. I feel that so much of what happened was my fault. Kim was the best friend I ever had but I got her killed."

"Roe, I told you before. I know you wouldn't have intentionally hurt Kim. Why don't you start at the beginning and tell me what happened?"

Roe didn't say anything for a couple minutes before she took a deep breath and the floodgates opened.

CHAPTER 25

Roe Estes

1986-1988

"During our first semester Kim and I went to a party at an apartment near campus. I don't even remember how we got invited or even whose apartment it was. It was just another party and there were a lot of people there including a woman named Charity. Kim and I both were uncomfortable because the people there were older and not the usual college crowd. Somehow Charity cornered me and asked me to come dance at a topless bar. I thought it was a joke. When I realized she was serious, I said 'No thanks.' Kim started teasing me and calling me Gypsy Rose when I told her about Charity's offer. Before we left the party, Charity put a piece of paper in my hand with a telephone number and a note that read, 'Call me for a guaranteed thousand per week.' I stuck it in my purse and forgot about it.

"It was a couple weeks later, when I found out that my dad had been downsized out of his job that I thought about the note again. I was concerned about the financial pressure my parents were under and I didn't want to put any more pressure on them. So, out of both necessity and I'll admit, some degree of curiosity, I called the number Charity had given me. A man answered the phone, and I could hear loud music in the background. I told him Charity had given me the number and I might be interested in learning more about her offer. He told me to come to a bar called Teasers on South Orange Blossom trail the next morning.

"Teasers was on one of the worst sections of the trail. I was uncomfortable even at ten thirty in the morning, but I was feeling desperate. The parking lot was deserted but there were a couple of junky cars parked toward the rear. The front door was open, so I walked on in. There was a guy working behind the bar counting bottles and he stopped and looked up at me but didn't say anything, so I asked him if Charity was there. He laughed and said, 'I doubt it. Not this time of the morning. You probably want to talk to Luke. Hold on and I'll gitem.'

"He went through a door in the back and when he came back, a huge guy in a tight T shirt came out with him. He was totally bald, and every inch of his arms was covered with tattoos. He was the scariest looking person I'd ever seen and if I'd known then what I know now, I'd have run for the door. Luke looked at me like I was a piece of meat before he said anything.

"'Charity told me you might come by. She tell you what you need to do to work here?'

"'I assume I'm supposed to dance,' I said. He laughed and told me to get up on the stage and dance.

"I stepped up on the stage and he walked over to an adjacent room and turned on the music system. It was really loud and intimidating but I started to dance and after a minute or two both he and the guy behind the bar were laughing. When he finally stopped laughing, he told me, 'Take your damn clothes off. Why do you think guys pay to come in here?'

"I took off my sweatshirt and jeans and kept on dancing in my bra and panties until he yelled, 'Take it all off, dammit.'

"This was probably another moment in time that I should have left but I didn't. I took it all off and both Luke and the bartender were staring by now. I felt used and abused, but I kept on dancing until the music suddenly stopped and Charity stepped out of the DJ's room behind the mirror and clapped her hands.

"'You'll do just great,' she said.

"I scooped up my clothes and quickly dressed and got off the stage.

"'Go back through that door into the dressing area and I'll be right there.'

"As I walked into the dressing area, I could hear Charity getting into Luke's face about something. A minute later Charity followed me into the dressing room and unlocked a door. It was a walk- in closet with one wall lined with hangers loaded with brief costumes of all colors.

"'Pick yourself a couple of these outfits. You might want to take both pair home and put them through the washer. If you want to go and buy something later you can, but I'd start with one of these until we're sure this will work out. Another word of advice. Don't ever let Luke get you alone. He's a convicted rapist, wife beater, and an all- round nut case piece of shit. We keep him working here because he's the best bouncer I've ever had. Now, why don't you go home and come back around eight o'clock for the night shift?'

"I quickly picked a white and a black outfit, rolled them up and left the bar. Charity lit a cigarette and watched me intently as I walked out.

"As I went out Luke leered at me, and I could almost see him drooling. It was such a relief to step out the door into the sunshine and I kept telling myself that I would never go back. But I kept thinking about the money. If what Charity said was true, a few weeks of dancing would pay my tuition and expenses for the entire semester.

"When I got back to the dorm, I tried on the outfits Charity had given me and Kim walked in while I was looking at myself in the mirror. Her eyes nearly popped out of her head.

"'You're really going to do it? I can't believe it.'

"'Only for a little while. I'll get rich and quit.'

"'Can I come and watch you?'

"'No way. You'd need an armed escort to go down there. And besides, I'd be too embarrassed. I'll tell you all about it.'

"Kim was really cool about the whole thing. She never told anyone, and she gave me space even when I started going over the edge."

Roe paused and looked out at the river as if she were searching for the right words.

"It started out okay. Most of the other girls were nice at first. I think I was a novelty to them, and they didn't really expect me to last very long. At some point, I became serious competition. One girl who helped me a lot was Jasmine. She was a black girl who didn't feel threatened by me. The guys who liked her, liked her because she was black. For her, it was a kind of positive sort of reverse discrimination. Anyway, she liked me and became a kind of mentor to me. Right from the start she told me how to dance effectively so guys would want to tip me while I was dancing and later want to pay for private dances. I learned right off that guys don't like heavy girls and don't like loudmouthed aggressive girls. It didn't take long to become addicted to having a roomful of guys wanting you and willing to pay good money as well. I couldn't believe how much money I was making. I was trying to balance studying with dancing and the long hours started to take its toll. There was just no way to go to class during the day, dance until four a.m. and keep up in school.

"One night I was really exhausted and one of the girls offered me something to pep me up. I was so tired I wasn't really think-ing straight, and I took it. She called it a Green Devil. It was a methamphetamine, and it was a first for me. I suddenly felt like I was on top of the world. But I wasn't prepared for the letdown when it wore off. As you might imagine, I wanted more. They were available, but for a price. All of a sudden, my hard-earned money began to disappear. Later I learned that this was routine procedure for gaining control of the dancers. Amphetamines are only one of the drugs used by the dancers. That's one of the ways they're kept on a tight leash. Charity, who I thought was a benefactor of some kind, was really a queen bee who recruited girls and also kept them in line. She didn't give a rat's patootie about my welfare when she warned me about Luke. She just didn't want to lose a profitable dancer because of him.

"By now I was dropping behind at school and I was becoming short tempered with everyone around me. Kim really tried to help, but eventually even Kim gave up. I dropped out of school and moved in with Jasmine who lived with her older brother Loften in a sleazy apartment near the bar. Jasmine and her brother both were using crack cocaine but I somehow managed to stay with alcohol and uppers. Often Jasmine would bring a 'date' home from the bar. I would have to go into Loften's room and wait until her date left. I woke up several times to find Loften's hand in my pants but after I bit out a piece of his ear, he left me alone.

"I rarely saw Charity. She spent most of her time in Tampa. I found out from other girls that she managed the bar in Orlando as well as a larger bar in Tampa. Her boyfriend was one of the bar's owners. By now, I was starting to noticeably lose weight from the pills and alcohol. One night I had drunk a lot, popped too many pills and I was really flying high. There was a group of guys in the bar that were in Orlando for some kind of convention. They were partying hard and throwing money around like crazy. One of the younger ones seemed to have formed a crush on me and was stuffing twenty-dollar bills in my garter every few minutes. When he asked me to go back to his hotel with him, I laughed at him and told him he was too young for me. I didn't think anything of it when he went to the end of the bar and spoke to the bartender. Later when he got up and went to the back of the bar, I thought he had gone to the bathroom. I didn't realize he was having an animated conversation with good ole Luke. Luke had tried on several occasions to talk me into leaving the bar with a guy, but I had always put him off. He wanted to pimp for me and get a cut like he did for several of the dancers. When the guy came back and brought me another drink, I still didn't realize what was happening. Then things started really going south. The room began to spin, and people's voices started to sound like a forty-five-rpm record running at thirty-three rpms. I began to have lapses in memory. One minute I'd be dancing on stage and then I'd be sitting on this guy's knee. I remembered getting hot and wanting some fresh air. Of course, you know who was helping me go out for the fresh air.

"I somehow had gotten my clothes on, and I had my purse with all the money from the evening. I vaguely remember being helped into a taxi by Luke but nothing after that. I woke up with a maid banging on the hotel room door saying, 'Room service.' I managed to make some noise so she would go away before I looked around. I had no clothes on, and my head was exploding. There were bed sheets and towels scattered around the room. My clothes were partially visible on the floor. My handbag was lying open on a chair. When I looked inside my purse the money was gone. I looked at myself in the mirror and I wanted to throw up. It was a rude wake up call.

"I got dressed, tried to comb my hair, and left with two maids in the hallway looking at me as if I had leprosy. I went back to Jasmine's apartment and woke her up. She told me she tried to tell me the night before that Luke was spiking my drink with something, but I was too far gone by then. When I heard what he'd done, I lost it. I got the few dollars I had hidden under a mattress, packed what few clothes I had in a cloth duffel bag and left. I went back to the bar which had just opened. There were only a few customers and a few of the day shift dancers had started working them for their dollars. The bartender gave me a strange look when I walked up to the bar.

"'I thought you were working the night shift?'

"'I left something. Where's Luke?'

"'He went out for a minute. He should be right back.'

"I went back to the dancer's dressing room and put on a pot of coffee and waited for it to brew. I waited a few minutes before asking one of the girls if Luke was back. She nodded a yes and I picked up two coffee cups and took the pot of coffee out to where Luke was sitting at the bar. He had a leer on his face when he saw me coming.

"'Did you have a good night?'

"I bit my lip and managed a friendly smile.

"'It was very profitable,' I lied. Luke's eyes lit up like Christmas lights when he heard the word profitable.

"'We need to work a deal,' I said and held up the steaming coffee pot and cups.

"'Good idea,' he said. 'It's about time you got real,' as I held out a cup for him. He took the cup and held it up for me to pour the coffee. I'd already taken the lid off the coffee pot, and I took one step closer, raised the pot over Luke's cup, and poured, not into his cup but the whole pot into his lap. His expression went from a smile, to startled, to anguish, as the steaming coffee soaked through his pants. He screamed and reached out with his hands still holding the cup and the last of the coffee turned his hands beet red. As he ran for the restroom, I walked toward the front door. The door was blocked. Charity was standing there, backed by two unpleasant looking men. Charity was laughing.

"'You know how to make friends, don't you?'

"I told her 'To go fuck herself' and tried to walk past her but both of the men blocked the door. Charity took my arm and led me past them and out the door. She put her hands on both my shoulders and looked into my eyes. It was like looking into the eyes of a cobra just before it strikes. I was hypnotized. She told me how I was different from most of the other girls, and I had the potential to become rich if I'd let her help me. She wanted me to go to Tampa with her and help her there. I know you'll ask why I let her manipulate me. This should have been another point where I split, but I simply didn't have the courage and I was naive enough to believe her. I also didn't know where else I could go. I felt like most of my bridges had been burned. When she told me to get in the car parked by the door and wait, like the fool I was, I climbed in and waited while she went back inside.

"While I sat in the car, the two men who were with her waited outside the car. By then I realized that they had no intention of letting me leave anyway. One of them was the Hispanic guy who followed us to my house in Tampa. I doubt that he'll be following anyone again. The other man was a large heavyset guy with bleached white hair. I learned later that because he was gay, Charity found him to be useful in helping her manage the dancers. His name is Rick Sealy and he'd been a professional wrestler in the past. Both of them stood like sphinxes and watched me. After a few minutes, Charity came back out, and she was laughing again. She got in the back seat with me, the two guys in front, and we drove away.

"'Luke is going to the emergency room. You might have burned his dick off. He sure as hell won't be using it for a while.'

"Charity couldn't stop laughing at the thought of it.

"'I told him that no one would know the difference, but he didn't think it was funny.'

"She handed me a paper sack with everything out of my locker along with my duffel bag. In one hand, she held out a dozen pills.

"'These were in your locker.' She lowered the window and threw them out. 'You're not going to need these. It's time for you to sober up. You're going into the big time now.'

"It really didn't bother me to see her throw them out. The previous night had been a wake-up call for me and I'd decided that regardless of what plans Charity had for me, drugs weren't going to be a part of them. We left Orlando on I-4 and drove to Tampa stopping once to eat at a fast-food place. They took me to the house in Tampa that we just torched. Charity took me inside, pointed to a bedroom, told me to make myself at home and wait for her. She was gone for a short time and when she came back alone, she had some new dancing outfits. She took me to the Bottoms Up and showed me the dressing area and gave me a locker.

"'I think you'll like this place. You can make a lot more money here than in Orlando. This bar is famous and guys come here from literally around the world. They drop a lot of money here.'

"She introduced me to a small wiry guy with a handlebar mustache.

"'This is Hank. He's one of the managers. Do a good job and Hank will make sure you're left alone.'

"She also introduced me to two other girls who lived in the house she'd taken me to. Charity told me to work the evening shift for a few days and she'd be back. By that time, I had to change and start dancing."

CHAPTER 26
A Deeper Hole
1988

Mark listened intently as Roe continued her narrative. He was almost afraid to ask a question fearing it might interrupt her train of thought. He knew that when Roe reached the point where Kim entered the story, he was going to have a hard time facing the reality of what happened.

"Charity was right about the money. I made just under two thousand dollars that first evening. A visiting Japanese business-man spent at least a thousand dollars. He wanted me to leave with him and I couldn't believe what he offered for me to go with him. I refused but he still tipped me well. Even after giving the bar a cut, I left with a bundle of bills. The bar stayed open till four a.m. and by the time I rode back to the house with one of the girls and took a hot shower, it was five thirty before I crashed.

"It was early afternoon when I woke up with Charity shaking my shoulder.

"'Get up and get dressed. We've got things to do today before your shift starts.'

"She took me to a shopping mall and into a sporting goods store that carried a lot of clothing. She picked out some outfits for me, but what was surprising was some of the clothes were what you'd wear on a camping trip, even down to a pair of hiking boots. She was paying so I didn't complain. We stopped at a restaurant as we were leaving the mall and ate something. I asked Charity why all the attention. I still didn't trust her.

"'You're different from the typical dancer. I've watched you closely. I really didn't think you'd take me up on my offer to dance in the first place, and even then, I didn't think you'd last more than one night. You not only stayed, you've done well. If you took away the heavy drinking and the uppers, you'd get a high score for survival. I've been looking for someone to help me do small jobs here and there. It could develop into big money if you work out.'

"I'll admit, I was flattered and the almost twelve hundred dollars sitting in my wallet from the night before felt good. When I asked her what kind of jobs, she only smiled and said, 'If you can drive a car and talk on a cell phone, you can do the job. In fact, this coming Monday evening you're going to help me.'

"I could only nod in agreement. Charity dropped me off at the Bottoms Up and told me to never say anything to anyone about our conversations or anything about what we did. She looked right into my eyes and said 'it would be very dangerous for my health' if I did.

"Every night I worked at the bar I made good money. I'd change it into hundred-dollar bills and hide it in the refrigerator. The bouncers at the bar were okay. They did their jobs and left me alone. I managed to get along with the girls I was staying with. I think they somehow sensed that I was under Charity's protection and none of the girls dared to piss her off. There was never a good time at work to ask anyone questions about Charity. But one of the girls I lived with had worked there for a couple of years and seemed to know a lot about her. And she didn't seem to mind talking about her. Her name was Blaze. At least that was her dancing name. I never knew her real name which wasn't uncommon since most girls never used their real names. Blaze told me the bar in Tampa as well as the one in Orlando were owned by the same person. She didn't know the owners name because there were dummy corporations protecting the owner. She said that occasionally a limo would bring in two or three well-dressed men and Charity would be kissing their ass. It was always the same group of men and she suspected they might be the owners. One of the apparent owners was Charity's boyfriend, a Columbian named Andre Mendez. He would sometimes come in with some other men who appeared to be Hispanic. There were lots of heavy gold chains and open necked silk shirts. Apparently, Charity was responsible for both bars and handled the day-to-day management. Blaze thought that Andre had some type of import business that dealt in flowers and leather furniture."

Mark couldn't help but smile at Roe's description of Andre's business.

"Hold that thought and let me get some more coffee."

Mark came back with the pot and poured more for them both and Roe continued to talk. It was as if she were purging herself of something that had been bottled up inside for a long time. "Sunday, Charity told me to go home early, and she would pick me up around nine. She told me to dress in boots and jeans and to pack one extra change because we'd be staying overnight. Again, she told me to tell no one. She picked me up right on time. She was in a four-wheel drive Suburban, and she was not alone. The two guys were the same two who picked me up in Orlando, Rick Sealy and his amigo sidekick. I got into the back seat with the amigo whose name was Fernando. We headed west toward Clearwater and then north on US19. We drove for three hours stopping once at an all-night convenience store. No one talked during the drive, and I slept most of the way.

"When I woke up the car was parked in front of a motel room and Charity was already opening the back of the Suburban. There were several fishing rods and tackle boxes visible in the back as well as a tarpaulin covering something. Rick helped her take out two large suitcases hidden under the tarp and take them into the room, which was directly in front of the car. Rick and Fernando went into a room next door. I followed Charity into a small room with two beds. It was close to one a.m. by then.

"'Get some sleep. I'm going to go out for a while. Rick is going to stay in the room until I get back. Don't worry. Rick is safe as long as you're female.'

"When she opened the door to leave, Rick was waiting there and came into the room as Charity left in the Suburban with Fernando. Rick had a thick paperback novel that he threw onto the bed. He reached behind his back and pulled out a large black pistol, threw it on the bed next to the book and lay down. Turning on the lamp next to the bed he started reading as if I didn't exist. I climbed under the covers with my clothes on and went to sleep. I vaguely remember Charity coming back but I have no idea what time.

"The noise of outboard motors woke me up. I looked out the window and saw that the motel was right across the street from a marina. I found out later it was the Steinhatchee River, and we were just inland from the Gulf of Mexico. Charity was still asleep and snoring and there was a gun on the nightstand near her head. Somehow, I thought the guns were related to the, as of yet, unopened suitcases on the floor next to Charity's bed. I got out of bed and took a shower. When I came out of the bathroom, Charity was awake.

"'I'm going to take a shower. Under no circumstance do you open the door. Not even for Rick or Fernando.'

"She moved the end of the bed around, so that it was pushing against the inside of the door, took the gun from the nightstand and went into the bathroom. I still didn't understand her paranoia. She left the bathroom door halfway open before turning the shower on. Even with the open door, the angle prevented her from seeing me seated on the side of the bed. I waited until I heard the shower running before reaching for one of the suitcases. It was one of the hard type cases and didn't have a visible lock. I leaned it over toward me and snapped the clasps and it popped open. It was packed solid with green stacks of hundred-dollar bills. I started to take out a bundle and count one when Charity yelled for me. I was lucky when I jumped at the sound of her voice. The involuntary motion caused me to snap the suitcase closed rather than opening it wider. Charity wanted me to hand her a small travel case with her shampoo. I was sure she would notice my shaking hand when I reached around the door and handed it to her.

"We spent the entire day killing time but someone, Charity, Rick, or Fernando always stayed in the room with the suitcases. Steinhatchee would be a great place to visit under different circumstances. It was a quaint village right on the river. There were a few small motels like the one we were staying in that catered to people who came to fish. The town was situated inland enough to be on high ground and partially protected from gulf storms. There were several marinas that rented and stored boats. I would really like to have stayed there for a few days. It was so quiet and peaceful. There were a few restaurants, mostly seafood places as well as a few honky-tonk bars. The premier eating spot I learned was Roy's. People routinely drove from as far away as Gainesville and Tallahassee for the food. Charity and I ate lunch there and it was the best seafood I'd ever eaten.

"By late afternoon the three of them were visibly becoming more and more agitated. Charity kept checking her watch and looking outside as it got dark. I was watching TV when Charity told me to get some sleep and she'd wake me when she needed me. I lay on the bed and half dozed until Charity woke me and said it was time to go. I glanced at the bedside clock while I tried to clear the cobwebs out of my head.

"It was two a.m. when Charity carried the two suitcases outside and put them back in the suburban. We all four got in and Rick drove a short distance to a bar on the outskirts of the village that you could hear before you saw it. The bar consisted of one small wooden building that seemed to be a huge amplifier. You could almost see the structure shaking. There must have been some kind of party going on inside. We parked on a dark side of the dirt parking lot next to a black colored Bubba truck. It was an F-150 sitting on huge jacked up wheels. Fernando got out of the Suburban without saying a word, climbed into the driver's seat and cranked it up. Fernando drove the truck back onto the road and headed north while we followed in the suburban.

"I had looked at a map Charity had in the room and had an idea of where on the coast we were. I remembered that state road 361 ran north out of Steinhatchee, parallel with and just inland from the coast. Within a few seconds after leaving Steinhatchee there is nothing but pine forest for the next twenty miles to the fishing village of Keaton Beach. There was a full moon which created a surreal image as we drove north on the deserted road. Fernando was leading the way in the truck, and I could see an occasional dirt trail leaving the pavement and leading into the pine forest. I soon stopped trying to count the deer grazing by the side of the road.

I could see the odometer over Charity's shoulder. I think we went between eight or ten miles before the pickup began to slow down before turning onto a dirt road angling off to the left. It was nothing more than two ruts in the dirt. I might be able to remember it because it forked soon after leaving the highway. One part angled off to the left and the one we followed went straight west toward the coastline, which must have been close. We only went a short distance before we seemed to be absorbed by the forest as the tree branches closed in over the trail, blocking out even the moonlight. We couldn't have traveled more than a half mile before we stopped at a small clearing next to a huge live oak tree. Charity backed the Suburban into the open space under the tree and turned off the motor. She reached into the center console, took out a two-way radio and handed it to me.

"'It's turned on. You just push the button and hold it down to talk. Sit down by the tree. You need to be outside the car to hear better and for the radio to work well. Don't move. Just listen. Use the radio only if you hear another vehicle turning off the main road and coming this way.'

"She handed me a spray bottle.

"'This is insect repellant. You'll need it. We'll be gone for a while.'

"Charity and Rick got out of the Suburban and opened the back. They took out both suitcases before they pulled the tarp back and took out two AK47s with long clips. They each had a large lantern type flashlight which they checked before climbing up into the truck with Fernando.

"Charity and the others disappeared into the forest leaving me sitting by the tree. The sound of the truck's engine was quickly swallowed up by the thick forest. The silence was profound, and the moonlight gave an eerie glow to the trees surrounding the clearing. Even with the insect repellant, the mosquitoes and bugs were soon eating me alive. I never had a chance to get scared because I was too busy slapping at insects. At one point, I imagined I could hear the faint whine of a boat motor coming from the direction of the gulf.

"I don't know how long I sat there before I heard the sound of a motor, but it must have been at least an hour. I was relieved when I was certain the truck was coming out of the woods and not from the highway. When the truck stopped at the clearing, Fernando and Rick quickly jumped out and each one took out what looked like large army duffle bags from the bed of the truck and put them into the back of the Suburban. Charity took the AK47's out of the truck as well and put them in the back of the Suburban. Rick got behind the wheel of the suburban, and Charity told me to get back in as she got in the front passenger seat. Fernando got back in the truck and headed back toward the main road. Neither vehicle turned on headlights, only using the light from the moon to navigate the trail. When we reached the highway, they paused to be sure there was no visible traffic coming from either direction before they switched on the vehicle's lights and turned onto the highway.

"Charity seemed to be in a relaxed and almost euphoric mood. We stopped at the same bar on the outskirt of Steinhatchee and Fernando parked the 150 in its original spot. He got back in the backseat of the Suburban next to me and Rick drove through a deserted Steinhatchee and eventually back onto US19 going south toward Tampa. Charity was quite talkative on the drive back. At one point, she told Fernando to be sure the tarp was covering the duffel bags and the AK47's. He made sure the fishing rods were on top of everything.

"'Roe, you're a successful smuggler now. The stuff in those bags is worth at least ten million on the street.'

"By then I had already figured out what was going down. I asked Charity, 'Why me? Anybody could have done what I did.'

"'First, because you're a smart girl. You were needed on this trip because two women with two men going on a fishing trip are far less conspicuous. We're tourist, we're here to fish and eat seafood. Also, we always need a fourth person as a lookout by the highway. You're going to help me do a lot of things. This is only the beginning.'

"I was afraid to ask what things but whatever they might be, I knew I was getting in way over my head. Dancing was one thing. I thought I could leave dancing one day, go back to school and live a normal life. But drug dealing was something else. I knew that if I were ever caught up in dealing drugs, my future chances would be limited forever. By then my head was clear of the amphetamines and I was thinking rationally again. All the way back to Tampa, I was thinking of nothing but ways to leave. It was early morning when we reached Tampa and I was dropped off at the house. As she left, Charity told me to rest and be ready to work the night shift at the club."

CHAPTER 27

No Where To Run

1988

"After I was sure they were gone, I packed my bag, called a cab and had it take me to the bus station. I bought a ticket for Orlando, but I had a two hour wait before the bus left. I really didn't think anyone would miss me until I didn't show up to work at six, but I was getting paranoid by then. I finally got on the bus and had an uneventful ride to Orlando. Going back to Orlando was a big mistake. When I look back, I could have gone anywhere but at the moment, I just wanted to get away from Tampa. I should have thought it through, but I was so consumed with running that I just didn't think straight.

"When the bus pulled into the station in Orlando, I was looking out the window and I saw Luke and some other guy standing just inside the station watching the buses come in. They must have known my bus was coming from Tampa the way they were watching it pull into the station. I dropped my head down behind the seat and pretended to look for something in my bag, which was under my feet. There were only about ten or twelve people on the bus and they were all getting up and heading for the door. I stayed in my seat and let the bus empty out.

"After a few minutes, they had unloaded all the baggage from the bus, and it was clear of people. I slowly raised my head and looked out at the platform. I saw Luke and the guy with him walking back into the station. I waited a few more minutes and slowly stood up and headed for the door of the bus. There was another bus that had just parked next to mine. As it was unloading, I joined the group getting off and went into the station trying to blend with them. I kept looking around for Luke, but I couldn't see him anywhere. I followed three women into the restroom and stayed in there for a long time before I came out. I was sure I was safe, and I headed for the exit. I walked out of the front door into sunlight so bright that I was blinded for a minute and that's when Luke took me by the arm in a grip so tight it took my breath away. A second later, the guy with him had my other arm and they picked me up and carried me across the parking lot to a plain commercial type of van. They opened the rear doors and threw me inside. The guy with Luke was about six feet tall but he must have weighed three hundred pounds and smelled like he'd bathed in some cheap cologne spiced with garlic. He was missing at least two front teeth and the ones that were left were black and green. He climbed into the van behind me. When I tried to sit up, he hit me so hard my head hit the wall of the van. I was stunned and couldn't move.

"'Don't hurt her,' Luke said. 'She's mine.'

"'Oh, there'll be enough to go around,' the fat man said and smiled a repulsive smile that highlighted his rotten teeth.

"Luke drove the van out of the parking lot and headed somewhere fast. I just lay still and tried to think. My arm was lying across my bag, and I gradually moved my hand to the top and found the zipper. I carefully inched my hand into the bag and searched until my fingers wrapped around a can of hair spray. I wished I had looked at the door handle more closely, but I couldn't see it because of the fat guy. I knew I would only get one chance. I waited until the van was stopped at a stoplight before I brought the can of hair spray up in front of his face and sprayed right in his eyes. It caught him by surprise and when he covered his face with his hands, I lunged for the rear door. I found the handle with no problem and pulled. It didn't budge. I tried again with everything I had, but it still wouldn't open. Luke had put the van in park and was getting out of the driver's seat to come back where we were. Fatso was beginning to open his eyes trying to locate me and I kicked him in the nose with my foot as hard as I could and lunged toward the back of the van. I shoved on the back-door handle with all my weight behind it and like a miracle the double doors flew open. My momentum carried me out the door and I rolled onto the pavement. By now, cars were backed up behind the van. I ran through a line of still moving cars, crossed a median with horns blowing, tires screeching, and people yelling, before I crossed the road. I could see the fat man rubbing his eyes and trying to cross the road behind me, but the fast-moving traffic slowed him down. I knew Luke couldn't turn the van around and I was sure I could get away from the other guy, but I wasn't taking any chances.

"I ran through a huge apartment complex and into a neighborhood of small rundown homes behind it. I walked for the longest time carefully looking behind for any sign of the van. I finally went into a seedy looking launderette, found a chair with a day-old newspaper laying on it, sat down, and pretended to wait for my wash to finish. Fortunately, while I was sitting at the Laundromat, I found a couple of dollar bills in my pocket, and I changed one for some quarters. I waited until dark and started walking again. I finally found a street I recognized and followed it until I got close to The Trail. I desperately wanted to find a pay phone, so I walked down a street parallel to Orange Blossom and cut over to a convenience store on the street. I used a pay phone outside the place and that's when I called Kim. I only told her that I was in trouble and needed help. She said she would come right away and pick me up. I hoped I could spend the night with her and then get my brother to come down from Gainesville and pick me up. I really didn't want to spend the night at the sorority house. I could already imagine some people laughing at me, but by then I was desperate for a safe place and a familiar face.

"There were no questions, no judgment, and no hesitation, from Kim. She was ready to help and after giving her directions, I went into the store to wait for her. I pretended to look at magazines while I kept watching the parking lot. I hadn't seen anyone I recognized but someone must have recognized me. When I saw Kim pull into the parking lot, I went out and walked toward her car. She had already gotten out, had locked her car, and was walking toward me when she saw me.

"I can remember how she looked at me, smiling as she hugged me and said, 'You look like bloody hell.'

"'Believe me. I feel even worse.'

"We turned and started walking toward her car. Before I could say another word, Luke's van had pulled up beside us. Three guys were outside so fast there was no time to run. The van was between the store and us so we were hidden from the view of anyone inside who might have helped. Kim and I both were thrown inside the van. The three men, one of whom was the fat man with the bad teeth, and another was Fernando, piled in on top of us. They were not taking any chances this time. They used duct tape on our hands, arms, and legs. They even put a piece on our mouths so we couldn't yell for help. The van was out of the parking lot and moving down the road within seconds.

"Luke, who was driving, looked around and said, 'Nobody touches her until I'm done with her.'

"The fat man asked what to do with Kim and Luke said, 'Whatever you want.'

Mark sat listening to Roe and wondered if he could bear to hear more. Tears were flowing down Roe's face. She had to stop talking until she regained her composure.

"Roe, you've got to tell me everything. We both have to face our demons in our own way. I've got to know everything that happened, and you have to tell me to help yourself as well."

CHAPTER 28

Honesty and the Anguish It Brings

1988

Roe had regained her composure as she looked out across the river and spoke as if she were in a trance.

"They took us to some kind of warehouse and drove the van inside and pulled us out. We were taken through a deserted office and thrown into a small room with no windows and a bunk bed. They threw us on the floor still tied up with duct tape. We tried to wriggle around on the floor so our hands could try to loosen each other's tape. We couldn't do it. They had done a good a job in tying us up. By then my hands were numb from having the circulation cut off. It seemed like an eternity that we were there. I finally gave up trying to hold it and peed in my pants. When the door finally opened, we were jerked to our feet, and they pulled the tape off our faces. Charity was standing in the door and Rick Sealy was standing behind her. I'll never forget how cold Charity's face looked. She stood in the door staring at me as if I were a piece of garbage.

"'Luke, you've been wanting a piece of this bitch. Take her next door and give her a lesson she won't forget. The rest of you can have this one,' and she looked at Kim. I screamed as loud as I could and spit at Luke. When he reached for me, he hit me in the stomach so hard I couldn't talk or make a sound. As Luke dragged me next door, I heard Rick ask Charity if this was the best thing to do. She told him to butt off. Luke threw me on a mattress on the floor and every time I tried to yell or fight, he would pound me with his fist until I was senseless. I heard Kim scream a lot, but they beat her too. Before the night was over, all of them except Rick had a turn with both of us. The fat man was the worst. He finally dragged me back into the room with Kim. They had beaten her even worse than me. Charity was sitting in a chair where she had apparently been watching the whole time. I remember she casually lit a cigarette and looked at me and smiled.

"'This is what happens to disloyal people. I trusted you and you let me down. You know too much now. You're going stay in line or else.' She nodded toward the fat man who left the room for a minute and came back with a syringe in his hand. Rick followed him back into the room very agitated and ask Charity, 'Charity, why are you doing this? It's not necessary!'

"'I'm doing it because it's part of Roe's lesson.'

"She told Fernando to get him out of the room and Rick was shoved out the door protesting the entire time. Luke was holding Kim's arm while the fat man pushed the needle into her arm and shoved the plunger down. Roe's voice was only a whisper now and barely audible by then. Kim looked right into my eyes and instead of accusing me, she smiled at me like she was trying to say, 'It's okay.'

"Kim died smiling at me. Charity grabbed me by the hair and told me that I was hers now and if I ever tried to run away again, she knew where my family lived. They would do the same to my mother and she would even let Rick have my brother."

Roe put her head in her hands and sobbed uncontrollably. Mark sat frozen unable to absorb Roe's words. Tears were streaming down his cheeks as well. They both cried until there were no tears left. Mark reached out and took Roe's hand.

"Will you help me get them? For Kim's sake? And for yourself? You know they'll never let you live now. You know too much."

Roe could only nod a "yes."

After they had both sat in silence for several minutes, Mark stood up.

"Why don't you rest? I need to go out for a while. You know your way around the house so make yourself comfortable. Don't answer the phone unless you hear my voice on the answering machine."

Chapter 29

A Start

1988

There had been a message from Moshe Gersten's office on the answering machine earlier telling Mark that the papers were ready to be signed.

Mark left Roe sitting on the patio when he left to drive to Moshe's office. Moshe wasn't there but everything was ready as he'd promised. It only took a few signatures witnessed by two paralegals to finish all the paperwork. From there he stopped by a branch of the bank he used and after convincing a teller that he wasn't being kidnapped, he withdrew several thousand dollars in cash.

When he got home, he found Roe sitting on the dock. She was sitting in a deck chair in the shade looking out at the river. From a distance, seeing her sitting there, Mark had the fleeting image of Kim and he had to choke back the emotions that rose in his throat.

Roe looked up as Mark approached.

"Mr. Price, I still can't understand why you don't hate me."

"Roe, if I had any idea that you wanted any of this to happen, you'd be dead. I do believe there is a devil. I equate the devil to the evil in the world. I have no illusions of wiping out all evil, but I am going to deal with the devils that have hurt us. My religious beliefs are dictated by the Old Testament. There should be an eye for an eye and a tooth for a tooth."

Roe sat quietly for a minute before answering.

"I'll do whatever you need me to do."

"Good. Let's start by having lunch and making some plans."

Roe seemed to summon up extra strength, stood up and headed up the steps.

"Give me five minutes and I'll be ready to go."

"Be sure to bring the diary you brought from Tampa."

Mark took Roe to his favorite restaurant at the Landing where they got a table outside with a large umbrella for shade. After ordering, Mark spoke first.

"Roe, I want to go over some of the details of things you've told me. Try to be objective and unemotional. I need to know everything you can remember."

Roe smiled for the first time as she reached into her handbag and took out the small notebook that she had taken when they escaped the house in Tampa.

"This is how I planned to get some revenge no matter what happened to me. It's a diary I started after they took me back to Tampa. After they'd killed Kim, Charity and Rick shoved me into the back seat of the Suburban. Charity wouldn't even let me get dressed. I rode all the way back to Tampa curled up in a ball on the floor wearing nothing. They left me in the same house in Tampa and Charity told me she would come back for me later. She made it clear to me once more what would happen if I tried to run again."

"Did you write down what happened to Kim in Orlando? Names and descriptions?"

"As much as I could remember. I never got the name of the fat man with the green teeth."

"We'll get to him in time. Do you think you could find the warehouse they took you to?"

"I don't think so. I was being held down and beaten going to it and I was on the floor in the backseat when we left."

"Well, we know we can't ask Fernando but I'm sure Rick can help with that." Mark had a funny smile on his face when he said it.

"How many trips did you make to Steinhatchee?"

"I've only been once more. They rotate a couple of people each time, so they always have a backup. Charity and Rick always go. One of the girls living in the house is on the rotation and I learned a lot from her."

"When they took you to help with the drug pickup, did they ever say how often they schedule it?"

"Nothing specific, but I got the impression that they did it once a month. They liked to bring in the drugs during a full moon because there's enough light from the moon to avoid using car lights. They also time the pickup during a high tide so the smugglers boat can get further inland to a dry landing point. The group I went with had obviously done it many times before because during our trip they often joked about things that had happened on other trips. One time they ran into a poacher when they got close to the gulf. They laughed about killing him and driving his truck miles away before leaving it. The smugglers that came in by boat, took the body out into the gulf and dumped it. On the drive back to Tampa, Charity made a comment about Andre being proud of them for their loyalty. Rick even commented, 'He does pay us well.'"

"Tell me every detail you can remember about the pickup spot." Mark made notes as she again described what she could remember about the turn off from the highway. He also asked questions about the people involved, taking careful notes all the time. Roe told Mark that even though he was openly gay, Rick Sealy spent a lot of time at the Bottoms Up. He was not a threat to the girls, and he seemed to act as a gopher for Charity and Andre. He was also known to have spent a lot of time at a gay bar not far from the Bottoms Up club. He lived alone in a small condominium development near the Air Force base.

"What are you going to do?" Roe finally asked.

Mark had a distant look in his eyes as he carefully replied, "I'm going to start collecting information. For starters, I'm going back to Tampa for a while, maybe even a few days. I want you to stay here and only answer the phone if you hear my voice on the answering machine. We'll stock up on groceries and movies and you'll be safe."

"I'd like to call my mom and let her know I'm alright."

"You can call from a pay phone. You'll need to tell your mom not to tell anyone you called. If anyone calls her or questions her, she should tell them she hasn't heard from you for months. This is important. I have no doubt that Charity's people will be looking for you. I think they'll do anything to get to you and we don't want to do anything that might lead them to your family."

By seven p.m. Mark had bought groceries and helped Roe call home to speak with her mom. She didn't tell her where she was and even if they saw the area code on caller ID, it covered a large area. She was able to convince her mom that she was okay. She made her promise not to tell anyone they'd talked. She said she'd see her soon. The wish to ask her mom to come pick her up was almost overwhelming, but she resisted the urge. Her mom was happy just to hear her voice and know she was okay.

When they got back to Mark's house, he put everything he wanted to carry out on the bed to be sure he had everything he might need. He put everything in the same small duffel he'd used before. He also put in one change of clothes and his shaving kit. He thought for a minute and went out to his garage, opened the door of his old Explorer. Reaching under the front seat he pulled out a dusty leather covered lead sap. He put it under the front seat of his newer Explorer.

Before he left, he gave Roe Detective Garcia's phone number. "If anything happens to me, call him and tell him everything. Trust me. Garcia is our friend. Don't leave this house unless you've talked to him first."

CHAPTER 30

Andre Mendez

1988

Mark reached Tampa around midnight and checked into a motel on Del Mabry Ave. within walking distance of the Bottoms Up Club. He paid in cash for two nights. The clerk didn't blink when he signed the register as John Smith. After finding an address for a Richard Sealy listed in the phone book, he went to sleep setting his alarm for six a.m.

By seven a.m. he had showered and eaten. He double checked his Model 39 to be sure he had a chambered round, and the safety engaged before he put it inside his waistband. The address listed for Sealy was in a condo complex in an area that catered heavily to military personnel. It was neat, clean, and well maintained. There were numerous large live oaks and the shrubs were thick and lush, creating the appearance of a resort setting. After circling the inside of the complex once, Mark parked several doors down in a well shaded area. He had a newspaper and a cell phone in case someone walked by. He would look like a good citizen who parked to have a conversation on his phone. It was quiet and there was little traffic coming and going. Most people with jobs had long since left for work. Mark reasoned that Rick's activities were mostly nocturnal and he wouldn't be on the same schedule as the traditional work crowd. At this point Mark was acting on the law of probability. Sealy might not even be the right place to start, but he had to start somewhere. Also, he didn't want to risk calling Rick either at home or at the club. He didn't want to set off any alarms in Sealy's mind.

Around ten forty-five the door to Rick's condo opened and a young male who looked to be in his early twenties came out. He was wearing tight jeans and a leather vest. Mark knew it couldn't be Sealy from Roe's description. According to Roe, Sealy also had a goatee mustache that he was continually touching. The young Brando wannabe got on a boat tail Harley, gunned the motor, and left. An hour later Mark was rewarded as a large middle-aged man with a goatee came out. He was not really fat, but he was only a few more burgers and fries short of getting there. He locked the door with a key, tugged on the handle to make sure it was locked and headed for his car. He got into an import sedan of some type and rolled down the windows. He didn't leave immediately but instead he lit a cigarette and sat as if trying to decide what to do. Mark slowly slid down in his seat so he couldn't be seen and waited. When he heard a car start and drive toward the exit he slowly sat up. As soon as he was sure Rick had passed him, he followed him out of the complex.

Rick's first stop was at the Bottoms Up. Mark parked across the street in a strip mall parking lot so that he had a clear view of the entrance. There were a few cars in the club's lot already. Rick was only inside for a few minutes before he came out and headed north on Dale Mabry. He turned left on ML King and into an area that seemed to be a mixture of every enterprise you could imagine. If there were such a thing as schizophrenic zoning, then this would be it. There were contractor's fenced compounds with guard dogs barking in their daytime pens. There were auto repair shops, junkyards, plumber's warehouses, adult video stores and theaters, and small questionable restaurants. Nestled in and around all of the commercial businesses were modest private homes, most of which were protected by tall wood or chain link fences. He passed a nude modeling place with a flashing neon sign located close to a daycare center. It was such an incongruous and interesting mixture of humanity that Mark had to concentrate on keeping a respectful distance behind Rick's car.

When he saw Rick stop in front of a large cinderblock building, he made a turn on a side street and turned around. When he eased back into view, he watched someone slide open a heavy steel gate and Rick drove into a fenced area on the side of the building. Within the fenced area was an asphalt parking lot and loading docks. When gate closed behind Rick, Mark drove past the warehouse and pulled into a small dirt parking area behind a small restaurant. The restaurant was definitely ethnic Latino, and the patrons were mostly of Hispanic origin who worked at the surrounding businesses. He got a couple of surly looks as he walked in and sat down at a small table close to the front where he had a view of the warehouse across the street. He was an obvious "Gringo" and he stood out to most of the patrons. A pleasant older lady came over and speaking English, took his order for a beer and left him a menu. Mark answered her in English, intentionally not using Spanish.

He was halfway through his beer when a door in the building opened, and Rick emerged. He was accompanied by a slim man who looked to be in his late thirties or early forties. The man had jet black hair pulled back into a ponytail. He had very European features that seemed almost out of place with his black hair and ponytail. Mark knew immediately from Roe's description that it had to be Andre. He walked straight toward the restaurant with Rick following behind like a pet dog on a leash. When they entered the restaurant, Mark could see that he wore a light ivory colored tailored suit with a black silk shirt. He had a solid gold Rolex on one wrist and a heavy gold necklace hung down on his hairless exposed chest. Mark held his breath as he turned in his chair so that his face was not visible. He didn't think that either Andre or Rick would recognize him but there was the possibility they might have seen him on surveillance cameras at the Bottoms Up. He could hear the woman that brought his beer greet the man as he entered.

"Good afternoon, Senior Mendez. Your table is ready as always."

Out of the corner of his eye, Mark could see them heading for the table toward the rear. They sat down without speaking and the lady asked if they would like the usual lunch.

"Si," Andre replied.

Andre and Rick started an animated conversation, but Mark was too far away to hear any of it. When the waitress came back to Mark's table to take his order, Mark ordered one of the special lunch plates and another beer. After a few minutes, he realized that Rick and Andre were no longer talking but were staring at him intently. Mark held his breath as Andre got up and approached his table.

He looked down at Mark and spoke in Spanish.

"*Eras un hijo de puta.*"

Mark had a blank expression on his face as he answered in English, "I'm sorry. I don't understand."

Andre then switched to English.

"Haven't we met before?"

"I don't think so. This is my first time in Tampa."

"Your face is familiar. It will come to me."

He turned and went back to his table with Rick and the two were soon quietly conversing again, but Mark could feel an occasional glance from Andres. If Mark could have heard their conversation, he would have heard them discussing the details of the next shipment of drugs.

When Mark had finished his meal, he walked up to the counter to pay. When he'd finished paying, he couldn't help himself as he spoke in perfect Spanish loud enough to be heard through the small room.

"*Gracias. La comida estuvo excelente. Seguramente vulvar a comer aca nuevamente.*"

Both Andre and Rick stared at Mark as he left the restaurant but neither made a move toward him. Mark walked back around to his car which was parked out of view of the restaurant windows. As he backed back down the alley to the next street and drove away without them seeing him leave, he realized what a stupid thing he'd done to bring attention to himself. He drove back to his motel, lay down and shut off his mind while he waited for the evening.

Dark was approaching before he dressed in jeans and a black T shirt. He used a pay phone to call home. The phone rang until the computerized voice answered before he spoke, "Roe, it's okay to pick up the phone."

Roe answered immediately.

"Is everything alright?" Mark asked.

"Yes. There was only one call from a Moshe who left a message saying he was sorry he missed you."

"Good. I should be back tomorrow. Stay in the house and off the phone."

CHAPTER 31

Rick Sealy

1988

As Mark left his room and was walking to his car, he passed a large dumpster that was overflowing with trash. He stopped and stared at it for a second and then looked around to see if anybody was nearby. There was no one in sight so he quickly picked up an empty pizza box that was spilling over the top of the trash before he walked to his Explorer, got in, and left the motel.

After eating at a fast-food drive in, Mark drove until he found a large discount store and went inside. He picked out several items, paid cash in the express lane, and left. When he reached Rick's apartment complex, he made sure that Rick's car was parked in front of his unit. By now it was almost dark, and he parked close to the spot he'd used earlier in the day. While he watched the apartment, he opened the bag from the discount store and took out a roll of duct tape, and a pair of rubber gloves. These he placed in the empty pizza box. Reaching under the car seat, he picked up the lead sap and put it in his rear pants pocket. He sat and watched the apartment until he saw a light come on before he put on a baseball cap with the visor turned toward the rear. After carefully looking around and seeing no one, he quickly got out of the car. Still trying to stay in the shadows, he carried the pizza box as if he were making a routine delivery. When he reached the door of Rick's apartment which was partially shielded by heavy shrubbery, he paused one more time to look around. When he was confident no one was walking by, he knocked firmly on the door.

There was a peephole in the door, so Mark held the pizza box up at face level and turned his head around, so his face was hidden. He knocked again and this time a voice answered.

"Who is it?"

"Pizza man."

There was a pause and Mark knew Rick was looking through the peephole to see who was knocking. The door opened suddenly, and Rick was standing in the doorway.

"I didn't order any," was as far as he got before Mark hit Rick in the head with the lead sap while pushing him back into the apartment at the same time. Mark stepped inside slamming the door closed behind him. He thought the blow from the sap would have totally incapacitated Rick, but he had underestimated him. Rick shoved a chair at Mark's feet throwing him off balance and turned to run toward a hallway. Mark tackled him from behind about halfway down the hall and their momentum carried them into the wall at the end of the hallway. Rick's head hit the cinder block wall with a solid thud and this time he lay limp and still.

After putting on the rubber gloves, Mark quickly retrieved the duct tape and secured Rick's hands and feet. He locked the front door and quickly checked the rest of the apartment. They were alone. He made sure all the blinds and drapes were tightly closed before returning to Rick. He dragged Rick back into the living room and looked around. The room was furnished with heavy wood framed Mediterranean furniture. Mark picked a solid heavy chair and lifted Rick onto it. Using a copious amount of duct tape, he placed Rick into a sitting position with his arms and legs taped securely to the chair. He had to move fast with Rick's last leg because he was beginning to regain consciousness. When he was sure Rick was totally immobilized, he tore off a piece of duct tape and pulled it tightly over Rick's mouth.

There was a large screen TV which was turned on but until now, Mark had not even noticed it. There was some sort of creature movie playing and Mark turned up the volume He then turned out the other lights in the room and the TV created an eerie flickering light in the dimly lit room. Rick's eyes were beginning to open as Mark pulled up a chair and sat down directly in front of him. As Rick's awareness returned, he stared at Mark's face. Mark reached over and in one quick motion, ripped the tape off Rick's mouth leaving it dangling on one side.

"You son of a bitch! You don't know who you're messing with. You were the guy at the restaurant today."

"I just want some information."

"Kiss my ass you prick."

Mark reached over and took the loose end of the duct tape and pulled it back over Rick's mouth. He got up, went into Rick's kitchen, and looked in some drawers. Not finding what he wanted there, he looked in a pantry closet and found what he was looking for. He returned to where Rick was sitting with hatred in his eyes, pulled the small clear plastic kitchen garbage bag over Rick's head and tightened the drawstring around Rick's neck. Rick's belligerence quickly turned into panic when he realized what Mark was doing. He started to fight the tape holding him in the chair, but Mark had done a good job taping him to the chair. It only took a couple of minutes for Rick to use up the air in the bag. Mark let him fight it for a couple of minutes and took the bag off his head and pulled the tape off his mouth again. As soon as Rick got his breath back, he started to yell more obscenities at Mark. Mark immediately pulled the tape back across Rick's mouth.

"Rick, to use a famous movie line, 'I guess what we have here is a failure to communicate.' I'm going to put the bag back over your head and give you a little more time to think. I'll be outside smoking a cigarette."

The chair was facing away from the front door and after pulling the bag over Rick's head and tightening it again, Mark went over to the front door. After looking through the peephole to be sure no one was standing outside, he opened the door and closed it again letting Rick think he'd left the room. Rick went crazy trying every way to get loose. Mark waited until his air was gone and just before Rick lost consciousness, he pulled the bag off his head.

Again, Mark took the tape off Rick's mouth. This time it took a lot longer for Rick to get air back in his lungs and Mark was beginning to think he'd left the bag on too long. When Rick opened his eyes again, he was no longer defiant and cocky.

Mark asked again, "Are you ready to talk now?"

"What do you want from me?"

"Only information."

"What information?"

"You work for Andre" Mendez."

"So, what?"

"You help with his pickups out of Steinhatchee, right?"

Rick took a deep breath and hesitated a minute before he replied.

"If you know so much, why are you asking me?"

"I'm just curious about some things. Who's bringing in the drugs?"

"I only know what they want me to know. Andre sets up everything with his family in Columbia. All I see is a flat-bottomed skiff coming up a tidal creek. I don't know where it comes from."

"How many people come in on the boat?"

"Always three. One counts the money; one stands guard and the third one stays in the boat keeping it running. Nobody hardly ever says anything. The guy throws the suitcases in the boat, and they disappear back toward the gulf. We haul ass away from the gulf."

"Will the next drop be at the same place?"

"As far as I know it will."

"When?"

"If I tell you that we're both as good as dead."

"Rick, you're already closer than you think."

As he spoke, Mark picked up the plastic bag and moved toward Rick.

"Okay, okay! It's going to be at the same place on Monday night two weeks from this Monday. It's supposed to be me, some guy from Orlando and a woman from Tampa."

"The woman being Charity?"

Rick had a confused look on his face.

"How do you know so much?"

Suddenly, a look of comprehension crossed Rick's flushed face.

"Roe! You're the guy she left with. We tried to trace your license plate, but it was a stolen plate. Who are you?"

"One more question Rick. What guy from Orlando?"

"Everybody calls him Greaser. I don't know his last name."

"Does he work with Luke and is he fat with green teeth?"

Rick was still trying to comprehend how Mark knew so much and why. Mark reached into his back pocket and took out a picture of Kim. He held it up close to Rick's face. Rick said nothing as he stared at the picture with a look of astonishment and fear.

Mark finally spoke softly.

"She was our only child."

A shock wave of realization finally hit Rick.

"I didn't touch her," was the last coherent word Rick uttered as Mark quickly pulled the duct tape back over Rick's mouth.

"You didn't help her either and I'm sending you to hell for it. Your last sight on this earth will remind you why."

He held up Kim's picture one more time before he struggled to get the bag back over Rick's moving head. He finally managed to get it back over Rick's bobbing head and closed it tightly around his neck again. Rick kicked and bucked while Mark watched with absolutely no emotion. At one-point Mark was afraid Rick was going to break the arms off the chair, but it held together in spite of Rick's desperate efforts to get air into his now empty lungs. When he finally stopped fighting his head collapsed to one side, and after a couple of shudders, was still. Mark looked at Kim's picture once more before he put it back into his pocket and said to himself.

"Four to go."

Mark went back into the first of two bedrooms and looked in the closet. This was obviously not Rick's main bedroom. There were two single beds, both neatly made up. He found nothing of interest and moved into the second bedroom, which was furnished in early French whorehouse decor with an ample abundance of mirrors and red velvet. A nightstand by the bed had a stack of pornographic men's magazines stacked on top. When he looked in the closet, he found a bulging leather briefcase packed with papers. There was also a Colt 45 semiautomatic pistol with two extra clips and a small plastic bag filled with a white powder in the briefcase. Mark didn't have to taste the powder to know that it was not powdered sugar. He lay the gun, and bag of coke on the bed and dumped the remainder of the contents on the bed. There was a spreadsheet with figures, dates, and a Florida map that had a lot of notations. He continued to search the closet and found two heavy shoeboxes. Both were tightly packed with hundred-dollar bills. Rick must not have trusted banks. He laid the boxes on the bed as well.

Going back into the living room, he removed the plastic bag from Rick's head and took it back into the bedroom. He dumped in all the papers from the briefcase as well as the money in the shoeboxes. Taking the bag back into the main room, he added the roll of duct tape to the contents and set it by the door. He left the briefcase on the floor by the bed and took the Colt and a pillow back into the main room. Mark turned up the volume of the TV even more, placed the pillow against the back of Rick's head, cocked the Colt's hammer, pushed into the pillow, and fired. The shot was muffled and with the noise from television, would be hard to be heard outside the apartment. It did have a big effect in that it removed a large part of Rick's face. He wondered how long it would take the coroner to determine cause of death. He released the magazine, jacked the shell out of the chamber and dropped the unloaded colt and magazine into the bag by the door. He intentionally left the empty shell casing on the floor where it had been ejected.

Next, he went into the kitchen and quietly opened the back door. Picking up a small empty ceramic pot sitting outside the back door, he used it to break a pane of glass in the door from the outside. It would look like someone had broken in. He then closed the door leaving it unlocked. The last thing he did was to spill the bag of coke on the floor leading to the back door and turn down the volume of the TV. After looking around one more time, Mark carefully avoided stepping in the blood and brain scatter across the floor in front of Rick, wiped any fingerprints off the front door where he had locked it earlier and picked up the kitchen bag and pizza box. After making sure there was no movement in the parking lot, he slipped out the front door and casually walked back to his car. He felt confident that no one saw him leave Rick's apartment.

When he got back to his motel, he threw the pizza box back into the dumpster where he'd found it. When he was back in his motel room, he sat down on his bed, took out Marge and Kim's picture, placed his face in his hands and cried. His outpouring emotions were both anger and sadness as he thought of them both. Mark let his emotions run their course before he placed the photograph back in his duffel.

After a few minutes, he took a deep breath, stood up, picked up his belongings, and left the motel. By ten o'clock he was on the interstate headed back to Jacksonville.

On the drive back, Mark called Roe to let her know he was coming back earlier than he'd planned and it would be well after one a.m. before he got back.

Roe was obviously relieved to hear Mark's voice.

"What did you find out?"

"It's going be a long story. Wait until I get home and I'll tell you what I've found. I will say that it's been a profitable trip."

"I'll have coffee waiting."

CHAPTER 32

A Growing Friendship

1988

Mark drove into his garage at one thirty a.m. When he walked into his kitchen, he was met with the strong smell of brewing coffee and frying bacon.

"I thought you might be hungry."

"If I wasn't before, I am now."

They sat at the kitchen table and ate eggs, toast, and bacon while Mark gave Roe a censored version of his trip by leaving out the details of his encounter with Rick. As far as she knew, Mark had only burglarized Rick's apartment. When they had finished eating, they took cups of coffee into the dining room and Mark emptied the plastic bag with all the contents from Rick's apartment onto the table. Mark had forgotten that the roll of duct tape was in the bag along with the rubber gloves. After the initial shock of seeing all the money, Roe saw the duct tape. She picked it up and looked at Mark with a curious expression.

"Just in case," was all Mark could say but he made a mental note to safely get rid of the tape and gloves the next day.

Mark took a small hard suitcase out of his closet and filled it with the money from the shoeboxes. They went through the pile of papers taken from Rick's briefcase. It didn't make much sense until Roe finally realized that it was Rick's crude way of accounting for the money he was skimming from the club, mainly at the expense of the dancers.

What really interested Mark was the map of the coastline. It clearly showed the trails and creeks they'd been using to make the drug pickups. It fit what Roe could remember as well. As Mark compared the coastline map to a state map, a plan began to formulate in Mark's mind. At the same time, fatigue was beginning to set in, and Mark stood up from the table. "Let's sleep on all this and we'll plan our next step in the morning."

They both got up from the table and Roe came around to Mark and kissed him on his cheek.

"Thank you." she said before she went up the stairs.

They both slept until close to noon the next day. When they were both up and had eaten another breakfast, they sat on the patio in the shade and talked.

"Roe, what would you like to do if you knew you no longer had to worry about these people?"

"I wish I could start over. Go back to school, get a degree, lead a normal life. I don't mean like before. I'll never be a sorority girl again. And I'd rather die than go back to the world I've been living in."

"If I could help you, would you let me? No strings attached. Somehow, I think both Kim and Marge would want me to."

"Mr. Price, I can't take your money."

"You're not going to take any of my money. I did a rough count of the money I took from Rick's apartment. There's at least three hundred thousand there. Just look at it as being rightfully yours. If you were willing to go to the university here in Jacksonville, I'd fix up the apartment over the garage and you could live there. There's enough money to get an undergraduate degree and for grad school if you wanted."

Tears streamed down Roe's face.

"I'm not sure I deserve any of this, especially from you."

"Roe, both good things and bad happen in life. If it's good, embrace it. If it's bad, then fight it. It's all we can do, one day at a time. And, speaking of fighting, I have a lot left to do. If we don't finish what we've started, then neither one of us will ever be safe."

"You plan to go after Andre and Charity?"

"Yes. I do. You don't have to be a part of any of it."

"No way. I'm responsible for starting it all and I'm going to finish it with you."

"Okay. We have almost two weeks before we do anything else. So far, I don't think they've connected me to anything, and they have no idea where you are. Hopefully we can keep it that way. I do want you to learn how to shoot a gun. I want you to be able to protect yourself if necessary."

"I like the thought of that."

Later in the afternoon Mark opened his gun safe and took out a Smith and Wesson Chief's Special that he kept stored in a soft padded case. It was a classic snub-nosed revolver in thirty-eight special caliber that had been a favorite concealed carry gun for generations of law enforcement personnel. While he was in the safe, he also took out the Thompson submachine gun as well as a Twelve Gauge Model 37 Ithaca police riot gun and left them both covered on his workbench in his small shop.

Mark took Roe to a large gun store that had an indoor shooting range. After fitting her with ear protectors and tinted shooting glasses, he proceeded to teach her to shoot the small revolver. He explained to her that he picked this revolver because of its simplicity and ease of use. There were no confusing levers or buttons to push. You only had two choices when shooting it. If you were in a hurry and didn't have time to aim, you simply pointed it and pulled the trigger. If you had time to aim, you simply cocked the hammer back, aimed at the target, and then pulled the trigger.

Roe was a natural. After flinching at the first few shots, when she realized that the gun wasn't going to hurt her, she settled down and shot like a pro.

"I'm pretending that I'm shooting at Charity. It helps my aim."

They went back to practice twice more over the next few days. During each trip, Mark bought a couple boxes of forty-five ACP caliber ammunition as well as a box of Twelve Gauge 00 buckshot. He spent some time in his shop working on the Thompson and Ithaca, carefully cleaning, and oiling every component. The Thompson was a real collector's item. It had been originally manufactured for the military as a "Submachine Gun, Cal 45 M1928A1, Thompson." By flipping a lever on the left side, it could be switched from semiautomatic fire to fully automatic. There were several magazines with the gun but the one that Mark focused on was a very rare one hundred round drum. Mark remembered once as a teenager, going out to the town dump with his dad and firing the gun with the large magazine. He could still remember lining up dozens of glass bottles and jars of all sizes, around an old refrigerator. From twenty yards, the Thompson killed all the bottles and ventilated the refrigerator. It was probably the only time the gun had ever been fired. Using surgical gloves to prevent leaving any fingerprints on the shell casings, Mark carefully loaded the drum until it was at almost, but not quite at full capacity.

He and Roe developed a routine of getting up earlier and jogging several miles each morning. Roe was becoming more relaxed and proved to be a comfortable person to be around. She was bright and she was beginning to shake off the trauma she'd undergone. Mark realized how much he'd missed having someone that he was so relaxed around. Still, his feelings toward Roe were totally paternalistic, in large part because she reminded him so much of Kim. It was hard to look at Roe and not see Kim. Roe seemed to sense how Mark felt and was grateful for the friendship.

One morning after jogging and having breakfast, they were sitting on the patio reading the morning paper when Roe sat up straight in her chair and said, "My god."

"What is it?"

She passed the section she was reading over to him. Under the section marked State News, was an article from the Tampa Tribune detailing the brutal murder of a Rick Sealy during an apparent robbery. Drugs were suspected to have been a factor. So far, no suspects had been identified.

Roe stared at Mark with wide eyes.

Mark simply said, "Rick lived in a dangerous world."

Mark didn't know how Roe would react to the fact that Mark was obviously responsible for Rick's death. He was relieved when she didn't ask any further questions but simply smiled and said,

"I hope he died a hard death."

Mark continued to read a section of the newspaper before quietly replying, "He did."

Mark intentionally hadn't shaved since his last trip to Tampa, and he was getting a nice growth of facial hair. He and Roe were getting groceries when Mark asked her to get some black hair dye for herself. Mark also began laying out the things he wanted to take on his next trip. The submachine gun and shotgun which had been fit with a sling, were carefully wrapped up in a small soft rug. He added a powerful flashlight with new batteries, a coil of nylon rope and a new roll of duct tape. He packed a large soft duffel bag with several changes of clothing, which included cameo hunting clothes and boots. He had Roe pick out several pair of jeans and shirts out of Kim's closet, packing them in a separate bag.

Mark had decided to use his old Explorer since his new one might be recognized. Plus, it was an even darker shade of grey than his new one and darker might be better for this trip.

Using Roe's description of her trips to Steinhatchee as a guide, he put an ample supply of rods, reels, and sundry fishing tackle in a visible position in the back of the car as well. They would appear to be another couple on a fishing trip to the coast. There was an obvious difference in their ages but with Marks beard, Roe's dark short cut hair, sunglasses, and wide brimmed hat, it wouldn't be that obvious to the casual observer.

CHAPTER 33

The Fishing Trip

1988

They left Jacksonville on Friday afternoon before the drug deal scheduled for the next Monday. Mark had grown enough facial hair by now to disguise his face but Roe's change in appearance was even more dramatic. She looked like a different person with her shortcut jet black hair.

Mark stayed on I-10 before turning south and going through the small town of Mayo. After following multiple two-lane county roads, they entered Perry, Fl. Perry sat on what was once another popular north south route on the west coast of Florida. The main road had once been lined with grand motels but only a few not so grand ones remained. Mark pulled into one that looked to be well maintained with a busy looking restaurant in front. Before he got rooms, Mark drove into an empty parking lot and quickly exchanged his license plate for the stolen one. When he went into the motel office, he registered as Joe Smith for two connecting rooms, paying for three nights in cash. The lady at the front desk smiled and asked, "You must be going fishing?"

"That's the plan."

"You're lucky to get rooms. In a couple more hours we'll be full. Lots of people fishing this weekend."

He backed into a parking spot directly in front of their rooms. They had been recently remodeled and were better than he would have expected. The first thing Mark did when entered his room was to put on a pair of surgical gloves. Roe looked at him as if he had grown a second head.

Mark smiled. "I know I'm being paranoid, but my fingerprints are on file with the military. If any law enforcement ever needs to check on occupants of local motels, I don't want to be identified. As long as you've never been arrested or applied for any government position there's no record of your fingerprints to worry about."

"No. I've never been fingerprinted."

The restaurant proved to be a pleasant surprise as well. Although it was busy, they were seated at a table in a corner with some degree of privacy. Mark had brought the maps he'd taken from Rick's apartment and while they waited for their order, Mark spread them out on the table. The one that proved to be the most useful was a satellite image of the area. From studying a state road map, Mark could see that the highway called Beach Road, left highway 27 just south of Perry and went west to the coast before turning south toward Steinhatchee. The majority of the route went through pine forest but the fifteen miles north of Steinhatchee was desolate land owned almost entirely by large paper companies. There were numerous logging roads leading into the forest from Beach Road and the key was in being able to identify the right one on the satellite image. Without Rick's notations on the county maps and the satellite image, finding the exact exchange spot would have been impossible guesswork.

Mark put away the maps when their meal was served. There was really nothing more he could do without actually driving to the area. The food was typical southern fare and was superb. Mark ordered the "all you can eat" fried catfish, hush puppies, grits, and fried okra. Roe had homemade meatloaf with green beans and mashed potatoes. As they left the restaurant, the waitress asked if they were staying at the motel.

Mark hesitated a moment before replying,

"Yes, we're going to a place called Dark Island to look at a house. We hope to get in some fishing as well."

"That's a pretty place. You'll like it. Before you leave be sure to come in for breakfast. It's really good."

They were up and dressed by six the next morning. Both were dressed in jeans and boots. The breakfast was as good as advertised and by seven a.m. they were headed for Beach Road. After reaching the coast at Keyton Beach they soon passed Dark Island and Piney Point. Mark had thought it would be easier to go all the way to Steinhatchee and backtrack since the directions and landmarks were referenced from that point.

Even growing up in the Florida panhandle, Mark had never seen a more desolate area than the drive north of Steinhatchee. It was almost a relief to drive into the small town and see human activity again. They drove past the motel where Roe had stayed but there was no suburban in sight. They really didn't expect Charity to arrive until late Sunday, so they took a few minutes to drive around the town.

Steinhatchee was a beautiful place just as Roe had described. Since it was a Saturday with a blue cloudless sky, it was alive with people heading out to fish. The marina parking lots were full of trucks and boat trailers. The Steinhatchee River was alive with anglers coming and going from the Gulf of Mexico, their heads filled with dreams of fish wells filled with trout and redfish.

They checked the odometer as they left Steinhatchee and retraced their route. After eight miles, they slowed down and started watching for the turnoff. It was easy to see because it had recently been used by logging trucks. Soon after they turned off Beach Road, the trail split.

Roe was watching carefully.

"This feels right."

Mark knew from studying the satellite image that the trail continued straight ahead and made a loop that eventually reconnected with Beach Road. There were multiple logging roads connected to this one loop and they all ran parallel and west, straight to the Gulf. Again, without Rick's detailed map, there would be no way to identify which one to take. Fortunately, as well, the area was experiencing a dry spell and the trails were easily passable. The trail was soon swallowed up by the forest before Roe pointed and said, "There. That's the tree."

It was hard to miss. It was a huge live oak with its wide canopy creating a large open area under its branches. They stopped, got out of the Explorer, and walked around the clearing. Evidence of cars driving over the grass was apparent. There were also empty water bottles and wrappers of various sorts.

"Probably my gum wrappers," Roe said as she picked up a piece of paper.

"That's where I sat next to the tree."

They got back in the SUV and Mark locked the Explorer into four-wheel drive.

"Now we need to go to the fourth trail to the left."

They had to pay close attention because the trails turning off the main one, were almost obliterated by overgrown pine branches. Mark wondered how anyone could find the correct one at night and his question was answered at the fourth turn. A few of the lower branches had been hacked off revealing a small red reflective lens attached to the trunk. They turned left and followed the trail. At times, it was open and easy to navigate and sometimes they thought they'd gone as far as they could possibly go. Mark watched the ground carefully to be sure they were staying on firm ground. This would not be the time or place to get stuck.

Eventually they emerged from the thick pines onto a beautiful open vista. They drove out onto a point of high dry land that extended well out into the waving, green marsh grass. In front of them, the open marshes spread out to meet the dark blue waters of the Gulf of Mexico. It was a breathtaking view. They sat quietly for a minute, literally absorbing the beauty. Mark was the first to speak.

"I want to walk around and get a good feel for how they do the exchange."

They both got out of the car and walked toward the marsh. A tidal creek came out of the high marsh grass right up to a muddy bank. It was almost low tide and the creek had only a few inches of water flowing back out toward the gulf. Mark could see the high tide mark and knew that a flat-bottomed boat would have no trouble navigating the creek at high tide. There were a few scattered cabbage palm trees. He noted a small clump of three or four trees off to the side of the open bank that had been butchered for the palm hearts. The heart of young palms had a high value as components of salads. The taste was exquisite, but the price for cutting out the heart, was a dead tree. Mark walked over to the clump of palms with broken, browned, drooping branches and looked around.

"This is perfect," Mark said.

From the clump of dead and dying palms, he had an unobstructed view of the creek bank and the spot where the truck would likely be parked. The palms were no more than ten yards from the spot the boat would have to pull up onto the bank.

Roe watched Mark as he walked around the bank and up to the clump of dead palms. He kicked at a few branches and looked out toward the landing area from where he stood.

"What are you going to be able to do but watch? There will be at least six of them."

"That's going to be their problem. Not mine. Let's go before the mosquitoes find us."

They drove back up to the main trail and turned left. They followed it until they found the next trail running parallel to the previous one. They followed it back toward the gulf as well. It didn't quite reach the open gulf but ended in a small turnabout area just before the open marshes. They turned and went back up to the main trail, turned left and followed it until, as indicated on the satellite picture, it reconnected with Beach Road.

They drove back to Perry, stopping at Keaton Beach to eat a healthy meal of fried shrimp, oysters, and mullet at a small seafood diner which hung out over the water.

Sunday was spent trying to make time go faster. After buying newspapers and magazines from a big box pharmacy, they spent the day and evening resting in their rooms. After breakfast on Monday morning, Mark dressed in his camouflage hunting clothes and boots. Although she didn't have camouflage clothing, she dressed in boots and jeans as before. The last thing Mark did before leaving the motel was to carefully wipe his fingerprints from the front door of his room which was the only thing he'd touched without gloves.

As they drove back to Steinhatchee, Mark explained his reasoning to Roe.

"Before we sit in the woods for hours feeding mosquitoes, I want to be sure they're here. As long as we're careful, there shouldn't be a problem. I also want to know for certain how many there'll be."

As they entered Steinhatchee, Mark pulled a hunting hat low over his head and Roe put on her dark sunglasses and a straw fishing hat. With his new growth of facial hair and Roe with her dark hair, sunglasses, and wide brimmed hat, they looked like typical Steinhatchee visitors. The parking lot for the motel was in the rear of the building and off the main street. A side street ran behind the motel and connected to a small structure that housed a medical office. There were several cars in the office lot and there was an unobstructed view of the motel's parking area from there. They parked between two cars in a space that gave them a view of the motel's parking area. Mark hadn't even turned off the engine when Roe spotted the black suburban sitting next to the motel.

Roe suddenly blurted out, "They're here."

"Good. Let's watch for a while. We've got plenty of time."

"This is about the time we went to eat at the seafood restaurant," Roe said.

They watched for almost an hour before a door next to the Suburban opened and the man called Greaser stepped out. Roe almost had a panic attack, gasping and sliding down in her seat the minute she recognized him. Mark had to bite his cheek and grip his seat to stop himself from getting out of his car, walking over, and putting a bullet in his head. Greaser was followed by a large black man that Roe didn't recognize. They knocked on the door of the adjacent room and the door was opened by Charity. She stepped outside and behind her came Jasmine, Roe's old roommate from Orlando. The four of them stood there with Charity apparently giving orders. Greaser was shaking his head, but he soon disappeared into Charity's motel room.

"It looks like the Greaser is getting guard duty while the others get to eat."

Roe was peeking over the dash again. "He must be the low one on the totem pole."

"Lower than he'll ever know," Mark replied through clenched teeth, still fighting the urge to go after him.

Mark and Roe watched as Charity, Jasmine, and the black guy, got into the Suburban and left the motel. As soon as they were out of sight, Mark started the car and drove back north on Beach Road.

This time they had no trouble in identifying the spot to exit the highway and they quickly reached the trail with the red reflector. They didn't turn this time but went on to the next parallel trail and turned left toward the Gulf. Again, they followed the trail to its end. After looking carefully at the thick underbrush Mark identified a solid spot that let him back the Explorer off the trail and into underbrush so thick that even if someone were to venture down the trail the Explorer would still be difficult to see.

After covering himself with insect repellant, he put on his cameo hat. It had a protective mosquito net that dropped down to cover his face and neck. He checked carefully to be sure he had his knife, flashlight, a cameo poncho, and a coil of nylon rope. He put all the items including the drum magazine for the Thompson in a comfortable cameo backpack. Opening a box of the 00 buckshot shotgun shells, he loaded seven in the magazine and jacked the eighth one into the chamber. He put a few more of the shotgun shells in the backpack for good measure before pulling on thin leather gloves. After Roe helped him position the straps of the backpack and get it into a comfortable position, he put the sling of the shotgun on one shoulder and picked up the Thompson.

"Roe, I'd recommend getting in the car before it gets dark. It'll be a lot better than staying outside with the mosquitos. You've got your gun, but I don't think you'll need it. Even in the car, you'll hear it when something happens. You might roll down a window around midnight. Based on what you've told me, I don't expect anything to happen before then. If I'm not back within an hour after you hear something, get the hell out of here. Go out the back way the same way we did yesterday and go back to Jacksonville. Don't stop. When you get there, take the suitcase with the cash, and hide it someplace safe. Then call Detective Garcia in Orlando. You've got enough information to have them all put away."

Roe held Mark's arm tight with both hands.

"Please be safe. I'm depending on you now. You're the only thing I've got."

"No, Roe. You can take care of yourself now. Never forget it. I've got to go now. I need to be in place before it gets dark. I want to be sure I'm not snuggling up with a water moccasin, a rattlesnake or even worse, sitting on a fire ant bed."

Mark only had to walk a short distance before he reached the open marsh. Even so, he stayed inside the tree line and worked his way toward where he knew the other logging trail came out onto the point. He had to walk several hundred yards working his way around thick palmetto thickets and wild myrtle underbrush. He didn't know when the people bringing in the drugs would leave the mother ship out in the open gulf and start up the tidal creek. It was reasonable to assume they might get in as close as possible during daylight and wait for high tide and a signal before making their final approach. In any case, he was going to err on the side of caution. The only problem he encountered was having to cross over a small creek coming out of the forest about midway. Except for getting his feet wet, it was no problem now, but he wondered what it would be like when he re-crossed it in the dark at high tide?

When he reached the site where the other trail came out onto the point, the sun was already beginning to set out over the gulf. Mark built himself a nest in the clump of dead palms. He did make sure there were no snakes or fire ant nests in the spot before spreading the poncho on the ground to sit on. His camouflage clothes were a good match for the dead palms and once he placed several dead palm branches over and around himself, someone would have to step on him to see him, especially at night. He firmly inserted the heavy drum magazine onto the bottom of the Thompson, making sure that it was locked into position before he pulled back the bolt and chambered a shell. Verifying that the switch was set on automatic fire, he lay both it and the shotgun carefully across the backpack.

When he was sure everything was arraigned to his satisfaction, he tried to relax and watch the sunset. He knew he had several hours of waiting but that was no problem for him. The ability to retreat into his mind for prolonged periods of time was easy for him. Sitting there watching the sunset, he mentally revisited his wife and daughter in a better time. It wasn't because he needed to rationalize what he was doing. In his mind, it was totally justified and the people he had hurt and those he planned to hurt, were travelers on the roads they had chosen of their own free will.

CHAPTER 34

Armageddon Day

1988

It was after two a.m. when the faint sound of approaching vehicles shattered the solitude of the night. The moon was full and loomed huge it the sky. Everything not in a shaded place was illuminated almost as in daytime. The sounds grew louder until a truck jacked up high on Bubba wheels, came out of the woods and onto the open point. The truck made a tight circle and stopped, pointing back toward the way it had come. The headlights were off and only the running lights were being used. They were cut off when the truck stopped, and the doors were opened. Three people climbed out. One of them reached back into the truck and brought out two AK 47s, which the two larger forms took. The smaller figure carrying two suitcases, walked toward the edge of the tidal creek where the high tide had brought the water up to the edge of the bank. The small figure that was obviously Charity, used a lanternlight to flash a signal toward the gulf. A faint light blinked in return and almost immediately the sound of an engine could be heard. Mark realized he was right about the boat having come in closer during daylight.

The two men with the guns stood on either side of the suitcases waiting for the approaching boat. When the boat appeared out of the marshes and reached the banks edge, one of the three men jumped out onto the muddy bank and pulled the front end of the skiff out of the water. Another man on the boat dragged what looked like two military duffel bags to the front of the boat, stepped out and both men lifted the duffels up onto dry land. Mark was amazed at the lack of any verbal communication between the figures. It was like a well-rehearsed choreography, and they each knew how to play their part. One figure remained sitting in the boat and held a compact Uzi machine gun pointing toward the people on shore. The two men from the boat set the duffle bags down on the ground as the woman handed them the suitcases. One of the men from the truck stood guard like his counterpart from the boat, holding his AK at a ready position. His companion helped Charity open the duffels to check their contents.

Mark was almost hypnotized by the entire scene, and he had to force himself to move. With the exception of the man sitting on the boat, all of the remaining figures formed a group within a twelve-foot-wide area. Mark was no more than thirty feet away as he rose to a kneeling position, braced himself against a leaning palm trunk, bringing up the Thompson at the same time, and depressing the trigger.

The Submachine Gun, cal45 M1928A1 Thompson, was originally named "The Annihilator" by its developer, General Thompson. As an early act of political correctness, our government changed the name. A different name didn't change its purpose. For the six individuals on the receiving end who had time to see, it must have looked like a blazing apparition from hell as Mark emptied the entire drum in one long sweeping burst. Within ten seconds, a virtual hailstorm of 230 grain lead projectiles traveling at eight hundred feet per second was unleashed. As soon as the magazine was emptied, Mark dropped the Thompson, picked up the shotgun, and stepped out of the clump of palms. The only sign of resistance came from the man on the boat. He'd been knocked flat in the boat but was trying to raise his Uzi.

Mark fired a round from the shotgun toward the man while yelling in Spanish.

"Drop it and I won't kill you."

Still dazed by the machine gun volley and the shotgun pellets roaring past within inches of his head, he dropped his gun and it splashed into the water. Mark quickly checked the other five on the ground. Charity, who had been kneeling behind the duffel bags, was still alive. It looked as if her right arm had almost been severed from her shoulder. The bags had partially protected her by absorbing several rounds from the Thompson. He leaned down and took the pistol from her back jeans pocket. She wasn't going anywhere anytime soon. He turned toward Greaser who was struggling to sit up. Mark stood over him and without any hesitation, jammed the barrel of the shotgun into his mouth breaking off green teeth in the process. He paused for a minute to give Greaser time to open his eyes and stare up at him. Mark smiled down at him and pulled the trigger. The sudden blast literally exploded Greaser's head and caused Charity to let out a wailing scream. Ignoring her Mark looked at the two men from the boat who had both been hit several times and showed no signs of life. The large black man was dead as well.

He went over to the boat and spoke to the terrified man who had been watching wide-eyed.

"Buenos tardes amigo. What's your name?"

The man stared at him with eyes filled with fear.

"Hernando."

"Do you think you can steer your boat out of here Hernando?"

"Si."

"Take a message from Andre to your boss. Andre doesn't need his help anymore. He's taking this shipment as payment for the times your boss has cheated him. Comprende?"

"Si."

Mark helped him move behind the wheel and restart the engine. He pushed the boat off the bank and pointed it back out the creek toward the gulf. Mark thought there was maybe a fifty-fifty chance he would ever make it back to the mother ship the way he was losing blood. There were several holes in the boat, and it was beginning to take on water, but it would be a plus if he did survive and relay the message.

Mark stood still thinking for a moment as the sound of the skiff disappeared out toward the gulf. From a distance, the sounds of the Thompson would be interpreted as an engine of some sort and not as gunfire. The shotgun though, could only be heard as a gunshot. If he was lucky, there were no game wardens on duty in the area tonight. He now realized he'd have to change his plan because there was no way he could carry the suitcases back the way he'd come. He quickly made a decision by carrying the suitcases and duffels over to the truck and throwing them in the truck bed along with his backpack. His guns went into the cab where he found the key still sitting in the ignition. After he was sure he'd put everything in the truck he went back to where Charity was sitting on the ground clenching her arm.

"You son of a bitch. Who the hell are you?"

"Good question. Rick asked me the same thing. Give me a minute and I'll enlighten you."

Mark went over to where the large black man lay and checked his pockets. He had been hit in several places, the most obvious being a gaping black hole where his left eye should be. As Mark had suspected, he was the driver and the keys for the Suburban were in his pocket. He knew they wouldn't have left them in the Suburban with the lookout.

Going back to the truck, he took the rope out of his backpack and walked back to where Charity sat.

"I need a doctor. I can make it worth your while. You'll need my help to survive after what you've done."

Before she could move, Mark had tied the rope tightly around both her feet and began dragging her across the ground to within a few feet of the truck. She screamed in agony with each step Mark took. He quickly tied the free end of the rope to the trailer hitch of the truck.

As soon as Charity realized what he was doing, her face turned white.

"Wait a god dam minute. This isn't funny."

Mark knelt down beside her.

"No, it's not funny. It never was. You wanted to know who I am?"

He took out the ever-present picture of Kim and used his flashlight to shine on the picture. He gave her a moment to realize what she was looking at and then she looked at Mark who had pulled back the netting covering his face.

"No. No way."

"Yes Charity. Kim was my daughter and my only child."

Mark stood up and headed for the cab of the truck leaving Charity trying in vain to untie the rope from her legs with her one good hand. Charity began to scream again and tried to stand up, but her screams were drowned out by the loud muffler exhaust as Mark started the truck and shifted it into gear. All the parallel trails that ran to the marshes from the main trail were straight lines and Mark drove as fast as possible until he reached the main trail, turned left, and went to the next trail where he turned left again toward the gulf. When he was halfway down the trail toward Roe and the Explorer, he stopped, got out and went to the back of the truck. What was left of Charity wasn't pretty. The only clothing left on her were ragged shreds of her jeans. Everything else was raw torn flesh. Parts of her skull were visible, but her face was gone as well as the injured arm. Mark quickly untied the rope from the trailer hitch and dragged her remains well off the trail into the forest before heaving her into a thick clump of palmettos. If she wasn't found within a day or two, she would never be found after the raccoons, fox, and bobcats, worked on her.

"RIP Charity," Mark muttered to himself as he started up the truck.

When he reached the end of the trail, he turned the engine off and got out.

"Don't shoot, Roe. It's me."

Roe stepped out of the underbrush gun in hand.

"Thank God. Are you alright?"

"I'm okay but we need to hurry. I'm going to turn the truck around. Bring the car out behind me."

As soon as the truck with the Explorer following behind, were pointed out on the trail, Mark quickly took his guns and rewrapped them in the rug. He transferred the two suitcases with the money into the back of the Explorer. The two duffel bags of drugs, he left in the truck bed.

"I want you to follow me out. I'm going to stop at the clearing where we assume Jasmine is waiting. When we get there, stay well behind me, and don't get out of the car. I'm going to turn on my bright lights so Jasmine can't see much. We don't want her to see you and she won't be able to identify me either."

"Yes. I understand. I just want to get out of these woods."

"You and me both. We've pushed our luck a long way. Let's hope it holds for a few more minutes."

Mark drove the truck with Roe following him, back up to the main trail and turned right toward Beach Road. When they reached the clearing where the Suburban was parked, Mark turned the truck toward the Suburban and turned on the truck's bright lights. Jasmine was standing by the car blinded by the headlights of the truck. Mark let the mosquito net on his hat drop over his face as he got out of the truck.

"Jasmine, get in the car in the driver's seat now!" Mark shouted as he pulled the duffels out of the back of the truck and dragged them to the Suburban's tailgate. Panicked and confused Jasmine did as she was told.

"There's been a change in plans," Mark said as he shoved the duffels into the rear of the Suburban. Walking up to the driver's side door, he handed the keys to Jasmine.

"Do you know how to get to Andre's warehouse in Tampa?"

"Yes."

"Good. Now listen carefully. Go straight to the warehouse and make sure Andre gets the bags I just put in the car. Do you have money for gas?"

"Yes. But what about Charity and the others?"

"There's been a change in plans. They won't be going home. Not now. Not ever. If you don't leave now, you won't be going either. Now go!"

She did. Without another word, sensing that she was lucky to be alive, Jasmine started the Suburban and headed toward beach road.

Mark checked once more to be sure he hadn't left anything in the truck before he had Roe move over into the passenger seat of the Explorer and he got behind the wheel. He approached Beach Highway slowly without the car lights on, making sure Jasmine had turned south. As soon as he was sure the road was deserted, he eased onto the highway, turned on his lights and headed south staying well behind Jasmine. He took the shortest route possible by using State Road 51 from Steinhatchee up to I-10, back to Jacksonville and home.

CHAPTER 35

The Last Act

1988

Roe slept like a rock all the way back to Jacksonville. Mark was still energized from the encounter and had no trouble staying awake. Roe didn't wake up even when Mark stopped at a rest stop on the interstate and used a payphone after first replacing the stolen license with the correct one. While getting ready for the trip to Steinhatchee, Mark had looked up phone numbers for the DEA and FBI offices in Tampa. He got an answering machine at both numbers and left messages saying that a shipment of drugs was being brought into the warehouse owned by Mendez sometime today. He included Andre's warehouse address and a description of the black Suburban on both calls.

It was only after he had pulled into his garage in the early morning and lowered the door that the fatigue hit him. He and Roe both struggled to their rooms and crashed leaving everything in the Explorer. It wasn't until early afternoon after they were both awake with large cups of coffee in hand that Mark told Roe what had happened. He left out the part about dragging Charity only relaying that she died with the others in the firestorm from the Thompson. He also explained his earlier phone call to the DEA and FBI.

"Andre is going to be exposed from two fronts. It's hard to predict which one will be the worst. His Colombian connection will be after him because they've lost both the drugs and the money. If law enforcement finds the drugs at his warehouse, he's going to have a tough time walking away from it. Regardless of his legal problems, the Columbians won't forget what he's cost them and eventually they'll get to him, in jail or out. Andre is going to be looking over his shoulder for a long time to come."

"Roe, for better or worse you know you've become a part of this whole thing. If we're ever connected to this either by the drug cartel or by law enforcement, you know we're in big trouble?"

"Mark. I know that. I also know that you've been whitewashing some of what you've done, thinking you're somehow protecting me. Leaving out details isn't going to make me any less guilty. So, from now on, treat me as an equal partner. I'm choosing to be here of my own free will. Not knowing details won't excuse me of accountability."

Mark had to look away to cover the moisture rising in his eyes. There was a level of maturity beginning to show in Roe that he would never have suspected. He hid his emotion by telling Roe, "I need to take the guns out of the car. Would you mind cooking up a breakfast for us while I clean it out?"

"You read my mind."

Mark went out to the garage, took out both suitcases from the Explorer, and carried them into his walk in safe. The suitcases were large, and metal cased. He didn't remember them as being so heavy. Inside the safe, he opened them. They were each packed tightly with equal size packets of circulated one hundred-dollar bills. He had no idea how much the total would be, but it would have to be in the millions. He'd have to count it all later. He left the rug containing the guns on his workbench. He'd clean them later.

After eating Mark told Roe that he had one more thing he needed to do and how she could help. Without going into minute details, he explained that she needed to stay at the house and provide an alibi for him if it was ever necessary. When Roe questioned him about what he planned to do, he simply responded, "Trust me on this Roe. It's the last thing I need to do to finish a promise I made to Marge and Kim."

"I'm pretty sure I know what you mean. I'd like to help."

"I know you would but this time the second person might be a liability. What if I promise that I'll tell you everything when I've finished?"

"Okay. But I'd still rather go with you."

Mark left alone for Orlando the next afternoon. He returned late in the afternoon on Friday. He didn't go straight home but instead went to Marge and Kim's gravesite at the cemetery. The sun was setting in the western sky and the panorama of colors reflected off the clouds was spectacular. He stood motionless for a long time before he knelt down on his knees and placed a hand on both granite slabs.

"I promised you they would pay. They have. I don't know if this brings you any satisfaction. It has for me. I'll always love you both."

Mark finally stood up and walked away.

CHAPTER 36

Closure

1988

When Mark finally arrived home, it was after dark. He'd called ahead to let Roe know he was almost there and to please not shoot him. When he walked into the house Roe was startled at his appearance. He had still not shaved and his unkept beard had continued to grow. But it was not just his beard. He was dressed in Salvation Army reject clothing. His hair was matted and disheveled and it looked as if something might crawl out at any moment. His shoes were what had probably once been someone's running shoes but now were nothing more than rubber soles barely held together by shreds of canvas.

"My God Mark. I'm glad you called before you got here. I'd still be shooting at you."

"Roe actually, it's really comfortable. I've gotten used to not shaving or taking showers. People tend to leave you alone." Mark's smile was barely visible through his matted beard.

"Including me," Roe replied.

"Just give me thirty minutes and this homeless person is going to disappear."

Mark got a plastic trash bag from the kitchen and went into his bathroom. When he emerged, the beard and matted hair were gone and he was dressed in old jeans, an orange cotton Gator sweatshirt, and flip flops. In his hand, he carried the plastic bag containing the old clothing, which he carried to the open grill on the patio. He doused the contents with charcoal lighter fluid and lit it.

"Roe let's fix ourselves a drink and I'll tell you what happened. He poured Roe a glass of chardonnay and himself Tanqueray over ice with a wedge of lime.

"I need to watch this fire to make sure I don't burn down the house."

While tending the burning clothes, Mark proceeded to tell Roe about his trip to Orlando. She listened quietly and when Mark finished, she only said, "Thank you."

"Roe let's talk about you now. Are you still serious about going back to school?"

"Absolutely. The more I think about it, the more excited I get."

"Then let's get started. I'm going to get a contractor I know to fix up the garage apartment. That way you can have all the privacy you want. You can drive the old Explorer unless you want something newer."

"No. It's fine. I don't want to do anything that would attract attention."

"Roe, you're reading my mind."

Mark checked the Tampa and Orlando newspapers every day after he returned. On Sunday, the Orlando Sentinel featured a story of a self-immolation in front of a nude dancing establishment on Orange Blossom Trail. The article went on to say that the identity of the individual had not yet been determined because of the severity of the burns. In addition, they were asking the public for help in identifying an apparent homeless man who had been seen at the scene. He was a person of interest, and he might be able to provide some helpful information. When Mark showed Roe the paper, she smiled and said, "Homeless person? Isn't that interesting?"

On Monday Morning, the Tampa Tribune front-page headline read, "Bodies Found in Forest, Possibly Drug Related". The article went on to read that on Sunday, a game warden working in Taylor County was investigating a site where a large number of vultures were circling. Expecting to find evidence of a poaching operation, the warden discovered the bodies of four men instead.

The deaths were described as, "Obvious foul play." Local, state, and federal authorities were involved in the ongoing investigation.

Again, Roe laughed and asked, "Obvious foul Play? That's an understatement, isn't it?"

Mark only shrugged his shoulders and remained silent, but it was only a second before Roe looked at Mark with a curious expression.

"Four men? What about Charity?"

"Charity was still alive, so I took her for a separate ride behind the truck."

"What do you mean by a separate ride?"

"Roe let's just say that Charity died like she lived. Hard."

"Oh, you don't need to say anything else. Now I understand what you used the rope for. I just wish I could have helped."

Chapter 37

Loose Ends

1988

Over three weeks had passed before Mark got the call he'd had been expecting.

"Mr. Price, this is Detective Garcia from Orlando."

"Yes Detective. Do you have any news?"

"Yes, we do. When it rains, it pours. I hate to try to give you all that we've discovered over the phone. Would you mind driving down here and letting me update you on what we've found?"

"Absolutely. Just answer one question. Have you found Kim's killers?"

"Yes. I think we have. Can you be here by ten a.m. tomorrow?"

"I'll be there."

Mark left early the next morning for Orlando. He asked Roe if she would clean out Kim's rooms for him. He would tackle Marge's stuff in the master bedroom later. There was no good reason to make a museum of any part of the house. Clothes could be donated to Good Will. Expendable things Roe couldn't use were to be thrown out. Personal effects such as jewelry, letters, and photos, could be packed in boxes. Mark knew that eventually the time would come when he would be able to go through it all. He just hadn't reached that point yet. The thought had occurred to him earlier that he could let Roe take over Kim's two rooms, but he decided against it. Roe wasn't trying to be Kim, and Mark didn't want Roe to take Kim's place either. By letting Roe live in the garage apartment, she would be able to keep her own identity.

Mark left for Orlando by seven a.m. At ten, he was ushered into Detective Garcia's office. He was surprised to see Major Rankin in the office as well. Both Rankin and Garcia greeted him warmly before Rankin spoke.

"We like it when we can give some degree of closure to a family. In this case, it's providing closure to several things but it's also raising many questions. Mr. Price, does the name Luke Travis mean anything to you?"

Mark's face was blank when he answered, "No."

"What about the name Charity Langer?"

"No."

"Have you ever heard of a bar called Teasers on South Orange Blossom trail?"

"No again. Why are you asking me? What's this got to do with Kim?"

Garcia said, "These names have some connection to Kim's death, and we wanted to know if any of these names had ever been mentioned by Kim before she disappeared. Let me start with last Thursday evening and go from there. Around eleven o'clock, a figure steps out of the shadows of an auto repair shop across the street from Teasers and ignites like a torch before he reaches the middle of the street. He'd left an empty gallon gas can on the sidewalk after apparently soaking his entire body with the full can. His cigarette lighter was on the ground at the edge of the street. Two patrons leaving the bar at that instant heard the man shout, "I'm sorry," just before he ignited. Traffic from both directions stopped. The fireball was so hot it melted the asphalt on the street. The two men who were leaving the bar as well as a couple of people in the stopped cars, said they saw what looked to be a homeless man standing at the spot the victim had appeared from. He disappeared during the commotion and wasn't seen again. The victim was burned beyond any recognition by the time someone came up with a fire extinguisher. We didn't get an ID on the man until Saturday morning. A dancer who had come out of the bar during the excitement, called our office to say one of the people running the bar had not shown up for work on Thursday or Friday. She thought she'd seen a necklace glowing on the victim's neck. She told us that the missing man, Luke Travis, wore a heavy gold necklace.

No one answered at Travis's apartment, so we got a warrant and went in. There was no one there and there was no sign of a struggle. What was peculiar was an empty pizza box on the floor just inside the door and a long hand-written note on the coffee table. A Colt automatic forty-five pistol was laying on top of the note. Next to the note was a picture of Kim that had been cut out of the Orlando Sentinel. Basically, the note was a long rambling confession. It was handwritten and signed by Luke. He expressed remorse for having been involved in Kim's death and he couldn't go on living with the guilt. He claimed that he and four others had mistaken Kim for someone else. In his note, he mentioned a Charity, Greaser, Fernando, and Rick as all having been involved. There were no last names. Everything Luke said in his note about Kim's death is consistent with the evidence we have. With the first names, we've been able to trace and eventually identify the people he mentioned. Fernando was killed in an unexplained gas explosion in Tampa. Rick was also murdered in Tampa. Greaser was one of the individuals found in the drug massacre on the coast in Taylor County. Only Charity is unaccounted for. Luke claims that they were all connected to a drug cartel out of Tampa run by someone named Andre Mendez whose name was associated with the convoluted corporate structure of the bar's ownership. Luke claimed that he was responsible for killing Rick at Andre's request. The pistol Luke left on his coffee table was determined to be same gun used in Rick's murder in Tampa. So, after putting everything together, we've found that four of the five of the people connected to Kim's death are accounted for and each one has met a violent death."

Mark sat motionless without expressing any emotion until Garcia finished. He realized that they were both watching him intently. Finally, Mark spoke. He was pretty sure what they were searching for, and he saved them from asking the question that he knew was coming next.

"Did you ever find out why Kim ended up on South Orange Blossom Trail at night?"

"No, Mr. Price, we haven't. We've hit a blank wall on that. In addition, we're not listing Luke's death a suicide. We think he was murdered. Even with the severe burns, the autopsy indicated his wrists, legs, and neck had been bruised from some sort of ligatures before he was set on fire. In addition, the lighter had no finger-prints on it. Because all of these deaths are in some way connected to your daughter, we'd hoped that by now you might have found or remembered something that would help us."

"Let's hope you never make that connection," Mark thought to himself.

He maintained a neutral expression when he answered.

"No. I have no clue. You still haven't told me why Kim was targeted?"

Garcia spoke, "No, we don't and apparently all the people who were involved are dead or missing. We're looking hard for Charity but so far, no luck. She was last placed in Steinhatchee with the people who were killed, including Greaser, during the drug deal gone bad. She hasn't been seen since. The Andre character apparently was the headman and he's wanted by a number of peo-ple, including a Columbian drug cartel. He's disappeared entirely. Somehow, he evaporated just before his warehouse was raided by the DEA. It's as if the wrath of God descended on everyone who was connected to Kim's death."

Mark had to stifle a smile at the thought of getting any infor-mation out of Charity, and Andre was probably wearing cement boots by now.

"Let's hope you can find this Charity character although I wish her all the worst. I don't have room for sympathy for any of them. And I'll always wonder why Kim ended up on Orange Blossom Trail that night. I'll never believe that she was looking for drugs."

Major Rankin stood up to indicate the meeting was over.

"I understand how you feel Mr. Price. I promise you that if we ever get more information, we'll let you know."

Mark breathed a sigh of relief. If they'd made any connection to Roe, he wouldn't be walking out of their office. And they were right in saying that the people who could make a connection, couldn't. He was still very uncomfortable with the way Garcia was watching him as he stood up to leave. He had a feeling that Garcia knew more than he was saying.

He left the sheriff's office and headed back toward Jacksonville with a heavy heart but a deep sense of closure.

Mark carried through on his promise to Roe. The apartment over the garage was cleaned out, remodeled and refurnished. Roe completed her undergraduate degree in Criminology within two and a half years. She aced the LSAT and was accepted into law school. She stayed at her parent's home in Gainesville which was only a few blocks from the law school, for classes during the week. She came back to her apartment over Mark's garage, which she now called home, on weekends where she could study without interruption. Her parents were overjoyed with her new course in life. They had no idea what her relationship with Mark meant but whatever it was, they were grateful to have their daughter back.

PART TWO

1998

There are times when even justice brings harm with it.
—Sophocles,Philoctetes

Chapter 38

Mark Price

1998

Mark had been able to live life on his own terms over the years since Kim and Marge died. He had received good advice from Moshe on how to safely handle the cash money he'd accumulated. And Moshe was very discreet, asking no questions about the origin of Mark's money. Although he was well off financially from his property leases alone, the additional millions of cash gave him options that few people ever enjoy. His biggest extravagance was his travel. There were few places in the world he hadn't visited. He had enabled Roe to get her degrees without incurring debt and she was now working as a prosecutor for a statewide task force combating human trafficking. Regardless of where her current operations were based, Roe still considered the apartment over Mark's garage to be her permanent residence.

Her relationship with Mark continued to grow stronger as the years had passed. They each seemed to lead totally separate lives but still they were closer than ever. Roe never tried to take the place of Mark's daughter Kim but they each seemed to draw strength from the other. In many ways it was like a father-daughter bond but neither ever assumed authority over the other. It was especially confusing to Roe's family because she refused to discuss her relationship with Mark. The only comment she would make about Mark was, "He's my best friend in the entire world."

Mark was intrigued by Jim Herbert's situation. Mark wasn't a psychiatrist, but he had always been adept at judging people. He just didn't accept the idea that Jim was capable of committing such a brutal act. He had to laugh at himself though because he had committed horrific acts himself. But he had been driven by the motivation to avenge his wife and daughter's deaths. What could Jim's motivation have been? He just didn't buy Jim Herbert's guilt. Since he was between trips, it would be interesting to look at the evidence to see if he could satisfy his own curiosity. He decided to start in Orlando. He had nothing but time to lose and time he had plenty of.

One of the things that Moshe had emphasized to Mark was that he should maintain a low profile. Avoid flashy cars, jewelry, anything that would bring attention to possible wealth. Mark's only obvious show of excess was his purchase of a year-old Toyota Land Cruiser. He brought it from Honest Abe with a cash transaction that worked well for both he and Abe. He did belong to a local gym, and he used a local shooting range regularly. He had never been in better shape physically and he couldn't bear to go more than two or three days without a heavy workout. The perk he enjoyed that was not obvious were the spiderwebs of LLC's that owned a condo in Boynton Beach as well as an offshore fishing cruiser.

Although he carried a major credit card, he used cash whenever possible. So, before he left for Orlando he went into his safe and took out several thousand dollars from one of the many stacks lining a metal storage shelf. A lot of the cash was stored safely away in multiple safe deposit boxes along with more gold than he could carry at one time. He packed a suitcase with enough clothes for a few days and before he left his house, he made one phone call to Roe's cell phone.

"Hey, Roe, Mark."

"Mark, what's up?"

"Will you do me a favor and look up the Jim Herbert murder case? Somehow, with being in and out of the country, I missed it completely. I know the guy and I'm just curious about the case."

"I'm aware of the case but I really don't know much. I'll ask around and see what I can learn. By the way, you realize it's been over two months since I've been home?"

"It is far too long. I'm on my way to Orlando now. Where are you?"

"I'm in Tampa right now. I may have to drive over to Orlando for a case I'm working on. I'll let you know if I do."

"That would be great. I'm staying at the Doubletree on Ivanhoe. Let me know if you hear anything interesting about the Herbert case."

"Will do. Bye."

It took Mark a little over two hours to get to his hotel, which was conveniently, located just off I-4 in Orlando. As soon as he had checked in, he looked up the office number of Karin Stills. He identified himself as a friend of Jim Herbert and was immediately put-on hold but only for a moment.

"This is Karin Stills."

Mark explained his meeting with Jim and asked if he could meet with her.

"I'll pay for your time."

"I talked to Jim this morning. He wanted me to meet with you. Can you come to my office early tomorrow morning?"

"Tell me when and where and I'll be there."

"Can you make seven? I start early and it'll be the best time for me to talk. I'm located near the main courthouse. The office won't open until eight thirty, so I think I can answer most of your questions. And Mr. Price, there won't be any charge for my time. I'm desperate to do anything I can to help Jim Herbert. If you have anything to offer, I'm all in. I'll even have coffee ready."

"I'll see you at seven."

Mark was up at five a.m. and did a thirty-minute run around a couple of the small lakes near the hotel. After showering and dressing, he picked up several fresh pastries from the hotel coffee shop and took them with him. By six thirty, he had located Stills' office building and parked in a lot designated for the building. Her office was one of several listed occupants of the two-story building a couple blocks from the main courthouse. As he got out of his car in the mostly deserted lot, he watched a grey Mercedes convertible pull into a marked parking space next to the building. From the limited description Jim Herbert had given him, he knew it had to be Karin Stills when she got out of the car. She looked across the parking lot and when she saw Mark, she immediately walked straight toward him.

"You must be Mark Price."

Mark was taken back by how small she was but at the same time at how attractive she was.

"I hope you don't trust everyone in your parking lot this early in the morning."

"Don't worry. I'm armed and dangerous."

"Duly noted. And yes, I'm Mark Price. Jim Herbert had a lot of good things to say about you."

"I wouldn't expect him be so kind considering where he's sitting right now."

'I'm anxious to know more."

"Follow me and I'll put on the coffee."

Mark followed her around the back of the building and watched as she unlocked an unmarked solid door. She turned on lights as they went inside, followed a hallway to a staircase leading to a second-floor landing with a door on either side of the landing. She opened the door on the left and they entered what looked to be a large break room with a kitchen on one side. Stills quickly and efficiently put on a large pot of coffee and as it began to perk, she indicated for Mark to sit at one of the several tables in the room.

"We'll go into my office as soon as the coffee's done. Tell me how you know Jim."

Mark gave her a condensed version of his relationship with Herbert.

"Jim told me you lost your wife and daughter. I'm sorry. I have one child who's in med school now. I can't imagine losing her. Losing my ex, not so much though."

"Cream and sugar?"

"Black."

Stills took the pot of coffee, two cups out of a cabinet and led Mark down a hallway with offices on each side. He followed her into a large corner office with plate glass windows. It was furnished simply but elegantly with thick carpeting and a lot of dark wood paneling. The wood was matched by her desk and bookcases filled with law books along two walls. There was a small sofa and two matching chairs with a coffee table in one corner. The only personal items Mark could see in the room other than her law degrees, was a framed picture on her desk of what must be Karin and her daughter.

Mark sat on the sofa and Karin took a chair and poured coffee into the two cups. Mark laid the pastries on the coffee table.

"Breakfast?"

"Thanks. They look good."

Mark started the conversation by reiterating his difficulty in accepting that Jim Herbert could have committed such a barbarous act.

"Mark, I agree. From the moment I took this case, I've never once questioned his innocence. Although none of them can publicly admit it, most of the law enforcement people who've been involved in the case, don't believe it either. The circumstantial evidence is overwhelming. It's almost too cut and dried. First of all, there was no motive for Jim to do it unless he'd experienced a drug induced, total breakdown. That just didn't happen. At the same time, there are other people who might have had a motive. He's passed a barrage of lie detector test at his own request, all indicating he's telling the truth. There is nothing in his background to indicate any predilection toward anger or violence. There's something wrong about someone calling from a payphone at that hour on a rainy night, to report seeing him leave her apartment. Then that unidentified person makes the effort to write down his tag number. Why at two thirty a.m. do you write down a tag number of someone simply leaving an apartment and then call the police to report a murder? Why was the only trace of blood identified in Jim's car his own? Based on the victim's injuries, Jim should have been covered in her blood. There was no sign of anyone showering off in the apartment so Jim couldn't have washed off her blood before he left."

"Was there blood on the door leaving her apartment?"

"Yes. There was blood on the outside of the door. There were even traces of blood on the floor outside her apartment door. The back door was locked with a key operated deadbolt lock.

It was still raining enough that the blood trail stopped at the bottom of the stairs. Why was there not blood all over Jim's car? How do you leave the victim's blood on the door as you leave, track it down the stairs and not leave any trace of it in your car? This lack of evidence was buried by the state during disclosure. They weren't going to use the results from testing Jim's car. I had to dig it out and bring it up. In the trial, they brought in an expert witness who said it was washed off by the rain. That's BS. Although Jim's semen was found, there was evidence indicating a condom had also been used. That doesn't make sense. And there was no condom found at the scene. They found Jim's fingerprints everywhere. There was no attempt to wipe them off. But at the same time, there were traces of powder indicating some type of medical gloves had been used.

This trial was toxic from the beginning. We were denied a change in venue in spite of the intense media scrutiny and the political implications locally. I've never had a jury that was as hostile toward the defense right from the start. I hate to say it, but the conviction was a predetermined fact. We only went through the motions. I think even the judge was concerned that the jury deliberated for less than an hour. The jury then proceeded to vote unanimously for the death penalty. In Florida a unanimous jury vote is required to receive a death penalty. The courtroom cheered when it was announced. I've never seen a decision influenced so much by public opinion."

"How did you stop his execution after the first death warrant had been signed by the governor?"

"I used the only bullet I had left. Jim had left his bloody shirt in the trashcan in his hotel room. The maid took it and was going to wash the blood out and keep it. She'd stashed it in her purse and taken it home. She dropped it in the bottom of a clothes hamper at her house and initially forgot about it. During the following week, all the carts were searched for any evidence. The maid was now scared shitless. She originally told them she'd thrown the shirt away in the trash when she cleaned Jim's room. Later, after the maid was fired by the hotel for some minor offense, she contacted an attorney in another office here in this building. At some point during her meeting with the attorney, she let it slip that she'd kept the shirt. Plus, she still had it in her possession laying unwashed in the bottom of her clothes hamper. The attorney realized what he was hearing and with the woman's permission, came straight to me with her story. When the revelation was presented to the courts, we were given a temporary stay on Jim's execution so the shirt could be evaluated and that's where we stand. That was my last bullet. That's why I'm willing to talk to you now. Jim said that you seemed to possess an unusual ability to get information. Maybe there's something or someone either my office or our investigator overlooked. I'll gladly make all the transcripts available, and I'll tell our investigator to give you anything he has as well.

"Could I look at the trial records this morning? I'll try to reach the investigator this afternoon."

"Absolutely. I'll have my staff set up a room for you. To be sure we're on the same page, I expect you to let me know immediately if you find anything useful or recognize that we've missed anything."

"Believe me, that's my goal as well."

By the time Mark finished his meeting with Karin, the office had come to life and was humming with activity. One of the office staff took Mark into a small unoccupied office that only contained a desk, phone, and computer. She told Mark that he was free to use the computer and she would bring in all the files on the Herbert case. She also showed Mark how to access material online as well. She brought in a large pile of documents, which he went through quickly. He didn't really expect to find anything, but he wanted to get a good feel of the flow of the trial. He wanted the names of all the individuals who were deposed in relation to the case. By noontime, he thought he had gotten all he would from the trial history and was anxious to talk to the investigator. His name was Dick Holmes, which Mark thought appropriate for a private investigator. Mark had to leave a message on Holme's voice mail but received a call back almost immediately. After hearing his reason for calling, He agreed to meet Mark for lunch. Holmes gave Mark directions to a small sandwich shop downtown near Still's office.

Chapter 39

Dick Holmes

Mark reached the restaurant first and after being seated at a table that gave him a view of the entrance, ordered coffee. There was no mistaking Holmes when he walked into the shop. He looked like an old-time gunslinger in a class B western movie. Instead of Western clothes he was dressed in a loose-fitting black suit with a white dress shirt and no tie. His jacket was unbuttoned, revealing a shoulder harness holding a big bore revolver which he made no attempt to conceal. He was tall and lean with dark, brown weathered skin which had never seen a drop of sunscreen. He was also totally bald and wore it proudly. Karin had told Mark that Holmes was an ex-Orlando cop who had grown up and lived his entire life in the area. She added that no one knew more about the history of Orlando and its people than he did.

Mark stood up when he walked in and without pausing, Holmes came straight to the table where Mark was standing. In spite of his intimidating appearance, he smiled warmly when he shook Mark's hand.

Mark returned his warm greeting with a smile as well, "Thanks for meeting me so quickly."

"If Karin vouches for you, you've got my attention, especially if it's related to Jim Herbert."

"It is," and Mark briefly explained his interest in the case.

"Mark, I've never been so convinced of someone's innocence. Jim was set up. I know it. The judge in the case knows it. The police know it. This was a crime of opportunity and Jim Herbert happened to be in the wrong place at the wrong time. I believe he was the victim of overwhelming circumstantial evidence and a social and political wave of class warfare. Herbert had absolutely no defense. Karin Stills is the best criminal defense attorney I've ever worked with, but she was helpless in this case. I think there are some prominent people involved but we've not been able to prove anything."

"I saw in the trial record that numerous people were deposed but almost nothing about following up after the depositions. Can you tell me about them?"

"Absolutely. Let's start with the ex-husband, Charles Griffin, a low life lawyer and wannabe politician. His father died from a heart attack while he was still an infant. His mom, Grace, who is a real piece of work, remarried her boss within a month of his dad's death. There is still some speculation about why a young man with no prior history of heart disease died so suddenly. Grace got unusual help from her boss who was a big-time heart surgeon. Her boss also happened to be the heir to a huge fortune and had serious political connections. Somehow, with the good doctor's help, there was no autopsy or any form of forensic investigation. The body was cremated before it got cold, so no one will ever know if the cause of death was anything other than a heart attack.

"Charles never got to know his biological father. He was adopted by Dr. Griffin and his name was changed to his stepdad's. By all indication, the stepdad was a good father and meant well. But Charles was a problem from the beginning. I think his mother was responsible. There was never any discipline. She protected him from the stepfather, from schoolteachers, and even eventually covered up run ins with the law. Somehow, she totally controlled the stepdad and he stood by and let her do whatever she wanted. Charles was given a new Corvette when he was sixteen and when he promptly wrecked it, it was replaced with a new Porsche. He was kicked out of a couple of private schools, and he tried to imitate Animal House during the time he was in college at Florida State University. There must have been a lot of strings pulled to get him admitted to a small private law school. He did get his degree and somehow with a lot of tutoring, he passed the Florida Bar on his second try."

"What does he do now?"

"Besides running for state representative? He's our local race baiter. And he represents some shady people. All of his cases, drug offenses, prostitutes, and parole violators are always race or gender related. He also has some connection to several nude bars where he spends a lot of his time."

"How did he meet Tanya?"

"She was a dancer at one of the bars he frequented. He fell hard for her probably because she ignored him. She had a regular boyfriend who took it hard when she did start spending time with Charles."

"Who was the boyfriend?"

"He's another figure that's connected to this entire soap opera. He's a hardcore biker named Vernon Jost. When Tanya asked him to back off, surprisingly he didn't interfere. At least not at the beginning. I think he thought that Charles was a passing fancy who would eventually get bored with Tanya and drop her. It didn't work out quite that way. Charles didn't lose interest in Tanya until she told him she was pregnant. He told her it was her fault and T.S. There are a lot of rumors on what happened next. I have a good working relationship with a couple of guys in that bike club who were eyewitnesses and I believe what they've told me. They told me that Tanya went crying back to Vernon and told him what was happening. My sources say Vernon made Charles the sort of offer he couldn't refuse.

"The night after Tanya had cried on Vernon's shoulder, Charles was leaving his apartment when he was surrounded by a group of bikers. They forced him into the back of a van, used duct tape to tape his arms behind his back and his legs together. He resembled a mummy before they threw a hood over his head and drove him to a remote scrub area south of Orlando.

"Vernon was there to meet him when they took him out of the van and stood him upright. The first thing Charles immediately realized as his eyes adjusted to the bright lights, was that they were in a clearing surrounded by scrub palmetto and scattered small pine trees. The bright lighting came from the headlights of two pickup trucks and the van's lights. The lights were aimed at a point in the center of the clearing. There was loud country music blaring from one of the pickup trucks, but Charles wasn't listening to the music when he realized what he was looking at. They say he peed in his pants when he looked at the large freshly dug hole directly in front of him. Dirt was heaped on either side and there was a heavily tattooed man standing on either side with a shovel in hand. It didn't take a lot of imagination for him to speculate on what was coming next.

"Charles asked Vernon 'What are you doing?'

"Vernon told him, 'This is what we do with assholes who knock up a good girl and then walk away.'

"Before Charles could utter another word, he was picked up and carried to the hole and dropped in on his back. By then he was so scared, he couldn't do anything but shake his head. The two guys with the shovels began to shovel dirt over him starting at his feet. When the dirt started hitting him, he managed to blurt out, 'I'm sorry. I'll do anything you want.'

"Vernon told the two guys with shovels to hold up a minute.

"'Anything?'

"'Yes, yes!'

"Vernon then made Charles the proverbial offer he couldn't refuse."

Mark smiled at that comment.

"So, they let Charles live if he agreed to marry Tanya?"

"Right. Actually, they were married the very next day in a small Church of God whose minister was a member of the biker group. Charles's mother found out after the fact and went ballistic. She tried to get the marriage annulled but Charles was too terrified to agree to an annulment. He knew enough about Vernon's reputation that either Vernon or one of his biker friends would finish the job next time around. It didn't take Tanya too long before she realized what a jerk Charles really was before she finally left him. Again, she had Vernon's protection. Neither Charles nor Tanya contested any part of the divorce, and they were given joint custody of the child. Surprisingly, Charles's mom Grace had taken a likening to the child, and she was actually the one who kept the boy for Charles when it was his time to have him.

"Almost immediately, Grace Griffin decided that she didn't want to share custody of the child with Tanya, and she put pressure on Charles to take control and retain full custody. By then, Tanya was putting her life together. The child brought out the best in her. She was a good mother, she had a decent job, and her future was looking good. There was no way she was going to give up custody of her child. Grace tried everything, even offering Tanya a lot of money to give up her custody rights."

"Was there any way they could have been connected to the murder?"

"Nothing that I could ever find. They all had solid alibis and Karin deposed them as well. I still don't trust them any further than I could throw them, but we had no evidence to connect them to the murder. The prosecution had no motive to investigate anyone else because they felt they had a slam dunk case."

"Who has the child now?"

"Charles. Or I should say Grace. She got what she wanted, again."

"Who else could have had a motive?"

"I'm not sure what his motive would have been unless it was jealously, but I have questions about one of Tanya's coworkers. He's an insurance investigator named Lewis Lynch. I do know that she had an on off affair with him after she'd left Charles. Again, he had a rock-solid alibi, and I haven't found anything to connect him to the murder. Karin took a lot of depositions of other people like friends and coworkers but none of them had a motive or connection to the murder. The police and investigators did very little to look at anyone other than Jim. I've done far more legwork investigating this case than all of the police investigators put together."

Mark was silent for a moment before he spoke.

"What else could you have done that you haven't already done?"

"I would have used wiretaps on some of these people. The problem is, first I would never be able to get approval for one and if I did it without a permit, it would never be admissible in a court. And again, the prosecution was not motivated to dig any deeper. I even went back to some of the people she worked with when she was dancing, thinking maybe we were missing something."

"Nothing there?"

"Not really. Every dancer has a few lost souls who latch onto them and become a nuisance. Tanya had too many to count. She was good looking, and she knew how to generate the tips. There was one guy who worked for a landscaping company that they finally had to throw out and trespass from the bar. When Tanya stopped dancing, they never saw him again. I think if he'd continued to be a problem, Vernon would have intervened. Even though Tanya no longer had any romantic interest in Vernon, I think he would have done anything to protect her."

"Is there anyone else that you think might be involved?"

"Not necessarily involved. Tanya did have an older sister that I talked to on several different occasions. I always had the feeling that she knew something but just wouldn't say it. She was convinced that Herbert didn't kill Tanya. I do know that she and Tanya were close, and she would sometimes baby sit Tanya's kid."

"Can I get the names and contact information for these people?"

"Everything is in my computer. I'll forward it to your email address. There's one other thing you need to know. It's one of the reasons I'm so sure there's a lot about this case that we don't know. I've received two different warnings to back off the case. Both were phone calls to me. The caller, a male, basically said drop the case or

I would pay a price if I didn't. Both calls came from a throw away phone so there's no way to trace them. It's just my word that I was threatened. You should be watching your back if you start asking questions."

Mark only nodded, not knowing just how true Holmes's statement would prove to be.

CHAPTER 40

The Last Chance Bar

When Mark returned to his hotel, he had a message on his room phone from Roe, asking him to call her back. When he did, she answered immediately.

"Hey Sherlock. Are you still playing detective? I found out a few things. First, the prosecutor, Leonard Knotts, is a pompous, egotistical blowhard with political aspirations. For him, this high-profile conviction set him up to run for a state senate seat which fortunately he lost. He's developed a reputation for being a relentless prosecutor. The other interesting thing I learned was that the initial crime scene involved both the Orlando Police and the Orange County Sheriff's Office. The crime scene was close to the sheriff's central office, and they got to the scene first. Ultimately, the case was left to the sheriff to investigate, and the Orlando Police stepped aside. Guess who was on the crime scene representing the sheriff's office?"

"I give up. Who?"

"Your detective Garcia, who is now a Major."

"Interesting."

"Also, it was common knowledge that Knotts openly discouraged any attempt by any one in his office to investigate anyone else who might have had a motive. He was so sure he had his man, and he was riding high on popular opinion. The minute the jury saw the crime scene photos, Herbert had no chance. Let me save you time on another front as well. Don't even try to talk to anyone from the prosecutor's office or anyone in the Orlando Police department. They'll all tell you that everything related to the case is public record and everything is freely available to anyone who wants more details. No one wants to go on record contradicting the trial results.

"I was told that Stills did an incredible job with her cross examinations of Vernon Jost, Charles Griffin, and Lewis Lynch, but it backfired when Knotts was able to portray them as victims of Herbert's actions. Stills had nothing but supposition to connect them to the murder. Plus, they all had airtight alibis. By the way, I'm coming to Orlando tomorrow. Maybe we can have dinner tomorrow night?"

"That sounds good. Do you want me to reserve you a room where I'm staying?"

"No. The state already has rooms for my group somewhere out near Disney. I'll have my car so we can meet anywhere. I should be free after six tomorrow. I'll call you then. Think about where you'd like to meet."

After talking to Roe, Mark used his laptop to open his email and found one from Dick Holmes. Using a small notebook, he copied down the contact information Holmes had sent. It included addresses and phone numbers of the individuals that Holmes had mentioned. The only person without either a phone number or an address was the biker, Vernon Jost. Instead, it listed two biker bars that Jost was known to frequent. Since it was already late afternoon and he had nothing planned for the evening Mark decided to look them up. The addresses of the bars were included in Holmes's email and Mark looked them up on a map on his laptop. He made a mental image of their locations, which should be easy to find even though they were on opposite sides of Orlando. He changed into a pair of jeans, black t-shirt, and a light windbreaker that concealed the gun he placed inside his waistband. He stuck a pack of cigarettes and a lighter in one of his jean's pockets.

Mark decided to start at the closest one, which was named, "The Last Chance." It was a straight drive-up highway 17-92 toward Sanford. There was a preponderance of trailer parks, auto dealerships, liquor and ethnic food stores, and fast-food restaurants. The bar itself was easy to spot as it sat as a single two-story structure in a large lot between a tire store and a Hispanic food store. The parking lot was partially filled with pickup trucks and older model tired looking sedans. The entrance was in the middle of the building and the entire area alongside the building on either side of the door was reserved for motorcycle parking. There were more motorcycles than autos. A sign across the top of the entrance read, "Hot Beer-Cold Women."

Walking through the door was like walking into a dimly lit cave filled with smoke and country music blasting out so loudly he wanted to cover his ears. He stood there for a minute letting his eyes adjust to the dimness. He could barely hear the voice next to him ask, "Are you going to the bar, or do you want a table?"

Mark looked down at a small girl dressed or maybe one should say undressed. She wore nothing but what looked like a white string bikini with red tassels hanging off the top piece.

Mark had to lean down to yell in her ear.

"I'd like a table as far away from the music as possible."

"Follow me," she said.

A bar on the left stretched along the length of the entire room. On the right side was a stage where a couple of longhaired tattooed guys were setting up equipment for live music. Miss Bikini led Mark to the backside of the room somewhat away from the blaring speakers. It was noticeably quieter, and Mark thanked her as he sat down facing the room. Before Mark could light a cigarette, another girl appeared out of the dimness.

"What can I get you?"

This girl was tall and lean and was dressed exactly the opposite of the first one. This girl wore a red bikini with white tassels. Mark couldn't help but smile as he ordered a draft beer.

"Do you need a menu?"

"No. You tell me what's good."

"The fish and chips are good, but the hamburgers are the best."

Mark knew from experience that if a bar served food, then the burgers were usually a good choice.

"Let me have a cheeseburger rare with fries. Lots of mayonnaise on the side."

"You got it."

While he smoked a cigarette and nursed his beer Mark carefully looked around the bar. There was a group of eight to twelve obvious biker types clustered around the far end of the bar. None of them resembled the picture he had seen of Jost, but he couldn't be sure. Anyway, he wanted to enjoy his food before he put his hand in the hornet's nest.

The cheeseburger was excellent. It was thick, juicy, and messy with the tomatoes, lettuce, and excessive mayonnaise. The fries were crisp and greasy just like they should be. He had finished when Miss Bikini II came over and asked if he was ready for another beer. Although he didn't intend to drink any more, he ordered another.

"Would you also do me a favor?"

"Sure. What do you need?"

"I'm looking for Vernon Jost. I was told that I might find him here."

The smile immediately disappeared from Miss Bikini II's face, and a sudden look of apprehension replaced it.

"I'll ask the bartender."

"Thanks. I'd appreciate it."

Mark watched as his waitress went back to the bar and ordered his beer. She leaned over the bar and said something to the bartender who only nodded. She came back with his beer and said, "He's going to check for you."

"Good. Thanks."

Mark lit another cigarette and sat back in his chair in a relaxed nonchalant manner. He avoided looking directly at the bartender but instead watched him carefully out of the corner of his eyes. A mirror ran the entire length of the back of the bar and that helped to give a view of the bartender as he approached the group of bikers at the far end. Mark watched as the bartender leaned over the bar and spoke to someone in the group. It was as if someone had turned on some kind of switch as one by one the entire group looked toward Mark sitting at his table. Waiting to see what would happen next, Mark continued to act as if he were completely unaware of the group. Surprisingly, not one of the groups attempted to approach his table. Instead, they continued to watch him carefully. When Miss Bikini brought his bill, she told him that no one knew where to find Vernon Jost.

Mark left a generous amount of cash on his table and as he stood up to leave, he realized that the group of bikers were leaving. He saw the back of the last one going out the front door. Knowing what was coming next, he took a deep breath and headed for the exit.

When he walked out the door of the bar, Mark immediately saw the bikers standing around their bikes that were parked close to the entrance. He appeared not to notice and continued walking toward his car. He could both sense and hear footsteps behind him as he neared his car. By the time he'd reached his car door, the group had formed a semicircle around him.

One of the men who appeared to be the leader, stepped forward toward Mark.

"Who wants to see Vernon?"

"I do," Mark replied.

"Why do you wanna see Vernon?"

"That's between Vernon and myself. If I had business with you, I'd have asked for you."

"How about I make it my business?" he said as he took another step toward Mark.

The man was about Marks height but outweighed Mark by fifty pounds. He was obviously a serious weightlifter. Huge muscles bulged out of the single open vest he was wearing. His neck was so thick it made his head look undersized and almost comical.

Mark smiled and said, "Answer one question for me. Do you need all these people's help, or can you take me by yourself?"

"I'll tell you what, ass wipe. You get past me, and you can talk to Vernon. You don't get past me, and you'll get a trip to the emergency room."

"Sounds like a deal," Mark said as he took a step toward the big man.

The man was surprised and angered by Mark's aggressive movement toward him. They were only separated by three feet as the biker swung a huge right fist towards Marks face. Instead of trying to dodge or step back from the blow, Mark took a step forward and used his left arm to deflect the blow and at the same time, he used two fingers of his right hand to make a V and drove them into the biker's eyes. As the biker brought both hands up to his eyes, he tried to scream but before he could, Mark drove his knee into the poor man's groin. Not sure which pain was greatest, the man reached down to protect his groin and that's when Mark drove the heel of his hand upward into the biker's chin. The man's mouth was open when Mark's hand made contact, driving his mandible up into his upper teeth and maxilla. The result was brutal. Because the teeth came together off center, there were only a few teeth that weren't fractured along with a cracked maxilla. The sound of teeth smashing together could be heard across the parking lot. Blood was pouring from his mouth as he collapsed onto the ground moaning and shaking like a leaf.

Other than the poor man moaning on the ground, there was stunned silence. Mark leaned back against his car and lit a cigarette.

"Will someone please tell me how I can talk to Vernon Jost?"

One of the bikers was already making a call on his cell phone. He walked away out of earshot and had an animated conversation. When he returned, he simply said, "Follow me."

Meanwhile the other bikers were trying to lift the man up from the ground. He still couldn't stand up on his own. He, not Mark, was obviously the one making a trip to the emergency room.

CHAPTER 41

Vernon Jost

Mark got into his SUV and followed two of the bikers out of the parking lot and back onto the highway. They had only gone a short distance before they turned down a side road that immediately dead-ended at a mobile home park. They followed a winding road in the park and finally stopped at a home with a brick paved parking area in the front. It was not at all what Mark would have expected. Even in the dark, the mobile homes appeared to be well cared for and there were no rusted cars sitting on concrete blocks or yards filled with redneck detriment. There was a lot of green vegetation and well-kept lawns surrounded the homes. As he pulled into the parking area, he saw a large open carport area with two motorcycles and what he thought was a new model Range Rover. The two bikers pulled in behind Mark and remained sitting there. When Mark got out of his car, the front door to the house opened and a large figure came down the steps and walked up to Mark. He was less than six feet in height but what he lacked in height, he made up for in width. He didn't appear to be fat but instead he reminded Mark of a large Pit Bull. He was dressed in jeans and a Miami Dolphin sweatshirt. His hair was pulled back in a ponytail, and his beard was neatly trimmed. He stopped in front of Mark and looked at him with curiosity.

"I'm Vernon Jost."

"Vernon, my name is Mark Price. I'd like to talk to you about Jim Herbert."

"Okay Mark. If you'll leave the pistol tucked in your waist in your car you can come inside."

Mark was impressed at how easily Jost had recognized his concealed pistol.

Vernon looked at the two bikers who hadn't moved and said, "You can both go now."

They both seemed to hesitate and Jost spoke again with dripping sarcasm, "If Mr. Price had intended to hurt me, he'd have already tried it. I'm not sure how either of you two clowns could've helped me anyway."

With an embarrassed look on their faces, they started their bikes and left.

"Come on inside before the mosquitoes carry us off."

Mark took out his gun, placed it in his car and locked it. When they went through the front door, Mark was surprised at the furnishings. It looked like a suite that you would expect in a luxurious hotel. It didn't match his image of what the inside of a mobile home should look like. The entire back wall was all glass and looked out on a patio with a small pool and hot tub highlighted with indirect lighting. Jost motioned for Mark to sit, and he sat in a chair opposite him.

"Mr. Price, I'm talking to you mainly out of curiosity. The guy you put down, Henry Land, is one of the toughest men I've ever known. He's been a professional wrestler, a bouncer, cage fighter, and he's served hard time in rough places. As far as I'm aware, he's never been beaten in a one-on-one fight. I was told you didn't even work up a sweat. You didn't express any emotion of either anger or fear. That's impressive."

"Vernon, first, please drop the Mr. Price bit and call me Mark. You might tell Henry not to be so obvious with his moves. I really didn't want to hurt him."

"Henry can be a hothead and a little overprotective at times. You want to talk about crazy Jim Herbert. Why?"

Mark was already impressed with Jost. There was a lot more to the man than his outward image revealed. When he spoke, he reminded Mark of an English Professor and not a rough biker type.

When Mark went through his connection with Herbert and his doubt about his guilt, Jost replied. "You're wasting your time. Herbert is guilty as sin. Believe me, I checked on the alibis of everyone I thought might have a motive. If I'd had any proof that anyone else could have been involved, I'd have taken care of them myself. I don't deny the fact that I had strong feelings for Tanya, but Tanya could sometimes be her own worst enemy. She was always sexually permissive and took chances with men. She ran out of luck when she took Herbert back to her apartment. You're wasting your time looking for something that doesn't exist. You show me anything that points to someone else, and you'll get my full attention."

"So, you don't think there's any possibility the ex-husband could have been involved?"

"That pussy hasn't got the guts to kill anything or anyone."

Mark was convinced that Jost was sincere in his belief. He also felt confident that he could cross Jost off the list of suspects.

"Who was the last person to see Tanya before she went out to the bar?"

"Her older sister Keri. She had come by Tanya's apartment to pick up a couple of boxes of baby things that Tanya's boy had outgrown. One of her friends was expecting a baby and Tanya was in a clean out mode. Keri told me that Tanya told her to pick out a few old toys and videos while she was getting ready to go out. Tanya didn't have the heart to give away her kid's toys, so she let Keri pick out the older things and pack them up. They both left the apartment at the same time."

"Vernon, why do you think Herbert trashed Tanya's apartment? If he did kill her, what was his motive in doing that?"

"I think he must have had a total break with reality. He lost it. He went off the deep end. Who the hell knows why? He just did."

Jost's cell phone rang, and he looked at the number before he answered, "Yes."

He listened for a minute before closing his phone.

"That was one of the boys that took Henry to the emergency room. Henry has torn corneas in both eyes, a fractured maxilla, a cracked mandible, a lot of fractured teeth and a lower abdominal hernia. I'm glad you weren't trying to hurt him. He's not going to be any good for a long time."

Mark said nothing.

Vernon asked, "Are you interested in a job?"

Mark smiled and said, "Thanks for the offer but I'm not looking for a job. Plus, motorcycles scare the hell out of me."

When he got up to leave, Mark said, "Somehow I'd expected you to be living in a house hidden deep in the woods."

"I've got better control of my surroundings here than I ever could in the woods. Here I can know everyone around me."

"How so?"

"I own the park and I select who lives here."

"That would work."

Mark gave Jost his cell phone number and Jost reciprocated.

"I don't give this number out to many people. If you can prove me wrong, call me."

"I will. By the way, tell Henry no hard feelings."

CHAPTER 42

Major Garcia

Mark drove back to his hotel, stopped by the bar, ordered a double Tanqueray with a lime wedge, and took it up to his room. He tried to digest the information he'd gotten during the day, but he knew he'd have to do a lot more. Unable to come up with his next best step, he switched on the TV and watched a Carol Burnet Show rerun while he drank the gin. He went to sleep with a smile while laughing at Mr. Tudball.

Mark's inner clock woke him at sunrise as it always did except for the week following the annoying daylight savings time changes. The first few moments of waking were Mark's most productive moments of clarity and insight. If he had unanswered questions or problems, this was the time he would often have a flash of creativity. This morning as he lay in bed his mind summarized everything he had done and learned the previous day before his next steps were outlined in his mind.

After showering and dressing Mark ate a large breakfast of scrambled eggs, grits, corned beef hash, sausage links, and half a pot of coffee. Leaving the hotel, Mark drove west on Colonial Drive to the Orange County Sheriff's office. When he walked into the main lobby, he had an overwhelming surge of depression as his mind flashed back to his wife and daughter. He paused, took a deep breath to shake it off, and continued to the reception desk.

"I'd like to speak to Major Garcia if he's available."

The black female deputy behind the glass asked, "Do you have an appointment?"

"No. Tell him Mark Price would like to see him."

She picked up the phone, spoke to someone, and waited a minute more before hanging up.

"You're in luck. If you'll have a seat, he'll see you in a minute."

"Great. Thanks." Mark sat in a chair and waited.

When Garcia himself came out to greet Mark, he looked exactly as he did eight years ago except for his clothing. He was now wearing a uniform resplendent with badges and insignias indicating his rise in rank. Mark assumed accurately that the rank of Major was a big deal. Otherwise, Garcia seemed to be the same person as he held out his hand for Mark to shake.

"Mark Price. How are you? Come on up to my office and tell me what you've been doing."

"How do I address you properly now? Major or Officer?"

"How about Luis? I get more than enough ass kissing here."

Garcia's office was the same one that Major Rankin had been using before he retired. Mark experienced another wave of emotion when he entered the office and sat in the same seat he had sat in eight years ago when he was told his only daughter had been murdered.

"Mark, I've thought about you a lot over the years. Your case was one that got under the skin of a lot of people here. We see a lot of bad shit, but your case was hard to forget. How have you been?"

"Thanks, Luis. A person copes and moves on but it's not easy. The pain never goes away and after a while you realize that it will always be there. The only way to eliminate the pain would be drugs, alcohol, or suicide. I don't consider any of those to be good options."

"I admire you for that. What brings you here today?"

"Do you remember the Jim Herbert case?"

Garcia sat up a little straighter in his chair.

"That's another case that's hard to forget. What's your interest in the case?"

"Jim Herbert was a good friend."

Mark went through his usual explanation of his connection to Herbert.

"Mark, I'll tell you, it was one of the most brutal murders I've ever seen. Our office was running a late-night raid on some human trafficking establishments and that's how I happened to be in the office at that time of the morning. We got an anonymous call saying something was wrong at that address. The caller reported seeing someone covered in blood, leaving the apartment and driving away. The person even gave the make and license of the car. We sent a car around to the address which was not far from our office. We quickly got a call back from the two deputies who were really shaken. By the time I got there, the Orlando police had also arrived, and they were closing off the area. I only went into the apartment for a minute. We wanted to keep the traffic to a minimum until forensics could work the scene. The apartment looked like a tornado had blown through. And the victim was almost unrecognizable. It was not pretty. There was a belt pulled tight around her neck and her face looked like ground meat. Forensics later showed that Herbert used a large piece of broken glass to cut her up."

Getting straight to the point Mark asked, "Do you think Herbert did it?"

Garcia paused for a moment and leaned back in his chair before replying.

"It's hard to refute the circumstantial evidence. On the other hand, the act was so out of character for Herbert based on his background. Our office was involved in the investigation and the prosecution, but I was somewhat surprised at the intense focus on Herbert alone. If you quote me on what I'm about to say, I'll deny I said it. As bad as it may be, politics and justice are sometimes intertwined. Guilty or not, the timing couldn't have been worse for Jim Herbert."

"Nothing was missing from the apartment?"

"To my knowledge, no. The trashed apartment was excused as an example of a deranged mind at work."

"How did the prosecution explain the lack of the victim's blood in Herbert's car?"

"The jury accepted the explanation that the rain washed it off before he got in his car."

"Do you know anything about the ex-husband?"

"Everyone in law enforcement knows Charles Griffin. He's used every opportunity to attack law enforcement as being violent and insensitive to cultural differences. In other words, he waves the race card. I'll acknowledge that we've had Neanderthal cops in the past. Not so today. We lean overboard to ensure fairness for everyone. Unfortunately, there are some bad people out there and sometimes we can't play nice. Griffin takes every opportunity to turn law enforcement into a racial incident. The press has sided with him to the point that our police and deputies are turning a blind eye to things that we shouldn't be ignoring. It's actually hurting the people who need the help of law enforcement the most. To make it even worse, the man is running for the state legislature and stands a good chance of winning."

"That's too bad. I'm just having a hard time believing that Jim Herbert could have done something so out of nature."

Garcia gave Mark a strange look before he replied, "Mark, you've never known anyone doing something out of character?"

Mark suddenly had an uncomfortable feeling the way the conversation was heading.

"Luis, I guess you look at each case separately. Anyway, thanks for seeing me. I'll always be grateful to you for the way you handled my daughter's case."

As Mark stood up to leave, Garcia smiled and said, "I'm glad to see you're doing well Mark. I hope we won't have a rash of bodies showing up around Orlando. Oh, by the way, give my regards to Roe."

Mark tried to hide his surprise and almost choked before he averted Garcia's eyes and mumbled, "Thanks for the information."

Garcia made no other comments, and this was a conversation Mark didn't want to continue as he made a hasty exit.

CHAPTER 43

Keri Smith

Mark got back into his car and found a shady spot at the periphery of the parking lot, parked and rolled down his windows to let fresh air in. He was still trying to process Garcia's last comment. If he knew who Roe was, why had the authorities never brought either her or himself into the picture? In any case, eight years had passed since his daughter's death. He could only assume that whoever knew of his and Roe's connection had no intention of ever following up on it.

Looking up the phone number from the list Holmes had given him, he called the number listed for Tanya's sister, Keri Smith. When she answered, it was a cautious "Hello" which sounded more like a "Who's calling me now?" Mark hated to be deceptive, but he was anyway.

"Ms. Smith, this is Mark Price from Insurance Underwriters Group. There are questions about an insurance policy related to your sister, and I need a few minutes of your time. It shouldn't take more than fifteen or twenty minutes. Could I possibly stop by your place and talk to you?"

"I don't know anything about any insurance."

"I understand. That's why I need to talk to you."

Mark decided to take a chance when he added, "I'll be glad to give you the phone number for the home office and you can call and confirm that I'm legit."

"No. Don't bother. Can you come by now?"

"That would be great. Let me confirm your address," which he did.

"I'm on my way now."

Keri Smith's address was in the Pine Hills area that was only a short drive from the sheriff's office. Her neighborhood consisted of well-maintained duplex apartments. Keri's duplex sat on a heavily wooded lot. The landscaping consisted of mostly native Florida plants such as saw palmetto, cabbage palms and wild myrtle. There was a double carport set back from the street with a storage area across the rear and a newer model Toyota Camry sitting inside. A large live oak tree near the front of the duplex had limbs spreading almost over the entire building adding welcome shade from the Florida sun.

Mark pulled in behind the Camry and parked. A walkway connected the carport with one of the front doors. The second door didn't appear to be used. It was hidden by shrubbery indicating the duplex was being used as a single residence. Mark rang the doorbell, and the door was opened by a woman in her middle forties. Mark saw immediately the close resemblance to the pictures he'd seen of Tanya. She was dressed in jeans and a thin white T-shirt. It didn't take him long to realize she wasn't wearing a bra. He tried to maintain eye contact with her, but it was a challenge. The combination of the jeans and the T shirt emphasized her perfectly proportioned body. Mark guessed her to be around five feet eight and a hundred and ten to fifteen pounds. If Tanya was supposed to be good looking, her sister was drop dead gorgeous. She smiled and opened the door for Mark to come inside. The room was neat and furnished in inexpensive but solid furnishings. A nice oriental rug covered the center of the room's floor.

When he entered the room, he realized they weren't alone. Sitting on the far side of the room in a doorway was the largest, jet-black Doberman Pincher he'd ever seen. It made absolutely no noise, but its black eyes were focused like lasers on Mark. Even across the room, he could see the quivering muscles in its hind legs looking as if it was expecting a command to attack at any second.

A white scar that ran from its ear all the way to the corner of its mouth stood out in contrast to the black coat. Mark froze as Keri said, "Stay Brutus." The dog slowly relaxed and lay down with its head resting on its paws and its piercing eyes continuing to focus on Mark. He suddenly regretted the ruse he'd used to talk to Keri. One word from her and he was literally dog meat.

She pointed to a comfortable looking chair.

"Have a seat."

Trying to make small talk, Mark pointed toward the dog and asked, "How did the dog get the scar?"

"Water moccasin. Brutus hates snakes. The back of my house backs up to a wooded area with a small pond. We've always had a lot of snakes around our back yard. Most of them are harmless water snakes that Brutus will grab and shake so hard it snaps them, but there is the occasional moccasin. The first one that bit him nearly killed him, that's where the scar came from. He's been bitten since, but he's developed immunity to the toxin. He hates snakes even more now."

Mark didn't know how to tell her the reason he was there for and was looking for the right way to approach it.

Keri saved him when she spoke next.

"Come one Mr. Price. Couldn't you do better than the old insurance line? I had to bite my lip to keep from laughing on the phone. Dick Holmes called me yesterday and said you might be calling me."

"Thanks for not laughing. I'm not a good liar and please call me Mark. Did Holmes tell you why I'm interested in your sister's murder?"

"In general terms. Mainly he said you don't think Herbert killed my sister."

"That's true. I have a lot of doubts about it."

"You may be surprised Mark, but welcome to the club. I don't think he did either."

"That's a strong statement coming from Tanya's sister."

"When it happened, I assumed he was guilty as sin. As the case progressed there were too many things I couldn't reconcile."

"Such as?"

"Such as some critical facts not adding up. He passed the lie detectors twice. I don't think he was trained to do that. Then, how could he be dripping with Tanya's blood when he left the apartment and not leave a trace of her blood in his car? Her blood was on the floor of the hallway. What was his motive for trashing the apartment? He was acting normally when he returned to his hotel. Why didn't he try to avoid being seen by the hotel staff? The police said robbery couldn't have been a motive, but I know Tanya had several pieces of expensive jewelry that Charles had given her. They were never accounted for. Then there's the issue of character. I think that anyone who could commit such an act would have to have shown some signs of instability leading up to it. I'm going to admit something to you that I haven't told anyone. I met with his ex-wife Julie during the trial. I really expected her to tell me what a powder keg he'd been. Surely, there was a dark side to Jim Herbert that indicated that it was only a matter of time before he went off the deep end. That didn't seem to be the case at all. The wife didn't believe he could be guilty either. I also made one trip to the prison and sat face to face with Herbert. I wanted to look directly into his eyes. Jim Herbert is innocent. He is not a killer."

"Who do you think killed your sister?"

"I have two theories. The first is what I call a random act of violence. A true nutcase happens along when Herbert is leaving, goes in and kills her. The only problem there is the fact that Herbert swears he left the door passage lock on. The door was not forced open. My second theory is my conspiracy theory. It involves motive and the involvement of more than one person."

"I think I know where you're going."

"I think three people had a strong motivation to get rid of Tanya. The most obvious being her mother-in-law Grace Griffin and her ex-husband Charles. They wanted total custody of the child, and they knew they'd never get it as long as Tanya was alive. The other person I question is her co-worker, Lewis Lynch. He's married with two kids and if his wife found out about his relationship with Tanya, it would destroy his marriage."

"Didn't all of this come out during the trial?"

"The child custody question was brushed off because it was only speculative. Lynch who had his own attorney, brushed off the questions of an affair as being baseless rumors. The Prosecution had no intention of pushing either of these agendas because as far as they were concerned, they had their man. Plus, all three had solid alibis."

"Did you tell the investigators what your suspicions were?"

"Are you kidding? I talked to anyone who would listen. I even told them what Tanya told me about having information that would absolutely destroy Charles Griffin. They would only say, "Show us." As far as the prosecutor was concerned, I was only proposing inconvenient rumors."

"When did Tanya tell you she had something on Charles?"

"They'd been fighting the custody thing for a year or so and during all that time Tanya kept telling me she was going to have something on Charles that would get him off her back once and for all. It was probably a month before she was killed when she told me she finally had him by the balls. She wouldn't tell me any more than that. She only said, wait and see."

"And you think this information would motivate Charles into killing her?"

"I'm not sure about Charles. I don't think he has the guts to kill someone like that. His mother is another story. She's an iceberg. I think she's capable of anything. Tanya once told me that while she was still living with Charles, he got dead drunk one night and told her that his mother had murdered his father. That's a sad thing for a son to think about his mother. Also, since Tanya's death, Grace and Charles haven't allowed either me or our mother to see Tanya's child. That's a level of cruelty that's hard to understand."

Mark was quiet for a few seconds before he spoke.

"If Tanya did have something on Charles could that explain why the apartment was torn up? Maybe someone was looking for something."

"That's a possibility. Maybe they found what they wanted. I'm the one who cleaned up her apartment and packed up her stuff and had it moved out. I went through everything with a fine-tooth comb after the police finished their search. I didn't find anything unusual. The police had already been through everything. If they'd found anything that might have connected Charles to the murder, it would have had to come out during the trial."

"You would think so. Did Tanya have a computer?"

"No. She used her computer at work as her personal one. She always said that after she left work, the last thing she was going to do was spend time looking at a computer. She did such a good job at work that her boss let her get away with a lot. Her work computer was taken by the investigators and examined, and then I'm sure her office wiped it clean before someone else used it."

"She sounds like she was a smart girl."

"She was smart. At least about everything but her love life. But she also had street smarts. She went through a lot of shit early on. She was really getting control of her life when she was killed. Both of my kids had become really close with her."

"How old are your kids?"

"They're nineteen-year-old twins. I married when I was eighteen and was divorced at twenty. One of them is going to Florida on a baseball scholarship and the other is going to Vanderbilt on a football scholarship. Fortunately, their dad compensated for being a shitty husband by being a good father."

"You have to be proud of them."

"They're my life. That's one reason why I've never remarried."

"I can understand that."

Something was nagging Mark and he wanted to ask more questions, but he wasn't sure what to ask.

"If I think of any more questions, can I call you back?"

Keri smiled, "Anytime. Maybe we could go have a beer and look at other possibilities."

"That sounds good."

As Mark walked back outside to his car to leave, he was still trying to think of what more he wanted to ask her. As he got into his car, he noticed the doors to the storage room in the carport were partially open and he could see several stacked cardboard boxes. Then what he'd been missing hit him like a ton of bricks. Quickly getting back out of his car he almost ran back up to Keri's front door. She was still standing there, and she laughed as he approached her door again.

"Wow, that was quick. Ready for that beer now, are you?"

"Not yet. I do have one question. You were at her apartment the afternoon before she was killed, right?"

"Yes."

"Do you remember what you were there for?"

A sudden look of understanding appeared on Keri's face.

"Come on back in. Stay Brutus."

They both sat down again, and Keri leaned back on her sofa with her eyes closed thinking before she spoke.

"I picked up a few things that I knew Seth had outgrown. From there I went to our mom's house. Our mom has a large storage shed in her backyard next to her garage. Tanya and I have both stored stuff there because neither of us ever had enough storage space. This is the first time I've thought about that box. With everything that happened that night, it became so insignificant I just forgot it. When I cleaned out her apartment later, I just piled her stuff on top of whatever else was in the storage room. Mom hasn't mentioned it and I didn't want to look at any of it again."

Keri got up and walked out of the room for a minute while Mark sat still under Brutus continuing glare. She came back with an extension phone and dialed a speed dial number.

"Mom? Keri. Have you done anything with all of Tanya's stuff we put in your storage room?"

Keri smiled and pumped her fist triumphantly causing her breast to make a big movement under her T shirt. Mark smiled not sure whether he was more pleased with her reaction or at the sight of her breast, or both.

"Good news and bad news. Mom is leaving to go to a funeral in Deland and won't be back until after dark. There's no electricity in the storage shed and there's no way I'm going in there at night, even with flashlights. Mom told me that she'd seen a snake in there once. We can see a lot better in the daytime anyway. How about tomorrow morning?"

"Okay. What time?"

"Let's say nine. The sun will be up enough to give us good light by then. Where are you staying?"

Mark told her.

"Then why don't you come by here and pick me up? It's not out of the way and Mom's neighborhood is confusing anyway."

"Good. I'll see you at nine tomorrow."

CHAPTER 44

Roe Estes

When Mark got back to his hotel, the message light on his phone was blinking. It was a recording from Roe saying she was in Orlando and asking if they were still on for dinner. Mark reached her on her cell and made plans to meet her at six at a popular steakhouse in South Orlando.

Mark arrived at the restaurant right at six and the parking lot was already packed. When he finally found a parking spot and walked up to the entrance to the restaurant, Roe was standing there waiting for him. Roe's appearance was startlingly different from eight years ago. She was still as beautiful as she was then but now there was a sense of maturity and an aura of confidence about her. When she saw Mark approach, she opened her arms and gave him a long hug that could be interpreted in different ways. Mark took her arm and headed into the restaurant.

"You're looking good as always. How's your meeting?"

"Boring. You can imagine what a room full of lawyers would be like. A lot of Indian Chiefs but few Indians. I'm looking forward to hearing about your detective work."

The waiting area was packed shoulder to shoulder and the Maître D told Mark it would be at least a forty-five-minute wait. That's what Mark had anticipated he would say as he leaned in close and extended his right hand toward the Maître D with a fifty-dollar bill in his palm.

"Do you think there might be an earlier opening?"

With a big smile, the Maître D smoothly made the fifty disappear into his own pocket and simply said, "Follow me."

Ignoring the angry stares of people who had been waiting, Roe and Mark followed the Maître D to a booth toward the rear of the room. Mark had assumed correctly, that the Maître D probably kept this booth open for opportunities like this.

After they were seated, Mark looked at the wine list and ordered a bottle of Chilean merlot. While they were waiting for the wine, Mark began to tell Roe everything he'd learned since he'd been in Orlando. Roe listened closely, occasionally interrupting Mark to ask a question.

"So, at this point you've still only got your suspicions and opinion to go on. There is no hard evidence that would help Herbert yet?"

"Finding anything in the stuff from Tanya's apartment is a long shot but at least it's a try."

"You know one possibility would be to bug the homes of the three people you've mentioned and send some sort of message to stir up the pot. See if anyone reacted to it."

"That's what the private investigator Holmes suggested and it's not a bad idea. Now let me lay something on you that Major Garcia said as I was leaving his office. His last comment as I was leaving was, 'Give my regards to Roe.'"

Roe took a long deep breath before she spoke.

"Do you know what that means?"

"You mean how much does he know? I'm really not sure. Regardless of what he knows, it's been years, and nothing has happened. I think if we were going to be accused for anything related to all that happened, it would've already been done. I wasn't about to ask him how he knew your name. We'll let sleeping dogs lie."

Roe held up her wine glass to Mark in a toast, "I'll drink to that."

The T-bone steaks were thick, juicy, and rare. The loaded baked potatoes and wine were perfect compliments to the steaks. Roe commented on how good the meal was.

"The only way it could be any better would be if we were eating it on the patio in Jacksonville watching the boats on the river."

"As soon as I've gotten this Herbert thing settled in my mind, one way or the other, we'll plan on it. One thing you could do for me is to check with one of the technicians at state and tell me what's the best bug for sound only."

"No problem. I can find out tomorrow."

Mark insisted on walking Roe to her car, which was parked, on the opposite side of the lot from his. Roe laughed at his chivalry and showed Mark how she walked with her hand in her handbag holding a lightweight Smith and Wesson 357 magnum revolver with a two-inch barrel.

"If I can make it to my car, I also have a Kimber 45 Auto cocked and locked. I'll never be an easy victim again."

She reached up and gave Mark a kiss on his cheek. "I'll call you tomorrow. I hope you'll find something tomorrow that helps Herbert."

Mark walked back across the parking lot to his car and immediately saw a small piece of paper stuck under his windshield wiper. He unfolded it and read the printed message.

"Let Jim Herbert die for what he did. You will get hurt if you don't."

Mark read the note twice before slowly looking around. He had the feeling that whoever put the note there was still watching to be sure he'd read it and to gauge his reaction. There was no one standing around in the lot and he assumed they were sitting somewhere nearby in a vehicle. Getting in his car, he left the restaurant lot and instead of turning back onto the main street, he turned down a side street bordering the restaurant and then quickly turned his car around facing the lot and the main street. There was no traffic on the side street until a car pulled out of the parking lot and immediately turned onto the main street, spinning its tires as it left. The car didn't fit the image of most of the cars in the restaurant lot. It was a yellow, older model Camaro with a rust hole in the trunk and a door that was a different color than the rest of the car. Mark tried to follow but when he approached the main street there was a steady line of traffic. He was forced to wait before he could enter the main road. He drove as fast as he safely could but by then the Camaro had vanished. He filed the image of the car away in his mind. It would be hard to miss if he saw it again.

CHAPTER 45

Tanya's Tiger

After a good night's sleep and a good breakfast at the hotel buffet, Mark returned to Keri Smith's duplex. She was waiting and walked out of her front door to meet him when she saw him drive up. She was wearing jeans again, but she had on a white blouse and to Mark's disappointment she was also wearing a bra underneath. Mark still couldn't help but acknowledge how good she looked. She was carrying a large soft purse hanging off her shoulder and a large lantern type flashlight in her hand.

"Snake light," she said as she got into the passenger seat. She gave Mark directions as they went east toward Maitland Drive. Keri was correct when she said her mom's house was hard to find. The neighborhood was an older one in a heavily wooded area. The route seemed to go on forever and they made several turns before they entered a cul-de-sac lined with several homes. The house was a modest, well maintained frame home that backed onto a wooded area.

Keri's mom met them at the door and invited them in. She was probably in her sixties with graying hair, but her overall appearance and warm smile made it obvious that her daughter's good looks were not an accident. Keri introduced Mark to Vera, her mom, and they went inside. Her house was filled with older furniture but was immaculate. Mark looked at a large, framed family photograph on an end table. It showed a smiling Keri and Tanya as children standing in front of Keri's mother and father. Mark pointed toward the picture and asked when it had been taken. Vera smiled and said,

"It was taken in this room during a happier time. Let me get you some coffee. I have a pot already made."

After she had brought them coffee, Keri briefly explained to her mom what they were looking for.

"Keri, everything that came out of Tanya's apartment went into the storage shed out back. I'd forgotten about the things you brought over the night she was killed. I took it straight out to the shed when you left. I had friends coming over to play bridge and I wanted it out of the way. When her apartment was finally cleaned out, remember we just piled everything on top of what was already in there. After your dad died, we put a lot of his hunting and fishing stuff in there as well. I can tell you that nothing has been taken out of the shed since then. I just can't bear the thought of going through either Tanya's or your dad's things."

"Mom, I'll make it a priority to clean up the shed sometime soon. Right now, all we want to look for are the two boxes I brought over the night Tanya was killed. Did Tanya say anything to you about Charles or anything related to their custody fight?"

Vera looked up as she thought about the question.

"Just before she was killed, she brought Seth over for cupcakes and she made a comment that someone she worked with, I think she said Lewis was helping her get something that would get Charles off her back real soon. She was in a hurry, and it was after Seth's bedtime, so I didn't have time to ask for any details. Tanya didn't mention it again and I forgot about it. You know how Tanya was. Trying to get anything out of her was tough. She would tell you when she was ready and not before."

"Amen. God rest her soul. Mark, let's go look in the shed."

They went through the kitchen and out into a screened porch. The porch screened door opened on to a backyard shaded by large older trees. The storage shed was at the back of an open carport. There were only a few yards of scraggly grass that separated the back of the shed from the bordering woods. The shed was a corrugated aluminum structure sitting on concrete blocks that raised it about a foot off the ground. All sides except the side facing the carport where the door was located, were covered in vines.

The door to the shed was hard to open and had to be pulled forcefully before it opened. A strong musty smell of mildew and rotting papers was apparent when the door was opened. There were two windows in the backside that were crank operated cantilevered glass. They were so covered with the vines that the light coming in through them was minimal. It was obvious that the shed was packed full. When Keri turned on the flashlight, Mark could identify an old lawnmower handle and parts of fishing rods. What really caught his attention though was the huge snakeskin stretched out across the top of several cardboard boxes. Mark knew it came from a harmless rat snake but as far as Keri was concerned, it might as well have been a King Cobra.

Mark pointed to scattered rat droppings and loose pieces of torn paper.

"There are obviously mice or rats in here and if there are rats or mice, there will be snakes. There's an opening to the outside somewhere in here. You shine the light and let me start moving the stuff out until you can identify the two boxes you brought over."

Keri was only too happy to let Mark go inside while she stood just outside the door holding the light. Mark pulled several heavy cardboard boxes out into the carport giving himself a little room to maneuver inside the shed. The floor consisted of wide wooden planks which still seemed to be solid. After he had moved a small kitchen table and a couple of small chairs outside, it was much easier to see what was in the room. Keri got a little braver and stepped inside the door and looked around. She pointed toward the back at two boxes stacked one on top of the other.

"Can you pull out those two boxes? They look like the right ones."

Mark pulled them across the floor and out the door where Keri eagerly looked closely at both boxes.

"These are the ones! I remember the markings on the boxes."

"Great. We can end the snake hunt."

"Mark, will you get a couple of those lawn chairs off the back porch so we can look through these boxes here in the carport. I don't want to turn a mouse loose in mom's house."

"Good idea. You also need to watch out for spiders. This is perfect Brown Recluse habitat."

After Mark brought two folding chairs from the screened porch, he shook both boxes to see if anything scurried out. Satisfied that there were no visible holes in the boxes, they both sat down and opened the first one. The tops had been closed and then taped together with clear packaging tape. The first thing they saw was a small, ratty, well-worn stuffed yellow tiger. It sat on top of the contents in the box.

Keri picked it up with a smile. "This was Tanya's stuffed tiger. It was her comfort animal. After I'd finished packing the boxes, she handed this to me and told me to bring it back here and leave it in our old bedroom. She said Seth had his own favorite comfort teddy and she didn't want him to totally tear this one up."

Mark reached over and took the well-worn stuffed tiger.

"It's definitely well used. She even had to sew it up on one side."

He laid it aside and returned to the box.

They methodically went through both boxes, item by item, carefully looking for signs of anything that might contain a message. There were several children's books, and they went through them carefully, one page at a time. They turned each toy every way around trying to miss nothing. There were several VCR tapes with titles like Thomas the Train and The Three Bears, which they set aside.

While they were sitting in the carport going through the boxes, Mark glanced up toward the front of the house where a section of the street was visible. A car he suddenly recognized was sitting at the curb possibly a hundred and fifty yards up the street just outside the cul-de-sac. It was facing in his direction, but the model of the car and the yellow color gave it away.

"Keri, there's an older model yellow Camaro sitting down the street. Don't make it look obvious but stand up and stretch and look in that direction and see if you recognize it."

Keri stood up as if she was tired of sitting and looked in the direction of the car.

"No. I don't recognize it."

"I need the license number. I know if the driver thinks I recognize the car, he'll be gone in a heartbeat."

Keri thought for a moment. "I have an idea."

She casually turned and went back inside the house through the screened back porch. Within a couple of minutes, Keri's mom casually walked out carrying her purse and got into her car which was sitting in the driveway. As she backed out onto the street, she casually waved to Mark as if to say, "See you later." As she exited the cul-de-sac, she slowed down without actually putting on her car brakes and continued on down the street and out of sight.

Keri came back out and sat down again in her chair. Mark smiled.

"Your mom is good."

"She reads a lot of detective novels. This is exciting for her."

When they had finished going through and repacking the boxes, the only thing they'd kept out, were the videos and the tiger.

"Does your mom have a VCR player?"

"Are you kidding? It's a standard requirement for a grandparent," Keri said as she picked up the videos and the tiger.

They went back inside, and Keri opened a small entertainment cabinet containing a TV and a VCR player. One by one, they ran the videos through at fast forward while watching carefully to be sure they only contained what was on the labels. When the last one was finished, they were both disappointed.

"Maybe whoever trashed Tanya's apartment found what they were looking for," Keri said as she picked up Tanya's tiger off the sofa. Frustrated, she tossed it across the room into a wooden chair. When the bear hit the arm of the chair it made an audible click. Mark, who was watching her as she threw it, got up, walked over, and picked up the bear. He used his fingers to feel the sides of it as if he were trying to feel a pulse. He handed the bear back to Keri.

"Feel along the area where it's been repaired."

Keri took the bear and probed the area with her fingers as Mark had done.

"This isn't right. There shouldn't be anything solid in this thing. I should know because of the times Tanya hit me over the head with it when we were little. Wait a minute. Let me get a pair of scissors."

She went into the kitchen, came back with a pair of small scissors, and carefully cut open the threads where the tiger had been repaired. Putting her fingers in the opening, she felt through the white stuffing until her fingers emerged with a green scan disk. She held it up for Mark to see.

"Does your mom have a computer?"

"No. But I do. Let's go back to my place. Let me close the house and the storage shed."

When they went back outside to close the shed, the yellow Camaro was gone, and Keri's mom was entering the driveway. She had a big smile on her face as she got out of her car holding up a piece of paper in her hand.

" Got it. I don't think he had a clue that I was writing down his license plate number."

"Mom, you get a gold star," Keri said as her mom handed her the paper.

"Thank you. Did you find anything in the shed?"

Keri glanced at Mark as she answered,

"I found Tanya's old tiger that I was supposed to put back in her room. It's inside on the sofa and it needs some repair work if you don't mind doing it."

CHAPTER 46

The Insurance Policy

On the way back to Keri's house, Mark called Roe. "Sorry to bother you during the day but I need to get some info on a tag number." He told Roe about the threatening note and the coincidence of the yellow Camaro.

"Not a problem. I'm at one of our state offices now. Give me the number and I'll see how much I can find out. I'll call back as soon as I get something."

Keri gave Mark a quizzical look.

"You have friends in high places?"

"Let's just say I have friends in the right places."

All the way back to her house, Keri held the memory stick they'd found in a death grip in her hand. She wasted no time in jumping out of Mark's car as soon as they reached her house. She almost ran toward the front door with Mark close behind. Brutus was obediently waiting inside, and she gave him the order to stand down so Mark could follow her in. She led Mark back to her bedroom. The room had either once been a large family room that had been converted into a bedroom or a wall had been removed to create more space. One end contained a queen size platform bed backing up against a wall of solid cinderblock which created a medieval appearance. The other end of the room was an office area with a couple of upholstered chairs and a computer desk. A large computer monitor sat on the desk as well as a laser printer. The entire back wall was floor to ceiling windows with plantation shutters. The floor was finished with wide wood planks with oriental rugs covering each end of the room. The room projected a feeling of comfort and warmth. A heavy bedspread had been pulled up over the bed without being formally made up and there were a couple items of clothing lying around the room.

"Excuse my housekeeping Mark, but I just didn't take time to straighten everything up." Mark couldn't help but think to himself that her unmade bedroom looked a lot neater than his did even when it was made up.

Keri went straight to her desk, sat down, and turned it on. As soon as it booted up, she inserted the flash drive into the monitor under the desk and watched it open up on the screen. The first thing to appear was a menu listing three files. There were no names on the three files, only dates. All three dates were within a thirty-day period. Keri started with the oldest date and clicked on it. It was a video showing a man and a young girl who could have been anywhere between fourteen and sixteen but probably closer to fourteen. The video was recorded from a high vantage point in a hotel room, probably an air conditioning vent. Keri let out a sharp breath as the video continued to record a graphic sexual encounter.

"The man is Charles Griffin. I have no idea who the girl is."

Both of them having seen enough, Keri closed the file and opened the next one.

The next video was exactly the same setting except the participants were Charles Griffin and a young male who could have been somewhere in his early twenties. They watched it long enough to know that it was a true hard-core encounter before closing the file.

Keri shook her head, "That's enough there already to sink Charles's political aspirations."

"I agree. Let's look at the last file."

When the third and last file opened it only took a moment before Mark said, "Oh shit." Keri tried to say something, but she was speechless. This time the video showed Charles Griffin and a young female who left no doubt that she was underage. Mark and Keri watched only a moment before closing the file in disgust. They both were silent for a minute before Mark spoke.

"This is not a question about Griffin's political aspirations. This will put him in jail for a long time. Now we have a solid motive that can explain why Tanya might have been targeted."

"What can we do now?"

Mark sat down in one of the chairs next to the desk.

"I think we can throw a hornet's nest into the room and see what happens. I want to hear from my contact before I do anything. We're both going to have to be careful now. If anyone connected to this disk knows we have it, they'll do anything to get it back. I'm really surprised that you haven't had a problem before now."

"Probably because they did a thorough search of Tanya's apartment, and no one connected my visit with removing anything from her apartment. It's no secret that I was at her apartment the same day she was killed but I guess they would have assumed that if I had this disk, I'd have immediately turned it over to the police."

"The very second Griffin and whoever else may be connected think we have this stuff, we'll be targets ourselves."

"Should we go to the police?"

"Not yet. There's nothing here that would exonerate Herbert. I'm not even sure how hard the state attorney would follow up even if he had this in his hand. Yes, they would go after Griffin, but this disk might not even be admissible in Herbert's case. Let's wait before we go to the police."

Mark was thoughtful as he spoke again, "The next question is, who recorded this?"

"I'm pretty sure I know. Remember my mom saying that Tanya told her that someone named Lewis was helping her? It makes sense. Lewis Lynch is an insurance investigator. His job is to spy on people defrauding insurance companies. He has the equipment and the ability to do it. I can easily see Tanya having him eating out of her hand and getting him to do anything she wanted."

"That sounds like a reasonable guess. It opens a lot of possibilities. Talking to Lewis Lynch would be a logical thing to do. The first thing I want to do is to make a couple of copies of this disk."

"There's an office supply store a few blocks from here."

Mark was already heading for the door.

"Good." He hesitated a minute before turning around.

"Would you be interested in having that beer and maybe some dinner tonight?"

"That sounds great. I'd love too. What time?"

"Why don't we shoot for six? If anything changes, I'll call."

"This time let me pick you up at your hotel."

Mark smiled as he drove away from Keri's house with the disk burning a hole in his pocket. It made him uncomfortable knowing what it contained but he realized that it might be the key that would help his friend. He followed Keri's directions to the office supply store, taking precautions to be sure he wasn't being followed, where he bought two high-capacity thumb drives. His cell phone was ringing when he walked into his hotel room.

It was Roe and she seemed pleased with herself.

"Mark, I got the car's owner and more. I'm calling on a pay phone outside a grocery store because I don't want this to be connected to me in any way. I didn't go through approved channels to get this information. Got a pen handy?"

"Just a minute. Shoot."

"The Camaro is owned by an ex-con named Bo Layfield. I looked up his recorded history which is extensive. He is one mean son of a bitch. If it's illegal, then he's probably done it. He's suspected of having killed two of his girlfriends but was never convicted. Now get this. They were both strangled, and their throats cut. He had airtight alibis both times. He fathered a daughter with another girlfriend but would never acknowledge the child as his. Even with his abuse, the girlfriend will still let Layfield spend time at her home. That was twelve years ago. He's been charged with cruelty to animals, elderly abuse of his own mother, and he's served time for both drug and human trafficking. He's currently on parole so I was able to track some of his current activity. He's working for a landscape company called Clean and Green. I was a little curious because there are not many legitimate businesses who'll hire someone with a record like his, so I did some more off record research. Two LLCs removed from Clean and Green, I came up with the true owner. Take a guess."

"Tell me, Roe."

"Charles Griffin the Third. And that's not all. As you might guess, the co-owner is Griffin's mother, Grace."

"Roe, you are a genius. Now let me tell you what I've found."

Mark then gave Roe a synopsis of what he'd found with Keri's help.

"Unbelievable, Mark. That could put Charles away for a long time."

"Absolutely. Now there are so many reasons for Herbert to have been set up."

"Before I forget, I've got what you'll need if you still want to use a bug."

"Yes. I do want to. I already know where I'll put the first one. If I drove to Tampa right now, I could be there by five unless there's a problem with traffic."

"Sure. I'm staying at the Marriott on Westshore. If I'm not in my room when you get here, look for me in the bar."

"Why doesn't that surprise me?"

CHAPTER 47

Help From Roe

Mark called Keri and arraigned to meet her later than planned before he headed out to Tampa on Interstate 4. As expected, he reached Tampa during rush hour, but traffic was moving through Tampa with no delays, and he turned off onto West-shore by five thirty. He called Roe's room on a house phone and after getting no answer he went to the bar area. It was packed but Mark had no trouble recognizing Roe. She was sitting at the bar and was surrounded by several men all fighting for her attention. When Mark approached, Roe stood up and met him with a big hug. The looks of disappointment and jealously on several men's faces was obvious.

"Mark, do you want a drink?"

"No thanks, Roe. I need to be back in Orlando by nine."

Roe grinned, "Don't tell me. You have a date?"

Mark smiled back, "Probably wishful thinking. Let me pay your bar bill and we'll find a quieter place to talk."

"What bar bill? With all these guys around?"

Mark had to laugh. "Why did I even ask?"

They left the bar and found a quiet seating area in the large lobby that afforded privacy. In a few short minutes, they went over the things they'd both learned.

"Mark, I agree with you. There is ample motivation on the part of several people to eliminate Tanya. You still need something concrete to give the state attorney before a judge will act on it. Even if you get someone to incriminate themselves on a wiretap, it'll still be illegal and inadmissible in court."

"I agree, Roe. At least I'm doing something. I might be able to push someone to panic and do something stupid. One more thing I want you to do. I want you to take one of the copies I made of Charles Griffin. If anything happens to me, send it anonymously to Major Garcia. I may be overly paranoid, but I don't want any possibility for Griffin to get away with this. Put it away in a safe place."

"Don't worry. I'll hide it well. I don't want to be connected to it either. By the way, who are you meeting tonight?"

"Tanya's sister, Keri."

"Oh, a little fringe benefit for your troubles."

"Roe, it's all related to helping Herbert." Mark actually blushed as he said it.

"Let's get you back on the road then. The electronic stuffs in the trunk of my car."

Mark followed Roe out to her car, which was parked in a part of the hotel parking lot that faced Westshore Drive. Just as Roe opened her trunk, two very drunk men crossed the street. They had just left the popular nude dancing establishment across the street from the hotel. As they walked between Roe's car and the adjacent car, they both stopped and stared at Roe. They couldn't see Mark because of the open trunk lid. One of the men took a step toward Roe and reached for her arm.

"Hey sweetheart. Didn't we just see you dancing? How about coming with us and giving us a private dance?"

Roe was standing sideways toward the man and when she turned to face him directly, she held her compact 357 revolver in her right hand. She stepped up to the man and as she stuck the gun barrel up to his nose, she cocked the hammer back with a loud click. In her left hand, she held up a large badge next to the gun.

"Maybe you two stupid assholes need a private dance with bubba in a jail cell tonight. I'm staying in this hotel and if I see either one of you again, you won't be sleeping here. Now fuck off."

A stain began to appear in the man's pants as he backed up stumbling into the other man who was already moving away.

Mark had stood still through the entire exchange before he exploded in laughter.

"Roe, you really know how to spoil a man's night on the town."

Roe smiled as she put away her gun and badge.

"I saw them coming a mile away. They just needed an attitude adjustment. Now, everything you need is in the box, including all the instructions. It's all generic stuff and none of it's traceable back to me or the state. I included two of the bugs in case you need an extra. As a bonus, I included a mug shot of Bo Layfield."

Mark couldn't help but look in the box and take out a folder containing the instructions for the electronics as well as the profile shots of Layfield. Layfield had a pug nose that had probably been broken multiple times. His face was brown and leathery from a lot of sun exposure and his long blond hair was tied in a ponytail. Most apparent even in the photograph though, were his eyes. They were predatory and almost maniacal in their appearance.

"Thanks for your help. I'll let you know what happens. If you hear anything about the governor planning to sign another death warrant for Herbert, let me know."

"I will. Drive safe and good luck tonight."

After a hug, Mark put the box containing the electronics in his Land Cruiser and headed back to I- 4 and east toward Orlando.

CHAPTER 48

Mark and Keri

Mark was back in his hotel room by eight thirty, so he had time for a shower and change of clothes before meeting Keri. He was tucking his gun into its holster when his cell phone rang.

"Mark, this is Keri. I'm only a few blocks from your hotel but I'm sure I'm being followed by that yellow Camaro. He's not getting close, but he's been behind me since I left my house."

"Keri, Now I know who the car belongs to. Just use valet parking at the hotel for now. I'm not sure if he'd try to follow you into the garage or not. I'm not ready to deal with him just yet. I'll meet you downstairs."

When Mark reached the lobby, he watched Keri pull up to valet parking and get out of her car. In the background, he could see the Camaro drive slowly down the street in front of the hotel entrance. It was impossible to make out any features, but the ponytail was easily visible. When the driver realized that Keri was using valet parking, the car accelerated out of sight.

Keri got out of her car, took a ticket from the valet, and walked inside the lobby. Mark was watching her as she entered the hotel. She was dressed in a short one-piece dress made of a material that clung to her body as she moved and highlighted every point it touched. Her legs were long and tanned and her hair was long and loose. She wore no visible make up. Mark was again impressed with her stark beauty.

Keri smiled as she approached Mark. "I feel like I'm acting in a detective movie."

"Right now, I think we both are."

"When I just spoke to you on the phone, you said you knew who the Camaro man is."

"Let's find a place to eat and I'll tell what I've learned. We'll go in my car. I don't use valet parking so if the Camaro man is watching, we might be able to leave out of the back of the parking garage without being followed. Do you have any place in mind?"

"There's a nice quiet Italian place in Winter Park. It's close. Let's try it first. If it's crowded, they're several other good places within walking distance."

Keri was right. It only took a few minutes driving up Orange Avenue. When they reached Fairbanks Ave., Mark had flashbacks of many happy meals in restaurants around Rollins College. He remembered how he and Marge had wanted Kim to go to Rollins rather than UCF, but Kim had her mind made up about where she wanted to go. He couldn't help but wonder if things would have been different if Kim had made a different choice in schools. The restaurant Keri picked was not one that Mark remembered and for that he was grateful. It was a good choice, and they had no problem getting a booth which offered some privacy. The music was easy and low key which made it possible to have a normal conversation. Even better, they offered Peroni draft beer, which they both ordered.

Mark had given some thought about how much information he would share with Keri. However, after thinking about it, he realized that she knew more that he did about the case, and she had good reason to be involved because of her sister. The one thing he wouldn't do though, would be to link Roe in any way to the case. After ordering the house special lasagna, which Keri promised, would be the best he had ever eaten, Mark told Keri about Bo Layfield and his connection to the Griffins. Keri listened silently as Mark told her what he had learned before she spoke.

"I see a lot of probabilities but no proof of anything."

"Right. From where I sit, I see too many things pointing at Charles Griffin, his mom, Bo Layfield, and somehow Lewis Lynch as well. Mark then went on to explain what he wanted to do with the electronic equipment he had acquired.

"This is going into an area that you may not want to go. I don't want to put you in a dangerous or compromising position."

"Mark, Tanya was my only sister. She was taken from me as well as my nephew Seth. I'm convinced that Jim Herbert wasn't the one responsible. I want the responsible ones to pay. You've offered me the best chance yet to do that. I'm all in whatever happens."

"Good. Let's enjoy the lasagna and beer."

The Lasagna turned out to be as good as Keri had promised and Mark found himself enjoying Keri's company. She was intelligent coupled with common sense, and she seemed to be aware of current political and cultural events. He was surprised to learn that she worked from her home as a proofreader and contributing writer for a newspaper chain. She was able to work on her own time and terms. Mark now realized why she had such high-end electronic equipment in her home. Mark felt very comfortable talking to her and the combination of the atmosphere, food and beer led the conversation to Mark's past. When he gave Keri an abbreviated version of what had happened to Kim and Marge, she shook her head.

"I don't see how you kept your sanity. I can't imagine losing a child and your wife as well."

Mark smiled when he replied, "I'm not sure I did."

When they returned to Mark's hotel there was a minute of awkwardness as they stood in in the lobby near the elevators. They both stood looking at each other with an expression that seemed to say, "Well, what now?"

Mark broke the ice when he said, "I suppose you need to go home and let the dog out."

"I left him with my mom. I was a little worried about her after the Camaro incident."

"Then it might not be safe for you to go home tonight."

"Probably not. Any ideas on a safe place?"

Without either saying another word they were walking, in unison, toward the elevators and to Mark's room. They paused at Mark's door and Keri looked at Mark.

"No worry, Mark. We're only good friends. No more. No less."

And for the rest of the night, they were truly the best of friends.

Chapter 49

Lewis Lynch

The next morning, Mark called room service and ordered a large pot of coffee and one of almost everything on the breakfast menu. He and Keri sat on the small balcony, both wearing a hotel robe, and enjoyed every bite of the food. While Keri showered and dressed, Mark read the instructions on the electronics and made sure the batteries were functioning properly. Mark followed Keri in the shower while Keri read the instructions as well.

After dressing, Mark looked up the contact number that Dick Holmes had given him for Lewis Lynch, the insurance investigator. The number was answered by a recording that listed names and extensions. He entered the number for Lynch and the phone was answered immediately.

"Lewis Lynch."

"Lewis, my name is Mark Price and I'm an old friend of Tanya Griffin. I need to talk to you."

There was a long pause before Lynch responded.

"I don't recognize your name. What do you need to talk about?"

"Lewis, Tanya left me something recorded on a thumb drive that I think belongs to you."

Again, another long pause before Lynch spoke again. His voice suddenly becoming high pitched and uncertain.

"Maybe we can meet somewhere."

"We'll meet at your office. If you don't want to meet me there, I can just mail what I have to your office manager with your name on it."

"Okay, okay. Come by now. I assume you know where my office is?"

"I'll be there by eleven."

Lynch's office was located downtown in a large professional office complex on South Orange Avenue. The location was convenient to the many medical related offices that depended on the insurance company's support. There was a large outside parking lot as well as a covered area under the building. There were no available spaces under the building so Mark found a shaded spot on the periphery of the outside lot.

Mark had the listening and recording devices set up in the back seat of his Land Cruiser. Keri was sitting in the back seat with a set of earphones.

"We need to be listening and recording the second I walk into his office. Start recording the minute I walk into the building. I predict we're going to create some panic."

Keri put on the earphones. "Let's do it."

Mark double checked to be sure he had the original thumb drive in one pocket and a small device the size of a quarter in the other pocket as he headed inside the building. After checking the directory just inside the entrance, he took the elevator to the third floor and found the entrance to Lynch's office. A single receptionist sat at a desk in a waiting area. Behind the desk was a single hallway with several offices opening onto it.

"I'm here to see Lewis Lynch."

The receptionist seemed to have to make a supreme effort to just to point down the hallway, "second door on the right."

The door was open and Lynch, sitting behind his desk, made no attempt to get up as Mark walked in. Lynch was a heart attack waiting to happen. He was short, bald, overweight, and his ruddy face and red nose suggested heavy use of alcohol. Mark could almost smell it across the room. He wore a dress shirt and tie, but the tie was poorly tied, and his shirt could have used a good ironing.

He was obviously very nervous and even in the air-conditioned room, sweat was running down his face.

"What do you think you have that belongs to me?"

Mark carefully turned and closed the door.

"I don't think you'll want to publicize this," he said as he took the small drive out of his right pocket and held it up for Lynch to see. Lynch was turning white as Mark approached his desk with his hand holding out the device. Lynch tried to bluster, "What the hell is that?" but he knew exactly what it was, and Mark could plainly see it in his eyes.

Mark walked around the desk without asking permission, and reaching down to the computer monitor, inserted the drive into a USB port.

"Why don't we watch and see?"

With robot like movements, Lynch opened the drive, and the monitor came alive with its contents. While Lynch stared intently at the opening screen, Mark used his left hand to take the small listening device out of his left pocket. While appearing to be leaning on Lynch's desk, he reached under the corner of the desk with the small disk concealed in his hand. The device had an adhesive backing on one side adhering it to the underside of the desk.

By now Lynch's shirt was becoming wet with sweat and he was turning redder by the minute. "Where did you get this?"

Mark walked back around to the front of the desk, pulled up a chair and sat down.

"I think you know where it came from. This is how you were going to help Tanya get Charles out of her life once and for all. You recorded one for yourself and gave her a copy."

"You can't prove that."

Mark quickly got up, went around the desk again and pulled the drive out of its port in the computer, stopping the play only partway through.

"Sorry Lewis. These recordings are time stamped. If the pictures were enlarged, the specific hotel is easily identifiable. What sort of coincidence would explain why you happened to be renting the adjacent hotel room with a connecting door at exactly the same time every one of these were recorded. I'd say you were an active participant in this."

"No! I never had any part of this stuff. It makes me sick."

"So, why did you record it?"

Mark was beginning to worry that Lynch was really going to have a heart attack. His face was beet red, and he was struggling to find the right words.

"Tanya."

"Tanya? What about Tanya?"

"She talked me into it."

"Bullshit Lewis. What do you mean she talked you into it? Did she pay you to record this?"

"No! I thought she loved me."

"So, you were screwing her?"

"It wasn't like that. Even though she was divorced from Charles, she had to put up with shit from him and his mother. I really wanted to help her."

"You gave her this disk. Did she ever show it to anyone?"

"Not that I know of. I told her to wait for the right time. But the minute she had the recording she shut me out completely. I realized then that she'd been using me."

"So, that's why you killed her?"

"No way. I was hurt and pissed off, but I would never kill her."

"So, who did kill her?"

"Jim Herbert."

"How many copies did you make?"

"Only the one that I gave to Tanya."

Mark's instincts told him Lynch was lying. He had to have kept a copy himself. Mark was silent for a moment before he spoke again. He pulled his chair up closer to Lynch's desk and leaned forward over the desk. He tried to put a conspiratorial look on his face.

"Lewis, do you realize what we have here?"

Lynch was taken back by the sudden change in Mark's attitude, and he simply shook his head. "No."

"How much do you think this little disk would be worth to Charles Griffin and his mother?"

Lewis's face went from red to white and his reply was little more than a guttural reply.

"We can't do that."

"Why not Lewis? It'll be easy money."

"You don't want to do piss these people off. They're all crazy."

Mark leaned back in his chair and looked at Lynch.

"I'm sorry Lewis. I thought I was being generous to include you in on this. That's okay. I offered. If you're not interested it's just more money for me."

Mark stood up and walked to the door before a stunned and shaken Lewis Lynch could utter another word.

"I'm staying at the Doubletree downtown if you change your mind."

He didn't wait for an elevator but instead went down the stairs two at a time and crossed the parking lot to his car.

Mark got in the driver's seat of the car and looked at Keri in the back seat. She was listening intently and pumped her fist when Mark got in. Keri continued to listen for a brief time longer before she removed the earphones for a second.

"You're not going to believe what I just heard. Let me play it from the beginning. It'll continue to record anything new from his office while we're listening to this."

Keri turned on the audio to replay the recording and she put the earphones back on to see if Lynch was making another call.

Mark listened to his conversation with Lynch. He heard his last words to Lynch as he was leaving the office and he could hear Lynch get up and close the office door. He immediately began speaking to someone, probably on his cell phone.

"Grace, this is Lewis Lynch. We have a real problem."

After a pause, "I know I'm never supposed to call you at home, but this can't wait. A guy who said he was a friend of Tanya just showed up at my office with an exact copy of the disk I gave to you."

Another pause before, "How many times have I told you there were only two copies. I gave one to Tanya and the other I gave to you. I've kept my word on our deal. I'm not stupid. You've made it clear to me what would happen to me or my family if I ever asked for more money. He told me that the copy he had was Tanya's. It did look like the one I gave her. I assumed Layfield found the one I gave Tanya, or it would have shown up during the trial. The guy tried to sell it back to me, but I think he realized he was trying to get blood out of a turnip. When he left my office, he said the video was worth something to someone."

Another pause, "Price, Mark Price. He said he was staying at the Doubletree on Ivanhoe."

Pause, "What do you mean you already know who he is? Christ, this is getting out of hand."

Pause, "Yes. Okay. Okay. I know all hell will break loose if people find out that Herbert isn't the one who killed Tanya."

Pause, "Of course I won't talk to anyone. Why would I want too anyway? You're the one with the muscle. But you better understand Grace, I'm not going down for something I didn't do. You need to take care of this now."

Another pause, "What good would it do to meet? I've told you everything I know to tell. Alright! But I still don't know how I can help."

The conversation apparently over, Mark could hear the sound of a drawer being pulled open and the pop of a cork being pulled followed by heavy breathing.

Keri took off the earphones.

"I think he's scared shitless."

"I agree. He should be. Things are beginning to make sense now. Lynch apparently was blackmailing either Grace or Charles

Griffin or both. They were going on the assumption that Lynch was being truthful when he said there were only two copies."

"Mark, why did you give him your real name and where you're staying?"

"I want them to focus on me. I'm worried about you and your mother. Layfield and the Griffins have been watching me so they must know you're involved, especially you, being Tanya's sister. They now know there's another copy of the thumb drive with the videos. They've got to be wondering whether there are other copies. If I were in their shoes, I'd worry too."

"You're scaring me now Mark. Maybe we should go to mom's house and check on her."

"That's not a bad idea. Is there any place she could go for a few days just to be safe?"

"I have an uncle who lives in Lakeland. It's less than an hour away. My mom and he are close, and she'd be welcome there. He's also a retired cop who can still shoot straight. He'd love an excuse to walk around with a gun in his belt."

Keri's mom was sitting on her back porch shelling black eyed peas when they reached her house. Brutus was lying at her feet with his head resting on a pillow. He jumped up to greet Keri and looked at Mark without baring his teeth, but he seemed to be saying, "I'm still watching you."

Keri briefly explained to her mom what their concerns were without including all the details. Reluctantly her mom agreed to go.

"I was going to cook these peas with some ham hocks for us to eat tonight. I guess your uncle Rob will get to enjoy them instead."

Mark couldn't help but smile.

"I'd like to take a rain check on that offer."

Keri quickly helped her mom pack a few things including the peas and hocks, got her in her car and on her way.

As soon as she was gone, Mark called the number that Vernon Jost had given him. The call was answered immediately with only a gruff, "Yes?"

"Vernon, this is Mark Price calling. You told me to call if I had any additional information about Tanya's killer."

"And?"

"I'm here with Tanya's sister Keri. What we have is a game changer. We may also need your help. Can we meet, the sooner the better?"

"Can you meet me at the Last Chance at seven?"

"We'll be there."

Keri opened the back door to let Brutus have a potty break in the back yard before saying, "We have some time to kill before seven. Any ideas?"

"I was hoping for black eyed peas and ham hocks."

Keri had a big smile on her face. "I've always had a fantasy about making love in my old bedroom. I dreamed about it when I was a teenager, but it never happened. My dad was always a step ahead."

"I'm not sure I can rise to the occasion of violating such a shrine."

The pun wasn't lost on Keri as she called Brutus back in.

Mark looked at Brutus before saying, "I want a locked door between Brutus and the two of us."

CHAPTER 50

Vernon's Enlightenment

The sun was setting when they left Kei's mom's house at six thirty and drove to the Last Chance Bar to meet Jost. They planned to come back to Keri's mom's house after meeting Jost and pick up Brutus. The bar was busy with the usual group of Harleys parked close to the front. They were all parked pointing away from the building as usual.

When Mark and Keri walked in the front door they were hit with the loud, almost deafening music and funny smelling cigarette smoke. They stood just inside the door adjusting to the dimness, blue smoke, and booming music for a minute before one of the bar's bikini girls approached. Mark almost laughed out loud thinking to himself that the bikini girls were trying to outdo each other. This one wore a similar scanty outfit with a blue halter and a white bottom. There were flashing red lights imbedded in the halter. Mark immediately let her know that they were there to meet Vernon Jost. She didn't blink an eye but turned and said, "Follow me." As they followed her toward the back of the bar, Keri looked up at Mark and shouted above the music, "Very patriotic."

They followed Miss Patriotic to an alcove with one large booth set at the rear of the bar. It afforded privacy and the decibels were decidedly reduced. Vernon was sitting in the booth, and he rose to meet them as they came in. It was apparent that he knew Keri and he hugged her with a warm smile.

"Keri, I'm always glad to see you."

He pointed to the other side of the booth indicating for them to sit down. He looked at Mark with an expectant look before he said, "Okay, what's so important?"

Mark took a deep breath before he spoke.

"Vernon what we're going to show you is going to make you want to do something bad to some people. You've got to promise Keri and I both that you'll listen to everything we're going to say. We can show you beyond doubt that Jim Herbert didn't kill Tanya. But before you go out of here with guns blazing, we've got to be sure we can establish his innocence with the people that matter. This hasn't been done yet and if certain people just disappear, we may not be able to do it."

Keri was looking intently at Jost as she spoke.

"Vernon, he's right. Most of what we have wouldn't be admissible in court. We need someone involved to break."

"Alright, so show me."

Mark took the thumb drive out of his pocket and held it out.

"Do you have a laptop computer we could use to play this?"

There were two heavily tattooed bikers standing outside the alcove and Jost motioned for one of them to come over.

"Randy, go back to Marvin's office and get me a laptop."

Randy was back in less than three minutes with the computer which he handed to Jost. Jost let Mark turn the computer on and insert the flash drive. When the first file was opened, Mark turned the screen around at an angle, so it was only visible to Jost.

Jost sat and watched the three separate files play through without uttering a word. After only a few seconds of seeing the third, one he pushed the computer back across the booth top to Mark.

"That's enough. That mother fucker. I had a suspicion that he liked young girls. But would have never guessed he had a taste for boys. How'd you get this?"

Mark proceeded to explain how comments Tanya had made had led them look for it. It would have also accounted for Tanya's apartment being trashed. When Mark detailed being followed by Bo Layfield, Jost just shook his head.

"Mark, you should have called me earlier. I should have never let that cockroach loose. I had to have a heart to heart with him when he was harassing Tanya during the time she was dancing. He left her alone after that. I know he still runs a landscaping crew, but he keeps his distance from me. By the way the other guy in the video is a punk named Gary Sims. He's an errand boy who works for Layfield. But I still don't see how this changes what Herbert did."

"Vernon, there's more. You're not going to like what you're going to hear next."

Keri was carrying a large purse which she put on the table and reached inside. It was the small recorder they had used earlier in the day to record Lewis Lynch. She handed Jost a pair of earphones.

"Listen to this. This conversation was recorded just this morning. Mark put a bug under Lewis Lynch's desk."

Jost put on the earphones and Keri hit the play button. By the time the recording had ended, Mark thought Jost was going to explode. There were very few men that Mark Price had feared in his life, but at that moment Vernon Jost ranked at the top of his list. Jost remained silent as he stared past Mark and Keri without seeing them, his mind working in a distant place. He finally came out of his trance and motioned to Randy again. Randy seemed to understand what he meant and disappeared. He reappeared in less than a minute with three glasses and a bottle, which he sat on the table. Without asking he poured a generous portion of Woodford Reserve into the three glasses, pushed two of them across the table and kept one for himself.

Raising his glass in a toast, Jost spoke with obvious emotion.

"I have to give you credit for doing something I should have done. I only hope that if Tanya can see us now, she'll forgive me. What angers me the most is I that didn't see what you both saw."

With that he drained his glass in one swallow and immediately refilled it.

"I understand now what you meant about proving Herbert's innocence. I'll honor your request and help you get Herbert off the hook. I only want one thing. I want Bo Layfield for myself."

Mark started to answer when Keri's cell phone rang. She took it out of her bag and answered with a startled look on her face.

"What! I'm on my way."

Looking at Mark she said, "It was my next-door neighbor. My house is on fire!"

CHAPTER 51

Gary Sims

Mark and Keri left the Last Chance Bar with tires screeching and headed for her house. Close behind them was Jost and several men on bikes. They could see the flashing lights of the fire trucks, emergency vehicles, and police cars well before they reached her house. They had to park some distance from her house and run the rest of the way. They were stopped before they could get close but as soon as Keri identified herself as the owner, they waved them through.

By now, the fire had been brought under control and the firemen were already rolling up their equipment. At first glance, it looked as if the fire had been concentrated around the carport and storage room. The main body of the house seemed to be untouched. The explanation for the minimal amount of damage was explained when Keri saw the neighbor who had called her. He was standing in his yard next door still holding a water hose in his hand.

Mr. Abbott was a retired plumber who was also exceedingly nosy. For once, Keri didn't mind his nosiness. When she and Mark walked over to him, he was still so excited he could hardly speak.

"Keri, I just happened to be looking toward your house when I saw this guy walking up into your carport carrying a can of some sort. He set it down up by your storage room and he went into the shrubbery and was trying to jimmy a window open. You know we've had several break-ins in the neighborhood this year. I told Vera to call 911 and I opened my window and yelled as loud as I could. He ran back to where he'd left the can, poured it out, threw a match on it and ran like a son of a bitch. I ran out, grabbed a hose, and tried to put out the fire. Vera was watching out the window while she was on the line with 911. She told em it was a fire, so they came quick as hell. It's a good thing cause even with my hose it was no better than try'n to piss on it. In a couple more minutes, it would have been too late to stop it.

Keri walked up to Abbott, put her arms around him and gave him a hug.

"Mr. Abbott what would I do without a neighbor like you. Thank you. Oh, this is a friend of mine, Mark Price."

Mark reached out his hand to shake it. "Mr. Abbott that was quick thinking. You must have worked in law enforcement."

Abbot was obviously pleased by the comparison.

"No Mark. I was a prince of the porcelain parlors. But thank you anyway."

"Mr. Abbott, can you describe the guy?"

"Not really. It happened so fast. He was a young white guy wearing jeans and a white shirt. He left in a white van, but I don't know what make."

"Could you tell if he had a ponytail?"

"He didn't have a ponytail. It was more like a crew cut."

Keri had gone back over to talk to the police. She told them they should talk to her neighbor before they left. By now, most of the emergency vehicles had left and Vernon had come up into the driveway. The rest of his crew had left. When Keri and Mark walked up to him, Keri told Vernon what her neighbor had said. Vernon had a thoughtful expression.

"I know Layfield sometimes uses a white van to ferry his landscaping crew around. I think I'll check around and see if I can find Layfield."

Seeing the concerned look on Mark's face, Vernon smiled.

"Don't worry Mark. I'll hold back for now. I know what our priorities are."

After carefully checking the superficial damage the fire had done to her carport and storage room and making sure her house was locked up tight, she looked at Mark.

"There's nothing I can do here now. I'll have to deal with this tomorrow. Right now, I want to go get Brutus, come back here, take a long bath, and curl up in my own bed."

Mark drove Keri back to her mom's house. As they were approaching the cul-de-sac, they realized there was a white van parked on the street in front of the house. Mark immediately reacted by turning off his lights as he pulled over to the curb and turned the engine off. Both he and Keri quickly got out but not before Mark reached behind his seat under a blanket on the floor and pulled out his old but well-kept Ithaca Model 37 and a Maglite. There was only one dim streetlight within the cul-de-sac, so they stayed on the darker side of the street with Keri staying just behind Mark. As they approached the house there were no lights and the only sounds were the usual background hum of crickets and frogs.

They followed the tree line around the side of the house so they could have a clear view of the back-screen porch. With the overlying trees, the darkness prevented them from seeing much but they were able to slowly approach the porch without having to use the flashlight. When they got close enough, they could see the screen door was partially opened and they could hear a faint moaning sound. But the other sound he could hear made Mark's hair stand up on his arms. Carefully opening the screen door, he held out the shotgun with his right hand on the grip and trigger and his left hand gripping the forward pump handle and the flashlight. Once he was well inside the porch, he switched on the flashlight.

The door entering the kitchen was wide open and a gas can sat on the floor just outside. When the beam from the flashlight shone into the room Mark and Keri, who was close behind, saw a surreal scene. Sprawled out face down on the floor, covered in blood and emitting gurgling moans was a man with his arms trying to cover his head. Sitting on his haunches next to the man's head with blood dripping from his mouth and eyes that glowed blood red in the flashlight beam, was Brutus.

Keri turned on the kitchen lights and called Brutus who came over to Keri and sat next to her feet. Keeping the shotgun pointed at the man on the floor and nudging him with his foot, Mark said, "Turn over."

As he turned himself over, the man pleaded.

"Keep that animal off me."

"Maybe I will or maybe I won't. It'll be up to you. Keri, can you find me some tape or rope?"

Keri left the room for a minute and Mark could hear drawers being opened and closed. She came back with a roll of packaging tape.

"Here, hold the gun and if he moves anything at all, point it at his balls and pull the trigger."

Mark pulled a kitchen chair over and lifted the young man up into the chair. Using the clear packaging tape, he taped the man's arms and legs with generous amounts of tape. While he was taping the man up, Mark was assessing his injuries. He looked a lot worse than he actually was. There was hardly any portion of his body or limbs that hadn't been bitten or torn but although there was a lot of bleeding, they didn't appear to be life threatening. The worst areas were around his head where part of one ear was missing, and a piece of his scalp was hanging loose. He was a small man in his early twenties with a short crew cut and he couldn't have weighed more than a hundred and forty pounds.

Keri wet a kitchen towel and sponged the blood off his face. Mark and Keri both took a step back and looked at each other. This was the young man in the video with Charles Griffin.

Mark pulled a chair up and sat facing the little man who was becoming belligerent now that he was separated from Brutus.

"I need to see a doctor."

"Gary, when we're finished with you, there won't be any need for a doctor."

A surprised look appeared on the man's face.

"How do you know my name?"

Mark ignored his question as he took his cell phone out of his pocket and dialed a number.

"Vernon, this is Mark. Guess who was about to start another fire. That's right. Keri and I have Gary Sims sitting in her mom's kitchen. No, Gary's not going anywhere. In fact, he says he'd like to talk to you. Good. We'll wait for you. Keri said you know how to get to her mom's house. See you in a few minutes."

Mark was watching Sims while he was talking to Vernon. The belligerence had left his face and was replaced by a look of panic.

"Vernon who?"

"Vernon Jost."

"Why does he want to talk to me?"

"For the same reason I want to talk to you. Why did Bo send you out to burn houses tonight?"

"I don't know. I just do what Bo says."

On a hunch Mark said, "Gary, Bo's been bragging to one of Vernon's bikers that you killed Tanya Griffin."

The reaction was instantaneous. Sims tried to come up from the chair. Only a growl from Brutus made him sit back down.

"Like hell I did."

"Bo seemed pretty sure of himself. He said you raped her too."

"I never got anywhere near her. I never got out of the car."

"You mean you stayed outside Tanya's apartment while he went in?"

Sims suddenly realized Keri was staring at him with wide eyes and he immediately shut up.

"I'm going to let you explain what you mean to Vernon when he gets here. Somehow, I don't think he's going to be very sympathetic. I think he believes what Bo was saying. Tanya may have been the only woman that Vernon ever loved. Like I said earlier, you're probably going to need a mortician, not a doctor."

With that statement, Mark stood up and double-checked the tape wrapped around Sims' body. He wasn't going anywhere.

Keri said, "Stay Brutus" as they both walked outside the back door leaving Sims under the watchful glare of Brutus and thinking about meeting Vernon Jost.

When they were far enough outside so Sims couldn't hear them, Keri said, "That was a smart thing to do. Did you see how he reacted?"

"That was almost a confession on his part. I think if Vernon will work with us, we can turn him. The key will be getting him to confess in front of the right people."

They waited until they could hear the faint sound of engines, which rose to a crescendo as Jost, accompanied by four other bikers, entered the driveway. When they all cut off their engines, the silence was suddenly as ominous as the bikes noise. Mark quickly approached Vernon and spoke quietly but urgently. Inside the kitchen, Gary Sims felt a warm trickle of urine run down his leg as he stared at the kitchen door terrified with the thought of meeting Jost. He'd heard many stories about Jost and none of them were good.

The first person to come through the door was Keri who totally ignored Sims pleading eyes and said, "Come on Brutus. I don't want you to get hurt. This won't be pretty," as she and the dog went back out the door.

Vernon and the four men with him made no effort in entering the room silently. The noise made by the sounds of their heavy boots accompanied by clanking chains filled the room. Sims tried to shrink up and become invisible as Vernon pulled up the same chair Mark had used and sat down facing him. The other four found chairs and sat surrounding the terrified and hapless Sims.

Jost very slowly took a cigarette out of a pocket and lit before speaking. He blew the smoke directly into Sim's face causing him to cough violently.

"Gary, I don't think you and I've ever met, have we?"

Sims could only shake his head in assent.

"You know for the last three years I've been waiting for Jim Herbert to fry for what he did to Tanya. Do you know how pissed off I am now? All this time you've made me look like a fool for believing a lie. Now I find out that you raped and killed the only woman I've ever really cared for."

Gary began to shake his head vehemently.

"No! I didn't touch Tanya. I had nothing to do with it. I swear it."

"That's not what Bo's been telling people."

"He's lying. I can prove it."

Sims again realized that he was going too far and maybe it was time to shut up. Jost watched Gary for only a minute before he spoke again.

"Randy, see what you can find in one of those drawers over there."

Randy got up from his chair and walked over to a row of kitchen cabinets lining the wall. Gary could hear him opening and closing drawers until he said, "These should work well."

He walked back over to where Jost was sitting and laid several kitchen tools on the table within reach.

Jost smiled and said, "Good job Randy. I'm not sure which one I like best."

He picked up a large butcher knife and ran his thumb along the blade. "It's not very sharp but it'll work."

He lay it down and picked up a small curved serrated instrument used for removing grapefruit sections.

"This works great on eyeballs, even better than on grapefruit."

Next, he picked up a simple nutcracker.

"I think we'll use this first. It'll crack knuckles like nothing you've ever seen. There are at least twenty-eight knuckles in your two hands. Takes a while but it's a lot of fun. But this is the best one of all."

He held up a small device that looked like several loops of coiled thick heavy gauge wire. Both ends lead up into a wooden handle with an electric cord leading out of the end of the handle.

"I haven't seen one of these in years. I think they caused too many house fires, and they stopped making them. You know what it's for don't you Gary? You put the coiled wire end in a cup of water, plug it in and the resistance in the coil of wire makes it turn red hot. Presto, you've got a cup of boiling water. Now use your imagination, Gary. Guess where we're going to put this before we plug it in? I'll give you a hint, we'll dip it in that can of bacon grease before we insert it. You seem to like having things stuck up your ass, don't you?"

By this point, Gary Sims was ready to say anything to stay alive.

"I swear. I didn't have anything to do with killing Tanya. I was supposed to go with Bo and shake down her apartment to look for something. Bo only told me that Tanya had something that belonged to Charles, and he had keys to her apartment. I was supposed to be the lookout while he was inside, but Tanya came home only a minute after Bo went in. Bo had his phone on vibrate and I called him to let him know she was coming up the stairs. Bo hid in the kitchen broom closet and waited until the guy that came with her had left. I was watching the apartment window. It was in the front on the side of the street. A light came on when the man left, and I could see Tanya open a curtain and look out. She watched the guy get in his car and then the light went out. Bo should have left then too. But not Bo. He gets something in his mind and won't let it go. He could have searched her apartment another time."

"After Herbert had left, I don't know what Bo did, but it couldn't have been good. When he came down to the car and got back in the driver's seat, he was covered with blood, and he still had on his rubber gloves. I was scared to death. I think I actually screamed at him, 'What the hell did you do?'

"He reached over and grabbed the baseball cap I had on and rubbed blood all over my cap with the bloody gloves. He stuck the cap under his seat and told me, 'You'll never say anything to anyone about this. If I go down for this, I'll swear you helped me all the way. I'll just keep this cap as insurance.'"

The room was so quiet you could only hear the breathing of the people in the kitchen. Mark had quietly slipped inside the door and had heard what Sims had said. Jost had picked up the butcher knife during the time Sims was talking. He was stroking the blade slowly with his thumb as if testing its sharpness as Sims finished. Mark was holding his breath hoping Jost wouldn't do anything stupid.

By now, Mark knew he should never underestimate Jost as he listened to him speak slowly and carefully, "Gary, do you know what'll happen to you if you're lying to us?"

Gary answered with a plaintive and pleading wail, "Yes! I do. For the last three years I've worried about what Bo did and what he would do to me. He's batshit crazy. He makes me do things I don't wanna do. Now you're on my back. It looks like I'm fucked no matter what I do."

Mark looked at Jost and nodded his head and Jost looked back at Sims who was beginning to sob.

"Gary, you do have a way out of this."

Gary looked up at Jost.

"Gary, when Bo is charged with Tanya's murder, which he will be, he's already bragging about you being the killer. If you go to the authorities now, tell them what you've told us, and agree to testify against him, the worst thing that'll happen to you is a light sentence, if any at all."

"The minute Bo knows I'm talking he's coming after me."

Mark asked, "Gary, do you know where Bo is right now?"

"He said something about Charles wanting him to talk to Lewis Lynch."

"What time did Bo tell you that?"

"Same time he sent me to burn the houses. It was late this afternoon."

Jost looked directly into Sims' eyes when he spoke again.

"Gary, you can relax now. If you agree to cooperate, you'll be under my protection, and you won't need to worry about Bo Layfield ever again. One thing I am good for is my word. The boys are going to take you to a doctor I know who'll take care of you. They'll just say that one of the pit bulls mistook you for a burglar and it was an accident. We'll keep you safe tonight and tomorrow we'll start the process of nailing Layfield. It's your choice."

At this point poor Gary Sims felt like he had just dodged the biggest bullet he'd ever faced. Gratefully he kept nodding his head like a bobbing cork and mumbling, "Okay." Jost reached out with the butcher knife and made several quick slices through the packaging tape binding Sims to the kitchen chair, speaking as he cut.

"Gary, this may be the luckiest day of your life. Randy, see if the keys to Gary's van are in his pocket. Go get the van and you and Zero use it to take this guy to Dr. Kline's clinic. I don't think any of us want him to bleed on our bikes. I'll call ahead now so they'll be expecting you. Randy, you stay at the clinic with Gary and let Zero bring the van back here. I think we can put it to good use."

CHAPTER 52

The Plan

After Randy had brought the van up close to the house, they put Sims with his head wrapped in towels, into the back of the van and left. Dr. Richard Kline was a longtime friend of Vernon's and the two maintained a symbiotic relationship. Kline loved motorcycles and was enamored with the biker's lifestyle. However, his profession along with a wife and three children limited his participation in the biker's lifestyle. Vernon gave him limited admission to his group and in return, Richard was always available to treat the cuts, bruises, and various traumas the bikers seemed to incur on a regular basis. He ran a very successful emergency medical clinic that employed several physicians. Vernon knew he would take good care of Sims with no questions asked.

"Randy, tell Richard that I'll cover all expenses for Sims like I did for Henry Land. He's going above and beyond for these guys."

After the van had left, Mark and Jost discussed how to track down Layfield. Mark had already called Lewis Lynch's work phone number, which he'd saved on his cell phone. The call was answered by an answering machine. He looked up a home phone number for Lynch in a directory Keri found for him. When he called the number, it was answered by a sleepy sounding female. Mark told her he was calling from work about a case he was working on with Lewis and needed to talk to him.

The lady who answered must have been Lynch's wife.

"He told me he was doing one of his stakeouts and might be out all night. I'll give you his cell phone number."

Mark wrote the number down before dialing it. It went straight to voicemail.

Keri had been silent, but she finally spoke, "We've missed the obvious. The meeting Lynch spoke of on the tape from his office must be the same one Bo Layfield mentioned to Sims."

"You're right," Mark replied, "But where?"

Keri spoke again, "Let's eliminate the places they wouldn't meet. Grace Griffin wouldn't have any meetings at her house, nor would Charles use his condo. It would be risky, but Bo might go to Lynch's office after hours. Another place that occurred to me would be the warehouse that the landscaping business operates out of. I'm not sure where it is."

Jost was nodding his head. "It's out near the airport. I know because we went there once when I needed to talk to him about messing with Tanya. Let me send someone by Lynch's office. We can eliminate that real fast. Zero should be back with Sim's van by then and we can check out the warehouse. After that, I've got no idea where to look. I don't have a good feeling about Lynch though."

Jost went outside and talked to one of the bikers for a minute and the man left immediately on his bike, the roar of the Harley engine shaking the house.

While they were waiting, Mark was on the phone again. This time the call was to Karin Stills who seemed surprised.

"I don't get many calls on this line so I'm assuming it's important."

"Karin this is Mark Price. And yes, it's more important than you could ever guess. I have information you need to see and someone you'll want to talk to as well. Can we plan to meet later tonight, preferably at your office? Time is critical. It's important we meet tonight. If it'll make you feel more comfortable have Dick Holmes be there as well. Karin, pardon the expression but you're going to have Knotts by the balls after you hear what we've found."

Stills seemed to come alive after listening to Mark.

"I hope you do have something good. The governor signed another death warrant for Herbert late this afternoon. You're right. Time is critical. Mark, do you really have concrete evidence that we can use?"

"Karin, I've got the Rock of Gibraltar. Unless you hear differently from me, let's plan on one a.m. I've got several loose ends to tie up between now and then. Also, don't be alarmed if you see what look like Hells Angels around your office. Just consider them to be Angels. I've got to go. I'll see you later."

Jost's phone was ringing, and he listened for a moment, "Come on back here," and hung up. "Lynch's office was deserted. No cars in the parking lot either."

Zero was just returning in the van while Jost was telling Mark how he wanted to use the van if they found Layfield at the warehouse. Mark listened carefully and after making a suggestion, they all agreed on the plan.

"Zero, I want you to use your bike and let Mark and Keri follow you back to Kline's clinic to pick up Sims. Both you and Randy stay with them after you pick Sims up. Follow Mark's orders. I'll call you if I need you."

Before Vernon and the remaining two bikers, Cletus and Red, got in the van and started out to check on the warehouse, all three took out a handgun from their saddlebags. Mark added to their arsenal by giving his shotgun to Vernon. Mark and Keri took Mark's SUV and followed Zero to the emergency clinic to pick up Sims and Randy.

CHAPTER 53

All Hope Lost

When the warden approached Jim Herbert's cell on death row, Jim reached the lowest point of his life. Jim knew what was coming and could only stand up and accept it. The new death warrant issued by the Governor essentially meant he had two weeks left to live. The previous weekend he'd had a visit from Julie and Libby. Libby still thought that visiting her dad was a great adventure, but she still had a tough time understanding why she couldn't stay with him or why he couldn't take her out to watch the boats or get ice cream. Julie tried to appear to be upbeat but inside she was only a heartbeat away from breaking down herself.

Jim was led from his cell in the Death Row wing of the prison and back to a Death Watch cell. After being thoroughly searched, Jim was unshackled and watched as the door was closed with a clang. Except for the guard sitting outside in the hallway, he was alone in the Death Watch area. If there were a way, he would have taken his own life to avoid what was coming. But God forbid that a condemned man should take his own life. And every provision was made to ensure it couldn't happen. The guard sitting in the hallway had only spoken once.

"Jim, let me know if I can help you."

It was a kindly gesture, but both the guard and Jim knew there was very little the guard could do for him. What Jim feared the most was a last visit from Julie and Libby. He really didn't know if he could see them without going stark raving mad. He lay back on his bare bunk, closed his eyes and prayed that if he tried hard enough, just like he'd done many times before, he'd wake up from a horrible nightmare or at this point, not wake up at all.

CHAPTER 54
Clean and Green

Clean and Green Landscaping was located in a commercial complex near the Orlando International Airport. It was one of the older sections and there was a lot of accumulated debris contained within the many chain link fences surrounding many of the large metal buildings. Clean and Green was no exception. The building was contained within a fenced off section with a power operated gate on the street side. At this time of night, the area appeared to be deserted but there was a faint light coming from somewhere inside the Clean and Green building. There were two cars parked inside the fence and next to the building. One of the cars was a newer model Ford sedan and the other was an older model Chevrolet Camaro. The main entrance gate required a card to be opened and Jost made a calculated guess that the van was a familiar sight to whoever was inside. He drove up to the gate and tapped the horn several times. In a couple of minutes, a light came on toward the front of the building and a figure emerged, took a couple steps toward the fence, looked at the van and went back inside. A speaker next to the card reader blared out.

"You, stupid dipstick. Lost your card again? You're about as worthless as tits on a boar hog."

The entrance gate slowly swung open at the same time a large overhead door at the front of the building started rolling up revealing a cavernous interior. The van's windows were heavily tinted and Jost hoped it would give enough cover to get inside before Layfield realized that it wasn't Sims driving the van.

As Jost drove the van through the opening into the building Layfield turned his back for an instant and Jost signaled for Cletus and Red, who were riding in the back of the van, to jump out of the rear door keeping the van between themselves and Layfield's field of vision. But Layfield just as quickly turned back toward the van and rapidly walked up toward the driver's side door. He was within five feet when he realized that the driver wasn't Sims and a large revolver, he was carrying in his belt was suddenly pointed directly at Vernon.

Layfield fired as Vernon ducked to the right. The 357 Magnum projectile drew a red line across Vernon's forehead, and he was showered with fragments of glass. Before Layfield could squeeze the trigger a second time, Cletus fired a shotgun blast from the hip. He knew how to handle a gun and as Jost had stressed earlier, they needed to keep Layfield alive. If Layfield persisted in trying for another shot, the next twelve gauge round would be fatal. The buckshot pellets went just over Layfield's head and crashed into a metal partition at the back of the large room. At the same time Jost pushed the van's door open, crashing it into Layfield's revolver causing him to drop it on the concrete floor. Red was a small man but quick and strong and he hit Layfield with a tackle that would have made an NFL defensive back proud. Red and Cletus were quickly on top of Layfield trying to hold him down, but Layfield was big, he was strong, and he was mean. Jost shook his head, picked up the shotgun lying on the floor and clubbed Layfield in the head.

"I'll never understand why you guys always do things the hard way. Tape his eyes. The less he sees of us the better. Try not to talk around him either."

The sound of a door slamming closed caused Jost to pick up the shotgun and run toward the back where the sound had come from. A partition that only went halfway to the ceiling separated the first room from a back area that looked like a large workshop. A door at the rear of the area was partially open and by the time Jost carefully looked out, all he could see were the disappearing taillights of a car turning out of the alley behind the building. It looked like a red Porsche, but he couldn't be sure. He kicked himself for not looking to see if there was another entry, but it was too late now. He closed the door and turned back to the room and realized that he wasn't alone. He had been so focused on the rear door that he had missed what was in the other side of the room. Hanging by his hands from an open support beam was Lewis Lynch. He was gagged and his legs were tied tightly together. What made even Jost cringe was what he saw on the ground underneath Lynch. It was a large commercial grade woodchipper that could easily handle large tree limbs. Human legs would be child's play for a machine like this.

"Both you guys, get in here as soon as you have that SOB tied up tight.

"Just a second. We found some duct tape. He's not going anywhere."

When Red and Cletus finally came around the corner and saw Lynch hanging over the chipper, they both swallowed hard. "Jesus!" was all Cletus could say.

Jost had walked over to where the rope had been tied after Lynch had been hoisted up. "Be ready to catch him when I untie this."

After lowering Lynch to the floor, Jost removed the gag and quickly cut his legs loose. Lynch was semi-conscious and was saying over and over, "I don't have any more copies."

It took several minutes before Lynch was fully conscious and able to carry on a coherent conversation.

"Layfield and Griffin were going to kill me no matter what I said. I think they were using the chipper as a threat to make sure I really didn't have any more copies."

Jost had found a chair and had Lynch sitting up.

"Lewis, Layfield and Griffin are going down for Tanya's murder. By now, you should know they're going to try to shift the blame on you. We already have one person testifying against Layfield. If your story matches his, you might be okay. I think we can even get you legal advice before anything else happens. If you want to go it alone, we'll leave now. It's up to you."

"No. Don't leave me. I don't have a choice anymore. I didn't have anything to do with killing Tanya. Yes, I've lived with the probability that the videos had something to do with it. Now there's no doubt. I'll do what I need to do. Just get me out of here before they come back."

Jost lifted Lynch to his feet. "I'm going to help you into your car and have Red drive you. You've got at least one separated shoulder, maybe both. You'll be safe with Red. He'll stay with you until I can find out what happened to Layfield."

He let Red help get Lynch into his car being careful not to let Lynch see that they had Layfield trussed up out of sight. As an afterthought, Jost took a heavy crowbar hanging on a post and carefully placed it deep into the chipper blades where it couldn't be seen.

"Let's see if it'll chew this up."

After getting Lynch into his car, Jost gave instructions to Red.

"I want you to take him to that all-night restaurant on Colonial Drive downtown. Keep him there until I call you."

Jost opened the gate and watched him leave. He went back inside and double checked to be sure Layfield was securely taped up. Layfield was defiant and belligerent.

"What the hell are you doing?"

Jost said nothing as he took the roll of duct tape and wrapped tape around Layfield's mouth, shutting him up and leaving only his nose exposed for breathing. Cletus helped him pick Layfield up and literally throw him into the back of the Van. Jost knocked out the rest of the busted driver's side window before opening the gate again and quickly driving out of the Clean and Green compound.

CHAPTER 55

A Secret Place

Jost drove the van south on Narcoosseee Road away from the airport. He eventually turned left onto Cyrils Drive. Some of the area south of Orlando had been good for farming but a lot of the area was too wet for crops but good for growing gators. Since there was only going to be one Disney, most of the area had been subdivided into anywhere from five to twenty acre lots. There were many mobile homes and a lot of storage buildings ranging from small tool sheds to large barns.

Jost eventually turned onto an unpaved driveway that was overgrown with dogfennel and showed no sign of regular use. The drive wound through a grove of live oaks, palmettos and wild myrtle. He finally stopped at a small, dilapidated house with poison ivy vines growing up the sides almost reaching the roof. There was a utility pole at the edge of the clearing that was tilting precariously with loose wires dangling toward the ground.

Using the headlights from the van, they pulled Layfield out of the back of the van and dragged him across the rotting wooden porch and through the front door of the deserted house. The house had probably been the home of a farmer sometime in the past, but it was now rapidly deteriorating. They propped Layfield up against a wall where some of the drywall had been kicked in, exposing a two by four wall stud which they used to tape him down. Jost then unceremoniously ripped the duct tape off Layfield's mouth leaving the tape covering his eyes, prompting him to curse violently. Jost and Cletus went back outside to the van. Jost used his cell phone to make a call before telling Cletus what to do next.

"Cletus, I hate to leave you here, but we can't take a chance on his getting away. Jim Bobs is on the way with some chains to lock him down. We'll need to keep him in one of the rooms so he can't see outside. Don't let him see any of your faces or hear any names. I don't want him to be able to identify anyone else. Just shove his food in the door. I'm not sure how long we'll wanna to keep him here."

"No problem, boss. If the asshole doesn't shut up, I'll tape him shut again."

Leaving Cletus to guard Layfield, Jost drove back the way he'd come. He knew there was little chance anyone would be visiting the deserted house. The property had been in fore-closure for years, but the title was so screwed up between the family members of the original owner that the cost of getting a clear title would cost far more than the property was currently worth. He had used the deserted house on more than one occasion in the past. The house was so well insulated from the neighboring properties that there was no fear of a prying neighbor hearing or seeing anything occurring in or around the house.

After making sure Cletus knew what to do, Jost called Mark. "How's our boy doing?"

"Your Dr. Kline did a super job on Sims. He said that if you keep sending in patients like this, he may give up his dreams of becoming a real biker."

Vernon laughed at that. "Do you think Sims is going to be able to give a reliable deposition?"

"I think so. He's almost in a state of shock but I also think he wants to end his nightmare. Did you find Lewis Lynch?"

"Just in time."

Jost told Mark what had happened at the warehouse with one exception. He told Mark that Layfield had escaped along with Charles Griffin.

"So, we've got two people ready to talk. That's more than I would have hoped. Let's keep them separated for now. I'll let Stills know."

"I agree. You take Sims into Still's office. I'll keep Lynch safe for now. We might need to get some guidance from Stills on how to handle Lynch."

CHAPTER 56
Karin Stills

Mark, Zero and Randy were still waiting at the clinic for Dr. Kline to write out a couple of prescriptions for Sims. He gave Randy a bottle with a few potent pain pills for Sims to use through the night. By the time they left the clinic it was pushing twelve thirty. They drove downtown to Still's office.

The area was deserted this time of the night and Mark was a little uncomfortable with the isolation. Still's Mercedes and a new model GT Mustang were parked close to the building. Mark parked next to them and helped Sims out of his Land Cruiser. Randy and Zero supported Sims as they walked around to the back door that Mark remembered from his earlier visit. The door was locked but there was a button which Mark pushed. After a minute had passed, the door was opened by Dick Holmes. Holmes looked at Zero, who was wearing only a leather vest, jeans and many tattoos, and Randy who looked even worse, with some surprise but his eyes really opened wide in surprise when Keri stepped through the door as well. His only comment was, "Mark, I see you've been busy." Mark didn't want to say much in front of Sims until he'd talked to Stills, so he only answered, "We have."

They followed Holmes up the stairs and into Sill's office complex. They took Sims into a small conference room and got him seated comfortably. Mark saw Karin Stills coming down the hallway and he held his finger over his mouth as a signal for her not to speak. He walked down the hallway to meet her leaving Keri and Holmes in the conference room with Sims. Mark followed Stills down the hall away from Sims and into a deserted office carrying the recorder with the phone conversation of Lynch.

"Mark, I hope you've got something good. Time is running out for Herbert."

"Karin, let me start from the beginning. First, I want to apologize for not bringing you into what's happened until now. Things have moved so fast it really wasn't until tonight that I had anything concrete."

Mark did start at the beginning leaving out anything that would identify Roe's involvement. After playing the recording of he'd made of Lynch, he pointed toward the computer sitting on the desk in the room.

"Can I use this computer to play this thumb drive?"

"Of course."

Karin turned the computer on and inserted the drive that Mark handed her. Mark showed only enough of the first video for Karin to recognize Charles Griffin. When the second video started playing, Mark identified the young man as Sims who was waiting in the conference room.

"Just so you know, Sims doesn't know we have this video."

Mark skipped the rest of the second video as well.

"This last part isn't pretty."

When the third video started and Stills realized what she was seeing, she let out a gasp.

"This will send him to prison for a long time. Talk about motive. No wonder they wanted both copies of this. Will Lynch be willing to admit that he gave a copy of this to Tanya? He'll have to admit it to the States Attorney. That recorded telephone conversation will never be admissible in court."

"Karin, I hope so. Apparently, he had the scare of his life tonight. We weren't sure what direction you'd want to go with him. We have him in a safe place waiting. He can be here in fifteen minutes but after you hear what Sims says you may have a different idea."

"Okay Mark. Let's go hear what Sims has to say."

They went back to the room where Sims was waiting with Keri and Dick Holmes. Zero and Randy had been assigned to stay out of sight and on guard in the parking lot. Holmes had brought Sims a cup of coffee and he was holding it with two bandaged hands. Stills walked into the room and leaned across the table looking closely at him before she spoke.

"Gary, my name is Karin Stills. I'm a lawyer who helps people in trouble."

She continued to stare hard at him a minute more before she spoke again.

"Jesus, man. You look like you just chased a fart through a keg of nails."

The remark coming from such a small prim lady was so un-expected and unlikely that everyone in the room started to laugh. Sims had to set his coffee down so he wouldn't spill it since he was laughing as well.

"Yes mam, I guess I do need some help."

That comment by Stills broke the ice. From that point for-ward, Sims couldn't speak fast enough. It was as if three years of pent-up fear and frustration poured out. Stills had set up a video recorder on the table with Sim's permission and recorded the entire conversation. No one spoke except for Sims and Stills who occasionally would ask Sims a question or for a clarification.

Finally, Sims seemed to have run out of gas. The combination of both mental and physical trauma was taking its toll. Stills ended the session with a final question.

"Gary, are you willing to talk to the District Attorney in the morning?"

"Yes Ma'am. I will."

"We have a room with a couple of cots that we sometimes use when we pull an all-night session. Let's keep Gary here until I can talk to the DA's office first thing in the morning. Holmes here will be your babysitter for the night."

Chapter 57

Decision Time For Lewis

Meanwhile, Vernon Jost was parking the van in the middle of a quiet side street several blocks from Keri's mom's house. The area was quiet and deserted at that late hour. He took the can of gasoline that Gary Sims had brought to Keri's mom's house and doused the inside of the van before throwing in a match. As the flaming van lit up the night, he walked the last few blocks to the house and picked up his bike. He called Mark when he approached Karin Still's office. Randy and Zero were there to meet him and showed him the back door where Mark met him. Mark and Jost entered the same conference room where Stills and Keri were waiting. Stills stood up and took Jost's hand.

"Vernon, I'm Karin Stills. I'm sure you remember me from the depositions we took during the trial. That may not be a good memory for you. It looks like we now have a lot to thank you for."

"Karin, I've been had just like a lot of other people. But I'm not the one to be thanking. Mark here, with Keri's help, are the ones you should be thanking. The two of them have believed in Herbert's innocence all along."

Stills nodded for everyone to sit down before she asked Jost, "Where is Lynch?"

"He's only a few minutes away. I wasn't sure we should put Lynch and Sims together. Also, I'm not sure which way he'll go after he's had time to get himself together. He could very easily freeze up."

Stills thought for a moment before she spoke.

"He's going to need serious legal help. He got a pass during Herbert's trial. That won't happen again. If you can get him in here tonight, we'll see what happens."

Jost used his cell phone to make a short call.

"He's on his way."

Within thirty minutes, Lewis Lynch was seated in the conference room with Mark, Karin Stills, Keri, and Vernon Jost. His confusion was evident as he tried to understand how this group of people fit together.

"What are we doing here?"

Again, Karin Stills did the talking.

"Well, Lewis, for starters we're not going to feed you to a woodchipper. You have Mr. Jost to thank for that. Secondly, I'm recording this conversation with your knowledge and the fact that you aren't being held here against your will. Your car is sitting outside my office, and you can get up and go any time you please. You should also be aware that Tanya Griffin's murder case is about to be turned upside down. No one at this table knows how much or how little you know about her death, but we have a participant in her murder who'll be talking to the DA within the next few hours. We know Bo Layfield killed Tanya. We know the motive for Tanya's murder was directly related to this video that you recorded."

She held the original video up for him to see.

"This puts you in the middle of a brutal murder. A close examination of your bank records might also bring charges of extortion and bribery by use of the video. I need to also remind you that you'll probably be facing charges of aiding and abetting child pornography."

After his near-death experience, and the revelations he was hearing, Lynch seemed to hit a new low and he seemed to visibly shrink in his chair.

"I want my lawyer."

"Lewis, let me give you a little bit of advice. If you mean the insurance lawyer who represented you during Herbert's trial, you're screwed. You need a competent criminal defense attorney to help you. You're going to have to deal with the State Attorney's Office. And know this, you're not walking out of this without consequence this time. However, whatever knowledge you may have, related to any of this can be a plus for you if you've got good representation. Within the next hour, I'm going to be filing a motion for a full acquittal of Jim Herbert based on substantial new evidence exonerating him. This video will be a large part of that evidence. Meanwhile, your keys are in your car downstairs. I'm sure Mark will be glad to show you out.

Lynch hesitated before speaking.

"Where's Layfield?"

Jost shook his head.

"Lewis, last we saw of him he was hauling ass after taking a shot at me. I think I saw Charles Griffin's car leaving out of the back alley. Bo probably left with him."

"I can't just go driving off alone."

Jost shrugged his shoulders.

"Lewis If I were you, I'd be worried about my family even more. Layfield is one crazy son of a bitch. There's no telling what he might do next. Then there's Charles Griffin. He's got to be a little worried himself."

Lynch turned white at the suggestion.

"How can you help me?"

Everyone sitting at the table was silent. Jost, Stills and Mark looked at each other and nodded in silent agreement before Stills spoke.

"Lewis if you'll agree to cooperate with the State Attorney's office, I'll get you someone who will truly represent your best interest in the most ethical and competent manner possible."

Looking at Jost she added, "Vernon here has saved your butt once tonight. Maybe he'll be willing to keep you safe until tomorrow."

Lynch only thought for a minute, before he finally spoke quietly.

"Alright, I'll cooperate on one condition. You've got to protect my family."

Jost nodded his agreement.

"I'd suggest we go now."

Jost took Lynch down to his car where Red was waiting. He passed the shotgun to Red and explained that he wanted Red to take Lynch home and stay with him until someone came to pick him up the morning. Lynch was still unable to drive because of his injured shoulders so Red continued to drive as Lynch gave him directions to his home.

Lynch lived in an upper middle-class neighborhood that at one time had been a very restrictive gated community. But, because of recurring financial problems, the community association was no longer able to maintain any form of security at the entrance. His house was a one-story Spanish style that was set well back from the street. He told Red to pull up in the driveway that led to the garage doors on the left end of the house. As they approached the house, Red noticed a sports car of some type sitting by the opposite curb about a half block from Lynch's house. It was noticeable because there were so few cars parked in the street. Red had served in Viet Nam as a marine sniper and had never been able to lose the paranoia he'd acquired from always looking over his shoulder.

Two things happened at once. Lynch punched the garage door opener on the car's sun visor and the garage door began to open. The automatic light on the opener mechanism lit up the inside of the garage and left the car outlined in the light. As Red watched the car parked down the street, he recognized a tiny flash of light that appeared to reflect off the roof of the car. He knew immediately what it meant but Lynch, who only wanted to reach the security of his home, was already lurching up and out of the passenger side door. The reflection off the riflescope lens was followed by a much brighter flash and immediately by the unmistakable crack of a high-powered rifle. Lynch who was on the side of the car facing the street, was literally knocked back into the passenger seat. Without hesitating Red punched the garage door opener he'd seen Lynch push and grabbing the shotgun, rolled out of the driver's side seat. On hands and knees, he crawled to the rear of the car. By now, the garage door had gone back down leaving them in darkness again. Knowing that it wouldn't do any serious damage at this distance, he fired a shot at the car, jacked in another shell and fired again, this time aiming over the top of the car. He could hear shotgun pellets hitting the car as it started up and backed away down the street before turning around and accelerating away.

Expecting the worst, Red ran around the car to the passenger side to help Lynch. Lynch was sitting down in the passenger seat with the door closed against his legs that were still hanging out of the car. Red opened the door and looked carefully at Lynch whose eyes were open and staring in complete bewilderment. When Red finally realized that Lynch was not hurt, he breathed a sigh of relief. The bullet had struck the car door directly on the handle and all of the energy was absorbed by the door causing it to slam closed and at the same time pushing Lynch back into his seat.

By now there were several lights coming on in neighboring homes. Red helped the confused Lynch get back out of the car and led him around a walkway that led to a patio area at the rear of the house. He could see a light turn on inside and he tapped on a glass door to get the attention of Lynch's wife. When she reached the door, he made sure that Lewis was standing in front of the door so his wife would recognize him. An outside light came on, and after a second's pause, she opened the door. Lewis had regained some semblance of awareness.

"It's Okay," Lynch said. "This man is helping me."

Red followed Lynch inside as Lynch began to try to explain what had happened to his wife who was staring with wide eyes expressing total bewilderment.

CHAPTER 58

Glimmer of Hope

After Jost and Lynch had left, Karin looked at the remaining people in the room. "Why don't you all go and get some rest. My work is just starting. I want motions filed and on the court's desk when the sun comes up. When Knotts reads this motion, the shit will be hitting the fan. I'm sure he'll ask for an immediate hearing with the judge which is what I want anyway. I'd like to know you three will be close by if I need you tomorrow."

As he was leaving, Jost got a call from Red who told him about the attempt to kill Lynch. He turned back to Stills and Mark and told them what had happened.

Stills shook her head. "Lynch shouldn't have any more doubts about needing help."

Jost nodded in agreement. "I'll have two guys stay outside for the rest of the night."

He knew that Layfield posed no threat, but Charles Griffin was obviously desperate enough at this point to try anything.

Before they left, they all agreed to be back in Stills' office at eight a.m.

Jost left to check on his men while Mark and Keri drove back to Keri's mom's house. Brutus was waiting just inside the door. For a change he didn't bare his teeth when Mark walked in and Keri didn't have to order him to stand down. They immediately went to sleep, both exhausted, Keri on her bed and Mark on the living room sofa. After a short night's welcome rest, they let Brutus out for a minute and then went back to Mark's hotel for a much-needed shower and breakfast. Mark drove his SUV and Keri retrieved her own car from the hotel garage before driving back to Karin Still's office.

The office was already a scene of chaotic activity. Jost and Stills were waiting in the same small conference room. Mark was surprised to see that Lewis Lynch was present as well. He looked like an entirely different person. He was freshly dressed and seemed to have a better awareness and even a look of determination that he didn't have a few hours earlier.

When he saw the quizzical look on Mark's face he spoke up.

"After last night, I've got no more choices. I'm taking Ms. Stills up on her offer to get someone to help me."

Stills replied in turn.

"Stephen Blazer is a good friend and but also happens to be someone who is well qualified to advise Lewis. He's on his way now. He's going to talk to Lewis here in my office and Lewis will make his own decision on what he wants to do next. We'll let Lewis wait here for Blazer and we'll move to another room."

They went down the hall to Still's office and after everyone was seated with coffee in hand, Stills gave Mark and Keri an update on what had happened since the previous evening.

"After the second attempt on his life, Lewis realized he couldn't bury his head in the sand any longer. Things were only going to get worse, and he had enough sense to realize his only route would be to testify. Whatever he says will be a positive for us. Now let me tell you the results of what I submitted this morning. At eight fifteen, my phones were ringing off the hook. Most of the calls were from the States Attorney's office, specifically Knotts himself. Because a new death warrant has been issued for Herbert, he thinks I'm grabbing at straws to stop the execution. I told him that not only was I going to stop the execution, but Jim Herbert was also going to be a free man within the month. Furthermore, he, Leonard Knotts, was going to have to do a lot of explaining for his prosecutorial methods. He is aware that I've filed a Writ of Habeas Corpus directly to the Trial Court as well as a direct appeal to the Governor for a stay of Herbert's execution. He's not happy but he's agreed to meet me today. I really believe when he sees both the video and hears Sim's testimony, he'll be an asset. I didn't tell him anything else. He can work on his ulcers between now and when we meet."

Keri asked, "Where is Sims?"

Stills smiled. "He's getting the royal treatment from some of my office staff. They're giving him a hero status. He's used our bathroom to shower, and they've brought him in a bag full of Egg Muffins. I don't think anyone has treated him with any respect for a long time. He's really pitiful. He reminds me of an abused dog. Layfield must really be a heartless bastard."

Stills looked at Jost.

"Vernon, you made a good call to send Red home with Lynch. Thank you."

The phone on her desk buzzed and she picked it up and answered, "Good." She stood up and headed for the door.

"I'll be right back. I need to introduce Lynch to Stephen Blazer. I've already told Stephen everything we know about the video and its connection to Herbert."

She was only gone for a couple of minutes and when she returned her phone was buzzing again. Her conversation was as brief as before.

"One o'clock? Yes. I'll be here as well as a new witness that I think you'll want to meet."

After hanging up the phone Stills smiled broadly. "Knotts will be here at one."

CHAPTER 59

Leonard Knotts

Leonard Knotts made a grand entrance into Stills office at one p.m. on the dot. He was accompanied by another attorney from his office as well as a paralegal carrying a heavy briefcase. The trio was ushered into Still's office. She stood up to meet them as they entered.

"Karin, I'm here out of respect for you. I can't imagine what you're doing but I hope it's worth our while."

"Leonard, I think you'll all want to sit down. It was thoughtful of you to bring your paralegal to take notes, but I'll save you the trouble by recording everything if that's alright with you."

Knotts was taken back by Stills suggestion of recording their conversation.

"Absolutely not. At least not until I know what we're discussing."

Stills had planned her approach very carefully. She started by reminding Knotts that any testimony regarding potential motivations by other people had been squelched by Knotts during the trial. "I'm going to show you the contents of a thumb drive that was found by Tanya's sister Keri, two days ago. It had been hidden in a stuffed animal that Keri had taken from Tanya's apartment the same day she was killed. It's been sitting in a storage shed at their mother's house." She then brought out the original thumb drive.

Knotts immediately objected.

"Karin, this is ridiculous. We're supposed to believe that three years after the trial, that a video miraculously appears out of the blue. You are obviously grabbing at straws."

"Leonard, when you see the contents of this drive and hear the testimony of our two witnesses, you'll understand. You might want to let Miss Gibbs wait outside while I play this thumb drive. You can decide later who you want to see it."

Knotts nodded to his paralegal, and she left the room.

Stills walked over to the door to make sure it was closed before sitting back down behind her desk and turning the desktop monitor around so all three could see. Stills inserted the thumb drive into the side of the computer monitor. The files came up immediately and she clicked on the first file.

"I'm not going to play through the entire file. There's no doubt what it's about."

She did the same thing for the second file. When Knotts realized what they were seeing on the third file they both were speechless and Stills quickly shut it off. Stills took out the thumb drive and walked around the desk and handed it to Knotts.

"This is your hot potato now."

"Karin, you say you know who recorded these images?"

"Yes, Leonard. Mr. Lewis Lynch has retained Stephen Blazer to represent him. He will be willing to cooperate with the States Attorney's Office with Blazer's guidance."

"Karin, what you've shown me here raises a lot of questions about Charles Griffin, but I don't see how its directly related to Jim Herbert's case."

"Leonard, I want you to meet the young man you just witnessed in the recording with Charles Griffin. But first let me outline what we've discovered. The person who filmed this video, Lewis Lynch, gave a copy of it to the victim who planned to use it against Charles in a custody battle. Charles Griffin and his mother knew she had a copy and were desperate to find it. The young man who's sitting down the hall from us, Gary Sims, will testify under oath, that he observed Bo Layfield enter Tanya Griffin's apartment on the night of her murder just before she arrived home with Herbert. Sims believed that Layfield had been sent to search Tanya's apartment at the request of Charles Griffin. He remained in Layfield's car as a lookout to warn Layfield in case Tanya came home early. When he saw Tanya coming back with Herbert, he called Layfield on his cell phone to warn him.

He will also testify that Herbert left the apartment long before Layfield did, and he saw the victim looking out of her apartment window as Herbert was leaving. Layfield remained in the apartment for nearly another hour after Herbert had left before he returned to the car where my witness had been waiting. Layfield had what appeared to be bloodstains all over his clothes. He threatened to blame my witness for murdering Tanya unless he kept his mouth shut. He actually took my witness's hat and wiped his bloody hands on the cap and stuck it in his pocket. It's more than a coincidence that a company owned by Charles Griffin employs Layfield. My witness will tell you how Layfield sent him out just last night to torch the homes of Tanya's sister and mother. He was partially successful with one house, but a guard dog prevented him from burning the second house. Layfield told him the houses needed to be destroyed on orders from Charles Griffin. Given all of these revelations, Jim Herbert's execution must be put on hold And further, if this latest information is all proven to be true, Jim Herbert's conviction should be immediately overturned."

Knotts and his companion, sat in stunned silence. Finally, it was Knotts who broke the silence.

"Let's see this witness."

Stills was quick to respond.

"Leonard, Sims has agreed to forgo all immunity for his testimony. I'm turning him over to you because there are going to be several criminal investigations coming out of this. He has been a victim in this entire affair and he's giving himself up to the mercy of the state."

Stills went to the door, opened it, and spoke to someone. In a few seconds, Gary Sims was led into the room and seated. As soon as Knotts saw the bandages covering Sims's head, he immediately jumped up.

"Karin. This is bullshit. This man has been beaten to a pulp. It's obvious you've forced him to testify."

Sims was offended by Knott's statement and without any prompting responded loudly.

"No. It was the damn dog that chewed me up. If they hadn't showed up, I'd probably be dead. I've never seen a dog as mean as that one."

Stills had to cover her mouth to keep from laughing out loud. From that point forward, the prosecutor's case against Jim Herbert began to unravel. By the time Sims had finished describing the events of the night Tanya was killed, Knotts was almost hyperventilating. Between the contents of the thumb drive and Sim's testimony, Knotts knew that the entire case against Jim Herbert was wrong. He knew in his heart that Sims was telling the truth about the night of the murder and that further investigation would support his story. Suddenly he was thinking about the implications this case might have on his career as a prosecutor and what he could do to mitigate the damage.

Stills was one step ahead of Knotts as she spoke.

"Leonard, in light of what we've heard here, there is now a great deal of doubt about Jim Herbert's guilt. Certainly, enough to stay his current death warrant until some of these new revelations can be investigated. I'm hoping you'll support my appeal to the Governor for a stay of execution. Also because of these new revelations I feel sure that the Trial Court will accept the Writ I've filed, and we'll sort things out there. I'm counting on you, as an arm of the law, to move as fast as possible to bring in Layfield and Griffin. I'm sharing everything I know with you."

Smiling as she said it, Stills continued, "You may be a hard person to deal with in court, but I know you to be an honest man who wants justice to be served. You're probably thinking how you're going to look for convicting an innocent man, but you can still make this work for you. From this point forward, you can be the honest prosecutor who saves an innocent man. It's still your case to win."

Knotts suddenly realized what Stills was saying and he knew she was offering him a way to turn everything to his advantage. He wasn't so naive to think Still was doing it out of the goodness of her heart. It was simply a means to an end for her. By letting him be the one getting the credit for saving Herbert from a tragic miscarriage of justice, she was successfully defending her client. All in all, serving justice was a win-win for them both but most importantly, for Jim Herbert.

CHAPTER 60
A Tangled Web

Following up on his plan to exonerate himself, Knotts unleashed all the powers he had at his disposal to show how concerned he was that justice be done. His first action was to have Charles Griffin arrested for having sex with a minor based on the contents of the video. He started in motion an investigation of Lewis Lynch's bank records but as long as Lynch cooperated with the state, he was not going to charge him. An arrest warrant was issued for Bo Layfield on suspicion of murder. Gary Sims remained in custody and the more he was questioned, the more apparent it became that he was telling the truth. He invoked a simple and somewhat sympathetic image. After a certain point, everyone who had contact with him found themselves feeling sorry for him and Layfield looked more and more like the monster he was.

When detectives went to Layfield's apartment in a rundown complex with a search warrant, they found several things of interest. Even though the apartment was in a low rent complex, the apartment was lavishly decorated in French Bordello. There was a lot of red velvet and several large nude paintings along with a Highwayman Elvis lining the walls. Layfield also had a state-of-the art entertainment center. The reason was soon apparent to the detectives. Layfield was an aficionado of porn. He hadn't made any attempt to hide it. His collection covered the gamut including pedophilia, bestiality, and snuff. The searchers realized that going through all of it was going to be an extended task. In his bedroom, they found a dresser drawer containing multiple pieces of jewelry.

Another drawer contained a huge stash of condoms. He had left a laptop computer on a nightstand as well. Layfield's car, his prize yellow Camaro, was found at the warehouse of the landscaping company and impounded. Since Gary Sims had described it as the car that was driven on the night of Tanya's death, a forensics team was called in to look at it even though it had been well over three years since the murder.

Knott's investigation was aided when Lewis Lynch walked into the State Attorney's office with his lawyer Stephen Blazer. There was a lot of bargaining between Blazer and Knotts as to how the state would proceed against Lynch. Ultimately, Knotts opted to give Lynch immunity for his testimony as long as he wasn't found to be directly responsible for Tanya's murder. Lynch did testify that he had filmed the video after following Charles Griffin long enough to recognize his habits. He paid the motel operator to give Griffin a predetermined room so he could set up his recording equipment in the adjacent room. He admitted that he gave a flash drive to Tanya so she could use it against Charles in their custody fight. After he gave Tanya the video and he realized that she no longer needed him, he decided to use the video to his own advantage before Tanya could use it. That's when he offered to sell his copy of the video to Charles and his mother. He told them there were only two copies, his and Tanya's. He was paid in cash for his copy and told by Layfield that if he ever said another word about the video, he was a dead man. He thought it was a forgotten issue until he got the phone call from Mark Price.

Another incriminating piece of evidence that connected him to Charles and Grace Griffin were his office phone records. They indicate that he tried to call Charles Griffin after meeting with Mark Price and after getting no answer, he called Grace Griffin. At the very least, it established a direct connection between Lynch and the Griffins in regard to the video. Lewis had one positive fact going for himself. None of the investigators found anything remotely connected to pornography of any kind after an exhaustive search of his home, office and all his electronic devices. That fact backed up his claim that he had only recorded Charles Griffin as a means of aiding Tanya in her custody battle. He also swore under oath that he had no knowledge of the identity of the young girl in the video with Griffin.

Charles Griffin was an entirely different story. From the moment he was arrested on suspicion of having sex with an underage victim, he admitted nothing and had immediate legal representation. The same thing occurred with his mother. She claimed that it must have been a plot hatched up by Tanya and Lewis Lynch and the videos must have been manipulated to incriminate her son. Knotts realized that he was going to have a hard time incriminating Charles mother Grace, but Charles was another story. The video hadn't been altered. What it depicted, happened. A search warrant of Charles apartment turned up nothing of interest except his desk top computer. It had recently been wiped clean. Forensics was trying to see if there was anything that could be recovered from the hard drive. Knotts wanted desperately to identify the young girl in the video. Her testimony would help ensure that Griffin would go away for a long time.

The one person who seemed to be immune to anything in all this, was Grace Griffin. Her only financial connection was through huge contributions to Charles political campaign. There was nothing except the phone calls to connect her to the blackmail and she had explanations for those. Charles misuse of campaign funds couldn't be traced back to her. In addition, she had excellent legal help and she continued to remain untouchable.

CHAPTER 61

Good News

Late in the afternoon, Jim lay curled in a fetal position on his bunk when he heard the door to his cell clang open. He still had a few days left to live but he was immobilized with despair. When he heard his cell door being unlocked followed by the warden's voice, he looked up. The warden was standing in the cell door with two guards behind him. He had the phone from the guard's desk in his hand and held it out toward Herbert.

"Jim, you have an important phone call. I think you'll want to take this one."

Jim stood up and hesitantly reached out for the phone putting it to his ear not knowing what to expect. "Yes?"

"Jim, this is Karin Stills. I've got good news. We have a stay from the Governor. I don't want to give you any false hope, but we've had new developments in your case. You can thank your friend Mark Price. He's been a real advocate for you. I can't tell you any more on the phone but I'm coming up there in a couple of days to go over where we stand. I can tell you that at the very least you're going to get a new trial."

Jim's knees buckled under him, and everything began to spin. Fortunately, he was standing next to his bunk, and he sat down heavily. He tried to speak but all he could do was to mumble, "Thank you."

The warden leaned over him and helped him stand up.

"Let's get you out of this cell Jim."

Jim felt almost giddy as a sense of relief surged through his mind and body. He would get to see Libby once more. But he couldn't help but wonder how many more times he would be brought to a death watch cell before it would be the last time.

CHAPTER 62

Redemption

Charles Griffin was in custody and Gary Sims was still being questioned. So far, there was no evidence linking Grace Griffin to anything. Jim Herbert was off death watch for the time being, but Layfield was still missing. That worried Mark because he knew Layfield had to be Tanya's killer. So far, the evidence was circumstantial and heavily dependent on Gary Sim's testimony. Mark had spent the afternoon after the hearing at Keri's home helping her clean up from the attempted arson. After leaving Keri at her house with Brutus as guard, he'd gone back to his hotel for a long overdue full night's sleep. He called Karin Stills first thing next morning and she suggested that he come by her office for an update.

When Mark arrived at Still's office, she was in her office and wasted no time in small talk.

"Mark, Layfield is still missing. We do have some good news though. Leonard Knotts has become my best friend. He's working like a defense attorney for Herbert now. In spite of his being an overbearing pompous asshole he is an honest man. He realizes now that Jim Herbert has been a victim of a perfect storm of circumstantial evidence from the start. Knotts is taking all the credit for discovering a miscarriage of justice at the last moment, and he's going to play it for all it's worth. If it means saving Jim, I don't care if he gets the Nobel Peace Prize for his effort. He called earlier to update me on what they've found so far. Among the items that were found in Layfield's apartment were the two pieces of Tanya's jewelry that Keri had claimed were missing from the apartment after the murder. Also, the condoms that were found in Layfield's apartment had the same lubricant that was found in Tanya at her autopsy. Located inside a kitchen cabinet was a half full box of surgical gloves and guess what? The powder on the gloves was a match for the powder found in the apartment. Again, these are circumstantial, but it all begins to add up. If you add Sim's testimony, there is more reason to question Herbert's conviction."

"There's one other thing that I'm waiting to hear back on. When forensics went over Layfield's Camaro, they noticed that new seat covers had been installed. When they asked Gary Sims if he knew when Layfield had them installed, he knew exactly when he'd done it. They were the do-it-yourself kind that he'd bought from an auto parts store. Sims was sure because he'd had to help Layfield install them on the day after Tanya was killed. Layfield did it because the driver's seat was stained from the night before. The fool just put the new covers over the old blood-stained ones. The material is at a lab as we speak. Also speaking of stains, there was an old baseball cap that was found in the back of one of Bo's dresser drawers. Sims identified it as being the hat that Layfield took from him the night of the murder. It adds to the credibility of Sims' testimony."

Mark let out a huge breath. "Is all this enough to have Herbert's conviction overturned?"

"Mark, I believe so. At the bare minimum, it will force a new trail. I really don't think it'll come to that. I think that with Knotts "Come to Jesus attitude," Jim Herbert will be a free man very soon."

"That's great. I just wish we could find Layfield."

"I asked Holmes if he had anything that might help but he said that other than knowing he was a dangerous man, he hadn't spent any time looking at him."

Mark stood, "Excuse me a minute Karin. I want to answer this call."

He went outside the office into the hallway before he spoke on his cell phone. Roe was laughing.

"Mark I've been following what's happening at the prosecutor's office. I see you've been busy."

"Roe, it's looking good for Herbert but there are still some loose ends. There's a warrant out for Layfield's arrest but he's disappeared. I remember that you told me he had an on again and off again girlfriend. You mentioned that Layfield still visits the woman occasionally."

"I did. I'll have to go back and dig it up. I can't remember her name off hand. It'll only take me a couple of minutes to look it up. I'll call you right back."

When Mark went back inside Still's office, she was talking on the phone.

"Leonard, I can't begin to tell you how much I respect you for what you're doing. From what I'm sensing from the public's reaction to all of this, you're going to be credited for saving a man's life. What you've done took a lot of courage. I think you'll be cited in law classes as an example of ethical behavior at its finest. Yes, thanks. I would like to be the one to tell him. I'm going up to the prison tomorrow."

When Karin hung up the phone, she sat without speaking. Mark realized that there were tears rolling down her cheeks. She got up and walked around her desk to Mark and hugged him.

"Thank you, Mark. I'm still not sure who you really are but I do know this wouldn't have happened without you."

She walked back around and sat down in her desk chair. She wiped her eyes and regained her composure.

"That was Leonard Knotts on the phone. He just got word from the Lab that the stains on Layfield's car seat were blood stains and were a positive match with Tanya's blood. The question I raised repeatedly during the trial about the absence of any trace of Tanya's blood on anything belonging to Herbert starts to make sense. When we go back to the trial court, Knotts is going to move for a reversal of the conviction and a dismissal of all charges against Jim. He's not planning on asking for a new trial."

Mark's cell rang and Mark again excused himself and went out into the hallway.

"Hey Mark, I've got a name and address of the girlfriend. There's a long history of domestic violence associated with the girlfriend and the address. This woman must be as mean as Layfield. What's that saying about matches made in heaven? Anyway, her name is Christie Morlan, and her current address is in Sanford. Her daughter should be fourteen or fifteen."

Mark wrote down the address. "Thanks Roe."

"Mark, how's it going with Tanya's sister?"

"You're not getting jealous, are you?"

"As long as I don't have to share my garage apartment, I'm good."

"Roe, you know that'll never be a problem. I'm hoping things here will all be resolved soon, and we'll be having our drinks on the patio."

"Great! Let me know if you need anything else."

After hanging up, Mark went back into Still's office.

"I'm going to follow up on one of Layfield's old girlfriends. It's a long shot but it's close and should be quick."

Stills looked at Mark with a quizzical expression.

"Mark, where are you getting your information?"

"Karin, if you keep digging back into Layfield's past, there's a lot of strange stuff. The woman's name is Christie Morlan. Her last known address was in Sanford. Does it ring any bells?"

"No. Until now, we haven't had any reason to look so closely at Layfield."

Stills stood up as Mark turned to leave.

"Alright Mark. You heard me tell Knotts that I'm going up to the prison tomorrow to see Herbert. I hope I can give him more good news. In any case, we've come a long way. Be careful. We all know how dangerous Layfield can be. If you find anything, give it to Knotts. He wants Layfield as badly as we do."

CHAPTER 63
Bo Layfield

After he was initially thrown into a room in the rundown house, Bo Layfield had tried, with no success, everything he could do to free himself. The worst part was the tape around his head which covered his eyes. He really thought if he could see his surroundings, he could get loose.

It was still dark when he heard a vehicle approach the house. He was soon being pulled across the floor and thrown into a room that he realized was a bathroom. He was soon secured with chains around his legs, waist, and neck. The men chaining him up were ominously silent and refused to rise to any of his insults. When they finished, they simply closed the door and left him alone. Now that his hands had some freedom of movement he immediately, slowly, and painfully, pulled the duct tape along with a lot of hair, off his head and face. It was still pitch dark and there were no windows in the room. He had enough range of motion to feel around and confirm that he was in what had been a bathroom. He could hear things crawling around but couldn't tell what it was. So, he sat propped against what must be the tub and waited for the light of dawn.

When dawn finally crept in, and he could see his surroundings, he soon realized that he wasn't going to free himself. They had done a professional job of chaining him down. Without a hacksaw or maybe a heavy-duty crowbar, he wasn't going anywhere. The only positive thing he found were two bottles of water they'd left him. Having experience with being locked up, he could wait. He would wait for them to make a mistake. But it didn't happen. During the first day, after a vehicle approached, the door to the bathroom cracked open and a bag of fast food was thrown into the room. His chains prevented him from reaching the door, but he was able to reach the bag with the food. The following day, the same thing happened. He never heard anyone speak nor could he see anyone. Sooner or later the Sons of Bitches, whoever they were, would make a mistake and he'd be on them like stink on shit.

CHAPTER 64
Amy Moreland

Mark drove out to Sanford and the last known address of Christie Morlan. The address was in an older part of the town and consisted mostly of small homes in varying degrees of upkeep. Many of the homes were being used as rentals with several cars parked randomly in the yards. Among the seedy homes was an occasional well-kept home, probably belonging to an older couple who had spent most of their life in the home and it was still their castle.

Morlan's house leaned toward the shoddy side with a yard sprouting more weeds than lawn grass. Most of the shrubbery that had once existed was dead from lack of water. A chain link fence surrounded half of the house. A broken up concrete driveway led from the street to an open one car garage which was cluttered with junk. There was a rusted swing next to the side of the house and within the fenced part of the yard. Mark parked on the side of the street a half block away. He parked behind a Bubba truck that had two flat tires and was covered in dead leaves. The leaves came from a large live oak Tree with branches spreading partway across the street. From there, he had a good view of Morlan's house, if it was still her house. Mark had a thermos of fresh coffee and an Orlando newspaper, so he opted to relax and watch the house.

By the time Mark had finished the last of the coffee and had read the last of the letters to the editor, which always got his blood pressure up, an hour had passed and still no movement around the house. He decided to drive up to the house and knock on the door. Just before he started his car, the front door to the house opened and even from a distance, he could hear loud shouting. A small figure came out, slamming the door with a bang. Mark could clearly hear the person yell toward the door, "Fuck you too." The young female walked over to the rusted swing set, sat down on the only remaining seat, and lit a cigarette. There was something vaguely familiar about the girl. Instead of driving up closer, he got out of his car and walked up a sidewalk that was cracked in many places with grass growing almost completely across its surface. When he was even with the girl sitting on the swing, he stopped outside the fence.

"Excuse me. I'm looking for someone and I'm not sure if I'm at the right place."

When the girl turned to look directly at Mark, he suddenly recognized her. She was undoubtedly the same young girl who'd been in the video with Charles Griffin. Even though she was three years older now, she still couldn't be more than fifteen or sixteen. With the cigarette dangling from her lips, she was trying to look older but without much success.

"Who you lookin for?"

"Do know a man named Layfield? Bo Layfield?"

The young girl's reaction was immediate. She jumped off the swing seat, approached the fence, and flipped her cigarette toward Mark.

"Did he give you my name? How much did he say I'd cost? Is my mom included in the deal?"

Mark took a step backward from the vehemence of the reaction.

"Miss, I'm not part of any deal. I'm only looking for Bo. I need to talk to him."

"Well, I haven't seen the son of a bitch in a long time. I'd be happy to know he's dead. That goes for my worthless Mom as well."

"Is your mom home now?"

"She's home. She's shit-assed drunk on dope or vodka or maybe both. She can't even stand up."

Mark was so focused on the girl that he hadn't noticed the three teenage boys who had walked up behind him until one of them spoke.

"Amy, are you okay? This asshole bothering you?"

Mark turned to see the three boys standing no more than five feet away. One was a kid at least six feet tall with broad shoulders. He wore tight jeans and a white wife beater T-shirt with a Che Guevara emblem across the front. His red curly hair stuck out from under a baseball cap sitting sideways and backward but somehow clinging to the side of his head. The other two were smaller but wiry with brown skin and features that suggested a Hispanic background. They wore jeans as well but if they sat any lower, they wouldn't have been able to walk without tripping themselves up. They both wore baggy Cuban style shirts that hung low. In stark contrast to the redhead, their hair was long, combed back and shiny black. The big kid seemed to be the leader and he was the one who spoke to the girl.

Before the girl named Amy could answer, Mark couldn't help himself and started laughing out loud while staring closely at the three.

The big kid obviously didn't like the way Mark was laughing at them and angrily asked, "What's so funny asshole?"

"If you three don't know how stupid you look then I can't help you."

The red head reached into his back pocket and brought out a knife that he flipped open and took a step toward Mark. Mark didn't move but he said with a smile on his face, "Kid you really don't want to do this."

But by now the big boy was committed and he had to make Mark an example in front of his two friends. He lunged toward Mark with a stabbing motion directed at Marks stomach. Mark rolled to the side while grabbing the kid's wrist and twisting it behind the boy's back. Simultaneously, using the forward momentum of the lunge, he used his right leg to sweep the feet out from under the boy who hit the sidewalk face first. The kid was stunned from hitting the ground and the knife fell from his hand. Mark picked up the knife and turned toward the remaining two boys whose eyes were staring in amazement. Their amazement turned to stark fear when Mark threw the knife toward them. They both cringed and ducked as the knife flew just over their heads and stuck, still quivering, in a telephone pole a few feet behind them.

"Why don't you two boys help your friend here. It looks like the sidewalk made his nose bleed."

They quickly helped the still stunned boy to his feet. Mark held out a handkerchief for the kid to hold over his nose as the fearsome trio limped off down the street.

Amy had watched the entire spectacle when she spoke, "Mister, I'd recommend you leave. They'll be back with a lot more of their friends."

"I'm sure you're right. I'd like to finish our conversation though. How about I buy you something to eat? I promise you I only want to talk."

"That's all?"

"That's all."

"Okay. I'm hungry. There's nothing to eat in this damn house anyway."

"Follow me. That's my car over there."

Mark started walking to his car and she followed. When she climbed into the passenger's seat, she kept her hands on the door handle just in case she needed to make a quick exit.

Mark remembered passing a business district with restaurants before he turned into the neighborhood, so he backtracked and turned into a restaurant that served breakfast all day. Her hunger was obvious as Mark watched her inhale enough food for two adults. Mark didn't press her for information but instead waited for her to finish her food. He let her be the first to speak.

"That was good," she murmured as she gulped the last of a large glass of soda.

Mark finally spoke, "How often do you see Layfield?"

"Mainly when he wants to beat up on my mom or take me on a date with someone."

"A date?"

"He wants me to screw someone."

"He forces you to do this?"

"If I don't do what he says, he'll beat up my mom even more then he'll work on me some too. He always tells her how he's killed his last two girlfriends and she could be number three."

"Have you ever considered running away or going to someone for help?"

"Of course. I've tried it. He found me and beat the shit out of both of us. He promised to kill us both if I tried it again. He gives my mom money and keeps her supplied with booze and pills. She's gotten used to it and I think she's okay with how it is."

"Do you remember a man named Charles Griffin?"

"Are you shitting me? I have to screw him at least once a month. At least he doesn't beat me like some of Bo's friends do."

"Does Bo ever abuse you?"

Amy turned her head away, but Mark could still see a tear roll down her cheek. She quickly wiped it away and looked back at Mark with a defiant expression.

"Only after my mom is passed out. I know she's worthless but even Bo knows she would go ape shit if she knew what he was doing to me."

"Amy, if I told you that I could help you and your mom, would you believe me?"

Amy looked quizzically at Mark.

"Help me how?"

"I can promise you that Bo will never touch you again. Bo has dug himself a hole so deep he's not getting out of it. I can also promise you that you can help make sure that Charles Griffin and anyone else that's touched you will go away for a long time."

"How do I know I can trust you?"

"Amy, you don't know. After all that you've had happen to you, trusting anyone is going to be a hard thing to do. You'll have to look in my eyes and make a decision to try."

"What about my mom?"

"We'll get help for her too."

"What will I have to do?"

"Just tell the authorities what you've told me."

Trusting anyone was something Amy had forgotten how to do but somehow, she sensed that Mark not a threat and that his offer of help was sincere. In spite of all that had happened to her, Amy was street smart, and she knew something had to change. She constantly dreamed of ways to escape her situation. What if this guy was for real? Anyway, her life couldn't get much worse, so she responded with a simple, "Okay."

With that statement, Mark used his cell phone to call Keri. He was brief and to the point.

"Keri I'm sitting in a restaurant in Sanford with Amy Morland. She is the daughter of Bo Layfield's girlfriend. She needs help in a big way. You'll recognize her when you see her. Can I bring her to your house for now?"

He nodded and closed his phone.

"Amy is there anything you've got to have from your house?"

"No. I don't want to go back in it if I don't have to."

When Mark and Amy reached Keri's house, Keri was outside still cleaning up the storage area that had been damaged by the fire. Mark and Amy got out of his car and Mark introduced Amy to Keri. Mark didn't have to say a single word' as Keri immediately recognized Amy as the young girl in the thumb drive video. Keri put her arm around Amy's shoulders and led her inside. Mark was relieved to see that Amy was accepting Keri as someone she might be able to trust as she allowed Keri to lead her. He could hear Keri telling her, "I have a daughter who has some clothes that should fit you well. Let's get you cleaned up and we'll see how they look on you."

Mark used his phone again to call Knott's office. After he'd explained that he was calling about the Griffin case, he finally got Knotts on the line. After he'd identified himself, he explained how he'd found Amy Moreland and her connection to Bo Layfield. When he told Knotts that she was the underage girl in the video with Charles Griffin, he had Knott's complete attention.

"That sorry SOB. I can't believe anyone could be that depraved. Where is she now?"

Mark explained where she was, but he also made it clear to Knotts that she would need to be treated gently if they wanted her cooperation. Someone needed to pay a visit to the mother ASAP as well.

"I understand. We'll need to bring in people from Health and Human Services who have experience with a situation like this. Don't worry. I'll make sure she's well cared for. I can see why she wouldn't trust anyone right now. If she can and will identify Charles Griffin, we'll have him dead to right and who knows who else might be implicated."

CHAPTER 65

Retribution

Bo Layfield had lost track of his time in confinement when he finally entered his personal hell. It was still early in the evening, and he'd dozed off into a fitful sleep when he woke to the sounds of engines approaching the house. He heard several people walking across the rickety floor approaching the room he was in. The door was thrown open and bright lights were temporarily blinding him. Before he could offer any real resistance, they were all over him. One of them covered his face with a cloth that reeked of a sharp and pungent odor. By the time his frantic mind identified it as chloroform, it was too late.

Bo slowly came out his chloroform induced stupor into a strange world with surreal characters. There was a dog, a mouse, and a duck, all staring at him in silence. By the time he recognized the masks, he also realized that he was sitting on the floor and leaning against a wall. The chains were gone, and he was completely nude. However, the worst of his nightmare was confirmed when he realized that there was something between his legs that was not right. Even the slightest movement brought sharp excruciating pain in his groin area. When Minnie poured the contents of a bottle of icy water over his head, he began to quickly regain his senses. The masks remained silent but stood with flashlights aimed at him as he began to realize what was happening. One of the flashlight beams was unwaveringly focused between his legs. As his mind continued to clear, he realized that his testicles were secured with a padlock between them and his groin. The padlock was small enough so that it was impossible to pull them back through. There was a 20-gauge wire rope looped through the padlock and secured to the wood floor with several large fence staples. They had been pounded so hard they were flush with the floor. He had about a twelve-inch length of play between the padlock and the floor. For one of the few times in his life, Layfield felt an overwhelming panic rise up in his chest. It didn't help when the four masks directed their flashlight beams across the floor illuminating a red metal gas can. The dog walked over, picked up the can and began to pour gas on the floor of the connecting rooms.

"What the hell are you doing? Why?"

The mouse answered with one word, "Tanya!"

"Tanya? Okay. I beat her up a little bit and I fucked her. So what? You think I killed her?

The mouse's reply was a bitter, "We know you killed her."

"No, I beat her up pretty bad. She was bleeding all over everything. She was crying in her bed when I left. I didn't kill her. This isn't fair. I'm telling you. I didn't kill her."

The mouse laughed, "Whatever you say," and with that statement, the mouse went into the adjoining room and threw a match on the floor. Bo could hear the whoosh as the gas ignited. The mouse knelt down next to Bo with a large drinking glass in one hand and a hammer in the other. She put the glass on the floor and with one firm blow of the hammer smashed it. Still holding the hammer, she stood up and walked toward the door.

"Bo, you know how to cut things with broken glass. We'll give you another shot at it."

By now, Bo was screaming as he heard the sound of motors revving up and fading out of earshot leaving him alone with the flames quickly spreading through the deserted house.

Larry Motts was feeding his horse at the back of his ten-acre home site off Cyrils Drive when he first noticed the plume of smoke rising from the neighboring property. His first thought was that someone had finally set the abandoned house on fire. He went back to his beat-up pickup truck and drove back out to the main road and the short distance to the overgrown driveway leading toward the abandoned house. By now, it was evident that the smoke was indeed coming from the house. Knowing it was a useless gesture he stopped and used his cell phone to call 911 and report the fire. He had no concern about the house, but he didn't want the fire to become a larger brush fire.

He'd stopped his truck well into the driveway, but he restarted his truck and slowly drove toward the blazing house, which was now visible in front of him. Not wanting to get any closer to the fire, he stopped at the edge of the trees surrounding the house. What he saw then was an image that would keep him awake on many nights to come. A figure somehow materialized out of the door of the blazing house as if it had emerged from hell itself. In a Frankenstein lurch, the apparition staggered across the porch and into the knee-high grass in the yard. As he continued to lurch across the yard toward Larry's truck with outstretched arms, Larry could see that he was completely naked. His hair was smoking, and one side of his body was blackened like a well-seared steak. But what was most obvious was the blood pouring out of his groin and running down his legs creating a sharp contrast against his scorched and blackened skin. Not knowing what else to do, Larry grabbed an old moldy horse blanket from behind the driver's seat, went to the wretched figure and wrapped the blanket around him as the figure collapsed to the ground. As the man collapsed, he kept muttering, "Mouse, Mouse." Larry felt as if an eternity had passed before the rescue vehicles finally arrived.

CHAPTER 66

Doubts

Mark had just left Keri's house as soon as several people from Knott's office arrived to help with Amy Morland. He was on his way back to his hotel when his cell phone rang.

"Mark, this is Karin. I thought you might want to know that they found Layfield. I really don't have any details except that he's in the hospital and is in critical condition. Knotts hasn't been able to talk to him yet, but he promised to let me know as soon as he's able."

"Karin, thanks for letting me know. I'm going to relax a little more now."

"Mark, there's another reason I called. I'm driving up to the prison tomorrow morning to see Herbert. Would you be interested in coming with me? You've been such a huge factor in everything that's happened."

"I'd love too. I appreciate the invitation. Let me drive."

"Alright. Pick me up at my office at seven a.m. We should be in Stark by ten thirty. Maybe I'll know more about Layfield by tomorrow."

After resting for a while, Mark showered, put on jeans and a sweatshirt before driving back to Keri's house. He stopped at a grocery store and picked out two thick rib eye steaks, a salad mix, and a key lime pie. Keri met him at her door with a glass and a shaker full of ice-cold Tanqueray and vermouth, not stirred of course but instead, very well shaken. Again, Keri didn't have to tell Brutus to stay put. He hardly looked at Mark when he walked in. They sat on her patio and enjoyed their drinks while the coals heated up on the grill. Mark told her about the call from Stills. Keri sat and listened without any expression until he'd finished. She looked off in the distance and smiled a strange smile before saying anything. "I know the bastard did it."

"What do you mean you know he did it? Of course, he did."

Keri seemed to wake up from her trance. "Oh nothing. I'm glad they've got him. I still hope he'll admit that he killed Tanya."

There was something about what she was saying or maybe it was how she said it that aroused Marks curiosity.

"Do you have any doubt at this point?"

Keri looked Mark in the eye and smiled.

"I'll just feel better after he makes a formal confession. Let's forget Layfield and enjoy the moment. By the way, I think it's great that Stills asked you to go with her tomorrow."

Mark could sense that Keri didn't want to talk about Layfield, so he dropped it and enjoyed the rest of the evening.

Mark left Keri's house in the wee hours of the morning, returning to his hotel for a shower and change of clothes before arriving at Still's office at seven. Her grey Mercedes was already in the lot along with three other cars of early arrivers. Mark didn't even have time to ring the bell at the door before Stills emerged dressed in a conservative black suit and carrying a stuffed leather briefcase.

As they had agreed, Mark drove, and Stills gave him an update on Layfield.

"Layfield is in critical condition in a burn unit. At least a third of his body has third degree burns but that's only a part of it. He'd been castrated and rather crudely at that. He lost a lot of blood from the wound. They're having to keep him well sedated for now and Knotts himself couldn't make much sense of what he was saying. Knotts told me he could only pick out a few coherent words that included cartoon characters."

Mark was driving north on the Florida turnpike while Stills was talking. A sudden flashback to the night before suddenly hit him and he almost drove off the road before he regained control. As he was getting out of Keri's bed earlier in the morning, he'd reached under her bed trying to find one of his shoes and he'd pulled out a Halloween mask. He pushed it back under the bed and thought nothing of it. But there had been no doubt because even in the moonlight shining through the windows, he'd recognized the mask as a mouse. All at once, Keri's comment about Layfield made sense. Her words echoed in his mind, "I know the bastard did it." What he couldn't understand was Keri's sudden doubt about Layfield being Tanya's killer. In any case he was sure Keri knew far more than she'd admitted. He'd have to call her the minute he got back to Orlando.

Mark stayed on the Florida Turnpike north to I-75 and cut over to 301 just north of Ocala. The drive from Waldo to Stark opened an old wound. There was minor change in the scenery and images of Marge and Kim kept flashing through his mind as he drove. Some things would never be forgotten and there would always be pain associated with his past. He knew he had to accept it, but it was still hard to do.

The death row wing of the state prison consisted of several rows of connected buildings. Because Stills had scheduled their visit beforehand, they only had to wait a couple of minutes before they were ushered through metal detectors and a thorough search before being led into a private room used by lawyers and prisoners. All the chairs were bolted to the floor and Herbert was sitting on one behind a table. When Karin and Mark entered the room, the guard removed Herbert's handcuffs, left the room, and closed the door. A glass window in the door allowed a guard to visually monitor the visit the entire time.

Going against protocol, Stills leaned across the table and gave Herbert a quick hug.

"Well Houdini, we've done it again."

A haggard looking Herbert smiled and replied, "I'm not sure how you did it but no matter, I'm grateful."

Stills went on to explain what had happened during the past week. Jim looked at Mark and said, "How can I ever thank you?"

"Getting you the hell out of here is thanks enough for me. I'm counting on us playing tennis again."

Stills went on to explain to Jim her hope of freeing him without having to have another trial. When they left Jim, his demeanor had improved considerably. For the first time in a long time, there was hope.

After they left the prison, Mark and Karin stopped at a Sonny's in Stark and ate large plates of barbecued baby backed ribs. Just before they reached Stills' office in Orlando, she answered a call on her cell phone. She mostly listened to the caller and closed the call with, "Thanks for letting me know. The son of a bitch can say whatever he pleases as long as Herbert is acquitted."

Stills looked at Mark and said, "That was Knotts. Layfield woke up long enough for Knotts himself to question him. Leonard says that Layfield is adamant that he only, to use his own words, "beat the shit out of her and fucked her," but he's still sticking to his line that he didn't kill her. That was all he could get out of him. Leonard did say that his goal was to have Layfield switch places with Jim Herbert on death row.

Mark dropped Stills off at her office and as soon as she had disappeared into her office, he immediately called Keri. "We need to talk."

Keri answered as if she had been expecting the call.

"Okay. Come on over. I've got plenty of gin left."

CHAPTER 67

Keri's Confession

Just like the day before, Keri met Mark at the door with a cold Martini.

"From the look on your face I know you need a drink."

Mark said nothing as they went out onto her patio and sat down facing each other.

He was the first to speak. "You knew what happened to Layfield all along?"

"I did. I didn't see any reason to put you in a compromising position by telling you about it."

"So, tell me about it now."

"Mark, before I tell you anything, I need to know how far I can trust you. There are other people involved with this."

"Keri, I have no doubt that Vernon is somehow connected to whatever happened to Layfield. I can only tell you that no matter what happens to Layfield, it can't be bad enough. By now, you know enough about me to put me in deep shit if you wanted. I think we have a mutual reason to trust each other."

"I guess I should know that. I'm sorry I even questioned you. Going back to the question of what happened to Layfield. Do you remember the night at my mom's house? Vernon went to the warehouse and found Louis Lynch. Vernon told us that Layfield was there, but he got away?" Well, Bo didn't get away. They took him to an abandoned farmhouse and kept him until yesterday morning. Vernon did like he promised. He waited to be sure there was enough evidence to get Herbert off the hook before he did anything with Layfield. A couple of days ago he told me he had Layfield and what he planned to do. He gave me the option of helping. I've been so certain that Layfield killed my sister that I jumped at the chance for revenge. You probably don't know what it's like to want revenge as badly as I did."

Mark could only nod his head at that and think to himself, "If you only knew."

Keri went on to tell Mark how they'd used chloroform to knock Layfield out, secure him with the padlock and then set the house on fire. During the time it happened, Jost made a big show of being present at the Last Chance Bar as an alibi for himself. They wore the masks to protect their own identity in case Layfield somehow survived.

When she was finished Mark asked her, "If you had to have an alibi, would you have one?"

"I was at my mom's house the whole time and she would go to her grave saying so."

"Keri, I still don't understand why you were questioning whether Layfield was the one who killed your sister."

"It's because of what he was saying when we left him in the burning house. Layfield is such a total ass that he brags about the things he's done. He was denying killing Tanya. He had no trouble admitting he assaulted her and beat her bloody but there was something about the way he denied killing her that rang true. I don't know why but I can't get it out of my mind."

"That's interesting. He's saying the same thing to Leonard Knotts. Everything points to his guilt just like everything pointed to Jim Herbert. Let's play devil's advocate. Suppose he is telling the truth. We know Jim Herbert didn't kill Tanya. What if Tanya was alive when Layfield left? Who else could have killed her? I know this is a big 'what if' but if Layfield is telling the truth who else would have wanted her dead so badly, they would have risked it?"

There was no hesitation from Keri.

"There are only three people who really had a motive to kill her. Grace Griffin, Charles Griffin, and Lewis Lynch. I've said that from the start."

"We can eliminate Lynch based on the conversation we recorded and what we've learned about his part in this. Charles Griffin was meeting with a group of ministers to push his house race. He was playing the role of protector for the down and out. After that meeting, he went straight to one of the nude bars he represented and made a big splash there for the rest of the evening. According to the timeline the prosecutor set, and based on multiple witnesses, his alibi was rock solid. Grace Griffin was supposedly at home with her husband and grandson. I'm not sure where we go with this theory. We could ignore your instincts and assume Layfield did kill Tanya. That would be the simple thing to do."

Mark was silent for a minute before he spoke again.

"It would be interesting to have a bug in Grace's house. Dick Holmes had even suggested doing it. It might be a total waste of time, but I think she's the queen bee behind everything. Even if Layfield did murder Tanya, I still think Grace still had some part in it."

Keri laughed, "Good luck on getting into her house. It's a secure compound and I'm sure she has every alarm known to man. Tanya was there once. Grace invited her in and tried to buy custody of her son. She thought Tanya would be vulnerable to the offer of money. Tanya laughed in her face and walked out but not before she saw the house from the inside and from the back patio. The house is located on Lake Seri and it's one of the most exclusive lakes in Orlando. There are only a few homes on the lake, most of them being large estates occupying most of the land around the lake. There was a guard house with a live guard at the front gate of the house. Tanya told me that she was taken out onto a rear patio overlooking the lake where she met with Grace. She said the compound's walls extended down both sides and even into the water for a distance. There was a dock extending into the lake."

Mark nodded. "Let's take a ride by the place and see for ourselves. There's always a way to get in if you look hard enough."

The drive to the home of Grace Griffin took them through a seedy section of town that evoked memories of his daughter's death. After turning into a nondescript side street and going a short distance, a body of water opened up in front of them. The street then split right and left in front of them, circling the lake revealing an enclave of affluence. The spring fed lake was well over a hundred acres in size. The homes were all large estates bordering the lake. Most were gated with tall walls or large, towering hedges. Griffin's home did indeed have a small guardhouse located next to a heavy, ornately decorated, iron gate. There was no sign of a guard in the guardhouse as they slowly drove by. The concrete wall covered in ivy, tapered to a point at its peak where it was capped with sharp iron spikes. It would not be an easy wall to climb over but not impossible. Mark immediately recognized that the problem would be the small wire that stretched across the top of the spikes. It was an alarm wire of some sort. He couldn't help but wonder why this much security was necessary. It seemed to be overkill unless they were expecting a zombie apocalypse.

There was no view of the lake from the street in front of the house, so they continued to follow the street back around to the point where it had split. Here there was a small finger of the lake that extended off its circular shape. It was shallow and was mostly a marshy area that would have not provided an attractive home site. It was at this spot that the road circling the lake almost touched the finger of water. There was no boat ramp visible, so the only boats on the lake were boats belonging to the homeowners. From this vantage point, there was a clear view across the lake. Mark pulled to the side of the road and stopped the car. Using a pair of binoculars, he could identify the Griffin house, which was directly across the lake. It was easy to identify because of the extensive use of native limestone on its exterior walls.

Keri watched as Mark looked though the binoculars.

"What are you thinking?"

"I'll bet the lakeside of the house isn't guarded like the front."

"So what? The front is guarded, and the compound wall goes all the way into the water." Keri laughed, "You'd have to swim across the lake."

Mark looked at her with a neutral expression on his face.

"No Mark. You've got to be kidding. You're not thinking about swimming across the lake?"

"It's not really that far. The water is calm with no current. My only concern would be alligators or water moccasins and they don't usually bother swimmers. I'll use a wet suit with flippers, and it won't be hard to do. Before I do anything though, I want to talk to Dick Holmes."

They left the lake as the sun was setting and drove to a fast-food restaurant and parked. Mark called Dick Holmes.

"Dick, this is Mark. I have a couple of questions. When you were working on Herbert's case, how far did you go in looking at Grace Griffin? Did you ever stake out her house or follow her movements?

"Mark, I spent a week sticking to her like glue. She doesn't go out much, but she has quite a few visitors. Her husband is now confined to a wheelchair, and I never saw him leave the compound. During that period, I'd hoped we could get permission to plant a wire in her house or to tap her phone. The police refused to consider it. I looked for possible ways to get into her compound on my own. I got to know one of the security guys who worked her gate and got him drunk one night in a local bar. He joked that you'd have to be a fish and swim across the lake to get into her compound. I took that to mean that the lakeside wasn't wired like the front. During the time I watched, the house seemed to shut down early most nights. Why are you asking Mark? I thought the case was solved."

There was something in the tone of Holmes' voice that seemed odd, but Mark shrugged it off.

"No, not really. I'm concerned about Keri and her mom's lack of access to the boy. They would really like to see him."

"I guess that is tough for them. At least they can have the satisfaction of knowing Tanya's killer's been caught. Anything else you need to know?"

"No. Thanks for helping."

Mark hung up and looked at Keri. "Strange."

"Strange why?"

"I suppose nothing. Holmes just sounded a little strange. Let's find a sporting goods store."

CHAPTER 68

The Long Swim

It was after nine p.m. by the time Mark had found all the things he needed. They stopped at a chain restaurant and ate a late dinner. Afterward, he and Keri drove back toward Grace Griffin's home and parked in a strip mall shopping plaza that was almost empty. Mark moved into the rear seat and struggled into a black wet suit. It was eleven thirty by the time Keri drove them back to the lakeside neighborhood and slowly circled the lake once again. There was a guard visible in the Griffins gatehouse and as they passed the gate, they could see lights in the main house as well. An older model Toyota sedan was sitting next to the guard gate and heading out of the compound. Keri slowed as much as she dared without attracting attention. The driver of the Toyota was an older female wearing a white nurse's cap.

When they reached the point where the street touched the finger of the lake, after making sure there were no cars visible in either direction, Keri stopped the car. Mark used the binoculars to identify Griffin's house across the lake before stepping out of the car. He pulled the wetsuit hood and pair of goggles over his head before putting on a pair of swim fins. When he lumbered toward the water, he looked like a creature from a grade B horror movie. In addition to a diver's watch, he wore a wide nylon diver's belt with a knife and a small waterproof flashlight attached on one side. A small waterproof pouch was attached to the other side. He had carefully checked the pouch before he got out of the SUV. The pouch contained the second listening device along with its' remote recorder, his cell phone, a black ski mask, a small lock pick tool and a pair of surgical gloves. When he reached the water, he pushed through several yards of tall grass and into a sea of Lily pads until the water deepened enough for him to flatten out and begin to swim. He'd seen several ripples in the water, and he hoped his biggest fear, water moccasins, were moving aside. Moccasins were known to be a highly irascible species of snake and were well known for striking out at anything that came close. At one point, he felt something slide across his leg and he tensed expecting a painful bite to follow. If it had been a snake, it must have been a harmless water snake because the bite never came.

As he swam past the Lilly pads and entered the main body of the lake, the water quickly deepened and turned noticeably cooler. He checked his bearing again to be sure he was swimming in the right direction. Making no effort to swim fast, he moved in a smooth manner by keeping his fins under water and making no splash or noise. The night was dark enough that he wouldn't be visible from any point on shore even if someone happened to be sitting on a dock looking across the lake. It took him nearly thirty minutes to cross the lake. At one point, he stopped to recheck his bearing and realized that the lights he'd been using as a reference point had been turned off. He had to look back at his starting point and recalculate his position, but he was soon moving forward again.

As Mark approached the shoreline, he stayed close to the dock all the way up to the sandy bank. Staying under the dock he removed his swim fins and reaching into the pouch, he removed the gloves, ski mask and remote recorder. After pulling the surgical gloves over his hands, he placed the recorder under the dock next to a piling near the shoreline. Since there was no way he or Keri could sit within range on the street for any length of time, the recorder would have to be hidden close to the house and retrieved later. He made sure it and the small listening device were activated. It was well hidden and would be almost invisible even in daylight. The swim fins and snorkel he left on the sand under the dock. Not wanting to leave any tracks in the sandy beach area, he boosted himself up onto the wooden dock. Looking up toward the back of the house, the only interior lights visible were on the second floor. There were outside security lights, but they seemed to be directed mostly toward the front of the house. While he was watching, the lights on the second floor were turned off.

Mark waited and watched a few minutes more before he pulled the ski mask over his face and began to move toward the house. He didn't think anyone would be watching but he still moved slowly and cautiously staying off the walkway and in the shadows of the shrubbery until he reached the large patio that overlooked the back yard and lake. From the configuration of the patio doors, it was apparent that there were several rooms leading onto the patio. He slipped out of the shrubbery on the right side of the house and eased himself onto the patio's surface. Moving along the wall, he stopped at the first set of tall French doors and looked inside. A faint flickering light made it possible for him to recognize a sitting room that adjoined a large room toward the right side of the house. The flickering light must have been from a television and in the intermittent flashes of light, he could see an empty wheelchair. It was probably the bedroom of Grace's husband, the doctor. It seemed logical that he would be on the first floor.

Seeing no other movement, he moved on past the two sets of doors to the next room. There was no light behind this set of doors, so he used his flashlight long enough to identify the room as a dining room. The next sets of doors were massive, and he could easily see that they opened onto a grand hallway that stretched the full length of the house from front to back. The lights on a front portico made it possible to see that the hallway was lined with large paintings and tapestries. Midway down the hallway, marble stairs curved upward. Crossing these doors, he came to the room he was looking for. Again, using his flashlight briefly, he could see a huge room with bookcases reaching up to the ornate ceiling. Otherwise, the room was black as pitch. Reaching into his pouch he removed the small tool that he hoped would help him unlock the door.

Reflexively, he turned the door handle before starting to work on the lock. The door opened outwardly, smoothly, and quietly, as if to say, "Come on in."

CHAPTER 69

Hurry Up and Wait

After dropping Mark off at the lake, Keri drove to a nearby all night donut shop and got a large cup of coffee from the drive through. There were some cars in the parking lot, so she parked and waited. She knew that what they were doing was stupid and dangerous as well. There was something about Mark though, that created confidence. He didn't seem to be reckless but neither did he exhibit fear. During the time they'd spent together over the last few days, he'd divulged nothing about his past except that his daughter had died tragically, and his wife died soon afterward. He did talk a little about his past as a history professor.

The other thing that had surprised her was the way he had accepted her description of what had been done to Layfield. His attitude was matter of fact and he didn't question either the brutality or the legality of the action. His attitude toward her was unusual as well. She wasn't looking for a permanent relationship but her experience with the few men she'd had a relationship with in the past always seemed to lead to a possessive attitude that turned her off. It was obvious to Keri that Mark could smile, wish her well, and walk away without any emotion. She had to admit to herself that it was somewhat annoying to realize this. Mark Price was an enigma to her but here she was ready to follow him anywhere. As she sat and brooded, she found herself staring at her watch and her cell phone, willing the phone to ring.

CHAPTER 70
Grace Griffin

Mark tensed, expecting an alarm to sound, as the patio door slowly swung open. His first thought was, "No, this is too easy," as an inner voice told him to turn and run like hell. But he hesitated for only a second before he took the bug out of his pouch and held it in his left hand. He promised himself that he would plant it under the huge desk and then haul ass out of there. He quickly slipped through the open door into the dark room and pulled the door closed behind him.

Standing still on the inside of the door in the dark, he listened for any sound or movement before he started across the room toward the desk, which was faintly visible across the room. That's when he heard one small click as the lights in the room were turned on. The second sound was a much heavier click that was the unmistakable sound of a large caliber revolver being cocked. That was followed by a voice he instantly recognized.

"Mark, I really wish you hadn't pushed it. For what? Everything was working out just as you wanted. Herbert's going free. Layfield's going down. You've even destroyed Charles."

Mark was only partially hearing what Dick Holmes was saying because his eyes were darting around the room looking for an escape route. To his right was a large set of double doors which opened into the main hallway, and he was judging his chances of diving through the door and into the hallway. That route was closed when Grace Griffin walked through the hallway door with a 38 caliber Ladysmith short-barreled revolver in her hand. Mark recognized from the way she carried it that she knew how to use it. This was the first time Mark had seen Grace Griffin in person. She had to be in her late fifties or early sixties, and she was a startlingly beautiful woman. She was dressed in a silk nightgown that clung to her and did little to hide a body that might have belonged to a much younger woman. Her hair was long, dark, and fell across her shoulders. But it was her eyes that Mark noticed the most. They were piercing and cold as ice.

Looking back to his left, he saw that Holmes was sitting in a leather chair with his cocked revolver pointed directly at Mark's midsection. Mark knew without doubt that Homes wouldn't miss at this distance. Knowing that he had no other option at the moment, he focused his attention on Grace Griffin and tried to buy some time.

"So, you're going to start shooting here in your own house? What do you say to your employees not to mention your grandson?"

Grace laughed. "Everybody's gone. We let the nurse go home and my grandson is at a slumber party with friends. My husband is zonked out on sedatives as usual. Why does it matter anyway? You're an intruder. I heroically defend my home by shooting you. Who'll question it? Really, this is more than I could have ever hoped for. You're the one responsible for my son being in jail so now it's payback time."

Trying to buy time, Mark remembered he had the bug in his hand, and everything was being recorded. Even if he didn't make it out, maybe someone would get to the recorder under the dock.

He looked at Holmes who stood up from the chair he'd been sitting in.

"Dick, I guess I've really misjudged you. You've worked both sides of the fence all along. You've known every step the defense was going to take. How long have you been working for Grace?"

"You do at least deserve to know the truth. Grace and I've been together ever since John, her husband, had his stroke. She hired me to check up on the backgrounds of some caregivers."

Grace interrupted, "That's right. I wasn't about to play nurse to a decrepit old fart who could only drool and piss in his pants. I needed someone I could trust to help me keep him medicated and out of my way."

Holmes smiled and continued, "We hit it off pretty well. Since I knew a lot about the law enforcement people in the county, I've been able to help Charles with his clubs. It's important to know who'll be helpful at the right times. Grace and I have also been extremely discrete with our relationship. That's why I'm able to continue working for Karen Stills."

"Does Stills know anything about your connection to Grace?"

"Are you kidding? I'd probably be dead or in jail if she had any idea."

Mark looked back at Grace.

"Why are you keeping your husband alive? I've heard you're quick to get rid of an unwanted spouse."

Grace answered with a big smirk on her face. "So, yes, the rumors are true. That was a long time ago. And you're right. I'd overdose him in an instant if it weren't for his estate. He has a niece that he's included in the estate. I'm working on a way to get her out of it, and I still need him to approve the changes before he goes away."

Mark smiled, "I sense a lot of love here."

Grace replied with a cold smile. "Fuck you."

"So, since you're unburdening your souls, who killed Tanya?"

Holmes took another step toward Mark still holding the revolver pointed directly at Mark's midsection.

"I did. Tanya messed up everything when she brought Herbert back to her apartment. We'd sent Layfield to look for the thumb drive. I was watching him, and I planned to finish her after he left. We intended to blame it on him all along. But Herbert entered the picture and was an even better set up. We didn't have to do anything but watch it happen.

"After I saw Layfield leave the apartment, I came up the back stairs to the back door of her apartment. I had a master key, but

I won't bore you on how I got it. I carried a bag with painter's coveralls, gloves, and clean booties like police wear at crime scenes. Tanya was alive but Layfield had done a number on her. She was unconscious and she never knew her throat was being cut. I cut her up a lot more with the broken glass to make it look even more gruesome. Before I left, I took off the coveralls and booties, put both in the bag and left out of the back door leaving it locked. I'm the one who called the police and gave them a description of Herbert as well as his tag number. You know the rest. If it hadn't been for Herbert, we would've made sure Layfield was blamed. But it wasn't necessary. Mark, I'll have to admit, we underestimated you."

Now standing within a few feet in front of Mark, Holmes nodded to Grace Griffin standing just inside the hallway door.

"Do it Grace."

As Grace began to slowly raise her gun, an explosion and a bright flash rocked the room. Mark was already rolling to his right in anticipation of Grace's shot. The sudden explosion caused her to jerk her trigger finger and fire prematurely. The bullet caught Mark somewhere under his left shoulder as he fell to the floor and instinctively rolled toward the hallway door where the explosion had come from. What he saw was beyond strange.

A wheelchair rolled into the room with Dr. John Griffin holding an over-under shotgun in his hands and a maniacal grin on his face. His robe hung open revealing a bony chest and his long white hair flared out from his head. Grace screamed and ran toward the other side of the room where Dick Holmes had been knocked back into the large leather chair he'd been sitting in. His eyes were open wide and staring at the huge hole in his sternum that was pumping out a geyser of blood. A three-inch magnum load of 00 buckshot at close range had punched a hole the size of a grapefruit through his chest, taking parts of lungs and heart and spraying them across the backrest of the chair he was now sprawled in. He tried to open his mouth to speak but before any words could come out, he seemed to collapse within himself. With eyes still wide open, he lay still.

Grace looked back across the room at her husband. Her face was filled with rage.

"What in hell are you thinking?"

"I guess you're surprised that I'm thinking at all. I stopped the meds a long time ago. You've just confirmed what I've suspected for a long time. You and your worthless asshole of a son can finally go to hell. You say you're worried about my niece getting part of my estate. If you'll check my will as of a week ago, you'll see that you and Charles have been removed entirely. Because of the original wording of our prenuptial agreement, you signed thirty years ago and thought I'd forgotten, I have the right to modify my will anytime I please without your permission. At the time, I wouldn't have asked for a prenuptial agreement, but I had a smart lawyer who was looking out for me at a time when I was infatuated with your charms. I just out lawyered you."

Grace was still leaning over the body of Holmes, but she stood up, walked over, and stood in front of her husband. She was still holding her revolver and with no hesitation she brought it up and at point blank range she fired four shots into John Griffin. He jerked backward in the wheelchair and then pitched forward on the floor. During this entire exchange, ignored by both John and Grace, Mark was lying on the floor next to the wheelchair as John Griffin pitched forward, dropping the shotgun as he fell. It didn't take an enraged Grace Griffin long to refocus her attention on Mark lying on the floor.

"You!" she screamed. "You caused all this just to help Jim Herbert. Why was he worth all this? He was nothing!" as she aimed her gun point blank towards Mark's face.

Mark could only watch as she squeezed the gun's trigger. He flinched at the loud click as the hammer fell on an empty chamber. She pulled the trigger repeatedly, forgetting that her Smith and Wesson revolver only held five rounds and she'd already used all five. When it finally dawned on her why the gun wouldn't fire, she dropped it, ran across the room, and picked up Holmes' large revolver which was lying on the floor next to his lifeless outstretched hand. The minute Grace turned her back on Mark, he pushed himself to a sitting position and picked up the shotgun that Dr. Griffin had dropped. He yelled at Grace as she turned, holding Holmes's large revolver.

"Don't do it Grace! Drop it."

But instead of dropping it, she took a step toward Mark raising the heavy gun with both hands. Before she could pull the trigger, Mark fired the second barrel in the over-under shotgun at Grace who was no more than five feet away. The effect was devastating as it knocked her backward. She fell at the feet of the lifeless body of Holmes, dead before her body hit the floor.

Mark sat still for a moment, stunned by the events and the ringing in his ears from the deafening gunfire in the closed room. The first thing he did was to look at his wound. He found where the bullet had entered, fortunately in a non-vital spot. He might have a broken rib or two, but the wound was not life threatening unless he bled too much. Thankfully, the wetsuit had prevented him from bleeding out on the carpet though there were a few drops visible. He wiped his finger through John Griffin's blood and across the few drops of his own blood on the carpet. Next, he looked for the bug that he'd dropped when he was shot. He picked it up and put it in his pouch. He took the shotgun, wiped off the parts he'd touched and placed it carefully next to Dr. Griffin with one hand wrapped around the grip and a finger still on the trigger. He did the same with Grace's gun by placing it back in her hand. After wiping Grace's fingerprints off Holmes gun, he placed the big revolver back in Holme's hand. He couldn't help but smile thinking what a field day the technicians were going to have with this scene.

Taking one last look around, Mark carefully opened the patio door making sure not to leave a trace of blood when he heard a loud voice calling.

Someone was coming in the front door and coming down the hall. He pushed the patio door closed and bolted for the lake, again staying off the main walkway. The pain in his side was becoming intense. By the time he reached the lake's edge he was doubled over from the pain. He remembered to use the walkway and to walk out onto the dock to avoid leaving any footprints in the sand. At some point, the house lit up with outside lights illuminating the entire compound. He dove for the cover of the dock and as quickly as possible put on his flippers and face mask at the same time putting the ski mask and surgical gloves back in the pouch. Retrieving the recording device, he put it in as well but before he closed the pouch, he made a call to Keri. By now, the pain was becoming almost unbearable, but his only way out had to be across the lake. He forced himself to ignore the pain as he focused on swimming back across the lake.

Despite the pain, Mark crossed the lake faster this time because he was making no attempt at stealth. As he swam, he could see lights flashing and could hear the sound of sirens as multiple vehicles circled the lake heading for the Griffin's home. By the time he approached the shoreline and the small lagoon, he had almost lost the use of his left arm and it was only his legs propelling him forward.

As another emergency vehicle passed close to the lake, he realized that he was not swimming alone. A dark shape was moving quietly in the water only a few feet from his left side. Gators were usually not aggressive toward humans unless they perceived them as prey. Mark suddenly knew why the gator was trailing him. He was bleeding and the scent of blood in the water was causing the gator to react naturally. It sensed wounded prey and was only doing what its reptilian brain was directing it to do. What really frightened Mark though, was not the gator he could see swimming behind him, but the one that might be moving underneath him.

As he approached the outer edges of the lily pads, he used what remaining strength he could muster to kick as fast as possible through the thick mat of vegetation until his feet touched the bottom. He turned toward the gator and plashed water toward it with his good arm and the black head turned away and disappeared in the dark.

Chapter 71

Dr Kline Again

An hour and a half had passed since Keri had dropped Mark off. She watched a lot of people come and go at the donut shop before her phone startled her. Fumbling and almost turning her phone off instead of answering, she put it to her ear.

"Meet me at the spot in thirty minutes starting to count now." Then went was silent.

She recognized the tension in Mark's normally calm voice, but he didn't give her any opportunity to question him. She looked at her watch. It showed one thirty. She tried to remember how long it had taken her to drive from the lake to the donut shop. She wanted to time it closely so she could avoid sitting by the side of the road at the pickup spot. She decided to give herself five minutes driving time as she forced herself to wait. She stared at her watch, while time seemed to stand still.

After almost thirty minutes had passed, Keri was sitting on a side street a block from the lake. She watched with concern as multiple responders raced toward the direction of the lake. At thirty minutes, she eased the SUV toward the lake and when there was a lull in the onslaught of vehicles she sped to the point on the shoreline where she had left Mark earlier. As she turned the vehicle at an angle so the headlights were aiming across the lake, she could see the dark form struggling out of the water and falling to his knees at the water's edge. Keri jumped from the car and ran to the slumping figure. She helped support him as he tried to move toward the car.

"Let go! Just drive," was all he said. She helped him stagger to the car and when she opened the back door, he collapsed across the back seat. She did a quick U-turn and left the neighborhood passing more flashing lights heading toward the lake. Her hands felt slippery on the steering wheel as she realized her hands were covered with blood.

Keri glanced through the rearview mirror and saw Mark trying to sit up. He'd pulled off the goggles and hood.

"Mark, can you talk? What happened?"

"Later. I need you to call Vernon and ask him to call his doctor friend. Take me to the clinic if it's alright with him."

When they reached the rear entrance of Richard Kline's office there was one car and a Harley in the otherwise dark and deserted parking lot. As soon as they had stopped, Jost came out of the door. Keri had already opened the back door and was trying to help Mark. With Jost's help they got Mark inside and up onto an examining table. As soon as Mark was on the table, Dr. Kline was slicing through the wet suit. So far not one word had been spoken. When the upper section of the wet suit was cut open, there was a pool of dark blood that poured out on the table. With Keri helping, they cut off the remainder of the wet suit and the t-shirt underneath. Kline was the first to speak.

"Mark I'm going to start an IV. You've lost a lot of blood and I'm going to need to put you out while I work on you. Are you allergic to anything?"

Gritting his teeth from the pain Mark could only shake his head in response. Within a few moments after Kline started the IV Mark felt a warm glow as he slipped into a deep sleep.

Over two hours later Mark could hear the sound of faraway voices that seemed to get closer. He was soon aware of faces watching him, but they seemed to come and go. He was vaguely aware of moving, a car ride and then more sleep.

When his eyes opened again, his mouth was filled with cotton, he was aware of sunlight coming through a window and best of all, the most wonderful smell of coffee. A smiling Keri was standing next to the bed holding a tray with the source of the pleasant odor.

"Good morning, Tarzan."

For moment Mark didn't know what she meant but it suddenly all came back. He closed his eyes for a moment as he realized how lucky he'd been.

"The recordings?"

Keri smiled and set the tray down on a nightstand. She leaned down and reaching under the side of the bed, she brought out Mark's diver's pouch.

"I like to hide things under the bed."

"Have you played it?"

"No. I wouldn't play it without your permission."

"Good. Right now, I'm not sure what I'll do with it. Now, tell me what the doc did to me last night?"

"He said you were lucky. A rib deflected the bullet but then it hit another. Both ribs were broken, and the bullet was just under the skin. They'll spend a lot of time looking for the that one. He said that normally what he did should have been done in a hospital operating room. When he finished, he said he'd done a dam good job considering."

"I'm not sure I like the considering part, but I really do owe him."

"Vernon is the one you really need to thank. By the way, Vernon took your car to get the back seat cleaned up. He's also disposing of what was left of your wetsuit."

"Does he have any idea what happened?"

"No. Vernon didn't ask any questions. However, the news all morning has been nothing but coverage of a triple homicide in a high-end neighborhood. Vernon has to know that you're connected in some way. The police are calling it possible murder suicide and they haven't even released the names yet, but Vernon knows who was killed."

Mark was able to sit up in bed and by evening, he was able to stand up and walk into a room with a TV. Again, the dominant story on the news was the murder of Dr. Charles Griffin and his wife. The wild card in the story was the third victim, Dick Holmes. Many theories were suggested to explain his connection to the deaths. Mark had to smile at the theories. The press interviewed Knotts at length. He was obviously playing a significant role in the investigation. What was surprising to Mark as he watched the news reports, was that there was no mention of any connection to the Jim Herbert case. Especially surprising since the Herbert case had been dominating the news.

"Keri, if you don't mind, I'd like to listen to the recording."

"Not a problem. Let me get it for you. I'm going to sit out on the patio while you listen to it."

After listening to the recording of the sounds from the Griffin's library Mark realized he had a difficult decision to make. There would be no doubt that it would identify Tanya's killer, but it wouldn't be hard for the authorities to identify him as the fourth person in the room. He finally decided to wait and see the results of the investigation which he knew would be intense. It turned out to be a wise choice.

CHAPTER 72

More Loose Ends

Mark spent the next several days recovering at Keri's house. Mark realized that Roe had left several messages on his phone before he returned her calls.

"Mark, where have you been? I've left messages at your hotel and your cell phone."

"Roe, I've got a lot to tell you but not now. Don't worry, I'm okay."

"Does it have anything to do with John and Grace Griffin?"

"Roe, like I said, I'll talk to you later."

Roe knew not to ask more questions and only said, "When are you going back to Jacksonville? From what I've heard, Jim Herbert is going to be a free man any day now."

"I've got a few things to tie up here. Hopefully, very soon. I'll let you know when."

After Keri drove him back to Kline's office to have his sutures removed, the new bandages were far less bulky and weren't even visible under his shirt. His chest would be sore for weeks, but the discomfort was tolerable. The news coverage of the triple homicide had died down and Mark called Stills to get an update on Herbert.

"Mark, I'm glad you called. I'm sure you've been following the news."

"I have and I wanted to wait until things were sorted out before I called you. What have you found out about Holmes?"

"It has been a little hectic here. I'm still trying to come to grips with what Holmes was doing. I'll admit I really trusted the man. In retrospect, it explains some things that happened. Leonard Knotts has kept me up to date with the investigation related to Tanya's death. Knotts told me that since Dick Holmes was never on the radar when they were looking at finances and communications, they missed some critical information."

"Such as?"

"For one thing, a lot of money passed into Holmes' hands from some of the businesses the Griffins controlled. They're continuing to look at the paper trails. But listen to this, a text message sent from Holmes to Grace Griffin on the night Tanya was killed simply said, "It's done." The second thing was what they found inside Holmes apartment. They found a pair of painter's coveralls rolled up in a closet. They'd been washed but there were still stains remaining that are suspected bloodstains. They're going see if they can get anything out of them including hair. The third thing they found was a master key for Tanya's apartment. Knotts doesn't want to publicly make any connections of this case with Tanya's death unless he can back it up with solid evidence. He wants to get it right this time. They may never know what went down in the Griffin's home. Knotts said it was a real clusterfuck. Regardless, he's continuing with steps to drop all charges against Herbert."

"Is Knotts still planning to try Layfield for Tanya's murder?"

"Unless they can prove otherwise, yes, they are. I think Knotts is not sure what part Holmes played in Tanya's murder. Fortunately, the one thing that is certain is, Jim Herbert didn't kill her. Apparently, Layfield tried to kill himself in the hospital. He's not adapting to being a eunuch and he's still claiming he didn't kill Tanya. So far, they haven't found who left him to die in that house. The main suspect of course was Jost, but he had an iron clad alibi and Layfield hasn't been able to identify anyone else except some cartoon figures."

"What's happening with Charles Griffin?"

"Charles is going away for a long time. Amy Moreland is testifying against him as well as a dancer from one of the bars. The dancer is accusing him of raping her two years ago and she was sixteen at the time. You may have heard from Keri that he's lost custody of his and Tanya's son Seth, as well."

"Yes. Seth is with Keri's mom now."

"What Keri and her mom may not yet be aware of is how Dr. Griffin changed his will. Seth and Dr. Griffin's niece are the two sole beneficiaries. Seth and his guardian, either Keri or her mom, will be very well provided for."

"That's good to know. Will you let me know when Herbert is actually walking out?"

"Mark, that's one call I'm looking forward to making."

After closing out the call to Stills, Mark walked out onto Keri's patio where she was sitting and reading with Brutus lying at her feet. Keri could read the expression on Mark's face.

"I know. You don't have to say it. It's time for you to leave."

"Keri let's don't say goodbye. How about so long for now? Once you get everything sorted out with your mom and Seth, I'd like for you to come visit me in Jacksonville."

Keri stood up, smiled and hugged Mark closely.

"I'd like that. We'll always have a lot of memories. I can never thank you enough for what you've done for us and Tanya."

Even Brutus tried to wag his remnant of a tail as he looked up at Mark.

After Mark went back to his hotel and packed up his things, he called Roe and left a message on her phone that he was on his way back to Jacksonville. He then called Jost. He answered on the first ring.

"Yes Mark."

"Vernon, I'm heading back to Jacksonville. I'd like to talk to you on my way out."

"Do you remember how to get to my home?"

"I think so. I'll call you if I get lost. I'm on my way."

Mark's cell phone rang as he was driving to meet Jost.

"Mark, this is Karin. I just got a phone call from Knotts. Layfield is dead. Apparently, Christie Morlan was begging to see him, and they let her into his hospital room. The officers guarding

Layfield swore they did a thorough search before they let her in. They think she had a razor blade hidden in her cheek and she used it to cut his throat ear to ear. When they went into the room to check on them, she was sitting in a chair relaxed and reading a magazine as if nothing had happened. Her only comment was that Layfield should have left her daughter alone."

"Thanks for letting me know Karin. My sympathy lies with Morlan. If there is a hell, we know that's where Layfield is headed."

When Mark parked in front of Jost's house, he was sitting outside in a chair waiting. Without saying a word, he led Mark through the house to the rear porch and motioned for Mark to sit.

Vernon spoke first. "You look a hell of a lot better than you did last week."

"I feel a hell of a lot better too. I wanted to give you money to pay Dr. Kline."

"Forget it, Mark. I told you before that Kline and I have an arrangement that covers expenses like that."

"Just let him know how grateful I am. The other reason I wanted to see you was to thank you face to face, for everything you did. Fortunately, most of which no one will ever know."

"Mark, I think I can say the same for you. I think you know what happened at the Griffin's house."

"Vernon, let me tell you a hypothetical story. Just suppose there was a fourth person present at the Griffin's house, that night."

Mark continued with an accurate account of what had happened and especially the admissions of guilt by Holmes and Grace Griffin. He left out the part about the recording of the event. When he finished Vernon sat quietly for a moment.

"So, we can be sure Tanya's death has been paid for. You know Mark, I thought I had connections up until now. Holmes was good. I just don't know how he stayed under everyone's radar for so long. I've got a lot to thank you for as well. Without your stirring the pot, they would have gotten away with everything."

With nothing left to say, Mark stood up to leave. Vernon reached out and shook Mark's hand.

"Mark, I consider you to be a good friend. Let's stay in touch."

"The same here Vernon," and with that Mark was finally on his way back to Jacksonville. He had slowed down to the forty-five miles per hour speed limit as he passed through Waldo when his phone rang. It was Stills again.

"Mark, I'm calling sooner than I expected. Herbert is going to be released tomorrow. I'm going up to the prison and I wanted to ask you if you wanted to come with me? Jim's wife and daughter will be there as well. It'll be a celebration."

Mark had thought about it, and he'd already made a decision.

"No Karin. This is your show now. Jim will be focusing on his wife and daughter. I'll see him later. Just tell him I said he'd better start working on his tennis."

Karin was disappointed but she understood and accepted Mark's decision.

"Thanks for everything Mark. Anytime you're in or near Orlando, call me."

When he drove into his garage and walked into his house, Mark suddenly realized how much he'd missed his home and the river. His house was musty from being closed up for so long, but otherwise in good order.

After unpacking, he poured himself a large Tanqueray over ice, added a generous amount of lime juice, and walked out onto his patio. Before he settled into his chair, he opened the tape recorder he'd used at the Griffin's, took the tape out of the recorder, put it on his grill and doused it with lighter fluid. After dropping a match on it and watching it blaze up, he settled down in his favorite chair. Taking large swallow of his drink, he looked up and raised his glass toward the sky and said, "Thank you."

CHAPTER 73

Libby, Julie, and Jim

The next day was a beautiful day in north Florida. There was a clear blue sky without a cloud in sight and a slight breeze blew gently from the east. While Mark was taking a slow walk along the river, a different scene was unfolding at the Florida State Prison north of Stark. Jim Herbert, accompanied by the smiling prison warden, walked out into a courtyard wearing civilian clothing and blinking under the bright sunlight. A small figure of a girl ran toward him with outstretched arms followed by a woman with a huge smile. Karin Stills was standing to the side with a large red-faced man dressed in a dark blue suit. A small group of reporters stood behind them. Jim scooped up the young girl and held her as tears poured down his face. Julie threw her arms around them both as her smile was replaced with tears as well.

By now, everyone watching was blinking back tears including the red-faced man, Leonard Knotts. Soon the reporters were crowding around Herbert, his ex-wife and child, each one trying to be the first to get a statement. Karin Stills, a tiny but authoritarian figure, pushed them all back saying, "No! Not here. Not today. Let him enjoy being a free man."

Stills, Knotts and the warden formed a protective ring around Jim Herbert and his family and led them out to Julie's car. Julie got in the driver's seat while Jim and Libby climbed into the back seat. Jim had to reluctantly peel Libby off his chest so he could buckle her into her seat. As Julie drove south into the North Florida countryside, the prison receded from view. Jim held on tight to Libby's hand and didn't look back.

Mark was back home from his walk and sitting on his patio enjoying watching the boats on the river when his phone rang. It was Stills who only said, "He's out and on his way home with Julie and Libby," before hanging up.

Mark smiled at the news but as he looked down toward the river, an image of Kim as a young girl, laughing and running up from the river unexpectedly flashed across his mind. At the same moment, his phone rang again. Roe was on her way toward Jacksonville.

"Mark, I'm about an hour away. I've got some news you'll want to hear. I just couldn't wait to tell you."

"Roe, I only want to hear good news right now."

"Well, I'll let you decide whether it's good or bad. I've been working on a human trafficking case for the last couple of months. I've gotten rumors but I didn't want to say anything about it until I was certain. Andre Mendez is alive and well. I don't know how he's done it but somehow the cockroach survived, and he's slimed his way back into business."

Mark was silent and Roe finally asked, "Mark, are you still there?"

"Yes, I'm here, Roe. I think it's time to go hunting again."

Acknowledgements

I want to thank my wife Ruth for her patience with me during the time I spent writing this book. I confess her observation, that at times I was just avoiding some household chores, was probably true. I also thank my three children, two lawyers, and a school principal, whose sometimes brutal honesty kept me in check. There were times that I would stray into social and political commentary which were anathema to the goal of my writing which was only to write a book that would be entertaining to all readers. I can't begin to name all the people who read my drafts and gave me suggestions and encouragement to continue. I'm afraid I'd miss someone so I'm not even going to try. You know who you are, and I thank you all.

Thomas Willis

About the Author

Thomas Willis was an Army officer during the Vietnam war, a practicing dentist and a university professor. He is retired and lives with his wife in South Florida.

Look for the release of the next novel by Thomas Willis, LAST NIGHT IN TAMPICO featuring Mark Price and Roe Estes as they follow the elusive trail of Andre Mendez. Go back in time and learn what happened to Mark during his "off the record military service."

LAST NIGHT IN TAMPICO is a story of how Emelia Rojas, a victim of human trafficking, can find the strength and will to survive even at her darkest hour. Her survival is tied to Mark Price, a man with a dark and violent history, Roe Estes, a young woman with a tumultuous past who now works as a DEA agent, and a Haitian/Chilean immigrant, Samuel Oreste, who has been caught up in events beyond his control. The unlikely trio follow a convoluted and dangerous trail that leads them from El Paso, Ciudad Juárez, West Palm Beach, and finally Tampico Mexico. The story revolves between Mark's questionable military actions in the past and the present search for Emelia. The end of the odyssey results in a bittersweet and life changing event for them all.